ARE YOU HAPPY NOW?

ARE YOU HAPPY NOW?

Richard Babcock

amazon publishing

The characters and events portrayed in this book are fictitious. Any similarity to real persons, living or dead, is coincidental and not intended by the author.

Published by Amazon Publishing
P.O. Box 400818
Las Vegas, NV 89140

ISBN-13: 9781612186719
ISBN-10: 1612186718

For Gioia and Joe

SUMMER:

The Pistakee Way

1

ALLEYS, THINKS JOHN LINCOLN. AT LEAST CHICAGO HAS alleys. He puts down his pencil and ambles the three steps from his desk to the small, round window—about the size of a medium pizza—in his cell of an office. If he were in New York right now, mounds of garbage piled higher than his head would be crowding pedestrians off the sidewalk. Without alleys, everybody's business is on the street. One spiteful strike by the sanitation workers and New York is turned into a landscape of dark plastic hills and vile odors, man's concrete universe overrun by gleeful rats.

Lincoln looks down through his round window at the wall of garbage bags now towering along one side of the alley below. At least in Chicago, people tuck the offal of their lives away, off the main thoroughfares, out of sight. That's one positive thing he could say about this place. One thing.

He returns to his desk and to the 462-page manuscript he has been fitfully editing for the last four days: *37 Rambles Through the Windy City*, by Norman Fleace. Lincoln is on page 226, halfway through the nineteenth ramble. Touched by inspiration, he flips to the title page and draws a sharp line with his pencil over "Rambles Through." What pretension, Lincoln tells himself. No one has rambled anywhere since Jane Austen was doddering around some Hampshire garden. For a moment, he considers the spare page in front of him and then strikes "37." What's with that number, anyway? No one ever uses 37. There's never 37 of anything. Now he pencils in three alternative words and studies the new title. *Walking Tours of the Windy City.* Prosaic, but it gets to the point, and cleaning up the verbiage creates alliteration, which will help hold the title in memory. Better.

Lincoln turns back to ramble—now tour—nineteen, a stroll from Clark Street in Lincoln Park twenty-five blocks south to the Loop. Past the site of the garage where somebody—maybe Al Capone's boys?—rubbed out seven members of the North Side Gang in the 1929 St. Valentine's Day Massacre (now an empty lot beside an uninteresting apartment building); past the ornate 1893 structure that once held the Chicago Academy of Sciences (snore); past the intersection where the Weathermen emerged from the park to begin a window-breaking rampage through Old Town during the Days of Rage in 1969 (all evidence was cleaned up within a week); past the Moody Bible Church (does anyone care?), the Chicago History Museum, the Latin School, and then block after block of sixties-era residential towers and forgettable mid-rises, a wall of vapidity that John Lincoln shudders to contemplate, let alone walk past. It's 2009. Get in your car and drive, he thinks.

In New York twelve years ago, the summer he was an intern at Malcolm House Publishing and living in an apartment on West 115th Street, he used to spend every Saturday walking. Usually the journey was the same: he'd start at Columbia University and head south on Broadway, just taking his time, hoofing it through the Upper West Side, into Times Square, around the Village, past City Hall, all the way down to Battery Park. The Broadway excursion took the whole afternoon. Every block, *every step*, he found something interesting to look at—a shop, a building, a celebrity. *That* was a walk. And you could repeat it all over Manhattan, in almost any direction. New York is a great walking town. Chicago, on the other hand…well, you've got the lakefront, from Hollywood Avenue to Hyde Park, and that's pretty lively, at least in summer, and then there are patches of mild interest—hipsterized Wicker Park, the Magnificent Mile of North Michigan Avenue, the old, struggling Loop, with a surviving Louis Sullivan building here and there (sparkling jewels compared to the blocks that have been turned black and somber by Mies). And in between are vast stretches of…vapidity. Close your eyes and you don't miss a thing. Sitting at his desk, Lincoln closes his eyes.

But try telling that to Professor Fleace, thinks Lincoln. The old coot is so decrepit, it's probably been decades since he left his University of Chicago office (in the geography department, naturally). The one time Lincoln visited him, the professor never got up from his desk, just sat there, a small clump of moldy clothes in clashing patterns topped by a scraggly white fur ball. But Fleace desperately wanted to bring out an update of his walking book (the 1987 edition offered only twenty-six rambles). And who better to publish him than Pistakee Press, friend of every hack, windbag, and literary aspirant who ever thumbed through a thesaurus?

Eyes open again, back to tour nineteen: "As we advance down the block, we find the imperious red form of the Chicago History Museum, its memorabilia-filled cavernous bulk secreting an imposing Saint-Gaudens statue of our beloved sixteenth president, standing, in a small garden just behind the building." John Lincoln's pencil is poised over the word "secreting" when a knock intrudes on his office door.

"Yes," he calls out irritably.

A compact round head with sandy hair peeks in. "Do you have a second?" asks Byron Duddleston, the owner of Pistakee Press.

"Of course," says Lincoln, quickly stiffening at the sight of his boss. "Come in, come in. Or 'Advance!' as Professor Fleace would say."

The owner takes a few steps into the small office, then pauses, lifts his chin, and sniffs the air. Given Duddleston's light brown coloring and taut, sinewy body, Lincoln thinks of a small woodland animal. "I wish they'd settle this damn garbage strike," Duddleston says. "The smell is starting to seep inside."

"Right," says Lincoln, wondering why he hadn't noticed. "Please, have a seat."

The two men sit and face each other over Lincoln's desk, a chaotic landscape of manuscripts, magazines, books, reference materials, and a computer. Duddleston is carrying a thick manuscript bound by a fat rubber band. "How are things going?" he asks.

Something shopworn and familiar about the manuscript in Duddleston's lap makes Lincoln uneasy. "Fine, fine," he tells his boss. "I've been working on Professor Fleace's walking book. A nice job, really—I'm just trying to tighten it up a bit."

"He's a beloved figure at the school," Duddleston interrupts. "In my time, students used to camp out in the halls overnight to be in line to sign up for his class on the geography of Illinois."

"I always wished I'd taken that course," Lincoln lies.

"Some teachers—they just have a way of looking at the world that stays with you," Duddleston muses. "In my time, the U of C was full of men like that. Women, too." He ticks off a few names, some faintly familiar to Lincoln. "I don't know if you had that experience there."

"Right, right." Lincoln nods eagerly. He wants to volley back the names of a few of *his* treasured U of C teachers, but his mind is suddenly scoured clean: he can't think of a single professor he studied under, even though at thirty-three, he's probably fifteen years younger than his boss.

"Well," Duddleston says, shifting warily in his chair, getting to the unfortunate point of his visit, "I wanted to talk to you about your editing on Bill Lemke's book on Wrigley Field."

"Yes?" Lincoln dreads what's coming.

"You're our most experienced editor, the one I rely on for the most delicate and sophisticated jobs."

Lincoln nods more slowly now. It's always griped him that Duddleston kept the editor-in-chief title to himself, a little trophy to put alongside his true role, moneybags. Lincoln's title, executive editor, makes him feel pinstriped and officious.

"Well, Bill came by this morning desperately unhappy," Duddleston continues. "He got your edit and your memo last week, and he said it depressed him so much he had to put it aside."

"I'm sorry to hear that," Lincoln offers, though he is not entirely surprised.

"He showed me your line edits on the manuscript, and ninety percent of them are fine, fine." Duddleston leans forward to emphasize his sincerity.

"Good."

"But…" He sits back again. "Look, Bill Lemke has been a writer all his life. He spent more than twenty years at the *Sun-Times*. I remember looking for his byline myself! And this"—he holds out the manuscript—"some of this is just way, way too harsh."

"I was trying to be candid," Lincoln says weakly. "Candid and helpful."

"But, but…" Duddleston starts leafing clumsily through the manuscript. He pulls out a page, crisscrossed by a giant X. In the margin, Lincoln had written in pencil, "Lose it, Bill. Trust me." Duddleston waves the page at Lincoln. "This is gratuitous." Then he digs some more. "And this!" he says, pulling out page 211, looking horrified. Beside one long paragraph, Lincoln had written, "I may vomit."

"That's the famous line from the great Kaufman and Hart comedy, *The Man Who Came to Dinner*," Lincoln explains. "I guess I was getting weary by then and trying to be a bit playful."

"'Playful?' What's playful about a remark like that?" Now Duddleston pulls eight single-spaced pages off the top of the wad of manuscript. "And your memo on how to fix the book—it's just way, way too harsh." He reads, "'Every page needs a cliché-ectomy.' You talk to Bill Lemke as if he's a child or an idiot."

Lincoln briefly considers pointing out that Lemke got fired from the *Sun-Times* years ago for being an incompetent drunk, and since then he's scratched out a living by writing about Chicago's blind love for its sports teams—the book in question, for example, *Wrigley Field: A People's History*. But that way lies more trouble, so instead Lincoln summons his best defense: "I've usually found that good writers—writers who really care about the craft and understand it—appreciate candor. They know I just want to help them bring out the best book possible. That's why I edit in pencil on paper—so the writer can see exactly what I'm doing. I spent two weeks working on that manuscript. That memo has got to be five thousand words long. I'm just trying to help."

"Writers are sensitive beings," Duddleston says, quietly, passionately. "They're fragile, their egos are fragile. They need to be handled delicately."

Now, Lincoln thinks, he really may vomit. Duddleston majored in English at the U of C, investing his undergraduate life in the dusty canyons of the old Harper Library—by his account, spending entire weekends in a favorite chair reading nineteenth-century English literature. But after graduation, to make a living, Duddleston took a job as a trader and spent the next twenty years in the wheat pit at the Board of Trade, screaming buy and sell orders at other sweaty, panicky men. He was good at it and parlayed his skill into a small fortune, and to his credit, he had the sense to walk away before an artery burst or he made a bad play and lost it all. In his heart, Duddleston always felt like an English major, so he took a chunk of his wealth and founded Pistakee Press, placing himself at the top. And even though small presses are notorious money pits, and the whole book publishing industry is going through a revolution, Duddleston retained enough of his financial acuity to turn the company into a nice little business. But because of that CV, he's never had to deal with writers as workers, as producers of a commodity that has to fight for success in the marketplace. He's never had to untangle their sentences (and their thinking), he's never had to convince them that their first, flatulent drafts are only first drafts and that it will take hours of more reporting and writing (and then many more hours of rewriting by the editor) before the tome can rightfully take its place as that underappreciated and overabundant product, a book.

No, Byron Duddleston still imagines that *Tess of the d'Urbervilles* sprang fully formed from Thomas Hardy's head, and if some snippy editor had jostled old Tom at the wrong moment, the whole classic story would have crumbled and blown away like sand.

"You're right, you're right," Lincoln tells his boss.

"Maybe it's different at newspapers, where you are working under draconian deadlines, but books!" says Duddleston. "Books are different."

Lincoln nods very slowly. His right forearm aches where he broke it so many years ago. He's heard stories of Duddleston's ruthless tactics as a trader and of his volcanic temper, but around Pistakee Press, the man always seems to be concentrating on talking slowly and deliberately. "What do you think I should do?" he asks Duddleston.

"Oh, call up Bill Lemke," the editor-in-chief/owner says, brightening. "Take him out to lunch. Flatter him. *Massage* him a little. All writers like that. I'm sure he'll come around."

"Righto," says Lincoln, wondering if Lemke can stay sober enough through lunch to absorb a few suggestions on his book.

Duddleston stands. "You're a brilliant editor," he tells Lincoln. "A brilliant man of words."

Lincoln forces out a smile. Duddleston has complained in the past about Lincoln's "abuse of writers"—Duddleston's term.

Now, something in the boss's precise delivery of the inflated compliment makes Lincoln wonder if he's about to be fired.

"We want to bring that book out next March, just in the middle of spring training, and it's July already," Duddleston reminds him. "Not much time."

"We'll get there," Lincoln assures his boss.

Duddleston starts to go but pauses at a bookshelf where Lincoln has placed some family photographs—the black-and-white portrait of his father, the Washington lawyer, posed somberly in a lugubrious dark suit; the fading snapshot of mom, dad, sister, and Lincoln himself at twelve, a basketball tucked under his arm; the picture of Lincoln and his wife, Mary, bumping shoulders, touching heads, standing in front of an inviting Tuscan café.

Duddleston turns to Lincoln with an avuncular gaze. "And how's it going with Mary?" he asks.

Lincoln shifts awkwardly in his chair. Maybe he should put away that picture, at least, for now. It was taken just a year ago, when he and Mary hoped the relaxation and distraction of a trip to Italy would enhance their surprisingly balky efforts to get pregnant. Not long after they returned, and with no success on the pregnancy front, Mary decided to put motherhood on hold until after she got an MBA. Three weeks ago, she announced that they needed "a vacation" from each other while she decided whether she wanted to stay married, and Lincoln moved out. "OK," he tells Duddleston. "Just trying to sort out our feelings."

"Seeing a counselor?"

"No, not at the moment. Maybe later."

"Well, whatever you do, don't rush into things," Duddleston says. "You've put in—what?—five years on this marriage, and that's not something you want to discard carelessly. Hold off on making decisions. Give yourselves time to cool off."

"Right, right."

Duddleston nods and smiles. “Go to it, Abe,” he says, closing the door carefully behind him.

John Lincoln takes a deep breath. His boss’s idea of an affectionate tic is to call his top employee after the adored president, even though John, as far as he knows, doesn’t carry a trace of the Great Man’s DNA. That’s another unfortunate consequence of landing in Chicago, Lincoln reminds himself constantly. From the moment he set foot in Illinois and introduced himself to his dorm counselor at the U of C, he’s had to explain to new acquaintances that he’s no relation to the state’s favorite son. “Oh, that’s too bad,” people often say. To which Lincoln, if he’s in the mood and the occasion appropriate, enjoys replying, “No, it’s not. Abe Lincoln was a chronic depressive and possible homosexual. Mrs. Lincoln went mad. Three of their four boys died young, and the survivor grew up to be a monumentally crass and greedy lawyer. Those are not the genes I prefer to be carrying, thank you very much.” But the retort is not much solace. He probably wouldn’t have to field the question if he lived in New York.

2

DESPERATE TO AVOID ANOTHER CRISIS, JOHN LINCOLN spends the next hour and a half going back over the manuscript of *Walking Tours of the Windy City*, erasing about a quarter of his careful pencil edits and laboriously eliminating traces of his most virulent marginal comments. He struggles particularly to remove all evidence of "ZZZZZ!!!" which he's scrawled in big letters on page 189, opposite a tedious digression into the natural properties of the winding moraine left along the Chicago lakefront twenty thousand years ago by the receding Wisconsin Glacier. Lincoln realizes that he must have been especially annoyed reading this geography lesson because even after he wears down an entire pencil eraser, the lingering imprint of "ZZZZZ!!!" is still clearly visible on the edge of the page, and even the watery eyes of Professor Fleace could probably spot it. Finally, Lincoln resorts to an old dodge and scribbles, "Well put!" in a heavy hand over the shadowy *z*'s, then erases the whole jumbled mess until he's certain the professor, even with the aid of a sharp-eyed young grad student and a magnifying glass, could never decipher the underlying offense.

No more angry writers. John Lincoln is not by nature a vituperative or even unpleasant fellow, but his caustic side began building when he landed in Chicago, and lately it's expanded to fill all corners of his life. And yet, he doesn't see himself as a bitter person—frustrated, rather, that things haven't turned out better. Confounded. During times of adversity, his father was fond of quoting what he claimed was an old Chinese proverb: This, too, shall pass. Lincoln has started to wonder: When?

Of course, the adversity that prompted his father was always national or global in scope, never personal. Lincoln may not be descended from the sixteenth president, but on both sides of the family tree, he comes from a long line of high-achieving WASPs whose gene pool hasn't deteriorated over the generations (perhaps, Lincoln reasons, because they never got rich). His distinguished ancestors feature a few doctors and businessmen, but most practiced law, frequently moving between private work and public service, staying largely true to their liberal principles (Eleanor Roosevelt was a dear family friend). Lincoln's father has followed the pattern, with two tours of duty in the Department of Justice under Democratic administrations. Growing up, Lincoln assumed that his future promised a similar course—at least, he so assumed to the extent that his thoughts of the future stretched beyond dreams of glory on the basketball court. But then he broke his arm the summer before his senior year of high school, delaying his playing season and diluting the interest of the basketball coaches at Dartmouth and Brown, whose attention might otherwise have overcome those pesky Bs on Lincoln's transcript. Lincoln's parents couldn't quite believe that the best he could do was the U of C, not so much because they had an unrealistic view of his record, but because he was *their* son, and certainly *their* son didn't default to the Midwest for college. Their disappointment inflated when Lincoln majored in English (not history! not government!) and then threatened briefly to pursue the subject as an academic career. But Lincoln found solace in the study of literature. He was good at it (in four years in Hyde Park, a sea of math and science geniuses, he never once met a student who could top his 780 on the verbal SATs), and in an odd way, literature offered an outlet for the competitive drive he'd previously exercised in sports. The right word, the best sentence, the most penetrating insight—this was a game Lincoln could play and play well. That summer as an intern at Malcolm House cemented the attraction, and Lincoln concluded he'd found an outlet for his curious personality mix of testosterone and aesthetics.

His parents sounded more baffled than dismayed when he announced he was taking a job as a news clerk at the *Chicago Tribune*. ("But where do you *go* with that?" his father had asked, as if Woodward and Bernstein, after taking down a corrupt president, had put away their childish things and gone on to productive and civic-minded careers.) Though he never discarded his original disdain for Chicago, Lincoln moved up quickly at the newspaper, and when his momentum seemed to stall as assistant metro editor, he made his move to book publishing, buying into Duddleston's promise that together they could build Pistakee into the premier house west of the Hudson.

But that was three years ago, and scores of flaccid, forgettable manuscripts later, Lincoln realizes that building a publishing house entails hours of tedium with dribble like *Wrigley Field: A People's History* and the constant hope that somewhere, somehow, he will find a book that makes a splash. He knows what he wants—at least, he thinks he does: get to New York, the publishing Mecca; land a job with one of the big houses, where he will edit *real* writers, the kind whose sentences leave you stunned and humbled; and bring out *real* books, the kind that get reviewed in the *New York Times Book Review*. Lincoln used to be in occasional touch with Jeff Kessler, the boss at Malcolm House (who was just a bright, friendly new editor when Lincoln interned there), and Kessler offered boundless encouragement, but never a job. The same with Angela Morrisroe at Pottersby, William Upswitch at Burling, and a handful of other top editors at New York houses. Even now, with the economy stalled and publishing in turmoil, several of them remain generous with their time when Lincoln makes his periodic trips to Manhattan. But he reads perfectly the subtext of their compliments about his budding talent: Prove it. If you think you're so hot out there in the flatlands, publish a book that somebody cares about, somebody besides a handful of ambulatory Midwest grannies and a few addled fans of the dipshit Cubs.

In her own way, Mary was probably saying the same thing. She told Lincoln that she was tired of just playing at marriage, playing at life (as if the failure to conceive in six months of trying meant they were amateurs). Selling houses on the North Side, she made half again what Lincoln did, and in the months before the breakup, she started the practice course for the GMAT. And where did she want to go to school? The U of C.

"Yes, the U of C," she cried furiously, when Lincoln greeted her announcement with a scornful face. "It's a great school, and Chicago is a great city. You live here, remember!"

Of course he remembers. In a perverse way, he feels fatally entwined with Chicago, as if he and the city are unspeaking partners in a two-legged race, contemptuous of each other yet forced to collaborate for the sake of the contest. He needs to show his wife, his parents, the publishing business—his own reeling ego—that he can carve out a success here, that he has not spent fifteen years (has it really been that long?) in vain.

Lincoln is blowing a storm of eraser bits from the pages of Professor Fleace's manuscript when another knock sounds gently on his door. "Yes," he caws disagreeably, since he knows it won't be Duddleston again.

The door opens tentatively, and a little ruffed grouse tiptoes in, the editorial assistant who started work just last week.

"What is it?" snaps Lincoln, stopping her in midstep.

"Mr. Duddleston forgot to leave the Wrigley Field manuscript," the young woman explains. "He asked me to drop it off." She has shaggy brown hair that frames dark eyes and a beaky little nose, and the few times Lincoln has noticed her, she was wearing a boxy peasant blouse, a formless bag of khaki that came just over her hips. The tiny face, the forest coloring, the nervous manner—Lincoln can't help but think of a ruffed grouse. Well, he's never actually seen one, not even a picture, but she looks like the name describes. She's draped in the blouse again today, wearing it over black slacks.

"Byron," Lincoln tells her grumpily.

She stares back, bewildered, and then her face lights up. "The poet?" she asks.

"No. That's his name. Byron Duddleston. No one calls him Mr. Duddleston. Byron. Or just Duddleston."

"Oh." The poor bird looks wounded.

"Just put it there," he says, nodding toward the far edge of his desk and returning his attention to tour nineteen and the Lincoln statue hiding behind the History Museum. After a moment, he's aware that she's hovering.

"What is it?" he asks irritably.

"On top of all these other things?" she asks. With her small, shifty eyes, she indicates the desktop's clutter, an accumulation that has the abandoned look of an unexcavated ruin. "I think Mr. Duddleston wanted you to get on this right away."

So the grouse has a bit of spirit, Lincoln thinks. "Byron!" he almost screams.

"Byron," she repeats meekly, looking thoroughly distressed.

"I'm the executive editor here," he reminds her. "I'll get to Wrigley Field when I'm ready. Now just put the manuscript on the desk."

She steps forward and carefully places the thick wad of pages atop a pile of unread magazines. Lincoln tries to ignore her, but still she lingers. "Oh, you've got Professor Fleace's book," she exclaims after a moment. "I loved his course on Illinois geography."

Lincoln puts down his pencil. "So you went to the U of C," he says drily.

"I just graduated in June."

"Congratulations." Lincoln wonders why it seems that everyone he knows in Chicago went to the U of C—six million stories in the naked city, and all of them feature a U of C weenie—everyone except Mary, who went to Northwestern but now wants her U of C dosage too.

"You went there." A statement, not a question. The grouse has been studying his résumé.

"Yes, yes, I did." When none of the Ivies took him, and his only other choice was the University of Maryland.

"My name's Amy O'Malley, by the way." She offers her hand across his desk, and Lincoln takes it without standing. He feels as if he could crush her fragile, bony fingers in his fist.

"How did you get this job, Amy?" he asks her.

"Mr. Duddleston…Byron…Byron was looking for an assistant, and he asked the U of C recruitment office for the best English major who was about to graduate."

"And that was you."

Amy's pale skin reveals a modest blush. "Well, I was at least the best one who wasn't going straight on to graduate school. I wanted to get out in the real world for a while, and the idea of working with books and writers…it was a dream come true."

Lincoln smiles condescendingly. He wonders how long that dream would survive an encounter with Bill Lemke, stinking of cigarettes and bourbon, thick patches of white hair on his neck that his razor has missed for weeks, babbling on about how the sports editor of the *Sun-Times*, that sniveling cretin, had maliciously envied Lemke's talent and torpedoed his career. "And I suppose you have the ambition to write a little yourself," Lincoln posits.

The blush expands from two small circles on her cheeks into a faint mask covering her entire un-made-up face. "Maybe, some time. I used to think so, and then I took a course with Professor Davoodi, and I realized how much I have to learn. It's one thing to imagine you want to write, but you have to have something to *say*, you know?"

"You took a course with Professor Davoodi?" Lincoln asks innocently.

"It was fantastic. He's a genius, don't you think? Was he there when you went to the U of C?"

"No," Lincoln muses ambiguously. "No, I think not." Cyrus Davoodi is a tall, imposing scholar from an ancient Persian family who made a name in academic circles by pioneering the application of postcolonial theory to American romance novels. Yes, he is a genius, everyone says, but a few years ago, he won a worldwide award for the worst writing of the year—a snarky designation, to be sure, but the newspapers paid attention. Out of curiosity, Lincoln had looked up Professor Davoodi's award-winning paragraph. Only a hundred words long, the paragraph was nonetheless a thicket of inflated phrases and run-on sentences so clogged with clauses—dependent, independent, and unrelated to any apparent earthly thought—that Lincoln had literally dizzied himself trying unsuccessfully to puzzle through it. Randomly stringing together big words from the dictionary would have produced a more readable narrative.

"He's so full of *ideas*!" the grouse offers.

"Maybe we can find a place for him on the spring list," Lincoln deadpans. And then arrange a joint reading with Professor Fleace and Bill Lemke, bring together all our stars.

Amy's tiny brow furrows as she tries to determine whether Lincoln is teasing her. "I hate it that Yale stole him away," she says.

Lincoln waves a hand. "Ah, well." He sighs and rudely turns back to his manuscript, but Amy doesn't leave. It occurs to Lincoln that she exudes the slightly aimless air of a college student who can drop into a pal's dorm room and chat thoughtlessly for hours since nothing really important is ever going on anyway. "These round windows are so odd," she says after a moment, running her fingers around the circular copper frame holding the pane of glass. "They really add something distinctive, don't you think?"

Lincoln doesn't look up. "Yes."

"Ahead of its time," Amy points out. "The square form was so dominant in those days."

"Mm-hmm." The building was put up a century ago by a former sea captain who, as legend has it, longed to recall the portholes on his ship. Never mind that the skimpy windows kept the interior shadowed and gloomy.

"And at least you have a window," Amy says. "I'm in a cubicle in the interior of the building." She leans forward to look down the alley. The movement hikes up her blouse, and as Lincoln glances over, his practiced eyes spot a delicate line of lace panty peeking above her slacks. Hmmm.

"In our business, all you need is a good fluorescent light," he tells her. Lovely lace panties? On the grouse? "Now, if you'll excuse me."

"Oh, I'm sorry. You have work to do." She bows and anxiously starts to back out of the room, bumping the edge of the bookshelf. "Oops." Finally she composes herself for a last exchange: "You know, you asked me earlier if I wanted to write?"

"Yes."

"Well, before I took the course with Professor Davoodi, I was working on a collection of short stories. One was even published in the new student literary magazine. Would you mind looking at them sometime?"

Lincoln imagines fragile, minimalist prose recalling incidents so evanescent, so utterly uneventful, that only a sensibility with exquisite perception could read their devastating impact.

"Pistakee doesn't publish fiction anymore," he tells her coolly.

Amy quickly adds, "I know, I mean, it would just really be helpful to have them read by a *real* editor."

How else is Lincoln going to get rid of her? "Just drop them off."

"Thanks!" she calls out, and scurries out of the office, leaving the door ajar.

A real editor, Lincoln thinks. I wish.

Outside in the alley, the Mexican busboys from the restaurant down the street chatter away in Spanish as they pile up more bags of garbage. Lincoln forces himself to rejoin Professor Fleace on his pedagogical stroll down Clark. A real editor. How can you be a real editor without any real writers?

3

At about six o'clock that evening, Lincoln puts his pencil down. He locks his desk, carefully folds his *New York Times* to expose the daily crossword puzzle, and walks into the small central lobby of Pistakee Press. The place is abandoned, utterly lifeless. The receptionist always leaves at 5:00 p.m. sharp, flipping the switchboard to automatic. The front panel of overhead lights has been turned off, leaving the area near the elevator in gloom. The handful of editors, secretaries, and bookkeepers—and Byron Duddleston himself—have all slipped out silently on their own, as always, never bidding good-bye to Lincoln, never, as far as he knows, even acknowledging each other as they leave. It's as if the place empties in shame, he thinks. He compares it to the rousing daily exits he recalls from his summer at Malcolm House, when he and the other interns and editorial assistants always looked each other up for news of the latest adventures and scandals, usually moving the conversation to a nearby bar. Sometimes some of the younger editors would join them, and often as not the roistering would carry on well into the night.

On the other hand, Lincoln reminds himself, the end of the workday was deadly at the *Tribune*, too. Maybe it's a Chicago thing.

Pistakee's offices are in River North, an old manufacturing neighborhood just north of the Loop that came alive with galleries in the eighties, when the art market was hopping, even in the Midwest. The galleries drew restaurants and shops, and by the late nineties the creaky, low-scale neighborhood was sprouting flesh-toned residential high-rises (lively colors don't sell) and multi-story parking garages, a building boom that threatened to engulf the original redbrick cityscape—at least until the real-estate collapse. Still, River North retains patches of funkiness, and most blocks remain open enough to feature late afternoon sun in the summer.

Lincoln walks west on Grand, checking the windows of the faux authentic Irish bar on the way; south on LaSalle, past what was once Michael Jordan's restaurant, shuttered after an unseemly tussle among the principals; west on Illinois; south on Wells; west on Kinzie; and on into the huge fortress of the Merchandise Mart, a commercial building that was long in the hands of the Kennedy family but never acquired any cachet from the association. In the Mart, Lincoln takes the escalator to the second-floor entrance to the elevated-train station. He dips his fare card into the machine and joins a crowd of mostly young, natty professionals waiting for the Brown Line train headed for revived neighborhoods to the north.

Lincoln enjoys the L and considers it one of Chicago's small wonders. When he was a student with more time in the middle of the day, he sometimes traveled the train just for the sport of it. The view from the L offers an unusual perspective on a city, Lincoln thinks—the track snakes through neighborhoods at about the level of a second-story window, and the train frequently thrusts with astonishing impudence past the living rooms and bedrooms in the buildings along the way. Twice he has spotted people fucking, and once, riding the Red Line just beyond Diversey Parkway, traveling through a gentrified old German neighborhood, he saw a girl, stark naked, with lovely, buoyant breasts and a small wedge of dark pubic hair, standing at a window, facing the tracks. Their eyes met in the split second it took the train to pass, and Lincoln was certain she gestured to him, beckoning, as the train rumbled on. How many years ago was that? Eight, maybe—well before he was married, before he'd even met his wife. In all the years since, he's never passed that building without looking and imagining.

Today, the Brown Line is running behind, as usual, and by the time a train arrives at the Merchandise Mart station, the cars are already full. Lincoln lets that train pass. The next arrives five minutes later, crowded also, but not hopelessly packed. Lincoln enters the rear door of the third car from the front. He shoulders his way through the cluster of passengers thoughtlessly gathered at the door and finds a spot of standing room in the aisle. Most of his fellow passengers are young and white, but because the train traverses a variety of neighborhoods, it occasionally provides a somewhat intimate mixing of race and class, one of the few places where that happens in Chicago despite the city's proud role as the hometown of President Obama. Lincoln is standing behind an older, rather heavyset black woman wearing a wide-brimmed, old-fashioned white hat and a ruffled, patterned dress with a stiff, white, crocheted collar. Standing a few feet away, Lincoln sniffs the dull fragrance of starch. He wonders for a moment why she's there—this hardly seems like the means or route for her to get to church—and then he privately notes with disapproval that none of the men sitting in the car has given her his seat.

Quickly, Lincoln turns to the *Times* crossword, which he typically completes in the fifteen minutes or so before the train arrives at his home station, Southport. He makes a good start, filling in the doglegged top left quadrangle, before his mind drifts back to his conversation that afternoon with Duddleston. Was his boss really preparing to fire him? There was something about Duddleston's tone—the soft suggestion of a simmering frustration, the hint that his patience has been pushed so far and would go no further. In glancing over a local book blog this morning, Lincoln had noticed a worrisome blind item: "Are changes coming to the editorial lineup of one of Chicago's top publishers?" The blog, *Big Shoulders Books*, is written by Marissa Morgan, a spacey, middle-aged North Shore housewife whose wide-eyed fascination with literature gets underwritten by her rich lawyer husband. She mostly carries cheerleading appraisals of local authors, but she's oddly well-connected and every now and then lands a surprising scoop. Did she know about something impending at Pistakee?

Lincoln realizes that he's in a precarious spot. He can't afford to lose this job—not if he has any hope of rallying his fortunes. Yet the harsh little secret of the business is that Pistakee could probably make the same modest profit publishing dreck that spilled straight from the computers of writers directly onto the pages of a Pistakee book without a touch from a seasoned editor. The public doesn't seem to care. Consumers will buy a book, or not, depending on the subject, the cover, the title, the fame of the author—and, increasingly, depending on the buzz stirred up by social media. Lincoln's injection of editorial professionalism probably doesn't make a whit of difference.

After several quick stops, the train pulls into the Wellington station and unloads some passengers, but then it sits there, doors open. Annoyed at the delay, Lincoln returns to the crossword puzzle. He scratches the answers out in pen, writing almost as quickly as he reads the clues. The car doors finally close and the train moves out, and after a bit Lincoln becomes vaguely aware of a commotion behind him. At about the same time, someone suddenly clamps a hand hard on his shoulder. The grip—like that of a stern father grabbing a child—is so out of place that Lincoln reacts almost nonchalantly. He stares at the hand—male, fully grown, with the trace of an inked stamp from a nightclub discoloring the pale skin—as if it were a familiar and harmless bug that had crawled onto his shoulder. Then he follows the arm back to its owner. Lincoln sees a young, short-haired man in a yellow polo shirt, his body awkwardly stiff, his gaze turned away from Lincoln and focused intently on the back of the car. Now Lincoln recognizes the source of the percolating commotion: a mob of stricken people is jammed in the narrow doorway between Lincoln's car and the one behind. As the first man and woman break through, they bolt down the aisle toward Lincoln, knocking aside standing passengers. Quickly a flood of panicked humanity is pouring into the car, escaping something, fleeing to the front of the train.

The young man in the polo shirt is still several reaction moments ahead of the other riders around Lincoln, and he abruptly uses Lincoln's shoulder for leverage to vault himself forward, past Lincoln and the black woman dressed for church. Shouts and pleas break out—"What is it?" "Slow down!" "Don't panic!"—and the car rapidly fills with a huge, shoving, pushing scrum of frantic passengers.

Since 9/11, it hasn't taken much to terrify residents of a big American city, but the papers recently have carried yet a new round of stories about official concerns over biological or chemical attacks, including the possibility of loading aerosol cans with anthrax. Lincoln recalls the stories, but he stands his ground, transfixed by the turmoil around him. The car is packed now, everyone crushed against one another, and the whole tangled mass of flesh is pressing forward, trying to force its way to the next car up. Near Lincoln, a man shouts, "Be cool, be cool!" But the frenzy continues. Meanwhile, the train inexplicably slows to a crawl.

Lincoln decides he should try to move forward too—maneuver himself to be near a door when it opens to the platform. Tucking his newspaper under his arm, he uses his strength and agility to squeeze past several layers of people. The train is still moving, and Lincoln knows it's now only a few blocks to the next station. The crowding is getting worse, however. Lincoln's right arm is caught between bodies behind him, and his left arm is pressed against his chest. He has trouble drawing a breath, and he has to fight waves of claustrophobic panic. Around him, the other L riders are locked in shocking physical intimacy, breath mingling, faces close, private parts pressed together. Stories of people being crushed and smothered in stampedes pour through Lincoln's mind. He flashes on the out-of-control helplessness he felt years ago when he broke his arm.

Finally, the train lurches into the Belmont station. The doors open, and the crowd shudders and presses onto the platform, the promise of escape fanning the terror, acting like oxygen on fire. Inside the car, the throng hobbles forward like a many-footed beast taking tiny steps, elbows churning. Slowly, agonizingly, Lincoln moves ahead until he's just inside the door, but a mass of people is milling on the platform, blocking the exit. The well-dressed, elderly black woman has made it out, but now she stands exactly in Lincoln's way. Though there's space beyond her, she seems hesitant, confused, her right hand holding tight to the broad-brimmed hat still on her head. "Lady, move!" Lincoln thinks. He holds his place, but behind him, the danger seems to be escalating. "Out! Out!" a man screams.

When Lincoln reconstructs the moment later, he convinces himself that if he'd been with someone he knew, he would have been impelled to show off his nerve and hold his own. By himself, however, he makes one of those instant calculations of behavior. In a nanosecond the decision is made: an anonymous display of courage doesn't trump the risk of being caught from behind by a suicidal terrorist wielding a can of man-killing Raid—or whatever other horror is slouching toward him through the L.

So Lincoln shoves the old lady out of the way, two hands on her back. But instead of meeting the resistance he expects—the weight and bulk of her body—she's as fragile and unbalanced as a feather. His moderate push sends her spinning, then sprawling on her back onto the platform, her flouncy dress riding up on her thighs, a shoe dislodged. "Aaiiee!" she cries, looking directly at Lincoln.

Immediately, Lincoln steps to safety and disappears into the crowd. The panic has erupted so quickly and the terror remains so palpable that Lincoln is only faintly embarrassed, but he knows he has to escape—at all costs, he has to avoid letting the situation take on the qualities of a personal encounter. The narrow space of the station platform is a madhouse. Passengers are spilling out of all the cars—the panic apparently carried through the entire train—and several other people have been knocked down.

Lincoln pushes his way to the stairway leading to the street. From the comments around him, he gathers that no one knows what happened. At the bottom of the stairs, two cops run past, knocking people aside on their way up. Lincoln doesn't wait to learn more. He leaves the station and walks the rest of the way home. He's still badly shaken, and he's peeved at himself for giving in to the panic. What if somebody saw him? He runs into his old classmates on the train all the time. Next, he'll read about it in the U of C alumni magazine: "News of graduates…John Lincoln, '98, the Chicago book editor, spotted recently assaulting an elderly black woman on the L…"

Halfway home, Lincoln suddenly feels something is missing. He stops and does a quick inventory. He's got his wallet. He left his briefcase at work. The *Times*. He's dropped the paper. "Shit!" Lincoln mutters out loud. He never finished the crossword puzzle.

4

IN THE WEEKS SINCE THE START OF HIS MARRIAGE VACATION, Lincoln has sublet two and a half furnished rooms on the second floor of a subdivided three-flat on a side street in the Lakeview neighborhood, just a few blocks from the lovely apartment he and Mary bought two years ago and where she still lives. This afternoon, he enters on the porch and climbs the narrow wood stairs to his landing. He almost wishes he would run into someone—he remains unsettled by the incident on the L, and he has an urge to talk it out. But the old building welcomes him only with stale, overheated air and deadly silence. In his apartment, Lincoln puts on Wilco's *Yankee Hotel Foxtrot* and listlessly checks the refrigerator. He could make scrambled eggs, as he did last night. He could call out for a pizza. But he's had that a lot lately, and a glance at the *Tribune*'s TV guide suggests there's not much to watch, just the dipshit Cubs playing the Astros in Houston. So Lincoln does what he's done increasingly over the last few years when Mary was out in the evening selling houses: he calls his friend Benjamin Flam, the *Tribune*'s literary editor. Does Flam want to meet for dinner? Of course he does—Flam never has anything going on. They'll meet at John Barleycorn, a bar near Flam's apartment that serves hamburgers and other modest food.

There's time, though—Lincoln decides he will go for a bike ride. He trades his slacks and blue oxford button-down for shorts and a T-shirt. In the tiny bedroom, he glances at himself in the mirror above the bureau, and for a moment he tries to imagine what Mary saw. At six foot two, he's still got the trim physique of his basketball-playing days. His light brown hair—still abundant—is parted high on his scalp, giving him a slightly detached, studious aspect. The nose is probably a little prominent and sharp, like his father's, but his strong, broad cheekbones balance the effect. Everyone said that he and Mary—an unquestioned dark-haired beauty—made an unusually handsome couple. A year or so before they married, they attended a friend's wedding in the suburbs and met Ed Paschke, long Chicago's reigning painter. "You two would make beautiful children," Paschke told them. Lincoln shuts off Wilco just as Jeff Tweedy is singing, "All my lies are only wishes."

Lincoln retrieves his bike from the basement and peddles to the lakefront, heading north up the busy path that meanders through the park along the shore. It's a typical evening for July, low eighties, rather humid, and Lincoln works up a good sweat passing the soccer fields and playgrounds, the softball games being played with the fat, sixteen-inch Chicago ball. Just below Foster Avenue Beach, he turns right and follows a gravel trail south for a few hundred yards to his usual destination, his rock. Well, it's not quite a rock, but a large, rock-like slab of concrete that long ago got laid along this area to protect the shore from the fierce battering of Lake Michigan's waves. In fact, this whole section of lakefront is fortified in concrete. Years of water and ice have broken and buckled the bulwark, however, lifting and tilting Lincoln's slab until it rests like a wide sofa facing east across Lake Michigan. Here Lincoln sits.

He discovered this perch not long after graduating from college and moving from Hyde Park to the North Side, and since then he has made the spot a regular retreat. Over the years, the view has changed dramatically. When Lincoln first arrived in Chicago, the lake was an unappealing grayish brown, colored by the churned muddy bottom and the countless tiny organisms that thrived suspended in the water. Since then, however, an alien species, the zebra mussel, has colonized the Great Lakes, probably arriving in the bilges of ships. The invader—a mollusk about the size of a fingernail—feeds on the tiny organisms and the particles of mud, seriously disrupting the lake's ecology. At the same time, the scouring effect has rendered an incredible aesthetic transformation: that dismal gray-brown water has turned glorious turquoise—under the sun, Lake Michigan now resembles a heavenly alpine expanse.

As he sits on his faux rock on the edge of a laundered natural resource, his gaze propelled east, over the waves, Lincoln finds something approaching a vanished contentment. He rode his bike here on the afternoon of September 11, 2001. He was working nights then at the *Tribune*, and by noon Lincoln had seen and learned enough. For more than three hours, he sat on his rock, looking out toward New York, aching over the loss and devastation, but aching, too, over the sense that he should have been there, that he was a New Yorker in his heart, and that somehow he could have, should have, done something. Now, as the late sun coming through the trees makes orange streaks on the quiet surface of the water, Lincoln wonders if he'll ever live in New York and make his penance.

Later that evening, Lincoln walks the leisurely blocks to John Barleycorn, taking the slightly longer but livelier route down Sheffield Avenue. The sidewalks are busy. Sheffield along here features bars and restaurants mixed among the houses and three-flats, giving the stretch a particularly youthful, informal character. On summer nights like this—with a light breeze coming off the lake a few blocks away—these North Side neighborhoods almost suggest beach towns, places you'd find in Florida. Old-timers tell him that a few decades ago, these were tough, working-class areas with some blocks controlled by Latin gangs. But now it seems as if every smooth-faced grad from the University of Iowa wants to hie over to the Big City, even these days, when jobs are scarce. Since Lincoln has been in Chicago, these hard-partying eager beavers have been taking over the ethnic neighborhoods, erasing the city's mottled character. Another lost facet of Chicago—the stockyards, Marshall Field's, Comiskey Park, Cabrini-Green, the mud-gray lake. Royko's dead, the *Tribune*'s in bankruptcy, even Bellow left town before he died. Maybe, Lincoln thinks, maybe the trouble is that Chicago's not Chicago anymore.

John Barleycorn has a brisk business going, but Lincoln slips past the bar and the big, dark dining room and goes out back, where tables have been set up in an open lot. Flam has grabbed a spot in the corner, and he's already at work on a beer.

"You beat me," Lincoln tells him.

Flam shrugs. "I live next door." Flam is a blond, spidery man with long, skinny arms and legs sprouting from a soft, round torso. Another U of C boy, he's a few years older than Lincoln. They met at the *Tribune*, where they bonded over their Eastern roots—Flam is from Boston—and became friends and confidants despite a lurking edge of competition between them. In fact, Lincoln had been the other finalist for the job of *Tribune* literary editor.

Lincoln orders a beer and a hamburger, and the two gossip about the newspaper for a few minutes. Even before the bankruptcy, the bean counters running the *Tribune* had shrunk book coverage, eliminating a stand-alone section and jamming reviews into a few pages in the anemic Saturday edition. "We're a dead zone," Flam laments.

"I still don't get it," Lincoln says. "Book readers are the most thoughtful, educated niche of the audience. You'd think advertisers would want their product nestled in there among the reviews."

"Book readers are old," Flam says, shaking his narrow head. Several strands of blond hair drop across his brow like bangs. "Advertisers want young, vacant minds with no brand loyalties. Advertisers want nitwits, they want Facebook." Flam sighs and uses both hands to balance his beer on his knee, his thin legs twined around each other. Lincoln recalls those awkward days before his marriage, when the two of them would go out drinking and try to pick up girls. After a while, Flam asks, "How are things at Pistakee?"

"Duddleston told me today that I am a brilliant editor," Lincoln reveals, trying to squeeze a touch of irony into his voice to lighten the boast.

"He's probably getting ready to fire you," Flam says evenly.

Lincoln covers his shock with a grunting laugh and a gulp of beer. "What made you say that?" he asks.

"You know, bloated praise, smoothing the skids—that kind of thing. Why in God's name would you overapplaud an employee if you didn't want him gone—happily, gently, of course, but gone?"

Lincoln thinks: Flam is the king of the weenies, but he's also amazingly astute. "Maybe I really am a brilliant editor," Lincoln suggests.

"I'm sure you are," says Flam, as if that has nothing to do with it.

The waitress plunks down their hamburger platters, and the conversation is diverted. Over the next hour or so, Lincoln drinks too many beers, and as the two men gab on about publishing and literature, he starts to let slip the frustrations with his job. "I need a hit!" he cries at one point, pounding the steel-mesh table and setting off a brief concerto of clinking empty bottles. "I need a fucking hit! Something to put this fucking midget publishing house on the map."

Flam, cool as always, tells him, "The problem is there are too many books being published, even today, when kids don't read and the economy is in free fall. The books pile up outside my office—literally like a wall. I can't even give them away. Who in the world has the time? With the Internet, movies, TV—who has the time to give a shit?"

"But they're still books, you fucking asshole! A pinnacle of civilization, of human life itself." Lincoln pounds the table again. He's aware that he's making a small spectacle and drawing stares from the people seated around. "And now you want to throw it all away just because we can fill our free time with *The Real Housewives of Orange County*?"

"I still like *Survivor*," Flam says. "They always throw in a few babes who walk around half naked."

"Come on, Flam. Look what's happening to us. You're the fucking literary editor of the *Tribune*, still one of the biggest papers in the country."

"Are you sure you're not conflating your own situation with the state of the world?" asks Lincoln's friend.

Even through a haze of beer Lincoln recognizes that Flam has trapped him in a dead end. "I just want a breakthrough book," repeats Lincoln, relenting.

"You just want to prove something to Mary," says Flam.

Lincoln smiles through his beer. Where would he be without Flam? When marriages fell apart in the Fitzgerald short stories that Lincoln devoured one college summer, the husbands always seemed to move into the Yale Club in New York, finding refuge in the clubby dining rooms, the dusty library, the moldy halls overseen by vintage portraits of the solemn teams of rowers and ballplayers. When it happened to Lincoln, he moved in with Flam, who fed him steaks and nursed his ego until Lincoln had recovered enough to get his own place.

"How often do you talk?" Flam asks.

"Oh, we talk," Lincoln says vaguely. In fact, his conversations with Mary—always by phone—have been rare, and then they've been cautious, almost scripted. After all, Lincoln tells himself, she said she needed a vacation.

As the two friends settle the bill and get up to leave, Lincoln asks, "How's *your* girlfriend these days?"

Flam knows he's being teased, since he has terrible luck with women. Lately he's enjoyed talking about his infatuation with the attractive girl who serves him coffee most mornings at the Starbucks around the corner. "I think I'm making progress," Flam says. "She sees me walk in the door and knows what to get before I have to ask—tall coffee, double lid."

"You better start shopping for the engagement ring."

"We've actually talked a bit," Flam goes on, ignoring the joke. "She's nineteen, a student at Loyola."

"You *are* making progress."

"She lives with her parents up in Avondale—you know, the Northwest Side. Working class."

Lincoln starts. "She doesn't even have her own place?"

"Not every girl comes with all the amenities," Flam points out with a smile.

Lincoln grabs a cab for home, but he gets out several blocks early and detours on foot past Mary's building, their old building. Flam warned him not to live so close, but Lincoln couldn't help himself. Was he nearby to protect her? To spy? Mary has insisted there is no one else, but Lincoln can't help wondering. Now he gazes up to the second-floor window in the stately graystone on this lovely, leafy street where he once lived. Lights off. All dark. Could mean anything.

Back in his apartment, despite too much beer, Lincoln lies in bed awake. In the distance, the passing roar of an L train, white noise for the North Side, rises and falls rhythmically. His arm aches in the broken place from pounding the fucking table at John Barleycorn.

5

IN THE MORNING LINCOLN RISES WITH A FEVERISH, UNSETTLED feeling, something between the wages of a night out drinking and an attack of free-floating anxiety. Well, it's not exactly free-floating—on opening his scratchy eyes, Lincoln remembers that he has specific and justified grounds for being anxious. His marriage. His job. Not to mention the lingering guilt over his lamentable behavior on the L yesterday.

He's already running late, but he takes the time to paw through the morning's *Tribune*. He finds the story he's looking for among the stacked short items devoted to neighborhood news.

> NORTH SIDE—Police arrested two Chicago men yesterday after a knife fight on a Brown Line "L" train during evening rush hour panicked passengers and led to several minor injuries.
>
> Enrique Gonzales, 19, and Ricardo Cabello, 21, were charged with endangerment and carrying concealed weapons. Neither was hurt, but their confrontation in a rear car as the train approached the Belmont Station frightened passengers, who then stampeded the front cars to escape.

> "Unfortunately, we've seen this happen before," said Dolores Jordan, spokeswoman for the Chicago Transit Authority. "I think a lot of the people who panicked didn't even know what was going on. They were just reacting to other people panicking."
>
> Several passengers were treated at the scene for cuts and bruises. One woman was taken to Advocate Illinois Masonic Medical Center and later released.

Lincoln reads the story over twice quickly. The woman who was taken to the hospital—could that have been the victim of his shove? He'll probably never know.

He's barely settled into his desk at work when Duddleston appears in the doorway, setting off a cherry bomb of bile in Lincoln's roiling gut. But Duddleston flashes his recently whitened teeth and gleefully announces that he's had an "epiphany" (what he means is a "good idea"): the Pistakee team will make an outing to the Cubs-Brewers game next Tuesday night! Bill Lemke will come along, so Lincoln can mend fences with the offended author in the low-pressure setting of Wrigley Field!

"Great!" Lincoln exclaims.

"It's impossible to stay mad on a night out at Wrigley."

"You're right about that!"

For several tedious minutes, the boss goes over the diplomacy of the encounter—the seating at the game, Lincoln's opening gambit, benign topics of conversation. (Lincoln has mused sometimes that Duddleston may have a touch of obsessive-compulsive disorder—precisely the neurosis that made him a rich trader: he knew how a flood in Kansas would affect September wheat prices before the first raindrop fell.) Lincoln nods robotically, his brain banging against the inside of his skull. The boss concludes with a gentle admonition: "We need to be supportive of our writers. That's the Pistakee Way."

When Duddleston finally leaves, Lincoln gulps two Bufferin, slogging them down with the last inch of cold coffee left over from yesterday's Starbucks.

Lincoln spends the remainder of the morning on *Walking Tours of the Windy City*. After a couple of hours, his father calls, out of the blue, ostensibly to remind Lincoln to drop a card to his mother, whose birthday is coming up, but probably, Lincoln suspects, to make inquiries about the status of Lincoln's marriage. "Any developments?" asks the old man. "Mary's mom told your mom that there were still some issues to deal with."

"They talked?" Lincoln feels as if his privacy has been violated.

"They're worried mothers. Nobody's happy about this."

"Well, neither are we, and we're working on it." (Issues to deal with? What did Mary mean?)

After Lincoln sullenly rebuffs a few more careful probes, his father gives up on the marriage and turns to another sore spot. "How's the job going? Working on any good books?"

"Let's see," Lincoln scrambles. He'd like to escape this conversation with at least a modest show of accomplishment or even just forward motion. "A history of Wrigley Field. A book about walking tours of Chicago." His father's silence on the other end leads Lincoln to embellish. "Quite a thoughtful book, actually, the walking book. There's nothing quite like it on the market now, and the pictures are fantastic."

"Those sound like little books," the father points out.

"Well, you know, those Cubs fans—there are millions of them out there, and they'll go for anything about the team... Wrigley Field. A landmark..."

After they bid farewell, Lincoln is too distracted to return immediately to *Walking Tours*, so he absently leafs through the latest issue of *Publisher's Weekly*, the book-business trade magazine. Arthur Wendt, a prunish Pistakee senior editor and occasional rival of Lincoln's, has pasted a Post-it on a page featuring a favorable review of one of his books, *Chicago's Richard M. Daley: The Mayor Who Works*, by Marcus DeBasio, hagiography from an ancient political hack. That makes four good *PW*s for Arthur so far this year. Pistakee's other senior editor, fidgety Hazel Lanier, who handles mostly children's books, has collected three. Lincoln has two—plus two pans and three other books that were entirely ignored by the magazine. Could Duddleston be keeping score?

Glancing through the front of the publication, Lincoln stops at the headline: "Malcolm House Taps *Time* Vet." Another cherry bomb goes off in Lincoln's stomach. He thinks: so this is how you get an ulcer. The brief story explains that Jeff Kessler has just hired Elizabeth Warner, a low-ranking editor at *Time* magazine. *PW* calls her a "vet," yet Lincoln reads that she's thirty-one, two years younger than he. Kessler didn't even call Lincoln for an interview.

He goes out alone for lunch and orders an Italian beef sandwich at a little joint on Wells, eating outside at a metal table on a concrete plaza. A handful of taxicabs idle nearby, coughing out noxious fumes. The garbage strike has finally ended, and now a monstrous truck parked in the alley grinds up bulging, black plastic bags of refuse. Something in the truck's racket, the stained air, the unintelligible chatter of Indian cabbies at a neighboring table, the sweet, brown gravy leaking from Lincoln's sandwich, messing his hands—the combination brings some solace, calms Lincoln's troubled insides. The world is foul, confused, cruelly indifferent. Think Don DeLillo, J. M. Coetzee, Cormac McCarthy. Fate only mocks our dreams, our efforts. Jonathan Franzen, David Foster Wallace. Why should Lincoln's life be any other way? He trudges back to his office, feeling slightly narcotized.

Shortly after he sits at his desk, his phone rings. "Got the date," Flam tells him from the other end.

"The date?" What's Flam talking about?

"The date!"

Lincoln's mind reels. Nothing makes sense anymore. Maybe he should just have the lobotomy and be done with it. Or maybe he's already had it and the operation has wiped out the memory of itself. Maybe that's it.

Flam throws a lifeline. "You know, my girlfriend. The girl from Starbucks. We're going on a date."

"Jesus Christ," says Lincoln.

"I got there late today, so the morning rush was over, and we started talking. I finished the entire cup of coffee right there, just gabbing away. She's really very sweet."

Lincoln thinks he's never heard Flam so upbeat, so enthused. "What are you going to do—on your date, I mean?"

"Yet to be determined. She likes the movies, so we might do that. Or maybe just a nice restaurant for dinner. I can afford it, and maybe she'd like that experience—you know, the older suitor, spend some of Daddy Warbucks's money. What's a hot spot these days?"

"Let's see." Lincoln is ticking down the names of a few popular restaurants, places he and Mary occasionally patronized, when a small, shaggy head peaks around the doorway into Lincoln's office. The ruffed grouse, clutching a manila file that of course contains her stories. Lincoln forces a smile and waves her in.

"Listen, Flam, I've got to run," Lincoln tells his friend. "Keep me posted."

Flam can't let go. He wants to bring flowers. Is that a good idea? "No one brings flowers on a date," Lincoln warns.

"I need to be different. She's nineteen."

"Roses," Lincoln suggests, and Flam is finally pacified.

Amy O'Malley steps tentatively into the office. She's discarded the boxy blouse for a snug, white T-shirt and jeans, and her face somehow looks brighter, more vibrant. Lincoln suspects she's spent time in front of a makeup mirror.

"How are you today?" he asks, trying to summon some enthusiasm.

"I'm sorry, I didn't mean to interrupt your phone call," Amy says.

"No problem. What can I do for you?"

"Oh, I just brought those stories I mentioned yesterday." She pads forward and holds out the folder. "If you had a chance to look them over..."

"Of course." Anything, as long as she tells Duddleston that Lincoln was a prince about it. He reaches across his desk to accept the bundle and leafs casually through the folder. There must be a dozen stories in here, he thinks, two hundred pages. Hours of dreary reading.

"There's one I kind of like," she natters, "one that feels a little more like *me*, you know? I wrote it when I was working for the sex survey at school..."

"You worked for the sex survey?" A small tingle starts at the base of Lincoln's back and moves gently up his spine, a caterpillar's crawl.

"One summer, and then part-time during the year. Clerical stuff. They paid me by the hour."

"I see." Lincoln nods gravely. For more than two decades, a team of U of C sociologists has been conducting the most comprehensive study of human sexuality since Kinsey. Lincoln has always been curious about the project.

Amy cautions, "Of course, everyone gets the wrong idea about the survey. It was very straightforward, very clinical. Nothing erotic at all."

"What do you expect? It was the U of C." He plops the folder down on his desk. "I'll take a look," he promises.

"Thank you so much," Amy exclaims, backing to the door. "There's no rush." She pauses. "Did Byron tell you about the Cubs game? Are you going?"

Before Lincoln has time to think, instinct takes over. "To watch the dipshit Cubs? Do I have a choice?"

Amy's face falls, and Lincoln realizes he risks a censorious report to the boss.

"Just kidding." He forces out another smile. "Wouldn't miss it!"

For the next two days, Amy's folder sits untouched on Lincoln's desk. No need to hurry into anything, Lincoln thinks. Better to give the impression that the work has been carefully considered. On Friday, Lincoln packs the folder into his briefcase and takes it home. Maybe this weekend, he tells himself, without really expecting that his days will be that empty. But a surprise rainfall washes out his bike ride the next afternoon, and none of the new movies look promising. So Lincoln figures he might as well get it out of the way and starts to browse through Amy's stories. He sees immediately that she shows flashes of talent. She's got a light touch and a good eye for detail. Still, the work is far from polished, and Lincoln can't imagine anything she's written being published, outside of perhaps a student literary magazine. He searches out the story about the sex survey—she's buried it toward the bottom of the folder—and finds it comes with a good title, *Standard Deviation* (for laymen, a somewhat familiar though uncertain phrase, with hints of kinkiness). But the treatment disappoints. The protagonist is a young woman interviewing other women about their sex lives, and early on, the story showcases some tantalizing scenes of anonymous subjects recounting the most intimate details of their lives. But the plot quickly detours into a cul-de-sac about the interviewer's relationship with her boyfriend (sexless in the story—Lincoln wonders if it's drawn from real life) and then dead ends in an ambiguous childhood anecdote about a little girl who gets stung by a sea urchin at a beach at a fancy Caribbean resort (does Amy come from money?).

After a rainy Sunday, Lincoln has read about half the stories in the folder, and that evening he considers the conversation he'll have with Amy, letting her down ever so gently. He rehearses the assorted kiss-offs that he got from editors back in the days when he was sending his own short stories to magazines. "Suggests a deeper literary intelligence that simply needs to be exercised." "Promising, but lacks felt detail. Keep working at it!"

Amy's stories are back in their folder, and Lincoln is sitting on the sofa, vacantly watching a familiar episode of *Curb Your Enthusiasm*, when something remarkable happens. The caterpillar Lincoln felt on his spine the other day suddenly molts its cocoon and a butterfly of an idea takes wing: Why not have Amy turn her experience as a sex researcher into a novel? Her months with the survey have no doubt given her reams of authentic experience, not to speak of endless insights into the secret sex lives of women. Hell, thinks Lincoln, if she can just put down on paper some of the elemental information and sketch out the personalities of some of the key players, he can rewrite it into something smart and sexy. And the book doesn't have to be long—a novel like that could come in at 150, maybe 175 pages, and everyone would go home satisfied.

Lincoln hops up from the sofa and pours a vodka on the rocks. Slow down, he warns himself—don't get too excited, you're getting way ahead of the game. He gulps a slug of vodka and waits for the alcohol to calm him. Way ahead of the game. Still, imagine the possibilities. Amy O'Malley is bright, verbal, and obviously ambitious. One encouraging word from him and she'll be spitting out copy like an old AP terminal. Plus, she's a promoter's dream—a petite, pretty U of C alum who spills about the cloistered world of sex research. Every talk show in the country would sign her up. Pistakee Press will have its first big hit, its first national best seller. And Lincoln…well, as the impresario of this cultural triumph, as the resourceful editor who spotted and nursed the talent, he will bathe at last in the recognition he deserves.

Lincoln pours himself another vodka. He'd like to talk out the idea, but he can't call Amy, even if he knew her number. Lincoln knows he's got to work up to this carefully—hint, suggest, let the book seem to germinate between them. Lincoln has been around enough to know that a writer has to feel proprietary about an idea for it to take hold. If you suggest a potential story line to an author, he or she will turn defensive, invent reasons that prove the idea is utterly idiotic.

There's only one person Lincoln can possibly talk to about the project, so he dials up Flam. "Yeah," says a morose voice on the other end.

"Flam?"

"Yeah."

"Did I wake you? You sound groggy."

"No. Just counting how many times the writers in Sunday's *Tribune* used variants of the verb *engage*. Three so far—a TV show 'never really *engages* viewers,' a modern dance comes off as 'provocative and *engaging*,' and a gallery exhibit of outsider art demonstrates the painter's 'fierce *engagement* with his subject.'"

Flam's sour mood has a specific cause: his Starbucks girlfriend postponed the Big Date—a teacher scheduled a makeup class, and the young woman doesn't have an evening free again for at least another week. (Lincoln thinks: the poor dear is trying to put off the unhappy event for as long as she can, maybe forever.) Lincoln doesn't want to jeopardize his excitement by having his aggrieved friend piss all over the book project, so after a few words of romantic encouragement, Lincoln tries to sign off.

"Hey, what did you want?" Flam asks. "You called me, remember."

"It was nothing. Just a book idea I wanted to run by you."

"Go ahead."

Why not? thinks Lincoln. So he tells Flam about Amy and her background with the sex survey and the idea of ginning up a novel out of the experience. "Think chick lit meets *The Kinsey Report*," Lincoln concludes.

"There's already been a novel like that," Flam says. "Several, in fact."

"Of course there have. Every idea has already been used." Lincoln remains undaunted. Then the vodka speaks: "But this one is mine!" He waits, slightly embarrassed by his ardor while Flam tortures him through a long silence.

"Why don't you just write it yourself?" Flam asks finally.

"Because what do I know about women's inner thoughts and sexuality?"

"You're married, aren't you?"

Lincoln thinks: if only that sufficed. "I don't have the experience. I haven't sat there for hours asking women what they fantasize about while their fat, boring husbands are rooting away on top."

"You're right, that's priceless," Flam deadpans.

After a few more minutes of diminishing skepticism, even Flam, with his punishing intelligence, concedes that Lincoln may be onto something. "It's all in the execution," Flam says.

"That's where I come in," says Lincoln. "I can rewrite anything. Just get me the material, and I can make it work."

"But can you make it a hit?" Flam asks.

"I've got to," Lincoln pronounces, with a ferocity that catches him by surprise.

6

ON MONDAY AT WORK, LINCOLN SEES AMY ONLY FLEETINGLY—once when she's talking to Duddleston in the hall and later across the lobby when he's going out for lunch. Lincoln decides she's avoiding him, trying to deflect any appearance that she's overeager to get his reaction to her stories. That's fine, he thinks. Let her marinate a bit, soften her up.

In the middle of the afternoon, Duddleston comes around to remind Lincoln of the ballgame the next night. "Bill used his connections to get us great seats, right next to the Cubs' bullpen," Duddleston explains.

"Fantastic!" says Lincoln.

"You might not want to get too much into the book yet with Bill," Duddleston suggests, still worrying over the diplomacy. "You know—bring it up, of course, but mostly use this as the occasion to reestablish the relationship."

"I'll be gentle," Lincoln promises.

"That-a-boy, Abe."

On leaving the office that evening, Lincoln notices a well-dressed, slender young black man studying the roster of the building's tenants posted on the wall near the front door. Lincoln is halfway down the block when he thinks he hears the man call after him, "Excuse me! Excuse me!" But Lincoln doesn't stop or turn around. He's not sure the man is calling to him, and, besides, Lincoln is tired of being accosted by panhandlers, who come in all colors and wardrobes these days. Still, the encounter is slightly disconcerting and rubs at Lincoln throughout his walk to the L.

The next day, Duddleston has arranged for a van to come at six to ferry the Pistakee team up to Wrigley Field for the Cubs game. Lemke will meet them there. The group waits for its ride outside on the sidewalk. "It's a perfect night for a ballgame," Duddleston repeats endlessly, and he's right—clear skies, high seventies, low humidity, a light breeze coming in off the lake. Chicago has about four days of ideal weather in a year, Lincoln thinks, and his rich boss has managed to land an event on one of them. Amy continues to be elusive, looking away whenever Lincoln glances toward her. He perceives with a small note of pleasure that she continues to elevate her level of stylishness, wearing jeans and a frilly blue blouse, with a blue sweater dangling over her shoulders. As she climbs into the van, he looks for traces of the lace panties, but the tight, thick denim crushes all evidence.

Avoiding his coeditors, Lincoln takes a seat next to Matt Breeson, Pistakee's dull, extremely competent comptroller. "I know you're from the East," Breeson says as the van moves through stagnant evening traffic. "But have you caught Cubs fever here in Chicago?"

"A serious dose," Lincoln replies, though, of course, he disdains the chronically dreadful Cubs and their bleached, arriviste fans who know nothing about baseball but treat a ballgame as a huge, chattering singles party. Not so long ago—before the Cubs started playing night games at Wrigley—the team was lucky to draw ten thousand fans to a midweek matchup in July, most of them babbling obsessives of the Bill Lemke variety, jabbering on about the sweet flick of Ernie Banks's bat and the unfairness of life.

"I was wondering," Breeson says, "did you ever consider publishing any mysteries?" He's a large, shapeless man of indeterminate age—somewhere in his late thirties or early forties—who has been with Duddleston since the trading days. Breeson has always treated Lincoln with a kind of distanced curiosity, if not awe, never able to grasp the messy, unquantifiable work of literary creation, but earnestly trying to figure it out.

"Not specifically," says Lincoln. "I'm not really conversant with the genre."

Breeson whispers conspiratorially, "I love mysteries. I like to try to figure them out before the end."

"Really. And do you?"

"Sometimes," Breeson says. "Sometimes."

The van finally drops them off at the corner of Clark and Addison, and the Pistakee group makes its way through the mob into Wrigley. Lincoln can't visit the place without thinking of the Roman Colosseum—not just because the entertainment within diverts the restless masses, but because, like its Italian counterpart, the ancient Chicago landmark is falling apart. Crumbling concrete forced the team to install protective netting. The interior walkways are narrow and decrepit. The foul and inevitably overcrowded men's restrooms feature long, communal troughs, a plumbing innovation Lincoln recalls from the public bathrooms at Pompeii. Still, after a visitor approaches Wrigley on a sea of pavement, passes through the stadium's gray walls, walks up the concrete steps to the field-level seats, he's suddenly confronted with an explosion of green—the outfield grass, the ivy walls, the huge, old scoreboard, all so lush and verdant it's almost dizzying. Lincoln thinks of that scene in *The Wizard of Oz* when Dorothy steps out of the uprooted house and the black-and-white movie turns Technicolor.

As promised, the seats are excellent, six rows back, just behind the Cubs' bullpen along the left-field line, and Bill Lemke is waiting. Duddleston orchestrates a clumsy minuet that sends Lincoln down the row to sit next to the author. "Hi, Bill! Great night for a game, huh?" Lincoln enthuses as he sits down.

Lemke nods slowly, barely acknowledging his editor. He holds a hot dog in one hand, and a daub of mustard colors the corner of his mouth.

Soon, however, Duddleston has corralled several vendors, and he's passing beer, hot dogs, and peanuts all around. The game starts, and as the beer continues to flow, Lemke's mood lightens. He's a balding man with a halfhearted comb-over across the back of his pate and a round, florid face marked by bumps and crannies. Lincoln can't be certain of Lemke's age, though his wardrobe—knit gray pants and a knit shirt with pale, green stripes—appears to come straight from a Sears sale in the 1950s. He's unhappy with the state of sports writing today, as he explains to Lincoln over the course of several innings. "It's a bunch of psychological crap," Lemke laments. "Where are the facts? You read a story and you don't even know what happened in the goddamned game."

"It's tough today," Lincoln points out. "The scores are out there immediately—on the Internet, TV. There's a lot of pressure to find new angles and ways to tell the story."

Lemke ignores the point and leans close, his breath reeking of mustard. "Twice I was voted Illinois Sportswriter of the Year," he confides.

Lincoln thinks: right, the only difference between Lemke and Nelson Algren is Algren didn't get any breaks. "That's a great honor," Lincoln tells him.

On the field, the Cubs' Alfonso Soriano overswings, as always, but gets enough of a fat pitch to send a ball high into the night sky and two rows deep into the left-field bleachers. The crowd stands and roars. The stadium lights pushing against the enveloping darkness create a dome of golden illumination over the playing field and the stands. The effect is so intimate that Lincoln feels as if he could reach out across the outfield and grab a handful of peanuts from a shirtless guy sitting in the bleachers. It's like having a ball game in your living room. Lincoln glances down his row and sees Amy at the far end, cheering and clapping around a beer in one hand. If he can maneuver his way beside her, he thinks, this would be a good night to drop the seeds of the book.

By the seventh inning, the home team is winning. The Cubs' pitcher is throwing a shutout, and Lemke is maundering on about his life and career as if Lincoln were his favorite nephew. When everyone stands during the seventh inning stretch, singing "Take Me Out to the Ball Game" under the direction of guest celebrity soloist Vince Vaughn, Lemke sings a few lines, then wraps an arm around Lincoln's shoulder. Swinging his head to indicate the buff young traders in Polo shirts, the suited businessmen in their expense-account box seats, the chattering girls showing off their navel jewelry, the suburban dads with their troops of restless kids—the whole nouveau Cubs family—Lemke whispers hoarsely, "These are my readers."

With the last call for beer, the Pistakee lineup shifts. Lincoln and Breeson go out for refills; Lemke slides over to recall his career triumphs for Duddleston. On his return, Lincoln manages to slip into the seat next to Amy. "Enjoying yourself?" he asks.

"This is a blast," she exclaims. "I love this place. I've never been to Wrigley Field before."

"I guess Professor Davoodi didn't organize too many field trips up here."

Amy eyes him coolly. Just then, a Cubs outfielder dashes in, flops on his stomach, and, sliding, grabs a soft line drive. Amy lets out a whoop, along with everyone else in the stadium. When the crowd quiets, Amy says, "You're disdainful of the U of C, but a lot of people who went there really liked it."

"I know the school has a lot of great qualities," Lincoln says, trying to sound reasonable. "Hell, in the fifties, the U of C was the hippest place in the country. While everywhere else was sleeping through the Eisenhower era, Hyde Park was overrun with smart, edgy, creative types. Mike Nichols, Elaine May, Susan Sontag, Philip Roth. Mostly Jews from the East. Children of immigrants. Second City started down there. They invented improvisational comedy—cutting-edge, intellectual stuff with real political bite."

"So?" Amy asks.

"Something happened. By the time I got there, the place had lost its spark—turned insular and crabbed. Nothing but kids who beavered away in the library all through the weekend."

Amy stares off at the field for a second, then says, "You know, you always seem so sour. You must be really unhappy."

The remark sets Lincoln back for a moment. Unhappy? Lincoln always thought he was just cynical—or maybe touched by cynicism's journalism-refined cousin, skepticism. But unhappy?

"What do you really want?" Amy presses. "Do you even know?"

"I'm an editor," he tells her. "I just want to make things better."

Amy shakes her head in exasperation, setting in motion her dangly silver earrings, showcased now with her styled short hair combed behind her ears. She and Lincoln watch the game wind down at a glacial pace. Though the Cubs are far ahead, the Brewers keep bringing in relief pitchers, prolonging the inevitable. Lincoln would like to lure Amy away to a neighborhood bar, where they can talk in privacy about his sex book idea, but he doesn't want to leave before Duddleston. Down the row of seats, Lemke is blattering into the boss's ear.

After a while, Lincoln tells Amy quietly, "I've been enjoying your stories."

"Really?" She turns to him, unable to mask her excitement.

"They're raw," he says, dialing back, trying to play this carefully, "nothing that could be published yet." He watches her deflate. "But you've got a nice touch. An eye for detail."

On the field, Soriano homers again. Everyone in the stadium stands except Lincoln and Amy. "Take 'Standard Deviation,'" Lincoln says over the commotion. "I think that story shows promise. The setting has possibilities."

"I *know.* That's such a weird situation—asking all those utterly private questions, in this totally clinical, sexless manner. I think I could really do more with that."

"Yes." Lincoln nods slowly. "Yes, you may be right." Bingo, he thinks.

At the end of the eighth inning, Duddleston announces he has to leave to tuck in his kids. Everyone from Pistakee gets up to follow the boss; only Lemke will watch the game to its last, staggering out. Lincoln jockeys over to shake the old sportswriter's hand. "I'll call you this week," Lincoln promises.

Lemke won't let go. "I was telling Byron about when the Cubs' outfielder George Altman ran over between innings and bought a hot dog from a vendor," Lemke says. "He thought we should put that in the book."

"Maybe, maybe. We'll talk." Lincoln manages to pull away.

The fans are already streaming out of the ballpark. The Pistakee gang falls into the pack and works its way toward the exit. Duddleston edges close to Lincoln. "Nice job tonight, Abe" he says. "I think you smoothed it right over. Bill's eager to get going again."

Outside in the mob on Clark Street, the group scatters. As Duddleston disappears into the crowd, Lincoln asks Amy if she wants to get a nightcap so they can continue their discussion. Of course, she does.

They join the crowd flowing south. The neighborhood is a riot of milling and shouting fans, lumbering buses, angry car drivers caught in the mess. An oblivious scrum of teenage boys barrels past, and Lincoln grabs Amy around the waist to pull her out of the way. His hand lingers on the taut muscles on the side of her stomach, then slides along her smooth back. Even though he's spent several days thinking on and off about her panties, her trim figure, her seeming makeover, for the first time a thought pushes into his head: Wouldn't it be lovely to sleep with her? He immediately processes one of those internal debates, the sort in which the pros and cons sound somehow familiar and now are laid out in a babble of overlapping contradiction: He's still married, and he hopes to get back again with his wife. (Well, they are separated for now, and the rules under those circumstances are muddy at best; and who knows if Mary remains faithful?) Amy's just an exuberant, ambitious kid—sleeping with a grumpy married man twelve years her senior is probably the farthest thing from her mind. (But hasn't she dolled herself up since he showed an interest, and isn't there a flirtatious glint to her manner?) She's a Pistakee employee, for fuck's sake; he's an executive, and this is 2009, when every accidental bump at the copying machine turns into a workplace sexual-harassment suit. (On the other hand, he doesn't supervise her—they're more like colleagues, and the law doesn't want to meddle with genuine office romances.) Put it out of your mind, Lincoln tells himself.

"Do you want to come back to my place?" Amy asks.

Lincoln stares at her, stupefied.

"Oh, no, no, no," she says, laughing, putting her hand on his chest and pushing him away. "I didn't mean it like that. I mean all the bars around here are going to be packed and noisy. We'll never be able to hear each other talk."

"I think I know a place," Lincoln says.

At a little round table in the Northern Lights Tap, Lincoln orders a Scotch on the rocks. Amy tells the waitress she'll have the same thing, but when it comes, she takes a sip and makes a face, so Lincoln orders two beers, too. He continues to compliment her on her stories, pointing out scenes he likes, characters that show promise. He discusses her work, in fact, until he starts to bore himself, though Lincoln has spent enough time with writers to know that they possess the endurance of Indian mystics—those fellows with towels wrapped around their loins who walk on coals—capable of withstanding unimaginable tedium and discomfort, as long as someone is talking about their prose.

Lincoln orders another round of Scotch and beer (I'll pay tomorrow, he thinks; on the other hand, Amy's eyes look as clear and bright as ever). He works his way back to the sex survey. "How much material did you leave on the cutting-room floor, so to speak?"

"One semester while I was working there, I was taking a writing course and the professor made us keep a diary." Amy touches Lincoln's arm. "I've got pages of the stuff."

"Hmmmm." Lincoln sips his Scotch, deep in contemplation. The bar is decorated to suggest a hunting lodge, with dark pine paneling, moose heads sprouting from the walls, fishing gear tacked everywhere. Lincoln wonders if the décor is pumping up his testosterone, because he has to fight an urge to nuzzle aside Amy's dangly earring and kiss her on the neck.

"Do you think I could turn the material into a novel?" she asks.

"A novel," repeats Lincoln, as if considering a fresh and intriguing idea.

"Oh, that's stupid," Amy chides herself. She sips her Scotch, then quickly follows with a gulp of beer. "I couldn't write a novel. I wouldn't even know where to begin."

Now it's Lincoln's turn to touch Amy's arm. "Wait a second. You may be onto something there." He lets his gaze wander the bar, seemingly searching for inspiration from the moose head, the decaying trout basket, the warped and nicked canoe paddle. "A novel. A young girl just discovering her sexuality who's thrust into an intense project to explore other people's sex lives. The experience is supposed to be clinical, anonymous, she's put off by it all, but then, slowly, she's drawn into the life of one of the subjects."

Amy is on fire. "I can write that!" she cries. "I can sit down and write that!"

"She enters a world that's dark, slightly shrouded." Lincoln speaks slowly. "Maybe there's the hint of a crime, a mystery unfolding."

Amy pulls away from his grasp. "Of course, it was nothing like that in real life."

"Who cares? It's a fucking novel! Anything can happen."

"And I do have pages and pages of notes."

"Exactly."

Amy looks at him with shining eyes. "Will you help me?" she asks.

"Well, I'd be happy to look the stuff over."

She leans forward. "You don't think Pistakee would publish a book like that, do you?"

Lincoln sits back and considers, the hoary old master. "Maybe. Who can say. We've done fiction before, though not for a while." Then, after a pause: "But let's not mention it to Byron just yet. This will be our own little project."

"Right!"

It's almost midnight by the time they leave the bar. The Wrigley crowd has disappeared, the leafy streets are quiet. Amy's apartment on Seminary Avenue is on the way home for Lincoln, so he walks her the handful of blocks. They are both a little unsteady on their feet and bump occasionally. The soft summer air coats Lincoln's feeling of accomplishment. After all the gabbing, they don't talk much. Lincoln wonders what she's thinking. Outside her building, Amy takes his hand. "Now I really do want you to come up," she says.

He follows without hesitation. It flits through his mind that Mary had said there was no one else. Hah! She's probably with her lover right now. In the elevator, Amy leans against him, and Lincoln rests his cheek on the top of her head. She's tiny, he thinks, she fits right under my arm.

They step into her apartment, and she flips on the light. Lincoln has only a moment to take in bright swatches of color, a collection of dainty bottles, other girly essences before they stumble to the sofa, bounce back to their feet, stagger entangled to the narrow bedroom, and fall onto the bed. Lincoln's head swims. He's on his back, naked, an overhead fixture making him blink, and Amy is in a white, frilly bra and panties, the cloth gorgeous against her tan skin. Lincoln closes his eyes, and he imagines a large cat, a panther, maybe, walking up and down his body, its soft, padded feet pressing gently into his flesh. With impeccable timing, the panther nibbles, then squeezes, and Lincoln feels as if he has let go of days, years of tension, his entire life in the Midwest, the flatness, the brown suits, the overweight children, the featureless gossip columns with the birthday greetings at the bottom, the stubborn plainness—all of it, washed away.

Afterward, Amy lies with her head on his chest. Lincoln feels too drained to breathe. Can you be so limp and exhausted that you just stop respiring, smothered by contentment?

Amy turns, arches her back to look up at him. Lincoln kisses her on the forehead.

"Are you happy now?" she asks.

SUMMER/FALL:

The Evinrude Doctrine

7

It's after three in the morning when Lincoln pecks Amy softly on her shoulder while she sleeps, then slips out of her apartment. The sidewalks are empty, and under the pressing light of the streetlamps, the storefronts take on a muted, Hopperish aspect—but without the melancholy, Lincoln thinks. In fact, Lincoln feels so buoyant that he briefly considers hiking over to his concrete rock on the lakefront to watch the sun come up. But he's expecting a busy day at work, and he should try to get a few hours of sleep. So he walks slowly home, his exuberance gradually giving way to...well, not to guilt itself, more like the anticipation of guilt. Actually, he doesn't know quite how to feel or how he will feel.

Later that morning at Pistakee, Lincoln applies himself diligently to rereading Bill Lemke's Wrigley Field manuscript, erasing or scratching out edits that aren't absolutely necessary, marking with a gentle little star suggestions that he hopes the author will continue to honor. But Lincoln really only has one object in mind today: talk to Amy. Tell her that last night was delightful, but it must not happen again, and it must remain their secret. There are so many reasons why. He still loves Mary. At least, he presumes he still loves her. He presumes that the brew of affection, regret, sympathy, memories, concern, interest, and, yes, lust he feels for his wife still combusts into love, even if their marriage is dormant for the moment.

But there are other, more practical, reasons why he and Amy must maintain a professional distance. Duddleston would fire him if he found out. In the sober daylight, Lincoln has no doubt. Duddleston is a Presbyterian family man, a Democrat, who nonetheless still grumbles about Clinton canoodling with Monica Lewinsky. In an era fraught with sexual harassment issues, you don't jeopardize the country's business (or a thrifty little publishing company) for a quick spot of animal pleasure. Besides, Lincoln reasons, he and Amy are onto a promising project. If they hope to haul the sex book through the writing and revision process, they must be clinical, objective. They can't get muddled by an emotional entanglement.

Amy will agree, Lincoln is certain. But she has disappeared. She's nowhere around the office, and he doesn't have her cell phone number. Several times Lincoln diverts past her cubicle on the way to the bathroom. The third time catches the attention of Duddleston's secretary, Mrs. Macintosh. "Something wrong, John?" she asks.

"No." She's noticed him frowning at Amy's empty desk.

"You look troubled," says the old lady.

"Just wandering the halls to exercise my imagination," Lincoln tells her. He doesn't want to risk asking where Amy is.

Mrs. Macintosh considers him suspiciously from beneath a tower of intricately curled white hair. Lincoln hurries away.

What if Amy's been so traumatized by their encounter that she's had a breakdown and even now is at home—unwashed, undressed, sobbing uncontrollably? Or what if she's one of those desperate, clinging women like Glenn Close in *Fatal Attraction*, and she's skipped work to plot her assault on his family, such as it is? What has he got himself into?

At around eleven, Lincoln gets a call from the office receptionist, Kim, a chunky blonde recently arrived from Iowa. "John, there's a policeman on the line who wants to talk to you."

"A policeman?" Lincoln's weary body immediately comes to attention. "What's he want?"

"I don't know." Kim sounds annoyed. "He says he wants to talk to you."

"Put him through." Lincoln's mind rushes through the terrible possibilities. Amy's dead. She flung herself out her window in humiliation at her lost honor. Or she's been murdered. Her boyfriend beat a confession out of her and then finished her off.

"John Lincoln?" says a deep voice with inflections of the South Side.

"Yes."

"This is Sergeant Evinrude of the Twenty-Third District. I wonder if you'd mind stopping by in the next few days?"

"What's this about?" Lincoln asks abruptly.

"Someone has filed a battery claim against you."

"What?" Lincoln is not prepared for this—he's still recovering from last night.

"A battery. They say you hit someone."

"That's impossible. There must be some mistake."

"Were you riding the Brown Line at about six fifteen last Tuesday evening?"

Lincoln's body rebels. Head, heart, stomach, arm. "There was a riot on the train that night," he squeaks through his tightened throat. "The *Tribune* had a story about it."

"Look, anyone can file a complaint. It's my job to investigate it. Can you stop by? We're on Addison, just east of Wrigley Field."

Lincoln tries to settle himself, think clearly. "Should I bring a lawyer?"

"Up to you," says Sergeant Evinrude evenly. "I just want to ask a few questions. You'll be free to go whenever you want. No need for any Miranda warnings."

Lincoln is dumbstruck. The sergeant moves them along. "How about ten tomorrow morning? Just ask for me at the front desk."

"Ah, OK," Lincoln mumbles.

"See you then." Click.

Lincoln sits holding the phone until it starts to whine from the disconnection. Even after he returns it to its cradle, the whine remains in his ears. A battery complaint? It must be from shoving the black woman. But that's ridiculous. He replays the incident over and over in his head. He was just acting in panic, like everyone else. Maybe he was thinking only of himself, maybe he was a little rough, but how could that possibly be criminal?

He stands and walks to the window, looking down on the alley, working to gather himself. He knows he's got to channel his father. Steely calm. Never admit, never concede. *His father.* An assistant attorney general for civil rights under President Clinton. The distinguished advocate for human rights whose son is being charged with battery on an elderly black woman.

"Lost in memory?" asks a voice from the doorway. Amy, looking relaxed and trim in jeans and a sleeveless green shirt.

"Where have you been?" he asks.

"I could ask you the same thing," she says, laughing. "I never heard you leave."

"Shhh." Lincoln motions her to sit.

"I've really only got a second," she tells him, sitting down nonetheless. "Byron has got me running all over the city picking up photographs for your Professor Fleace. I spent the morning at the History Museum."

"Were you able to find some good shots?" Earlier, Fleace and Lincoln had made a list of promising images.

"Lots. You could cut the text and add more photos."

"Listen," he says, sitting again, "we need to talk, seriously."

"OK." She looks at him with concern.

The phone rings. Lincoln picks it up.

"John, your wife is on the line," Kim announces.

"Ah…" Before Lincoln can decide whether to take it, the call clicks through.

"Linc?"

"Hiiii." In his distress, he turns the greeting into a yodel.

"Linc? You OK? You sound kind of funny."

"Yes, just in a meeting at the moment." Lincoln sits up and hunches over the phone, as if he could hide this conversation from Amy.

"Oh, sorry," Mary says. "This will only take a second." But then in a rushed, anxious voice she launches a monologue about how their insurance broker thinks Lincoln should take his name off the car insurance since Mary's the one using the Camry these days, and the premium will drop without Lincoln and his two speeding tickets, etc. They haven't spoken in two weeks, and this is what Mary wants to talk about?

Lincoln nods with the phone at his ear and smiles stupidly at Amy. His head is pounding, and he wonders if it's too soon to take more Bufferin, but he's too distracted to do the math and count the hours. Finally, he breaks in and tells Mary to go ahead, delete his name from the coverage.

Mary pauses. "How are things going?" she asks in a gentler voice.

"OK, busy, OK."

"Me, too. But I'm getting away. I'm leaving today for a week in Sedona."

Alone? Of course, not. Lincoln wants to ask, With whom? Instead, he jokes darkly, "Oh, a vacation from the vacation."

Mary doesn't get the reference. "Huh?" Then: "Sorry, I know you're in a meeting. I'll let you go. I miss you, Linc."

Really?

"Me, too," he blurts nonsensically.

Mary hangs up.

Amy stands abruptly. "I have to go. More photos to chase down."

"Wait!" Lincoln cries.

Amy sits again, but she cocks her head and studies Lincoln. "Are you OK, John?"

"Fine," he lies, then continues carefully, "I just thought we should maybe talk. Last night—I had a really good time, and you're terrific, but I think we ought to lay out the parameters… well, we probably should just cool it."

Amy aims a hard little smile at him.

"I mean, I'm still married, technically, and I don't know what's happening with that, and given that we work together…"

Amy lets a silence settle between them. Finally, she says, "I envy your ego, John. I really do."

"Ah…"

"Last night was last night. Get over it."

"Right, right." Lincoln nods frantically, though on top of everything, he feels let down. As a lover, is he really that fungible?

After another pause, Amy asks, "Why are you always rubbing your arm?"

"I guess I didn't realize I do it." Lincoln drops his hands to his lap. "It aches sometimes where I broke it once."

"How'd you break it?"

"It's a long story."

More silence. Amy stares at him evenly. It startles Lincoln, how she can make herself appear so different from those early impressions. Her layered, dark brown hair divides in a neat part stylishly askew from the crown of her head. Dark brows and lashes frame her chestnut eyes, and her thin nose is softened by surprisingly full lips. Even now, with all hell breaking loose, memories of last night tease him.

"What about my novel?" Amy asks.

"I love the idea."

"You know, I didn't sleep with you just so you'd help me."

"And I didn't encourage you just to get you in bed."

Amy rises to go. "I'm glad we understand each other," she says.

"Right."

At the door, Amy stops and sends a parting shot: "You know, it's terrible, when you think of all the damage Glenn Close did to one-night stands in *Fatal Attraction*."

Wisely, Lincoln says nothing.

8

OVER A RESTLESS AFTERNOON AND SEMISLEEPLESS NIGHT, Lincoln decides he will go it alone on the battery complaint, without a lawyer, at least for now. Some obsessive surfing of the Internet yields the intelligence that complaints filed by citizens are fairly routine and often amount to little. Hiring a lawyer will almost certainly turn the case into something larger. And what if Duddleston finds out? It's bad enough that Lincoln abuses writers. He also punches out old black ladies? Besides, Lincoln has enough confidence in his intellectual dexterity to assume he can parry the detective's questions without giving up anything. And if the discussion turns difficult, Lincoln will simply leave and then hire a lawyer, if necessary. He reminds himself repeatedly: he hasn't done anything wrong! Well, at least, not legally wrong. On another scale (what would it be—morality, courage, dignity?), he wishes he had a do-over.

The next morning, Lincoln calls Pistakee to say he'll be late and then walks the fifteen or so blocks to the Twenty-Third District headquarters, a surprisingly attractive Italianate red-brick building with green awnings and a green cornice. Inside, beyond a heavy wood door, Lincoln feels as if he's seen this place before on any of a hundred cop dramas. A motley assortment of citizens are milling around a cramped lobby papered with official notices. A high counter separates a crew of bored-looking cops from the bothersome public. A blonde policewoman with a rote manner fields questions from a line of petitioners.

Lincoln gets in line behind an elderly woman whose dog has disappeared and a suited man who insists his car has been towed unjustly. When Lincoln's turn comes, he gives the policewoman his name and tells her he's there to see Detective Evinrude.

"What's this about?" she demands.

"He called me. Something about a complaint."

She speaks into an intercom, and a minute or so later, a tall, powerfully built black man with graying hair emerges from the back. He nods and beckons Lincoln through a door and leads him on a twisting course deep into the building to a small, plain office with a gray metal desk and several matching chairs. "Have a seat," says the detective as he takes his place behind the desk. Buried this deep in the station house, Lincoln wonders whether just getting up and walking out would really be that easy. He's more anxious than he anticipated. (One slip of the tongue and he's under arrest?) Still, he takes a seat. He's brought his briefcase—it seemed a good prop, with suggestions of status, purpose, etc.—and he hugs it in his lap.

Detective Evinrude puts on a pair of wire-rimmed reading glasses and shuffles papers on his desk. "John Lincoln, right?" he confirms, reading from a sheet.

"Yes."

The detective stops himself and looks up. "Lincoln. Any relation to the president?" he asks.

"No, I'm afraid not. The only name descendant died in the 1920s."

"Really? I didn't know that." The detective nods to himself, as if this were a useful piece of information. He returns to his sheet of paper, and for several minutes he reads silently, apparently unconcerned that Lincoln is sitting with nothing to do but watch. Finally, he puts the sheet down and takes off his glasses. "So there was an incident on the Brown Line at the Belmont Station. The complainant says you got mad and knocked an elderly woman down."

Lincoln reminds himself of the rules he's established for this encounter: be terse; speak in generalities; don't volunteer a whit more than necessary. "There was a riot on the L that night," he recounts carefully. "Everybody was in a panic trying to get off the train. There was a story the next day in the *Tribune*. I've got it here." Lincoln has printed a copy from the newspaper's Web archive, and he pulls it from his briefcase.

Ignoring the story in Lincoln's hand, the detective says, "The old lady was African American." He brings this up with no particular inflection, as if it were just another fact to be considered—the time of the incident, the number of witnesses—but Lincoln feels acutely the divide between them. (He thinks: Should I have lied earlier? This is one occasion when it might actually help to be related to the Great Emancipator.) "It says here she was the only black person around," the detective continues. He stares unblinkingly at Lincoln. The man's bulk, his stolidity—Lincoln recalls playing ball against guys like that; they'd take a position near the basket and you couldn't move them. Implacable.

"It was chaos," Lincoln says. "There was a stampede. Race had nothing to do with it."

Detective Evinrude nods toward the newspaper story in Lincoln's hand. "Can I see that?"

Lincoln gives it to him and watches the dark eyes behind the wire rims scan the lines. Doesn't a Chicago police detective have more important things to investigate—a murder, an armed robbery? "I'm sure there's a police report on it," Lincoln suggests.

Again, the glasses come off. "So you say you didn't knock down the old lady?" the detective says.

"Everybody was pushing and shoving," Lincoln evades. "It was chaos."

"And then you just left the scene?"

Lincoln's heart jumps in red alert. (Is it a crime to be a hit-and-run pedestrian?) "I didn't think there was a problem," he responds, then pulls out another tactic he'd planned, turning interrogator himself. "Who is this person who filed the complaint?"

"Can't tell you, at least not until I've looked into it a little more," the officer says evenly. "We don't want people settling things on their own."

"Was the complainant even there?"

Detective Evinrude picks up his glasses and consults the sheet. "One of my colleagues took the report," he explains, "but he's been promoted." After reading for a few seconds, he says, "It appears not."

"How did my name even come up?"

"You dropped your *New York Times*. Had your name and your company on it." Said with just a hint of satisfaction, as if the detective has trapped Lincoln with this simple explanation.

Lincoln zips shut his briefcase. Time to flee. Probably past time. But Detective Evinrude has another question. "Pistakee Press. What do they do?"

"A book publisher. I edit books."

"What sort of books?"

"All sorts." (Does the cop suspect that I'm a pornographer? Lincoln wonders.) Lincoln does a rapid inventory of his projects, searching for a possible sympathetic connection. "Right now, I'm editing a book on the history of Wrigley Field."

"I grew up on the South Side. A White Sox fan."

The black South Side. The white North Side. Why does race have to come into everything in Chicago? "I'm mostly a Bulls fan myself," says Lincoln, dodging.

And then Detective Evinrude warms by a degree or two. "Maybe you should do a book on Comiskey Park, you know, the old White Sox stadium."

"Maybe I should!"

"I could tell you some stories."

"I'll remember that!" Lincoln takes advantage of the slight détente to get up to leave, but he dreads the thought of walking out into the warm summer morning burdened with uncertainty. So he asks, "On this L train matter—what happens now?"

The temperature drops again. "I'll look into it. We'll be in touch."

For all his planning and preparation, Lincoln can't help himself. He blurts, "I mean, it just seems like a waste of time. The whole thing was an accident, nothing more."

The officer waits, letting Lincoln suffer in the silent memory of his outburst. "Sometimes these complaints are just for the record," Evinrude says finally. "They're preliminary to the filing of a civil case."

"A civil case?"

"Do you have homeowner's insurance?"

"For a condo."

"Same thing. Sometimes your homeowner's insurance will cover it." The detective considers Lincoln, who is hugging his briefcase as if it were the stuffed polar bear he carried around when he was six. "Can you find your way out?" Evinrude asks.

Lincoln assures him that he can.

The detective hands Lincoln his card. "Let me know if you plan to leave town," he instructs.

9

LINCOLN LEAVES THE POLICE STATION AND WALKS SOUTH, too befuddled to go right to work. Why does everything have to be so ambiguous? He's accused of a crime or he's not. He's in good standing at his job or he's not. He's married or he's not. Where are the hard edges? How do you turn a corner when everything around you is curved?

The pedestrians he passes on this stretch of Halsted, the gay neighborhood known as Boystown, move with strong, purposeful strides. Lincoln feels as if his noodly legs can barely hold him up. He's a thoughtful drinker and hasn't touched booze before noon since college, but this day he needs a bracer, so when he comes to Leonard's Lounge, a small, nondescript dive, he enters and sits at the bar. He's alone with a bartender in a blue Hawaiian shirt and a television tuned to CNN with the sound off. While Lincoln sips a Bloody Mary, waiting for the vodka to stiffen his bones, he watches video of the disgraced ex-Illinois governor, Rod Blagojevich, who has made another appearance that morning on his media tour to proclaim his innocence. The boyish face, the mop of hair, the sad, pleading eyes—doesn't he realize that the whole world knows he's a crook? Yet, he natters on, making his ludicrous case. He has a way of acting hurt, surprised, victimized, but without rancor—like a wounded soldier who didn't realize until the moment of impact that the enemy was using real bullets. Sitting at a bar at eleven in the morning, Lincoln envies Blago's clueless certitude.

By the time he's finished his second Bloody Mary, Lincoln has vowed to be more *proactive* with his life (yes, he uses that clichéd neologism with himself, even though he has struck it from every manuscript that ever crossed his desk). To start with, he'll get ahead of the game on a possible civil suit by checking his homeowner's insurance, as Detective Evinrude advised. But the actual document is in a file cabinet in the condo he bought with Mary. She still lives there, but she's in Sedona by now. Lincoln can't even remember who the insurance carrier is, let alone the salesman on their policy. No problem: summoning his new firmness of purpose, Lincoln decides to call Mary and get her to call the superintendent to let him into the apartment.

Sitting at the bar, Lincoln dials her cell. She picks up after six rings, sounding breathless and not pleased to hear from him. Lincoln gets right to the point.

"Why do you need to see *that*?" Mary demands.

"A possible liability issue."

"What?"

Even with the separation, it stuns Lincoln how easily they slip back to the annoyed skepticism that characterized their conversations toward the end. "It's nothing. Just call the super for me," he says impatiently. "He knows I'm not living there, so he'll get suspicious if I ask him to let me in."

"Linc, you've got the goddamned key. Let yourself in."

"Oh." He somehow assumed she'd changed the locks. "OK. Just wanted to check with you."

"I've got to run, Linc." A pause. "I'm going mountain biking."

"Wow. Have fun."

"Bye."

"Bye."

Lincoln orders a third Bloody Mary, trying to recapture his resolve. She's OK having me paw through the apartment, he thinks. At least she has nothing to hide.

Working off the Bloody Marys, Lincoln walks west along quiet side streets until he comes to Mary's building, their old building. Taking a calming, deep breath, he unlocks the front door, then climbs the stairway to their apartment. Since that awful afternoon, he's only been back once, to pick up clothes, and now he wonders whether Mary has changed things, eliminated all markers of life with him. Inside, however, he finds the place almost exactly as he left it. They bought the apartment three years ago, and Mary took the occasion to exercise her decorating taste—sort of country French (reproduction, of course) with accents of Olde Chicago gleaned from the city's carelessness with its architectural heritage (a section of stained glass recovered from a leveled West Side church, a gargoyle saved at the last moment from the exterior of a doomed Loop building).

Lincoln goes directly to the little-used office in the second bedroom and riffles through a file cabinet until he finds the homeowner's policy. It's dense and legalistic—the definitions alone take up several pages. Better just hang onto it for later study. He closes the file drawer and glances around the room. The sleek, white desk is piled high with books, magazines, and bills, just as before. Mary's laptop is missing, but she probably took it to Sedona. Lincoln's small collection of workout weights, idle since before his marriage, sits against a wall. The light brown Burberry blanket adds a streak of color draped over the back of the dark blue convertible sofa, just as he remembers.

Emboldened, Lincoln inspects the kitchen (spotless and barren, as if she's stopped eating), and then he makes a daring tour of the master bedroom. It's here—and in the connected bathroom—where he'll find the evidence if Mary has taken a lover. But the graceful wrought-iron bed with its lacy white covering looks innocent. She's moved the alarm clock from his bed table to hers, but otherwise the setting is unchanged. He checks the two books stacked on her table: *The Lazarus Project*, the acclaimed new novel by the Chicagoan Aleksandar Hemon, and a paperback called *Your Successful Real Estate Career.* He opens the closet and reels for a moment under a wave of air fragrant with Mary's perfume, Blue Agava by Jo Malone. His old corner of the closet remains unpopulated save for a few jackets and shirts he never bothered to retrieve. OK so far.

Still high on the fragrance of Mary's perfume, Lincoln enters the sparkling bathroom and bravely opens the mirrored medicine cabinet. A colorful array of makeup jars, emollients, and aspirin containers line the shelves. Lincoln allows himself only a quick peek. All looks in order. Just as he's closing the door, though, he notices on the bottom shelf a thin, squeezed tube with a plainness that seems out of place. He takes it out and inspects: Tucks Hemorrhoidal Ointment.

My God, Lincoln thinks. Poor Mary. She needs me.

10

A WEEK OR SO PASSES WITH NO FURTHER WORD FROM Detective Evinrude. Meantime, with the arrival of August, a heat wave washes over the Midwest, smothering Chicago with a dense blanket of air. Daytime temperatures venture deep into the nineties four days running. The remorseless sun punishes anyone who strays beyond a shadow. Walking around outside, breathing the thick air streaked with faint, swampy odors, Lincoln has the odd sensation of being trapped in his high school locker room. At home, the air conditioning can't keep up. One evening, Lincoln rides his bike to the lakefront, hoping to find a spot of relief in a breeze coming off the water. All of Chicago has the same idea. The bike path along the lake is a mob of cyclers, skaters, defiant joggers gushing sweat, fast walkers, wanderers, oblivious children, glistening shirtless musclemen, overheated dogs, exhausted young parents pushing strollers, Indians in damp and clingy saris—people of every shape, color, and style except the old, who've been warned constantly by Mayor Daley not to move around in the heat.

Thwarted by the crowd, Lincoln dismounts and walks his bike north, but a group of Mexicans has colonized his rock for a picnic, and the entire park up here is a throbbing, multi-culti refugee camp of tents and grills and screaming children, families fleeing the torturous heat inside their tenements. Soaked with sweat, Lincoln turns and walks his bike back the other way. A cluster of gasping joggers—a running club, perhaps—staggers past, and Lincoln sees something familiar in the contorted rictus of their faces, their mouths like raw gashes as they suck for air. The group is well beyond him before he makes the connection: those are the faces on the human casts he saw on his visit to Pompeii.

And, yet, circling back to his apartment, he passes a popular Greek restaurant at the busy corner of Halsted and Webster. The proprietor has lined up tables outside along the narrow sidewalk, and each is filled with diners—Chicagoans gobbling their moussaka in the unbearable heat while a string of cars stopped at the intersection blasts hot and filthy exhaust at their feet.

"It's alfresco hysteria," Lincoln tells Amy the next day when he runs into her on the elevator. His blue linen shirt is stained with sweat. "It's as if these people are so crazed by the winter cold that they can't bear to miss a single moment to eat outside."

"You sound as if you need to get away for a weekend," she tells him.

Lincoln thinks: I'd have to warn Detective Evinrude.

When the elevator opens on the twelfth floor, Amy says, "Can I stop down for a moment? I'd like to talk."

Lincoln glances sideways at Kim the receptionist, who sits just feet away and whose Iowa goodwill acts as radar for subtle changes within the Pistakee family. She guessed the regular UPS deliverywoman was pregnant several weeks before the lady in brown announced it. "Give me a few minutes to settle in," Lincoln tells Amy coolly.

Ten minutes later Amy appears at his office door. She's wearing slacks and a silky print blouse, and she looks untouched by a drop of perspiration. Lincoln warns, "We need to be more discreet."

"What's the harm in talking?" asks Amy as she plops into the chair facing Lincoln's desk. Still, she lowers her voice to a whisper. "Listen: I think I've had a breakthrough on the novel."

"Really?" Lincoln perks up. "What happened?"

"I took a walk the other evening. I couldn't get any momentum; every sentence was a struggle. So I stepped outside. It was awful in this heat. I felt as if I were melting, literally, turning into a puddle. And I suddenly realized—that's it: that's the opening scene. Mary is in this sterile office asking these clinical sex questions, and then she steps outside onto a busy sidewalk in the middle of a heat wave, and she feels as if she's falling into a kind of tropical spell."

Lincoln interrupts: "Your protagonist's name is Mary?"

"Yes. I like using a classic name—you know, the biblical overtones. I thought about calling her Eve, but I decided that was maybe too much."

"Hmm." Lincoln nods carefully. (Does Amy know his wife's name? He's assiduously avoided mentioning it around her—there seemed to be something profane about it.)

"You don't like 'Mary'?" Amy asks.

"No, fine, just thinking."

"Anyway, I ran home and wrote the scene, and after that, the story just started flowing. Now, every day after work, I write until very late, midnight or later."

"That's great," Lincoln tells her.

"And I think I've got a story line. I've figured out the other main character, Jennifer, she's sort of based on a girl who lived in my dorm. She was a senior when I was a freshman, and she liked to scandalize us by saying she was on a mission to find the Ultimate Position."

"Huh?"

"You know—the perfect sexual position. The position that provides maximum pleasure for both partners."

In his mind, Lincoln starts running through pornographic flip cards.

"The story revolves around the interplay between the two women," Amy continues.

Lincoln is still enjoying the pornography. "The Ultimate Position," he says, nodding. "That's good."

"Maybe that's the title."

"So what was it?" Lincoln asks innocently.

"What?"

"The Ultimate Position. What did it turn out to be?"

"Oh, I don't know." Amy is annoyed that he'd ask. "I never checked in with her at the end of the year."

"Probably something from the Kama Sutra," Lincoln muses.

Amy hesitates, then asks, "John, do you really think I can do this?" She has a way of swinging between steely and vulnerable that Lincoln finds endearing; either quality alone might get on his nerves.

"Of course you can," he assures. He sends her off with lines borrowed from warmed-over motivational speeches given at halftime by his old basketball coach, and Amy seems bolstered.

At around eleven that morning, Kim calls from up front. "John, there's a man here to see you," she whispers into the phone.

"Who is he?" Lincoln asks.

"He says his name is Mr. Buford."

"What's he want?"

"He says it's personal."

Lincoln assumes immediately there's trouble. "Why did you let him up?" he growls. Their building has an annoying buzzer system—you can't even get in the locked front door without announcing your intentions.

"He sounded *important*," says the flustered young woman, as if that alone justified her breach of responsibility. When Lincoln doesn't respond immediately, she adds, "He's not going to go away, John."

"All right, tell him I'll be out in a few minutes."

Lincoln prepares himself. Maybe it's just an aspiring author. Every now and then, people see the sign for Pistakee Press on the building and wander in off the street. Or perhaps it's a particularly aggressive cold caller trying to sell him penny stocks. Someone's got to warn that receptionist to take her gatekeeper role more seriously.

Lincoln wastes a few minutes, hoping the visitor will get discouraged and leave, then plods out to the reception area and finds Kim chatting amiably with a nice-looking young African American wearing a white shirt, red tie, and a tropical blue blazer that hangs loosely on his slight frame. Lincoln has seen him somewhere before.

"John Lincoln, this is Antonio Buford," says Kim triumphantly, as if the two men had been clamoring to meet for months.

"Call me Tony," says the visitor, thrusting his hand.

For an anxious moment, Lincoln resists the gesture. The man appears to be about Lincoln's age, maybe a few years younger. His face, the color of light chocolate, is round and unlined, and he wears his hair trimmed close to the scalp. He's carrying an extraordinarily thin canvas briefcase, hardly big enough to hold the folded-up *New York Times*. Standing there dumbly, Lincoln suddenly recalls where he's seen Tony Buford before: this is the man who tried to talk to him on the sidewalk in front of the building not long ago.

After a quick handshake, Lincoln asks, "How can I help you?"

"Ah, could we speak privately?" Buford glances at Kim, then locks a friendly yet intense gaze on Lincoln, who senses immediately that there's something practiced about the manner: maybe he's just a therapist, coming around to hawk the idea for a book on a new self-help regimen.

Ordinarily, Lincoln would maneuver to keep any questionable visitors away from the sanctum sanctorum of his office, but with Kim sopping up every nuance, Lincoln decides to risk privacy. "Follow me," he says.

The two silently wend their way through the corridors of Pistakee, Buford pausing on the way to consider the wall of framed Pistakee book covers. In his office, Lincoln leaves the door open. Buford lingers at the porthole window. "I've never been in this building before," he says.

Lincoln starts to recount the story of the nostalgic sea-captain/builder, but Buford interrupts. "I know the history. I've just never been inside."

Lincoln forces a smile, settles into his chair. "What can I do for you?" he asks.

The visitor sits on the other side of the desk. He glances over the manuscripts and other effluvium cluttering the surface. "Working on something interesting?" Buford asks, as if he were an old friend dropping by for a casual conversation.

Lincoln considers briefly how far to play along. "A book about walking tours of Chicago."

"Ah, exploring the city on foot. I bet that will sell!"

He must be a cold caller, Lincoln thinks. In this economy guys like him are desperate. Any second now he's going to pull out a brochure about his nifty portfolio of horribly undervalued Midwest stocks. "What can I do for you?" Lincoln repeats.

The man is impervious. "I imagine book editing is one of the most satisfying jobs possible," he muses. "Working with words and ideas, collaborating with others. It's sort of like the theater in that way."

Maybe he's just out of his mind. "Yes. Now, what was it you wanted to see me about?"

"I really just wanted to make your acquaintance." That locked-in gaze again.

"Well, here I am. But I'm afraid I'm kind of busy." Lincoln sits up and tidies some loose pages of Professor Fleace's manuscript.

"I mustn't steal your time," says Buford. He reaches in his briefcase and pulls out a small snapshot, then hands it to Lincoln. The photo shows a hefty, well-dressed, elderly black woman, standing in front of a blank interior wall. The woman from the L. In the picture, she is wearing a large, white medical collar around her neck and looking profoundly mournful. "My mother."

Lincoln says nothing but simply stares at the picture. After a moment, Buford reaches across the desk and retrieves the snapshot from Lincoln's hand. "Ever since, she's had terrible neck pain and terrible headaches," Buford continues. "She can't get comfortable, standing, sitting, lying down. We've been to several doctors and a chiropractor. No relief. She may have to have surgery. You forget sometimes the fragility of our skeletal structure. Your head is like a big pumpkin sitting up there on a thin stalk." Buford places his hands on both sides of his face as if to brace his pumpkin.

In addition to his roiling stomach and the short blasts of pain shooting from the long-ago break in his arm, Lincoln's neck immediately begins to ache. "The detective said we aren't supposed to talk to each other," he says weakly.

"Achh, the Chicago Police Department." Buford shakes his head and returns the photo to his briefcase.

Lincoln quietly takes several deep breaths. He clears his throat. "I'm sorry about your mother," he says, trying to mirror the cordial demeanor of his visitor. "But what do you want?"

"Let's just say I'm exploring options. My mother is in a bad way, and we, the family, we need to make some accommodations. I'm pinpointing the responsibility for her condition, then looking at opportunities up to and through the courts."

"Why me?" Lincoln croaks. It's all he can think to say.

"You were the direct cause," Buford explains in the solemn tone a health official might have used in breaking the news to Typhoid Mary.

This is too much. "You can't be serious," Lincoln tells him. "The police aren't going to bother with this. Maybe, maybe you'd have a civil case against the CTA or the gangbangers who started the panic, but me—I was a victim too! It was an accident! You can't sue somebody for something like that." Before he's finished, Lincoln already regrets his self-defeating outburst—exposing anger, blurting presumptions.

Buford assumes the advantage gracefully. "Now, Mr. Lincoln," he says, sitting back in his chair, "my father, God rest his soul, practiced law in Chicago for forty years, and one thing he taught me was that you can sue anyone for anything. You might not always win, but you can always sue." Buford washes Lincoln in a warm smile. "But we are getting ahead of ourselves," he continues. "I just wanted to meet you, let you know about my mom, and test your sympathy, so to speak."

Lincoln works to gather himself. Never admit, never concede.

"You are involved in a very special enterprise here," Buford goes on, gesturing to take in the cluttered desk, the manuscripts stacked on the floor against the wall, the overflowing bookshelf. "Literature has interested me from my earliest days. I'd come home from school and lie on my bed, reading. I guess you could say I was kind of a nerd, but I loved books. I majored in English in college."

A gloomy thought presses on Lincoln. "The U of C?" he asks.

"No, Kenyon."

Ah. Lincoln feels a slight lift. The curse is broken. "Good school."

"I went to the U of C for my masters, in psychology."

So it's a conspiracy, after all. "You are a psychologist?" Lincoln asks.

"By training." He takes a business card out of his wallet and passes it to Lincoln. "At the moment, I'm a professor of happiness studies at DePaul. You know the field?"

"Uhh…"

"Rather new. Quite interesting. What makes people happy. You'd be surprised. We're just starting to quantify, but the results so far are remarkable. I must tell you about it sometime. There might be something there for you." Buford stands and extends his arm. "But I shouldn't take any more of your time. This has been most edifying for me. I'm so glad to have made your acquaintance."

Lincoln rises uneasily and shakes hands. Can his crisis really be passing so quietly? When they stop shaking, however, Buford doesn't let go. They remain connected, awkwardly, across the messy expanse of Lincoln's desk. "And now that we are acquainted, maybe you would be so kind as to take a look at something I've written," Buford says. "It's very modest. Just a small collection of poems."

In the silence, Lincoln feels acutely the grip of Buford's hand. "We don't really publish poetry," Lincoln says, hedging slightly since once, a year or two before Lincoln arrived at Pistakee, Duddleston unaccountably printed a small anthology of poems by mothers about their sons. Unsold copies used to lie around the office like old telephone books that no one bothered to discard.

"Well, you might just enjoy taking a look," Buford continues. He drops Lincoln's hand and pulls a rather thin manila envelope out of his briefcase, then places it directly in front of Lincoln in the middle of his desk. "Of course, my mother is a great fan of my work. I think it would ease her situation enormously if she had the pleasure of seeing it published." Buford studies Lincoln's face. "Looking forward to hearing from you," the visitor says before turning and marching out.

Seconds later Byron Duddleston appears in the office door. "Who was that?" he asks, gesturing down the hall in the direction of Buford's exit.

Lincoln is still standing behind his desk, asking himself whether he's being blackmailed. "Uhhh…a writer," he tells his boss. He slides Buford's business card under a pile of papers and casually moves the poet's package to the side of the desk. (Yes. Blackmail. Definitely.)

"A writer!" Duddleston repeats, pleased, as if he and Lincoln had accidentally spotted a rare and beautiful yellow-throated warbler well north of its typical range. "We need more diversity on our list."

"I've been thinking the same thing," Lincoln improvises.

As Lincoln sits again, the boss steps into the room and hovers, his maroon bow tie adding a menacing edge. (Why menacing? Lincoln has long wondered. Something about academic smugness, aggressive competence. Lincoln could never tie one.) "Bill Lemke has come to me with what I think is a fantastic idea," Duddleston says cagily.

Lincoln frowns. "Really?"

"Yes. He's been talking to the marketing people with the Cubs, and it turns out they'd really like to promote his book. In fact, they're doing a special night to celebrate the history of Wrigley Field, and they've offered to make Bill part of the event."

"That's great!"

"Yes. But here's the thing. They want to do it at the end of September, so we'd need copies of the book by then. Paperback, of course. Oversized."

Lincoln does a quick mental accounting of their normal production schedule. "That's impossible," he points out.

Duddleston's famous temper flares. "Nothing's impossible!" he snaps. "That's the trouble with the book business—everybody's stuck in the same old pattern. Of course, it's possible to publish a book in two months—companies do it all the time with annual reports, special issues, that sort of thing. We've already speeded our schedule way up. There's no reason we can't do it some more. If you can get the manuscript in shape, I'll take care of production and distribution. Bill's game, that's for sure."

So Lemke, that mothy and odorous fossil, is ready to march with Duddleston into the fast-moving future, while Lincoln, the brilliant young executive editor, is stuck in the sluggish routines of the past. "Wow," says Lincoln, trying to save his job, "We'll give it a try!"

"Good."

Lincoln pours it on: "What a great idea!"

"Maybe. It'll be expensive and risky." Despite the hedge, Duddleston's pleasure with himself dances around his face. "And this could even be the Cubs' year. They're hanging in there, despite the injuries. Wouldn't it be something if they made it to the World Series? Do you know how long it's been?"

Everyone who lives in Chicago and has avoided dementia can answer that question: "1945."

Duddleston stands, apparently satisfied that his top deputy has got with the program. "Why don't you give Bill a call and get it started."

"Sure thing," Lincoln says.

And lest there be any lingering question, the owner/editor-in-chief adds on the way out: "Today."

11

LINCOLN HAS PLANS TO JOIN FLAM IN THE EVENING AT AN advance press screening of the Coen brothers' *A Serious Man*, but throughout the afternoon, even through a long, somewhat disjointed conversation with Bill Lemke (had he been drinking? would the new production rush be Lemke's excuse to ignore all of Lincoln's editorial suggestions?), Tony Buford's trim package silently nags, forcing itself into Lincoln's attention, like a cell phone left on vibration. Finally, toward the end of the day, Lincoln surrenders and retrieves the envelope from the far corner of his desk, where he'd hoped he could forget it among other unread manuscripts. He opens it and pulls out a rather thin sheath of thick, expensive paper, the kind used for letters from rich people or executives. *L*, says the title on the top sheet. "*Poetry by Antonio Buford*. Copyright 2009." (Is that title a reference to the unfortunate incident?)

Lincoln skims through the pages. The poems are numbered, and most are contained on a single sheet. The titles are short descriptors of objects, places, or simple activities: "The Brown Easy Chair," "Shaving in the Shower," "Masking Tape," "North Wells Between Grand and Illinois." Fifty poems in all. Lincoln flips to the end, then returns to one called "The Remote," attracted by the possibly clever use of an adjective as a noun. No. It's about the author's Emancipation Day, when the family got a remote control device for the television and the father could change channels from the sofa instead of repeatedly ordering the son to schlep to the console.

Several pages on, Lincoln dips into "The Morning Paper," a sixty-word salute to the 6:00 a.m. delivery of the *Tribune*:

It pounds on the door, rude, oblivious
Reviving the household
Like that first rough CPR stroke
on the chest of a sprawled heart-attack victim.

Lincoln considers several others, "Sharpening a Pencil," "The DustBuster," "Maple Leaf." All the same—short, modestly thoughtful celebrations of the utterly ordinary. The collection could have been called *Ode to the Mundane.*

Finally Lincoln turns to the front and burrows his way through all fifty poems. He finds the language clean and accessible, and every now and then Buford summons an image that's mildly catchy. In a couple of instances, Lincoln realizes that he's been prodded to a fresh regard for an element of everyday life (the "calming" paper clip that "tames clutter, the unruly mind"). Overall, the quality is several grade levels above greeting-card verse. Still, the poems are palliative, thin. Unimportant. Given Buford's aggressiveness in pushing his work, Lincoln had been expecting something raw that drew on the African-American experience. But nothing in the collection even hints at the poet's racial identity. Sitting at his desk, holding the overweight pages in his hands, Lincoln thinks the work could easily be the creation of a widow from suburban Milwaukee, writing by the window in her sunset years.

Lincoln is late for the movie, and Flam is cross—he's finally had his big date, and he's eager to dish the details. Instead, they have to rush to claim the last two empty seats in the small screening room buried in a nondescript Loop office building. "Last-minute crisis," Lincoln whispers in apology as the lights go down.

Even during *A Serious Man*, which Lincoln likes, he can't stop brooding about Buford's poetry collection—or, more to the point, Lincoln can't stop worrying about how to get rid of the guy. Detective Evinrude must have been right: the criminal complaint was just a prelude to a civil suit (and the homeowner's policy won't be any help—the snippy insurance agent confirmed that). Buford seems to be offering a way out through blackmail, but Pistakee obviously can't publish him. The house has been working hard to build a reputation for quality, and *L* would deflate that in seconds. Lincoln can imagine the look on the faces of the Pistakee sales reps as he holds up the galleys and explains in feigned seriousness that this white-bread verse by a black man touches the pop-culture zeitgeist.

Maybe he can send Buford off to another small publishing house. Or a vanity press—for a few thousand dollars, Buford can pay to get his book printed. Lincoln slouches in his seat as the Serious Man watches his lush neighbor sunbathe in the nude. Whatever, Lincoln suspects darkly, Buford is unlikely to go for it.

After the movie, Lincoln and Flam walk north across the river to Harry Caray's, the noisy Italian steak joint founded by the late broadcaster for the Cubs. Their waitress is young and blond and offers a faint recollection of Scarlett Johansson. She wants them to order steaks, the expensive entree. Lincoln has been trying to ration his meals of red meat, so he goes with the linguine with clam sauce. Flam is happy to engage the young woman in several minutes of flirtatious discussion before finally settling on a New York strip, medium rare.

"You're not worried about your arteries?" Lincoln asks after the waitress has tripped off.

Flam smiles. "She was working hard," he says.

Lincoln considers his tall friend—curled in his chair, legs tangled and arms wrapped around his soft torso, his high, intelligent brow as smooth and white as an egg. No man has ever been less sexy, Lincoln thinks. "So tell me about the big date."

"I drove up to Avondale to pick her up. Met Mom and Dad. Very solid. Polish. Born over there. Both still have heavy accents."

"What did they think of you?" Lincoln tries to imagine this effete, thirty-six-year-old suitor making small talk with the Old World parents of a nineteen-year-old babe.

"They seemed fine with me," Flam says crisply, as if slightly put off by the question. "Editor at the *Tribune*, college degree, settled—I think they appreciated that I was interested in their daughter."

"Of course. So then?"

"First we went down to see *Whatever Works*, the new Woody Allen movie, then I took her to dinner at Brasserie Jo. I like that place. Very French, sort of romantic. The waiter even let us speak a little French to him. We stayed late, talking. Karolina—that's her name—Karolina really is bright and eager to learn, in the way that working-class kids embrace education without any of the quibbles and hang-ups of the rest of us."

"What's she studying?"

"Accounting, but she's talking about going to law school."

"So, what was the denouement?"

"After dinner, I drove her home. It was a beautiful evening, and we sat on the stoop and chatted. Very 1950s. Every now and then a neighbor would walk by and call out hello. It was late, but people were still out, walking their dogs. Finally, it was time to go." Flam sits back, his eyes drifting, as if he were recalling a moment from long, long ago. "I said good night—no kiss or anything, just a sweet *au revoir*."

"And that's it?" Lincoln asks. "That was the whole date?"

Flam stiffens. "Then I went back to my apartment, took out my collection of old *Playboys*, and whacked off. Twice."

Lincoln hoots. Heads turn at neighboring tables. "Jesus Christ, Flam," he says, lowering his voice, but still laughing.

"It was the most sensually satisfying evening I'd had in years." Flam's narrow face barely cracks a smile.

"Why *old Playboys*?"

"I don't like shaving."

Lincoln cracks up again. He thinks: Flam knows exactly what he wants and never reaches beyond—maybe that accounts for his unchanging demeanor of calm authority (the quality that won him the job of literary editor, Lincoln has always suspected). Or maybe (less charitably) he's calm because he lives a kind of meta-life, essential experiences several degrees removed from perilous reality. "Are you going to see her again?"

"I see her every day at Starbucks. Nothing has changed. Whether we go out again…" Flam wraps himself in his arms and shrugs.

The next morning at work, Lincoln tries to borrow some of Flam's cool detachment in an e-mail to Tony Buford. He thanks the writer for sharing his poems. He offers, somewhat honestly, that the work shows imagination and a care for language. He posits that the poems might well find an enthusiastic audience. With the cushioning in place, however, Lincoln gets tough: several years ago, Pistakee made a firm decision not to publish poetry, and the house intends to hold to that resolve. Lincoln names a few other small publishers in the Midwest who might be interested, but doesn't insult with the suggestion of a vanity press. Then he dropkicks Buford with a concluding sentence: "We appreciate your interest, and good luck with your writing career."

Seconds after hitting the SEND icon on his e-mail, Lincoln is tucking Buford's manuscript into a new envelope (all that heavy, expensive paper—the guy will probably want the hard copy back) when the phone rings. "Tony Buford is on the line," says Kim, the receptionist.

"Shit."

"What?" says the clueless young woman. "Oh, should I tell him you're in a meeting?"

Lincoln quickly decides that putting Buford off risks another office visit or worse. "I'll take it."

Waiting grimly for the connection, Lincoln stares at the keypad on his phone. Grime has built up around the numbers in a curious pattern. Heaviest on the "7," "5," and "3," light on the "2" and "0." Why? What does that say about the telephone numbers he dials? Then a click: "Mr. Lincoln?"

"Yes."

"I don't think you understand. I'm offering you the opportunity to publish my poems." The familiar voice is deep and resonant. Commanding. Since adulthood, Lincoln has been slightly disappointed in his own wobbly tenor.

"As I explained in my e-mail, Mr. Buford, we don't publish poetry."

"Of course you do."

"Excuse me?"

"Pistakee is a publisher. Its business is publishing books. This is a book."

"We are not a vanity press, Mr. Buford." (Who is this guy to lecture on the nature of Lincoln's job?) "We decide what we will publish."

"You decide?"

"Yes."

"You, personally?"

"I'm the executive editor here."

"You, personally." Buford has carefully moved from a question to a statement of fact, a crafty cross-examination ploy Lincoln recognizes from TV court dramas.

"Me, in consultation with my colleagues," he says carefully.

"Oh." Perkily. "And did you share my work with your colleagues?"

Be firm, Lincoln reminds himself. "No, I made the decision on my own."

"So you handled my manuscript differently from others?"

A frightening thought: Could Buford be tape-recording this conversation? "Look, Mr. Buford, I'm terribly sorry you're disappointed, but your book simply doesn't fit with Pistakee's plans. It may be fine for another publisher, but it's not for us."

The pause on the other end gives Lincoln a moment to hope his message has been accepted. Nope. "I really am surprised at you," Buford continues. "Surprised and disappointed. My mother's condition has not improved. If anything, it's deteriorated, and one of the things that has brought her solace—that's eased her pain better than the drugs, frankly—is the thought that she will see her son's book of poetry published. Perhaps she and I should come down there and have a meeting with you and your colleagues."

"That will not be necessary."

"I assume your office is ADA approved. You can handle a wheelchair."

The fragile psychological dam Lincoln has constructed to block his anger—the mental equivalence of twigs and mud—finally gives out. "Listen, Mr. Buford," he shouts into the phone. "Enough! I've had it. If you are going to sue me over that stupid accident, then sue me. I don't care. But I won't be blackmailed." Lincoln is vaguely aware that half of Pistakee Press can probably hear him through the flimsy walls, but he can't help himself.

"My God, Mr. Lincoln, what's this about blackmail?" The voice on the other end suddenly modulates. The baritone moves up several octaves.

"That's what you're up to."

"Oh, I'm sure you misunderstood. Blackmail? My God, Mr. Lincoln, I'm an academic."

"Well..."

"I'm simply a writer who believes in his work. You must know the type."

"Yes."

"Maybe I got a little offended when I saw your curt e-mail. I'm sorry."

"OK." Lincoln feels whipsawed. He's not sure he's off the hook, but he wants to push for conciliation. "I'm sorry I raised my voice."

"Listen, let me buy you a drink. Apologize in person."

"That won't be necessary."

"Please, I insist." The baritone again. Buford can tune it to accommodate an incredible range of emotions. "Look at it this way: you can tell me in person that you don't like my work, which will erase the impersonal offense of e-mail, and I can apologize in person for being too persistent."

Lincoln hesitates. The relief flowing through him at the sudden slaking of anger leaves him feeling slightly giddy. His clarity of purpose gets clouded, and for the moment, he forgets he's the object of a police investigation. "OK."

"Terrific! It'll be a couple of weeks. I'm about to head off on a little trip to Iceland."

"Iceland?"

"Beautiful country. You've never been there? Remarkably happy people. I've got a conference in Reykjavik that I'm turning into a vacation. But I'll send you an e-mail when I get back."

"OK."

"Terrific. Maybe in the meantime, you might just take another look."

"Another look?"

"See you in a few weeks." Click.

Lincoln gently places the phone back in the cradle, then stares dumbly at the machine. Did I just make another mistake? he wonders. How did this happen? Maybe, he tells himself, maybe this is like a hostage situation—better to keep the perpetrator talking, hope that he'll tire or that something serendipitous will happen. Maybe time will heal—even heal the old lady's neck.

After a minute or so, Lincoln gets up from his desk and pulls the last three years of Pistakee catalogs from his bookshelf, then makes an inventory: out of fifty-seven books the house published in that time, the period of Lincoln's employment, only three were by African Americans, and two of those were acquired before Lincoln arrived. This, in a city that is almost 40 percent black. That sent the first black man in history to the White House. Lincoln immediately confects a scene outside the Pistakee building—a crowd milling, traffic stopped, bullhorns blaring, the Reverend Jesse Jackson leading an angry protest with Tony Buford as the aggrieved centerpiece, the noise and infamy blowing away Lincoln's reputation, his dignity, his family's honor—and all his various hopes, up to and including the possibility of getting a job in New York.

12

Thank God for Bill Lemke, thinks John Lincoln. The washed-up sportswriter puts in a week of heroic work, e-mailing chapters to Lincoln that arrive at all hours of the day and night (11:44 p.m., 2:19 a.m., 5:05 a.m.—when does the man sleep?). Long ago, Lemke enjoyed an all-state career as a third baseman for Chicago's huge Lane Tech High School, and Duddleston's challenge has tapped the dormant competitive instincts of the vanished athlete (like extracting DNA from a fossilized bone). Lincoln has never heard Lemke sound so focused and thoughtful, so youthful. Lincoln crunches and polishes the new work, rationalizing sentences, excavating clichés, trimming lines, tightening scenes, inserting questions for the author that the two of them will go over later, though Lincoln finds that Lemke has done an admirable job of cleaning up his own text (apparently taking to heart many of the snippy and embittered suggestions Lincoln made on the original manuscript).

On the first weekend of the book's new, frantic publishing schedule, Lincoln spends most of both days at the office to keep up with Lemke's prodigious pace. Lincoln feels drugged by the stale building air and sodden with Starbucks coffee, but in a nice turn, Duddleston swings by late Sunday afternoon.

He's ostensibly come to pick up some symphony tickets left in his desk, but Lincoln wonders if the boss hasn't in fact found an excuse to check up, knowing the harsh deadline Pistakee faces to produce a finished manuscript.

"Hard at work!" Duddleston pronounces admiringly when he finds Lincoln in his office.

"Comin' 'round the bend," responds the executive editor, secretly thrilling, since he had been about to leave for the day and this small triumph of dedication could easily have been missed.

"Been here long?"

"Since about ten this morning." Lincoln pauses, then adds modestly, "I was here most of yesterday, too. Bill is really churning the stuff out."

Duddleston nods his appreciation. The two men consider each other's casual attire. Duddleston's trim white polo shirt and navy linen slacks outclass Lincoln's old Smashing Pumpkins T-shirt and khaki shorts, but that's OK with Lincoln (evidence of his utter focus on the task at hand). "How are you and Mary getting on these days?" asks Duddleston when the pause in the conversation grows uncomfortable.

"Oh, we talk."

"I hope this tough deadline doesn't get in the way of your reconciliation."

"Not a problem."

"Well, if you can manage it, take her out to dinner tonight and charge it to Pistakee. You guys deserve it."

"Thanks!" says Lincoln, wondering whether the offer would work for Flam, since he hasn't heard from Mary since their brief, prickly Sedona conversation.

"Give her my best," says Duddleston as he departs, and Lincoln decides, no, better not to have to explain Flam to the company's vigilant comptroller.

At the office several days later, Lincoln is finishing up a *Wrigley Field* chapter on the Bleacher Bums of '69 when a message from Duddleston pops up in Lincoln's e-mail inbox tagged with the bland subject "Personnel Communication." Lincoln assumes it's more on changes to the company health plan, which he can never understand anyway, so he continues editing. He only opens the message a few minutes later when he takes a break. "Senior Editor Arthur Wendt has resigned from Pistakee Press as of this morning," the e-mail reads. "Arthur contributed seven years to the success of the company, and we wish him the best in his next endeavor."

And that's it. No elaboration. Nothing about why he's leaving or where he's going.

Lincoln stares at the computer screen in disbelief. Wendt was the first editor hired by Duddleston. He didn't come up with a lot of interesting books, but he had connections in academia, and he could provide the slog of an edit to convert a professor's manuscript into something approaching readability. And his books sold steadily. Every now and then, Lincoln checked the numbers, and in fact, cumulatively, Wendt's books notched more sales each year than did Lincoln's.

What has happened? Lincoln has no one to ask. Wendt himself was the only gossip in the company. As comptroller, Matt Breeson must have some insight, but he'd never betray his vows of discretion. And as for Duddleston—Lincoln can't imagine asking his Presbyterian boss, who considers personal privacy the cornerstone of the country's founding principles and who conducts his business, and his life, on a need-to-know basis. Lincoln briefly thinks about calling up Amy, who might have picked up some intelligence sitting outside the owner's office, but her cubicle is just feet away from the desk of the loyal Mrs. Macintosh. Lincoln has no choice but to suppress his curiosity and get back to work.

An hour or so later, another e-mail arrives from the owner. In this one, the entire message is contained in the subject field: "Pls stop down." Lincoln immediately assumes the worst. So that's the way the word arrives—in the banal shorthand of officespeak. Duddleston must be picking off his editors one by one. Maybe the owner has suffered a sudden setback and now he's cleaning house. Is this the end of Pistakee? Lincoln prolongs his agony for a few minutes, wandering the Web, scanning the news on Jim Romenesko's media site, trying to distract himself and slow his heartbeat. Finally Lincoln does some deep breathing exercises and makes the *Dead Man Walking* march down to Duddleston's office. Just outside, Amy looks up at him and silently signals doom with her face. "Go right in," says Mrs. Macintosh solemnly.

Duddleston commands from a large, carpeted western-facing corner office, the scene of a constant war between the afternoon sun (here the building's renovators have replaced the portholes with wide windows) and tall, fusty shelves of Duddleston's first editions and favorite books. In winter's low light, the room can resemble a London men's club of Edwardian vintage. But on sunny days like today, even with the shades drawn, the relentless brightness reminds Lincoln of a hospital operating room. Duddleston sits at his desk, the taut, athletic body firmly erect. "Come in," he tells Lincoln. "Close the door."

Lincoln follows orders and takes a seat in an Aeron chair across the desk from his boss.

"You saw my note about Arthur?" Duddleston asks.

Lincoln nods.

"I need you to take on his books, at least until we can bring in someone else."

Lincoln blinks. Suddenly, the overbright office transforms from the clinical setting for a risky and perhaps fatal surgical procedure to a sunlit meadow on a lovely spring day.

"I know you've already got a lot on your plate, particularly crashing the Lemke book," Duddleston goes on. "But you're the only one who can handle this kind of work. It's not really Hazel's métier."

"I can do it!" Lincoln chirps. (Of course he can—he can do anything, as long as he still has a job!)

Duddleston bathes him in a patronizing smile, and the thought crosses Lincoln's mind that he's squandered a tactical opportunity—that perhaps he should have held out a bit, acted slightly beleaguered (finagled for a raise? a title change?). But the moment passes as the two men discuss the status of the two books Wendt has on the fall list and the handful that lie in the pipeline. By taking on Wendt's projects on top of *Wrigley Field* and *Walking Tours*, among other things, Lincoln realizes he's facing a frenzied autumn—where will he get the time to edit Amy's novel?

"I'll start looking for a replacement for Arthur immediately," Duddleston promises, perhaps sensing Lincoln's concern. "And if you have any candidates, don't hesitate to steer them my way."

"About Arthur," Lincoln says, then pauses, hoping Duddleston will take the bait and explain what happened. After a silence, Lincoln adds obliquely, "This was very sudden."

Duddleston fusses with papers on his desk, signaling the audience is over. "These personnel matters are never easy," he says, looking away. "The part of this business I like least."

"I understand," Lincoln consoles and takes his leave.

At about six that evening, after the rest of the office has cleared out and Lincoln is packing his briefcase, the phone rings. "It's me," says Amy. Lincoln can tell by the faint throb in the connection that she's calling from a cell.

"Do you know what happened?" he asks.

"You can't tell anyone. Byron would fire me in an instant."

"Of course I won't."

Amy pauses, takes a breath. "Sexual harassment. Arthur kept hitting on Kim."

Lincoln lets out a low whistle.

"Really," Amy continues. "He never did anything—just lurked. She used to complain to me about it, but I figured, grow up, the world is full of creeps. But apparently Arthur said something to her last week, and Kim went to Mrs. Macintosh."

"What did he say?"

"I don't know. I'm sure it was innocuous—he probably complimented her on her figure, or something. And she does have a nice figure. I mean, give the guy a break—he's got a wife and two kids."

"Whew." Lincoln sighs into the phone.

"Yeah." Amy waits, then says carefully, "Byron doesn't fool around."

Lincoln gets her meaning exactly.

On his way out of the building a few minutes later, Lincoln's curiosity leads him to detour past Wendt's office. The room is already bare, Gettysburg after the battle. Bookshelves emptied, family pictures gone. Lincoln thinks of a cheap motel room whose endless string of weary visitors leave no trace.

13

Because of what happened to Arthur Wendt, Lincoln and Amy go out of their way to appear indifferent to each other when they're at Pistakee. They pass in the hall without acknowledgement. Amy no longer visits Lincoln's office except when dropping something off, and then she enters and leaves wordlessly. On the few occasions when Lincoln finds himself together with Amy and Duddleston, Lincoln hints at a mild disapproval of her presence. Amy returns his chill at every possible moment, and Lincoln finds it somewhat curious that she appears to be as paranoid as he is that their indiscretion will be found out. After all, under the conventions of sexual harassment, she'd be presumed to be the victim of a predatory supervisor and thus not at risk of losing her job. Does her extreme caution reflect a grave concern about Lincoln's standing in the company? Or does she suspect that Duddleston would be so put off by their poor judgment that he would sweep both of them out the door?

In any case, the wall they build between themselves in the office has the effect of broadening communications outside, since Amy gets in the habit of calling Lincoln—her cell phone to his—minutes after he leaves work most days. At first she calls to pass on bulletins about the Wendt matter. It turned out to hinge on an adolescent joke. Kim had removed an earring to talk on the phone, and the faux pearl had accidentally dropped down her blouse. Wendt was hovering around the reception desk and cracked, "I'd like to go deep-sea diving." Later, in the women's room, Kim grumbled about the remark to Mrs. Macintosh, and that set the execution in motion. "That's incredible," Lincoln points out. "Arthur Wendt was utterly humorless. That's probably the first joke he ever made in his life."

"Maybe he really *was* getting dangerous," Amy suggests.

Afterward, Kim felt terrible. She confessed to Amy that she wanted Wendt to stop annoying her, but she never dreamed he'd be fired. After several days of remorse, she made an entreaty on Wendt's behalf to Duddleston, but the boss was unmoved. The senior editor's behavior was unforgivable.

Within a few days, Wendt recedes as a topic of conversation, and Amy's calls mostly provide updates on her novel, which she's writing at a frantic pace. Her innocent young protagonist is getting drawn deeper into the life of a survey subject, a woman exploring the far reaches of sexuality—the search for the Ultimate Position. Amy bounces ideas and plot points off Lincoln. He listens patiently and pushes back here or there, but he knows to stay somewhat distant, at this point letting her imagination roam.

Sometimes their conversations stray beyond the novel. Amy tells Lincoln about her family—her mother, a child of County Cork who's lived in Chicago since college; her father, a successful contractor in the south suburbs; her brainy, computer-jock, younger brother. The mother had wanted a large family, but after the brother's difficult birth, she was unable to have more children. By Amy's analysis, that disappointment turned her mother picky and demanding. It was bad enough that Amy abandoned the Catholic Church. But at the U of C, she turned from premed to the impractical precincts of the English department. "She's constantly on my case about how I can still go to medical school," Amy tells Lincoln one day as he pauses in his commute to make faces at the orphaned dogs in the windows of the Anti-Cruelty Society building on Grand.

"Did you tell her you're writing a novel?"

"God, no. She'd ask what it's about, and then I'd never hear the end of it."

"How often do you talk to her?"

"Every day, a couple of times," Amy says, as if it's the most normal thing in the world, and Lincoln wonders why his family only stays in touch every few weeks, usually when there's a specific piece of information to convey. The mixed collie breed stares out at him disapprovingly, and Lincoln hurries on.

Riding the L home one evening, shortly after hanging up with Amy, Lincoln looks up from the *Times* crossword puzzle, and the thought suddenly strikes him that the sexual component has been laundered from their relationship—their inappropriate attraction has been suppressed, and they now address each other as colleagues—maybe friends, too, but not quite. More like close acquaintances. Lincoln is pleased with the evolution, and he credits himself with a new maturity. Could it be that he's learned from the struggles of the last few months—the bust-up with Mary, the anxieties about his job, the threats from Tony Buford? Lincoln glances around at the other riders in the L car—mostly well-dressed young North Siders like himself, probably (like himself) working late to get ahead. Through the rattle and vibrations of the train, he feels a brotherhood with them, his generation, and with it an easing of tension, almost as if someone has turned a dial and slightly lowered his heart rate.

The restful mood lasts until the next day, when an e-mail arrives from Tony Buford. He's back from Iceland and wants to get together, as discussed. Buford invites Lincoln to meet him next Thursday evening at seven at the northeast corner of Wacker and LaSalle. Lincoln spends an hour or so considering the message. Meet on the street? What's that about, a set-up for a drive-by shooting? On the other hand, that corner is a bustling public spot, right along the river. And several restaurants in the buildings across the street feature comfortable bars; maybe they'll select one together. Or maybe Buford just wants to walk. Wacker along the river can be quite pleasant on summer evenings. Whatever, Lincoln knows enough from Chicago mob history not to get into a car with Buford, but otherwise, what's the risk? Lincoln e-mails back: "See you there."

On Thursday evening, Lincoln plans to arrive at the designated corner a few minutes early to establish a redoubt, so to speak. It's been a warm, muggy day, and now the clouds have dissipated and the departing sun shoots horizontal blasts of light through the spaces between the buildings. Walking south on LaSalle, he falls into a light sweat. As he crosses the bridge over the river, he sees that Buford has already staked out the corner. The professor is wearing a tan tropical blazer and a pale mauve tie; in one hand he holds a large brown shopping bag, and in the other he carries that curiously thin briefcase. He spots Lincoln and lifts the shopping bag in greeting.

"So good of you to come," Buford says. "Sorry to be a bit mysterious about the setting, but this is one of my favorite places in Chicago, and I wanted to share it with you. Follow me."

He wheels and heads down a wide stairway toward the river. Lincoln watches him go. The stairs lead to a narrow concrete promenade just a few feet above the surface of the water. Several couples are lounging on benches. A little farther east, tables and chairs have been set out for lunchtime dining. It looks benign enough, so Lincoln follows and takes a seat beside Buford on a bench facing the river. "Nice—don't you agree?" Buford asks.

It's several degrees cooler this close to the water. The dark expanse of the LaSalle Street Bridge dominates to the left, and across the river an ancient factory, long ago converted to offices, presents a handsome redbrick facade. But in a city that celebrates its views from on high (why else put up the world's tallest building?), this vista is low, blocked, urban. "Very nice," agrees Lincoln.

"And do you know what happened right here at our feet?" Buford points to the river below them.

"Ahhh…"

"One of the greatest disasters in American maritime history. On a Sunday in 1915, a tour boat, the *Eastland*, was docked on the river to make an excursion with the families of several thousand workers from the Western Electric Company. The ship was overcrowded, and when it pulled away from the dock, the passengers rushed to one side to wave good-bye and the *Eastland* tipped over. More than eight hundred people drowned."

Of course, the *Eastland* Disaster. A highlight of one of Professor Fleace's walks.

"Now, look." Buford waves his arm, indicating the buildings, the steel bridges, the concrete riverbank, nothing like the pilings and dirt that must have existed a century ago. "You get my point?" Buford asks.

"Not really."

"We are resilient! Hopeful, optimistic. That is man! We keep going. We bury our tragedies and construct expensive condos looking right over the graveyard."

"I see," says Lincoln.

Buford rummages in the shopping bag and pulls out a chilled bottle of Krug Grand Cuvee, two plastic glasses, a sliced baguette, a tin of caviar, a plastic knife, and a purple paper plate. "Provisions," he says as he pops the cork on the bottle. He pours Lincoln a glass, and the two click plastic. He opens the tin of caviar and paints several slices of bread with the black delicacy, arranging the treats around the purple plate.

As Lincoln helps himself to the hors d'oeuvres and sips champagne, the poet asks, "Did you have a busy day?"

"The usual." Mustn't get personal, Lincoln tells himself.

"Working on any exciting books?"

"A couple." Lincoln smiles insincerely.

"Well, I just read a wonderful book. *Undaunted Courage*, by Stephen Ambrose—do you know it?"

"The Lewis and Clark expedition. The book came out when I was in college. I haven't read it."

"Wonderful book," Buford repeats. "In fact, I'm thinking of adding it to my syllabus next semester."

"I thought you taught happiness studies."

"I do. As well as introduction to psychology. But Happy Talk, as the kids call the course, is the big draw. I have to turn students away."

"But doesn't Meriwether Lewis end up a suicide?"

Buford smiles in appreciation of Lincoln's knowledge. "Yes, Lewis ends badly, but that was well afterward," the professor explains. "The expedition itself, for all its hardships and dangers, was the happiest time of his life—it was probably the same for all the men on it. The focus. The *engagement*."

That word again, thinks Lincoln. It's like a virus.

"That's what I try to teach my students."

Loosened by the champagne, Lincoln nudges forward a provocation. "I thought that happiness stuff was mostly self-help hooey—you know, Oprah territory."

"Oh, academically, it's much more than that. Quite disciplined and scientific, in fact. They call it positive psychology. It's probably the most exciting thing going on today in the field." Pausing to nibble a slice of baguette, Buford spills a few beads of caviar onto his white shirt. He brushes the tiny black eggs away without a trace. "We used to focus on the unpleasant aspects of the human condition—depression, negativity, isolation, neurosis. Now we're studying things like love, altruism, companionship, the qualities that make people happy. It's astonishing—there was this entire side of the emotion spectrum that the so-called experts had virtually ignored. And the kids love it. I not only teach the science, but help the class apply it to their own lives. I always survey my students before and after the semester, and on average about seventy percent of them feel better about themselves after they've taken my course."

"That does sound like Oprah," Lincoln says.

"There's a reason her show has endured," Buford says with a laugh. "As an editor, you should appreciate this: studies show that if you're in a cheerful frame of mind, you'll be more creative—you'll do better on tests, you'll explore more options, your imagination will fire more freely than if you're depressed."

Lincoln loosely remembers an undergraduate course he took on psychology, and he recalls coming away with the impression that researchers could cook up just about any finding they wanted, depending on the experiment. "What do you do with Joyce, Faulkner, Hemingway?" he asks. "The literary canon of the twentieth century came from depressives. And it's the same in other fields. You think Van Gogh would have been Van Gogh if he'd been doodling smiley faces in his spare time?"

Buford laughs again. "It's true—for the most part, the works that have been anointed reflect the bleak visions of their creators. But who does the anointing? Academics. Intellectuals. The cultural elite, to use the disparaging term."

Lincoln tries another tack. "So where is this body of Great Happy Art?" he asks. "I suppose by your reckoning we should replace Chekhov in the curriculum with *Tuesdays with Morrie*."

"You should come visit my class, old buddy," Buford says. "The kids would enjoy this exchange." He refills their champagne glasses. "I agree, the sentimentalists and self-help gurus have polluted the water for people like me. Oh, there are a few books out there—*To Kill a Mockingbird*, for example. That's on my syllabus. But we need more."

So here comes the advocacy for his poetry, thinks Lincoln—Pistakee's opportunity to open Western Civ to a revolutionary aesthetic. But instead Buford veers off into a discussion of books he's read recently and movies he's seen. For almost an hour, as the shadow of the bridge stretches down the river, they sip champagne and nibble caviar sandwiches while chatting easily. Lincoln decides after a while that Buford actually makes pretty good company. Those Kenyon English professors taught him well. He's argumentative, but in a good way, nothing personal. Probing, ambitious, informed. Conscious of man's obligation to amuse.

"Want to get dinner?" Buford asks finally. "There's a pretty good seafood restaurant right across the street."

Lincoln hesitates. "No, I should get going—home fires and all."

"Fair enough." Buford starts packing the remains of their picnic into the shopping bag. "I really do appreciate you taking the time to have a drink with me—then to listen patiently to my crackpot theories on literature."

"My pleasure."

"You're a good man."

Lincoln smiles in gratitude.

"I'm surprised you didn't ask about my mother."

Fuck sake. "Ah, of course. How is she?"

A big sigh. "Not well, I'm afraid. Still a lot of discomfort. Many visits to doctors. Surgery may be the best option."

"I'm sorry to hear that." (Lincoln thinks: Is there any reason on earth to believe him?)

"It's been hard on the family. She's always been our rock." Buford sits back on the bench to watch while an architectural tour boat passes in front of them on the water, every seat on deck filled, the docent's amplified remarks about the twin corncobs of the Marina Towers echoing along the river canyon. When the boat has passed, Buford says, "You really should publish my book."

By now, Lincoln is prepared. He turns to the poet and addresses him earnestly. "Look, you're an educated guy. You majored in English at Kenyon, for Chrissake. You're extremely well read. You can't really think there's any quality to those poems."

Buford absorbs this mixed insult evenly. "I'm surprised at you, John," he says, for the first time addressing Lincoln by his first name. "Do you think you're living in the nineteenth century? We're in 2009. No one suggests there's a relation between quality and popular culture, except perhaps an inverse one." He reaches for his thin briefcase and unzips the top, then pulls out a copy of Pistakee's spring catalog. "Shall we consider some of the books you've been publishing? *The John Wayne Gacy Labyrinth: Inside the Mind of a Serial Killer.* Or maybe *The Lava Lamp Story.*"

Lincoln holds up his hand to interrupt. "But it's a business—it's all about sales, or potential sales. Before we take on a book, I have to convince Byron Duddleston, our owner, that the book will make money."

"Who do you suppose has a better sense of the consumer—a former trader of hog bellies or someone who has spent more than five years studying human desire?"

So Buford has done his homework. He knows Pistakee. Lincoln smiles but shakes his head. "I'm sorry. Byron would laugh me out of the room."

Buford sighs noisily. He has a way of exhaling through his nose that suggests both pain and menace. Tony Soprano featured the same tic. "You make things too hard on yourself, John. One of the lessons I've learned, one of the things the studies all show us, is that successful people know when and how to make compromises with themselves."

"But what about principles?" Lincoln protests. "What's the harm in sticking up for your principles?"

"Principles are fine. But like every other living thing, they should evolve." Standing, Buford takes a card from a leather wallet in his inside jacket pocket. "My brother," he says, handing the card to Lincoln.

The type is embossed:

Lucas Buford
Attorney at Law

Above the list of contact information, Lincoln recognizes the name of a Loop law firm. "Your brother is a lawyer?" Lincoln asks wanly.

"You'll be hearing from us," Buford says before climbing the stairs to Wacker Drive.

Lincoln places the card in the pocket of his shirt, then lingers for a few minutes by the river. The cheerful effects of the champagne have worn off. He leans on the railing above the water, communing with the hundreds of forgotten victims of the *Eastland* Disaster. Buford admires the march of progress, the erasure of folly and sorrow, but it hardly seems fair. Losers can't catch a break.

14

IT'S HARD TO LEAD A NORMAL LIFE WHEN YOU HAVE TO PLOT your movements to avoid a process server. Lincoln assumes Buford's lawsuit will drop at any moment, and his sketchy knowledge of civil litigation suggests that word will come when some shady guy in a soiled overcoat jams a legal document into his hands. Leaving home in the morning, Lincoln pauses with the door cracked to make sure no one is lurking outside. He alters his commute, exiting the train one station early so he can approach Pistakee's building from the rear, unseen. Rather than go out to lunch, he has a Jimmy John's sandwich delivered daily, and he reminds Kim not to buzz in anyone she doesn't know. Does any of this do any good?

Lincoln worries about his health. Stress is a killer. He's started to break into a sweat at the least provocation, or no provocation at all, and he seems to spend all day chilling in the office as the air conditioning hits his damp shirt. Sitting there one afternoon, feeling clammy and distracted, he wonders if maybe Buford is right, maybe Lincoln really is making things too hard on himself. He finds that he can (seemingly) lower his blood pressure simply by letting his imagination play with the preposterous notion that he might get rid of Buford by publishing him.

Lincoln never got around to returning the poet's manuscript, so he retrieves it from the side table and leafs again through the pages, not certain what he hopes to find. He absently recites titles, "The Typewriter," "Buttering an English Muffin." In Buford's poetic world, "The Brown Easy Chair" memorializes an avuncular hunk of wood, cushion, and corduroy that comforts a little boy. Lincoln lets himself wonder if perhaps he's grown jaded and too quick to judge. After all, Buford is probably right about one thing—Lincoln lives within the bubble of the cultural elite.

In this frame of mind, Lincoln comes up with the notion of shopping for a second opinion. But from whom? Duddleston hasn't yet replaced Arthur Wendt, and Lincoln has so little regard for Hazel Lanier that even her gushing endorsement (unthinkable, of course) wouldn't mean much. Flam—well, Flam would guffaw at this stuff and never let Lincoln forget it. Lincoln needs a fresh, unbiased eye, so when Amy stops in to drop off some photographs for the Wrigley Field book, Lincoln figures, why not?

By now, they've relaxed somewhat their frosty office interactions, but Amy still looks puzzled when Lincoln hands her Buford's manuscript. "See what you think," he says.

"A book of poems?" Amy asks. "You think we should publish it?"

"Just tell me what you think. But quickly. I've promised to get back to the author."

Early the next morning, Amy returns to Lincoln's office. Lately, she has reverted to her long, puffy peasant blouse, and her eyes look heavy. She drops Buford's manuscript on Lincoln's desk and flops into a chair. "Well, I read it," she says, "but first I had to work something out in my novel, and I didn't finish that until almost two in the morning. But I think I get it, I think there's really something there."

"The poems?" Lincoln asks optimistically.

"No, my book."

"Terrific," Lincoln says without enthusiasm. For a few minutes, the two discuss the progress of the novel. Amy says she might have something for Lincoln to look at in a month or so (he envisions a scene: poring over the manuscript in his office, trying to focus while Reverend Jackson's forces mass and chant outside the building).

As she stands to go, Lincoln taps Buford's manuscript with his finger. "Did you have any thoughts..."

"Oh! I completely forgot." Amy laughs and sits again. "Those poems are awful, John."

"I know, I know." (Lincoln thinks: well, at least my sensibility is reliable.)

"They're so un-modern."

"I know."

Amy laughs again. "On the other hand, I never really liked modern poetry."

"Nobody does."

"I call it 'about about' poetry."

"Huh?"

"You know—poetry about being about something. It sort of warms up to a subject without ever getting there." Amy taps the manuscript. "But you know what? I kind of like these poems."

"Really?"

"They remind me of my grandmother."

"She read poetry to you?"

"No. They remind me of *her*. Reeking of sweet perfume. Soft. Sort of unimportant. No demands."

Lincoln thinks of alternate titles. *The Granny Poems. Senior Theses. Here's Nana.*

"What's this guy got on you?" Amy asks.

"Ah..." The accidental precision of the remark stops Lincoln for a moment.

"You're not really going to recommend that we publish him?"

"No. Of course not."

After she leaves, Lincoln sits at his desk in a kind of trance. Blackmail. He's being blackmailed. Buford denied it, but that's exactly what's going on. He may not be asking directly for money, but Pistakee would incur expenses bringing out his book. Besides, what he's really demanding is that Lincoln pay with his reputation, the career he's built as a discerning editor. His personal brand! That's worth something, no? Blackmail. As he chews over the word, Lincoln thinks of Detective Evinrude. The officer never called back, and it's been more than six weeks. What would he make of Tony Buford's behavior? After all, blackmail is a crime.

On an impulse, Lincoln picks up the phone and dials the Twenty-Third Police District. Detective Evinrude is out. But after Lincoln gives his name and explains that he's already talked to the detective about a criminal matter, the cop on the other end of the line schedules an appointment for three the following afternoon.

Lincoln arrives early. The station house is busier than on Lincoln's previous visit, and even with two cops behind the counter taking inquiries, Lincoln has to wait ten minutes just to get to the front of the line and announce his presence. For another twenty minutes he occupies himself looking at wanted notices posted in the lobby. Finally, a young cop with a blond crew cut summons him and leads him down the hall to Detective Evinrude's office. On seeing the officer seated at his desk, Lincoln has a sudden failure of nerve. Evinrude's aging yet conditioned physique, his stolid bulk fills the small office and commands with presence. This is not Lincoln's home court.

Before Lincoln can bolt, the detective glances up from a document he's reading and gestures for Lincoln to sit. Then Evinrude returns to the document. Lincoln waits for almost a minute, beating back the urge to squirm. There's nothing in this tiny room to distract him—no family pictures, no framed diplomas, no sentimental calendar art, just sheets of printed matter pinned to the pasteboard walls. It's as if the officer exists as a concept, not a person. Finally, the detective takes off his glasses and looks up wearily. "Now, what's this about?" he asks.

Lincoln is not sure where to begin. "You may remember, I was here a month or so ago, in the matter of the riot on the L train."

Detective Evinrude frowns briefly, trying to bring the case back. "Oh, right, you're the publisher, right?"

"Well, editor, yes."

"I don't think I've got too far on that case. It seems like it's more a civil matter."

"Well, yes," Lincoln nods, "that's sort of what I came to talk about." As clearly and simply as he can, Lincoln explains that the man who has accused him of battery now seems to be promising to drop the claim if Lincoln will publish his manuscript.

Detective Evinrude frowns again as he takes this in. "You mean, you think he's blackmailing you?"

Yes, the magic word. Lincoln had discreetly avoided using it himself. Just give the officer the facts and let him draw his own conclusions. "That's what seems to be going on," Lincoln says indignantly.

"And he'll forget the whole thing if you publish his book of poetry?"

"Exactly."

The detective studies Lincoln carefully, as if his face might hold a clue—a fingerprint, maybe; residue of a gunshot? After a while, Evinrude says, "Well, why the hell don't you? It's only a book of poems."

Lincoln blurts: "But they're really bad poems." He regrets it immediately.

The detective chooses not to explore aesthetics. "How much can it cost?" he asks. "If you get sued for battery, a lawyer alone will cost you thousands of dollars, and who knows what you'll be out if you lose. Who cares about a book of poems? If you can get rid of him, go for it."

For a moment, Lincoln's instincts push him to argue. After all, what does this career law-enforcement officer know about the agonizing intellectual nuances of the publishing business? But his presence, that commanding certainty, ricochets off the pasteboard walls of the office and almost knocks Lincoln out of his chair. The detective speaks with simple, practical logic. Probably experience, too. Lincoln smiles and stands. "Can I go out of town without permission now?" he asks.

"Do whatever you like."

In the cab on the way back to the office, Lincoln chews on the Evinrude Doctrine, as he taken to calling it, and gives himself a pep talk. Amy's novel, a job in New York, a resurrected marriage—he has goals and hopes, real aspirations that link directly to his life. Stop wasting good mental energy fretting about an insignificant book of poems that would vanish on publication—unseen, unremarked, unknown by the world, a sparrow fart. (Maybe that should be the title: *Sparrow Farts.*) Move on.

Back at his desk, Lincoln sends a short e-mail to Tony Buford: "On further consideration, I will submit your ms to the editorial committee."

The response is almost immediate: "You're the man. You can make it happen. TB."

15

HOW DO YOU ARTICULATE THE TERMS OF A COP-OUT? IN A cell phone conversation with Amy, Lincoln test runs the arguments that he will make to the depleted editorial committee (only Duddleston and Hazel now round it out). "You're actually going to recommend that book?" Amy gasps when he tells her what he's considering.

"Just hear me out." Lincoln takes a deep breath. "To begin with, the book might find an audience. The poems are accessible and easy—you said so yourself. Once you start reading, it's hard to stop." Lincoln waits for a reaction. Nothing. He continues, "The language is clean and even witty in spots."

"Sort of," says Amy unhelpfully.

Lincoln aims higher. "You can even argue that Buford has confronted the narrow, faddish, textual analysis of today's academy, lifting the gaze off the flat page and turning it on the real, three-dimensional materials that make up life."

Amy laughs. "Are you on drugs?"

"Look," Lincoln says, taking yet another tack, "Pistakee has a terrible record with diversity. We keep talking about bringing in more African American and Hispanic writers, but we never do. Let's face it, we don't have great connections in those circles.

So here we have a black author coming to us—a South Sider, no less—with a manuscript that would be simple and cheap to produce."

"I agree," Amy says, turning serious. "We're a Chicago publisher. It's pathetic we haven't brought out more books by African Americans."

"This may not be the greatest work of poetry, but sometimes you have to reach out to get things going."

"You're right. I'm sorry I teased you." Amy's voice turns fluty through the cell. "You know, John, sometimes I think you really see things better than other people. I guess that's being a good editor."

The next day, Lincoln gathers with Hazel and Duddleston in the small windowless conference room in the interior of Pistakee's twelfth-floor suite. With the departure of Arthur Wendt and the rushed production for *Wrigley Field*, there are schedules to go over, backlogged book proposals to consider. The meeting drags endlessly. As noon approaches, Duddleston says at last, "Let's wrap it up. I assume there's nothing of interest in the slush pile"—a reference to the collection of manuscripts that have arrived unsolicited from agentless writers, the method of submission left to amateurs and wannabes.

"Actually," Lincoln offers, "something came in that's worth a gander." (A gander? Lincoln's anxious mind races: Where did that word come from? Endorsing this book is so beyond his nature that he's slipped into an alternate personality, the foppish host of a children's TV show.) For the next few minutes, he makes the careful arguments that he practiced on Amy, adding an emphasis (for Duddleston's benefit) on Buford's U of C masters. Lincoln passes out photocopies of one poem, "The Morning Paper," to give a flavor of the work. And he concludes by repeating the heartening call for diversity in the Pistakee list, noting carefully that responsibility for the house's negligence in that regard, if it is negligence, falls on him, as the executive editor (mustn't let the boss think you're calling him a racist slug).

The presentation is greeted with silence. Reading "The Morning Paper" a second time, Hazel squints as if she's trying find her route on a confusing map.

Eventually, Duddleston points out in a tired voice, "I thought we decided to stay away from poetry. Before you got here, we published some, and the books always flopped."

Lincoln has exhausted his lines of argument and can't bear to repeat previous points just to keep the discussion going. (So this is hell, he thinks. Is it worse than getting sued for battery on an elderly black woman or just another circle on the descent?) "See, the book is so out of the mainstream, you really can't compare it to anything we've published before," he responds.

"I don't remember you ever indicating any interest at all in poetry," the owner continues.

"These are different times," Lincoln says, hoping his ambiguous shrug is taken to stand for the collapsed economy, the wars in Iraq and Afghanistan, fractious politics, porous borders, weird weather, celebrity culture, and, above all, the continuing bad shake given black Americans.

Duddleston absorbs this dose of gloom and finally offers, "Well, why don't you let me look at the manuscript, and then let's talk."

"Of course," says Lincoln, and at last the meeting ends.

Several days go by without further word from the owner, and Lincoln gets increasingly agitated. It's one thing to compromise your principles to avoid acute personal embarrassment, but what if it doesn't work? To buy more time, Lincoln sends Buford a short, cryptic e-mail, saying that the book is "under consideration." The poet responds immediately: "Do the right thing."

Another day and then the weekend pass in uncertainty, but on Monday afternoon Mrs. Macintosh summons Lincoln: the boss wants to see him. Duddleston's office feels clubby on this overcast day, and he greets Lincoln with a welcoming smile and waves him to a chair. Buford's manuscript sits in a corner of the neat, expansive desk.

The owner's sunny mood has nothing to do with the book of poetry. "I want you to know how much I appreciate what you're putting in," he tells Lincoln. "Crashing the Wrigley Field book and then taking on Arthur's projects—well, you probably didn't expect to carry a load like this."

Lincoln shrugs modestly. "I want the company to do well, too."

"I want to do something for you," the owner continues, bathing Lincoln in a patriarchal glow. "When this push finally slows down, take an extra week's vacation. I've alerted Matt—you normally get two weeks; this year you get three."

"That's very kind of you," Lincoln says, though he would rather have a raise, a title change, the authority to green light books on his own.

"Just think of it as R & R."

"Thanks!"

With the benefaction out of the way, Lincoln watches the warmth slowly seep from his boss's face. "Now, about this book of poetry," Duddleston says.

"Yes?"

The owner winces and slides his tongue around his mouth, as if searching for the right word among his teeth. "Is this stuff really any good?"

Lincoln hops right to it and waxes for several minutes on the play of language in Buford's work, the animating humor, the clever and often counterintuitive choice of subject. But, no, as much as he wants to avoid being accused in court of committing a racist attack, he can't bring himself to say the poems are good.

Duddleston listens patiently and then poses another fraught question: "You said in the meeting that this would be a step for us in adding diversity to our list, but when I look these over"—he gestures at the manuscript without touching it—"I find nothing that even hints of the African-American experience. I mean, it's entirely pale-faced, as we used to say."

"See, that's it," Lincoln says. "It's post-Obama."

Duddleston frowns. "And that title—*L*—there's nothing in here about the elevated train. What's that about?"

"Good question. We might want to work on that."

Duddleston takes a deep breath and looks away. He holds the moment (hoping that Lincoln will capitulate?). "Well, what the hell," he says at last. "You deserve a shot. I assume we can get it cheap?"

"Of course." Lincoln realizes he has no idea—he and Buford never discussed money.

"Well, offer him five hundred dollars. And a small printing—say, a thousand."

"I'm sure that will work."

Duddleston slides the manuscript toward Lincoln. "It's all yours," he says.

Closing the deal is a snap. "Five hundred dollars," Lincoln tells Buford in a phone conversation later that afternoon.

"Excellent!"

"We'll put it on our spring list."

"Excellent!"

"Now, about that title—*L*. I'm confused. There's nothing in the poems about the train."

"Oh, no, no, no," Buford says with a laugh. "That's the Roman numeral for fifty. There are fifty poems in the collection."

"I didn't realize. Nobody will realize."

"It's subtle, but it works. *L* is the most beautiful letter in the English alphabet—so elegant, so simple. Plus, it's the beginning of *life* and *love*."

"Also *loser*, *ludicrous*—"

"You're thinking too hard. And just look at it—straight lines, stiff back, erect. The sexual component is just below the surface."

"I tell you, no one will get it."

"Well, I've written more poems. I suppose we could add ten and then call it *LX*—you know, sixty."

"No," says Lincoln. "Listen, we've got a month or so. Let's agree to think about it."

"Of course, whatever you say. And, by the way, don't you want to edit anything in there—the phrasing, the imagery?"

"No, I think it's fine as is." Lincoln explains a few other details of publication and promises to send a contract.

Buford responds with a minute or so of gushing gratitude. "Oh, and I thought you'd like to know," he adds in conclusion, "my mother is doing much better. Acupuncture. That seems to be doing the trick. Looks as if we can avoid surgery."

"Excellent," says Lincoln.

After he hangs up, he sits at his desk, staring at the closed door to his office. Beyond, the halls of Pistakee are silent. Outside in the alley, the Hispanic kitchen workers are chatting in their staccato Spanish while they smoke their cigarettes. Lincoln's stomach feels a little queasy and his arm aches, but those are just the effects of the tense afternoon. Done.

FALL:

Still Life

16

THREE DAYS BEFORE BILL LEMKE'S BIG PROMOTION AT Wrigley Field, copies of his rushed book arrive in a large carton at the Pistakee office. Duddleston makes a ceremony out of opening the box, calling the staff and Lemke himself into the conference room and serving celebratory champagne and pizza. Holding the book over his head like a trophy, the boss pronounces, "This is what we can accomplish if we put our minds to it. The old patterns are falling away. It's up to small, agile operations like us to find the new paths."

Unfortunately, two days later, the Cubs are eliminated from any chance of making the playoffs, and suddenly Wrigley Field Night at the ballpark turns into a meaningless contest against a lackluster team, the Pittsburgh Pirates. Duddleston belatedly discovers that his wife has tickets to the ballet that evening and asks Lincoln to call Lemke with the news that the boss won't be able to make it to the game, despite the front-row box seats that the team has provided. Lemke correctly reads the diminished interest from his publisher. "But you're still coming, right?" he asks Lincoln through his disappointment.

"I wouldn't miss it!" Lincoln assures, though he'd rather do anything else, short of reading another book about the team.

"Before the game, they're going to introduce me on the pitcher's mound and plug the book," the author reminds him. "And then I've got a signing scheduled afterward at the 10th Inning, the bar down the street."

"I'll be there!" Lincoln trills, already wondering how long he'll have to hang around.

"You're my guy!" Lemke crows.

But on the afternoon before the game, Mary calls for the first time in weeks. She wants to have dinner tonight with Lincoln.

"Tonight?" He is completely upended to hear from her.

"I want to see you," she says in a soft, pleading voice, and Lincoln imagines that his marital torture is over.

So he calls Bill Lemke again and apologetically explains the turn of events. The old sportswriter, whose long bachelorhood remains a mystery to Lincoln, can't believe that any man would pass up a Cubs game for an attempt to reconcile with his estranged wife. "You sure you don't want to see her some other time?" he asks. Lincoln is sure. "Well, if you can get away afterward, stop by the 10th Inning," Lemke graciously offers.

"I'll try to make it," Lincoln promises insincerely.

He spends a jittery afternoon anticipating the evening, not sure what to expect. Mary was always hard to predict, hard to categorize—that was one of her attractions. She grew up in Minneapolis, in a big Swedish family that had married outside the tribe enough times to provide her with luxurious dark hair and vibrant brown eyes, color schemes that contrasted dramatically with her pale white skin. They met when he was at the *Tribune* and she was a few years out of Northwestern, working as a paralegal for a downtown firm, trying to decide whether to pursue a graduate degree in literature or go to law school. Mutual friends had organized a *Ulysses* discussion group, and Mary and Lincoln had signed up. She caught his attention immediately. Mary was gorgeous, athletic, lusty, smart, and in love with books. Plus, Lincoln quickly discovered to his glee, she enjoyed exercising a small strain of cynicism—nothing sour or deflating, just enough to blast through the numbing Midwestern niceness.

But she never went to graduate school. Even before they married, she diverted into real estate. She'd always been interested in houses and décor, and a friend who'd become a broker suggested that Mary try it out, at least until she decided what she wanted to do. And Mary turned out to be quite good at it, her style and intelligence winning the confidence of buyers. She joined a small firm and carved out a specialty in North Side Victorians, and within a few years she'd become a star saleswoman. Since North Side Victorians remained popular even through the housing bust, she was one of the few real-estate professionals who continued to do reasonably well.

Did the fact that her career flourished while his stalled contribute to the troubles in their marriage? No, Lincoln decides that he enjoyed her success, admired her for it. Something else had gone awry. Their marriage was like a promising but flawed manuscript, a work-in-progress for which he couldn't quite find the editing solution. He loved her, he was sure of that (and he assumed she loved him in return), but love alone didn't prevent them from drifting. The effort to have a baby had been Mary's idea. Lincoln would have been content for them to go on as before, unencumbered and slightly unstable.

On the long, awful Saturday afternoon when she announced that she needed time apart to figure out her feelings, Lincoln was caught entirely unprepared. Through her sobs, however, he sensed that she was leaving him a small opening: that if he would seize her, whisper his love, demand she love him in return, she would wake from this madness. By then, though, he was so wounded by her desire for a break in their marriage that he couldn't bring himself to do anything but pack his things in an L.L.Bean duffel bag and leave. It took a day or so for Lincoln—lying on the air mattress in Flam's dusty spare bedroom—to realize that he'd missed his chance, that if he loved Mary, he should have fought for her.

But now, is she giving him a second chance? He entertains a fragile optimism: in their brief phone conversation, Mary had sounded confiding, intimate—as if they'd never been apart. He vows not to let this moment pass. Tell her what he should have told her before.

They've arranged the date for the restaurant Erwin, a slightly pricey, artisanal-tilted favorite from their marriage. Lincoln gets there first and sits at the bar, sipping a club soda with lime (better to take it easy until he gets a feel for the flow of the occasion). Within a few minutes, he sees her approaching on the sidewalk. On this pleasant fall evening, she's wearing a light gray sweater and a silky dark skirt that clings to her thighs as she walks. When she enters, he impulsively jumps up and takes her in his arms, giving her the sort of exuberant squeeze that dropped out of their marriage after a year or two. "Wow!" she says, gently breaking away. "It's been a while, hasn't it?"

A waiter leads them to their table. The light, coppery color on Mary's cheekbones—probably a souvenir of Sedona—reminds Lincoln of sexy excursions they made together to the Caribbean, and the dark hair curtaining her shoulders seems even more vibrant than he remembered.

The talk is awkward at first, but Lincoln orders a bottle of pinot noir, and soon the conversation eases and circles on subjects that are practiced and familiar. "I've been so busy!" Mary sighs, half exasperated, half pleased. "We keep signing up these corporate clients, mostly from New York, and the companies keep transferring executives out here." She looks up from her salad. "Frankly, I think a lot of nonfinancial businesses are nervous about New York these days."

"They don't like the association with Wall Street?"

She nods. "It should be good for us—at least, Jerry thinks so."

That would be Jerry Cirone, the owner of Mary's firm, a dour, middle-aged health-food nut who can't stop complaining about how his wife took him to the cleaners in their divorce.

"I could use some time off," Mary continues. "But in business you've got to seize the moment. With the economy as it is, you can't leave money on the table."

There was a time, Lincoln recalls, when conversations with his wife focused often on literary matters. Now he wonders if she misses those days.

"And how are things at Pistakee?" she asks as the waiter brings their entrees.

"Good!" says Lincoln, and in the glow of the wine (not to speak of Duddleston's acknowledgement of his hard work and the settlement of *l'affaire Buford*), he means it, at least momentarily.

They chatter on through dinner, finish the wine, order another bottle to go with dessert. Lincoln keeps looking for the opening to confess his continuing love, but for all the good cheer, their conversation remains solidly *informational*—a practical accompaniment to dinner. Let the moment arrive, he tells himself, channeling Zen. Yet as they continue through dessert—a shared helping of sour cherry pie, an Erwin specialty—still more information flows: Mary's sister's wedding last month; Lincoln's update on Flam's romantic ventures; Mary's plans to get an MBA.

"I love real estate, but I'd like to be smarter about it," she says at one point. "You know, really understand the way the economy works, the markets, the financing. I mean, I'm fascinated the way Jerry can explain how a tiny move by the Fed affects the banks, then the mortgage rates, and then the whole housing market."

At this second mention of the pinched, owly boss, the name falling so easily from Mary's lips, Lincoln suddenly gets a shivery image of the container of Tucks Hemorrhoidal Ointment he found in her medicine cabinet. In an instant, he's constructed an entire, terrible world of betrayal and secret love all squeezed from that skinny tube.

"You all right, Linc?" Mary asks. "You look funny all of a sudden."

"Just a little gas." Lincoln pats his stomach.

By the time they've finished the pie, Lincoln has given up on saying anything about his love. Mary gets up to use the restroom, and when she returns and says with a sigh, "Linc, we've got to talk," he has almost steeled himself for what is to come. She wants a divorce. The time apart has helped her realize that they weren't really serious about each other, about marriage, that they would be stuck forever in the feckless patterns of post-grad existence, the place they'd been when they met. She says that she wants to take her life to the next level. She'll always be fond of Lincoln, of course, but in the end this will be better for both of them.

Is there someone else?

"No. Well, yes, but he's not the cause. It would have happened anyway."

Jerry?

"Did you know?" Mary's surprise passes quickly, and she explains that her boss courted her for months. She resisted, succumbed, broke it off, then took it up again. She doesn't say, but Lincoln realizes, that this was all going on while he and Mary were still together.

At least Jerry's got hemorrhoids, Lincoln thinks. The plague would be better, but hemorrhoids help, if only a little.

Lincoln has drunk almost an entire bottle of wine, but he doesn't feel high so much as he feels hungover, as if he's skipped the fun part and gone straight to the consequences. He's limp, wasted, achy. A hole has opened in the top of his head, and a million thoughts and memories are crowding, shoving, struggling to get out, like the passengers trapped on the panicked L train. Every now and then one breaks free: The otherworldly silkiness of the hair on the ears of Cal, the family mutt when Lincoln was growing up. He can feel the sweetness now in the tips of his fingers. Or that time, a couple of years ago, when he accidentally ran into Mary at Macy's downtown, and when she saw him, as she glanced past a rack of dresses, her face opened up like a flower.

"You want some more wine?" Mary asks genially.

No, he tells her. No more wine. He'll take care of the bill.

She doesn't object, and with startling swiftness, they are on the sidewalk in front of the restaurant. There are so many issues, logistics, *details* to discuss. But Mary seems to feel they can wait. Lincoln rouses himself to say cavalierly, "Well, my lawyer will call your lawyer."

"Oh, Linc," says Mary, offering that bright face from the surprise encounter at Macy's. She puts her hand on his forearm, the one he broke so many years ago. For an instant, he feels connected. But then she pulls away.

Lincoln wanders the North Side for two hours. It's not so much that he can't bear to go home alone—though he does have the hazy premonition that if he enters his apartment now, he'll never emerge—it's more that he can't focus on any direction, any ending place. Even his eyes can't focus. The streetlights are harsh, glowing suns. Neon ads become rainbows of red and yellow, blue and green. After a while, he finds himself swimming against clumps of fans leaving the Cubs game. From snippets of conversation, Lincoln gathers that the team has lost again. The subdued traffic, the air of communal misery—it offers a kind of relief. Perhaps by subconscious design, Lincoln comes to the 10th Inning, the scene of Bill Lemke's book-signing party, and after a moment's pause, he plunges in. Lincoln has been here before, and the place is typically mobbed after games. Tonight, though, the bar is almost empty, just a few knots of people drinking beer from steins.

Lemke sits in the back corner on a folding chair in front of a card table adorned with a stack of his books. He's alone. There's not even any sign of the Pistakee intern who was supposed to handle credit card transactions. The author is slumped in his chair. His shoulders sag, his Cubs hat sits low over his forehead. With his faded green shirt, the enormous, flat collar like bat wings circling his throat, and his brown pants scarred with ancient stains, he looks like nothing so much as a pile of dirty laundry carelessly tossed by a Midwest golfer on the basement floor in front of the washing machine in the summer of 1956 and miraculously preserved in the decades since.

"How'd it go?" Lincoln asks.

Lemke looks up without interest. "They forgot to introduce me," he says.

17

"YOU WANT SOME XANAX?" FLAM OFFERS THE NEXT DAY when Lincoln calls to give him the news.

"I'll tough it out."

"Well, anytime. Just ask. I've got a nice supply."

Lincoln rises out of his funk just enough to realize that he has learned something new about his friend. "I didn't know you take tranquilizers," he says.

"I don't, almost never. It just bolsters me to have a stockpile. When things get bad, usually just thinking that the pills are there is enough to keep me steady. You should use them the same way."

"Let me see how it goes," Lincoln says.

He waits two days before calling his parents. Though they aren't totally surprised, given the prior separation, his mother wants specifics that Lincoln can't bear to furnish. She offers to come out to comfort him, but Lincoln tells her that's not necessary. His father hurries through the sympathy and moves swiftly to a dispiriting checklist of things Lincoln must do: cancel joint credit cards and bank accounts; notify the utility companies; warn the mortgage holder; sign up a lawyer. "Now, son," the father continues, "I don't know what was going on in your marriage, but, whatever you do, when you talk to Mary again, don't confess anything."

"Dad!"

"Just good advice. You admit something, and it can come back to haunt you."

"OK, Dad," says Lincoln, thinking of his tryst with Amy and feeling slightly cheered to have an incriminating secret to withhold from his wife.

On top of everything else, breaking up a marriage turns out to be a terrible drain on one's time. Lincoln spends countless hours on the phone following his father's checklist, though he stops short of hiring a lawyer (canceling a seldom-used joint MasterCard doesn't ignite the sense of helplessness and failure that comes with the thought of enlisting an actual human being—Lincoln will need more strength for that). But he also has to calculate whom to tell and how to tell them, then evade as best he can the inevitable questions.

On Friday afternoon, he trudges down to Duddleston's office. Amy is on vacation (writing her novel, she has promised), so Lincoln only has to navigate past Mrs. Macintosh to land an audience with the boss. Facing other acquaintances, Lincoln has come right to the point. With his employer, Lincoln serves up a few publishing matters before dropping the news casually as he's about to leave.

"My God, no!" Duddleston cries, reacting so strongly that Lincoln wonders for a moment if the good Presbyterian considers divorce a firing offense. After a moment, the boss proceeds in a more measured tone. "The two of you seemed so right for each other. Did you try seeing someone? A counselor? A therapist?"

"No, we decided not to do that."

"Every marriage has its bumps. Victoria and I..." Mentioning his wife, Duddleston falters. The angled October sun streaming through the window leaves his face in shadow, and Lincoln gets the sense that Duddleston feels buried suddenly, struggling in a dark place in his past. "It's important to talk," he continues, recovering. "Look, I'll pay for it. Find yourselves a good marriage counselor and have them send the bills to me."

"Jeez," says Lincoln, flabbergasted at his boss's generosity. "That's too kind of you, but I can't accept it. I'll talk to Mary, and maybe we'll see someone. But thank you so much."

"I'm serious. Get someone. Talk."

"Thank you, thank you," says Lincoln, hurrying out of the office.

Walking to the L station after work the next Monday, Lincoln turns on his cell phone and finds a fresh message from Amy. "Call me," she orders. He ignores the command. He's simply not in the mood. But later that night, after he's spent the evening with Flam at John Barleycorn, he calls Amy back.

"John, I heard," she says. Beyond the sympathy in her voice, Lincoln detects a pinprick of curiosity.

"Heard what?" he says, being difficult.

"About the divorce."

"Who told you that?"

Amy hesitates. "Mrs. Macintosh."

"The old bat shouldn't gossip."

Amy recovers enough to hold her own. "Well, is it true?"

"Yes."

"I'm sorry."

"It's one of those things."

"Do you mind my asking—what happened?"

No one else except his mother has been so brazen about getting the autopsy report. "It's a long story," he says wearily.

"I thought you two were trying to work it out."

Suddenly he understands: "You're not about to be named a correspondent, if that's what you're worried about."

"Fuck off," says Amy, and she hangs up.

Lincoln lies down on his bed and concentrates on Flam's little white container of Xanax.

Tony Buford calls the next day at work. “I thought I should check in and see how my editor is doing,” the poet says.

“OK,” Lincoln tells him. “The book’s in copy editing. I sent the manuscript over to our designer to get some ideas for the cover. And we need to think some more about that title.”

“I meant personally,” Buford corrects. “I was sorry to hear about you and your wife.”

Was there a story on the front page of the *Tribune*? Does all of Chicago know? “Who told you?” Lincoln asks bluntly.

“Matt Breeson mentioned it. I’ve been dealing with him on my contract.” Buford pauses, then continues, “Sorry—didn’t mean to be impertinent.”

“That’s OK. I’m just kind of sick of talking about it. And thinking about it.”

“Understood. So listen, I’ve come up with some ideas for the title of my collection. Want to hear?”

“Sure.”

“OK. Here’s the one I like best: *Still Life with DustBuster.*”

Lincoln says nothing.

“You know, because one of the poems is about a DustBuster,” Buford explains.

“I remember. What else have you got?”

“Well, I’ve got several. *Shards of a Man. Building Blocks. Facets. Taking Stock…*” Buford keeps rolling them out, and Lincoln listens, but he can’t hear. The words are white noise. His mind is drifting. Mary has left him for another man. A man with hemorrhoids. “*Surroundings. How to Get By. Reflections—*”

“OK!” Lincoln interrupts. “There’s a lot to think about there.”

“I’ve got more.”

“Listen, why don’t you just e-mail me the whole list, so I can chew it over.”

“Sure. I’ll put them in the order I like best, favorite on top.”

“OK. Now I’ve got to get back to work.”

"Sure, sure, you're a busy guy. But have you got just one more second?"

Lincoln sighs silently. "Of course."

Buford starts slowly, picking his words carefully. "I know it's none of my business—we've got the editor-writer relationship, nothing more—but, well, in all the back-and-forth over my mom and my book, I've come to feel pretty close to you."

"Yes?" Where in God's name can this be going?

"And I really hate to see you get torn up over the marital situation."

What has Matt Breeson told him? "I think I'm handling it pretty well," Lincoln says.

"Of course you are, of course you are. But just bear with me here. I've started a new group, a new process, really. I'm calling it Poetry Therapy, and it combines poetry appreciation with yoga, but yoga without all the New Age, spiritual crap. You get the best of both worlds—yoga to relax your body and poetry to sharpen your mind. I've got ten or so people in my group. We meet on Thursday evenings in the DePaul student center. I really think it would do you good."

"Ahhh." Lincoln can't find words to describe the horror of the image that has risen in his mind: ten rubbery nerds in body-baring Spandex, rolling around on smelly gym mats, sweating and sighing while someone in a pretentious voice reads aloud from *Leaves of Grass*. "Gee, I appreciate your concern," Lincoln says. "But I'm trying to get through this on my own."

"Sure." Buford doesn't sound entirely convinced. "Just keep it in mind. I really think this could help."

"Thanks. Send me the titles. Bye."

Flam remains heroic in his kindnesses, offering not just Xanax but a continuing patient ear and a willingness to talk Lincoln back from the cliffs of despair and paranoia. They eat together most evenings, usually at John Barleycorn, though occasionally they venture to some other inexpensive spot on the

North Side. "I'm not even mad," Lincoln confesses one night. "It's as if anger is beside the point. I'm mostly just dazed."

"It's probably like grief," Flam suggests. "There are stages you have to go through, and you'll get to anger eventually."

"I can't believe she was falling in love with someone else while we were living together. It makes me question everything—as if I've been wrong from the start. My whole reality is tilted."

"There is no reality," Flam says. "You just have to tell yourself a good story and stick to it."

Flam's companionship bolsters Lincoln through the first agonizing weeks, but in his misery Lincoln even grows short with his generous friend and frustrated at the awkward bachelorhood they share. Lincoln starts to lose patience with Flam's amusements, such as his habit over dinner of disgorging the news of the day, particularly items confirming the idiocy of somebody or some institution. Flam has become particularly enthralled by a story embraced by the tabloid *Sun-Times* about a man in suburban Schaumburg who weighs over nine hundred pounds and can't get out of bed. He needs hospital care, but the health authorities have decided that the best treatment is to keep him at home on a strict diet until he's lost enough weight to move. "They're starving the poor bastard!" Flam cries one evening at Barleycorn as Lincoln hides behind his mug of beer.

The next day, the news turns tragic. The fat man bribed a neighborhood boy to smuggle in several bags of hamburgers, fries, and candy. The man binged, then died, probably of a heart attack. "Murder!" pronounces Flam. "The state killed him."

Lincoln can't keep it in. "For God's sake, the man ate himself to death. The health authorities were doing what they could."

"Then it's suicide facilitated by the state. They probably didn't want to have to pay to get the fat guy to the hospital and take care of him there."

Lincoln carefully puts down the knife and fork he was using on his open-faced tuna-melt sandwich. He speaks in weary tones.

"The man was pathetic. He's not worth our time. Let's talk about something else."

"Suit yourself," Flam grumbles, and the dinner concludes in monosyllables.

By the time Lincoln is in bed at home, he's digested the evening sufficiently to know exactly what Flam is now thinking: no wonder Mary left that cold son of a bitch.

The next day, Lincoln gets to work line editing one of Arthur Wendt's manuscripts, *Revolutionizing Business*, a book on management principles gleaned from the Founding Fathers, by Mitchell Morgenthau, another beloved U of C professor. Lincoln is trudging through the second chapter when his phone rings. "Your wife," Kim tells him when he picks up.

Lincoln has a terrible taste of stale coffee in his mouth. He swallows hard, trying to wash it away. "OK."

"Linc? How are you? I tried to get you earlier on your cell phone, but it was turned off."

"I'm at work."

"I know. This was the other day."

"You didn't leave a message."

"I know. I didn't feel right just being a disembodied voice. I wanted to talk to you for real, and I figured you'd see it was me on your 'Missed Calls' function."

"I don't ever use that."

"Well, no matter, here we are. How are you?"

In the moment while Lincoln considers what to say, he reflects that her voice sounds different—a little higher, slightly tinny, something being held back. She's not calling to beg forgiveness. "I'm OK."

"Really? I worry about you. Are you hanging out with Flam?"

Flam. His friend. Lincoln flashes back to dinner yesterday and thinks: How could I be so ungrateful? "Yes."

Mary natters on for a minute or so about applying to business school. "Then I spent the whole weekend studying for the goddamned GMAT," she goes on. "Morning to night. I've never done anything so boring. I hope business school isn't like this."

The precise ease with which she describes this annoyance makes Lincoln assume that she spent the weekend in romps from the kitchen floor to the dining-room sofa to the bed in Jerry Cirone's expensive downtown condo.

"Have you hired a lawyer yet?" she asks abruptly.

"Not yet."

"Well, you probably should, so we can try to sell our apartment. It'll be tough, but I think the quicker we get it out on the market the better."

She's so, so far ahead of him. The world is ahead of him. "You should know," he says sullenly.

"Linc, I wish you wouldn't be that way."

For a moment Lincoln wonders: Would it really be possible to be any other way—wounded, confused, self-doubting, depressed, angry, and, finally, petulant as a teenager when confronting the source of the pain? "I've got to get back to work," he tells her. "I'm in the middle of editing something."

"Good-bye, Linc," she says simply and hangs up.

Lincoln gets up and walks slowly to the men's room, trying to recover some equilibrium. When he returns to his desk, first thing he calls Flam and apologizes for being a prick last night.

"You think last night was out of character?" Flam asks with a laugh. "No apology necessary. Does a barracuda apologize for its teeth?"

Then Lincoln works straight through the day, snacking on a tin of Starbucks mints in his desk, using the wandering sentences of *Revolutionizing Business* as the koan in which to lose himself and seek enlightenment.

He thinks often that he should just pack up and leave—abandon Chicago at last and move to New York. But that would defy another piece of advice from his father: don't quit your job until you have a new one. Lincoln has already sent out more than a dozen inquiries, some to the familiar New York editors, some to a new round. Like every other business, however, publishing is feeling squeezed. Most of the editors he contacted haven't even responded.

So rather than indulging in Poetry Therapy or Xanax, Lincoln devises his own prescription for coping: he jogs. Every evening after work, he heads east from his building to the lake. It's dark, but the streets and the lakefront path are mostly well lit and usually populated by other runners. Lincoln enters the park through the Waveland underpass and each time faces a critical choice: Should he turn left, away from the city, toward the lonely, quiet regions to the north, the path edging between the shadowy trees and the black oblivion of the lake? Or go right, running toward the jagged explosion of buildings and lights of downtown Chicago, the illuminated Ferris wheel on Navy Pier a kind of lighthouse to mark the shoals of inflated promises and manufactured joys? Lincoln never knows which way he'll turn, but lets impulse take over. And then he runs, pounding, gasping, sweating, punishing his body, exhausting his brain, driving out all thoughts but the deep, total awareness of physical discomfort. He runs for an hour, longer on some nights, stopping finally when he's circled back, walking the last few blocks to his building, soaking wet now, cooling in the fall night air, feeling for the first time all day a measure of relief. And sometimes walking back, the question drifts into his emptied head: Am I going to die in exile in Chicago?

18

By Thanksgiving, Lincoln's life has eased back toward homeostasis. He has adjusted to his furnished apartment and come to know the neighbors he'd hoped he could avoid (two young couples, a trader, and the elderly widow on the first floor who has lived in the building since long before the neighborhood gentrified); gently curtailed his evenings out with Flam; and hired a lawyer, who is now working out the details of the divorce. She is an attractive young mother of twins who assumes the attitude—presumably to bolster spirits—that getting a divorce is one of life's special pleasures: "That day when it becomes final, you'll experience a rush of emotion that will bowl you over," she promises. "That's what I call the Freedom High."

At the office, Lincoln's various projects are moving forward, though Duddleston has wisely decided to hold Professor Fleace's *Walking Tours of the Windy City* until spring, when someone in Chicago might actually dare to face the weather and walk around outside. The owner has also hired a replacement for Arthur Wendt: Warren Sternberg, who made a name bringing out *Deep Dish*, a history of Chicago pizza.

Through a bolt of serendipity, Lincoln and Tony Buford have found a suitable title for the collection of poetry. Lincoln had given the manuscript to Pistakee's multi-tattooed young designer, Gregor (just Gregor—he's also an artist, intent on becoming his own brand), and appended the title *Still Life with DustBuster* as a placeholder until they came up with something better. Either Gregor didn't understand or Lincoln failed to explain adequately; in any case, Gregor took the faux title as inspiration and designed a handsome cover, featuring his own photograph of a utility-closet corner with a DustBuster bedded among an old pair of shoes, a shopping bag of wire hangers, a used tennis ball, and a roll of heavy-duty extension cord. In his enthusiasm for his composition, Gregor neglected to leave sufficient room for all the words of the stand-in title, so he shortened it simply to *Still Life.* Perfect, thinks Lincoln when he sees the mock-up. Seldom has a title so exactly expressed a book's content. With a minimum of persuasion, Buford goes for it, too.

By then, Lincoln has also repaired his relationship with Amy. For several weeks after she hung up on him, they steered clear of each other, going beyond even the cool discretion they'd exercised previously. The Pistakee offices are too intimate for that to last, however, and eventually their grudging nods give way to terse greetings. Finally, one day after work, Amy calls on his cell phone. "I'm not mad at you anymore," she announces. "But I'll get mad again if you're not careful."

"Don't worry. What I said was stupid. I was just a little out of my mind because of what was going on."

"I know. I was ready to give you the benefit of the doubt, but then you never called back to apologize."

"I should have," Lincoln confesses. "I'm sorry." After Mary's deception, Flam's sarcasm, Duddleston's reticent management style, and Buford's manipulation, Lincoln feels as if he's been dealing with people who operate on several levels at once, and he appreciates Amy's candor. Turning upbeat, he asks, "How's the book coming?"

"I should have something to show you after Thanksgiving."

"Really? So soon?"

"Do you think it's too soon?"

"All depends. How many pages do you have?"

"Around two hundred."

Lincoln does a quick calculation in his head. That's around a hundred seventy-five or so pages in a book, depending on the design.

Amy asks, "What are you thinking? Is that too short? I'm used to writing short stories, so this seems enormous."

"No, that's probably fine. Some of the classics are short. *Gatsby, Billy Budd.*"

Through the cell, Amy's voice softens a notch, loses its hint of office efficiency. "I missed our discussions," she confides. "You pushed me. I wrote the last third of the book on my own, and I'm afraid it's not so good."

"I'm sure it's fine," Lincoln tells her. Fighting the nippy wind blowing from the north, he's struck suddenly by a mild melancholy. Just a few months ago, on those steamy summer evenings, his cell-phone conversations with Amy about her novel always gave him a shot of encouragement. Now, Amy's venture seems like a mere diversion. "I'm eager to read it," he adds.

For the first time since before he was married, Lincoln spends Thanksgiving with his family, joining his mother, father, sister, and her two kids at the family's weekend place in rural West Virginia. Lincoln had hesitated to accept the standing invitation, worried that he'd be repeatedly cross-examined about the end of his marriage. But it turns out that a newer crisis has inserted itself into the family circle. His sister's husband, an investment banker from Boston, has failed to make the trip, citing pressure from a mysterious deal. Lincoln's sister, Lillian, is elusive about the situation, and the husband, Brad, doesn't call on Thanksgiving Day. Rather than pushing to dissect this latest worrisome marital development, Lincoln's parents choose to avoid probing questions almost entirely. Just once, after the

Thanksgiving dinner, on a walk along the country road in front of their house, Lincoln's father brings up the matter, asking if Lincoln is happy with his lawyer.

"She seems fine," Lincoln says.

"I called a few acquaintances, and they gave her high marks," his father continues. "The divorce bar can be a snake pit, you know. Very few scruples. But she worked at Mercer, Epstein before starting her family. Quite a good firm."

"I know, Dad," says Lincoln, slightly disconcerted to learn his father secretly vetted Lincoln's choice. When he was a child and got invited on a playdate with a new friend, Lincoln's mother would quietly call around to check the reliability of the friend's family.

For the most part, his parents also avoid pressing Lincoln about the progress of his career, though on that same walk, his father casually asks how the job search in New York is going. "Got some letters out," Lincoln says briskly. "Waiting to hear."

In the silence that follows, Lincoln feels a grudging admiration for his father's restraint, given that the worthy Democrat so desperately wants to welcome his only son to the pantheon of civic accomplishment. It was bad luck for both of them that the old man is utterly uninterested in sports, considers games a frivolous waste of time, so Lincoln never even got credit at home for his achievements on the basketball court.

They scuff along the road for a few more yards before his father says almost wistfully, "Probably not too late for law school."

The family's West Virginia property features a lovely, square, two-story, nineteenth-century farmhouse with a porch around two sides and the original wood floors and trim. (A shame Mary never saw the place, Lincoln thinks—she might have stayed if she'd realized this thing of beauty was in the family.) Lincoln's room sits in one corner of the second floor, and he spends much of the holiday lying on his familiar old bed, reading books. Going back as far as Lincoln can remember, he and his mother and sister came out for the summer, his father joining them on weekends. Because of those summers, the contents of the room are like a core sample of his childhood, the layered detritus of assorted ages. The stuffed dog and stuffed bunny. A gorgeous wood train carved by a former hippie who moved to the area in the sixties and created a thriving cottage business. Swimming ribbons. Several generations of baseball gloves. Posters of Magic Johnson and Larry Bird. Trophies from a summer basketball league.

Sometimes when he wearies of his book, Lincoln lies back with a Proustian regard. After the order and calm of his suburban neighborhood, West Virginia came off as untamed and alluring—the river swimming hole with the rope swing over the water; the general store, with its unfamiliar offerings; the overweight natives with their twangy accents. Lincoln recalls those summers fondly, but his memories aren't entirely heartening. He's not far enough removed from his childhood to find comfort in nostalgia, and he has the nagging sense that he'll never quite get to that happy station until he accomplishes something—until he's tasted some success as an adult. Relishing his past would be so much more rewarding if it lay back beyond the Golden Era of his life, his Heroic Period. Instead, the divorce has returned him to a kind of adolescent limbo in which he's waiting to be let out of the house to get going again.

Back in Chicago, Amy strides into Lincoln's office on Monday morning and drops a heavy Kinko's box on his desk. "All yours," she says. She plops down in a chair.

"You finished!"

"I nearly got disowned. I spent the holiday holed up in my apartment, except for Thanksgiving dinner. My parents were pissed."

Amy's face is pale and lacks highlights, and her hair carelessly falls over her ears. She's wearing an old, bulky purple sweater with jeans. "You still haven't told them what you're working on?" Lincoln asks.

"I had to tell them I'm writing a book, but I wouldn't tell them what it's about. You're the only one who knows."

When she's gone, Lincoln removes the top of the Kinko's box to consider the first page of the manuscript:

THE ULTIMATE POSITION
By Amy O'Malley
(draft)

So she went with that title. Quickly he closes the box and places it with other manuscripts on the side table in his office. He anticipates the book with such a mixture of longing and dread that he knows he has to approach it at the right time and in the right frame of mind.

That moment arrives approximately three minutes later. He closes his office door and starts to read. He shudders when he sees the first word—"Mary"—but he plows on and rather likes the first sentence. "Mary Reilly considered the slender, attractive young woman sitting in the hard plastic chair, and something candid in the visitor's aspect—her willingness to ignore the tiny beads of perspiration forming on her upper lip, a condition brought on by the overworked and failing office air-conditioner—told Mary that this would not be the ordinary sex interview." The rest of the opening chapter has problems, but Lincoln's optimism builds through the day. With only a pause to get a sandwich for lunch, he reads the manuscript straight through.

He finishes about six that evening, and after coming home, he pours himself a vodka on the rocks. He sits in his nubby easy chair and gazes out the window, staring absently through the jagged tree branches to the darkened houses across the street. Jesus Christ, he thinks, this might work. The main character,

Mary Reilly, has a quirky inner life. The narrative flows. The dialogue's fresh.

And the book is all about sex.

Lincoln savors his vodka. Jesus Christ.

The story follows the outline that he and Amy had discussed. Mary Reilly, a young researcher for a sex study at a fictitious university in a Midwestern city, becomes fascinated with one of her subjects, a slightly older, somewhat mysterious graduate student in theology named Jennifer Blythe. Over the course of several weeks of interviews—and then over lunch and dinner as the two women fall into a friendship—Jennifer recounts a series of sexual escapades that turn increasingly bizarre (there's that search for the Ultimate Position). At first, Mary is intrigued, but soon she grows alarmed. There's something needy and finally degrading in Jennifer's obsessive drive to test the limits of her experience. Meantime, as Mary tries to investigate the background of her new friend, a sexual predator starts attacking women in the university town, and Mary comes to wonder if Jennifer knows something about the perpetrator—she seems to be engaging in the same sexual acts that later get unleashed on the victims. The book is too cerebral to qualify as a thriller—Amy cares most about exploring the growing relationship between the two women—but the ending holds Lincoln's interest, even though he knew what was coming: Jennifer turns out to be an unhinged fabulist who picked up hidden details from a cop acquaintance, then invented her lurid encounters to capture and hold Mary's friendship.

Lincoln rises and pours himself another vodka, then returns to his post in front of the window. Of course, the manuscript needs work. For one thing, the sex has to get better. Amy's renditions have such a mechanical quality that she could be describing how to vacuum the living room. Though Amy sets the story in the Midwest, the book offers no sense of place—the plot could be unfolding in Honolulu. Several of the secondary characters come off as one-dimensional buffoons. Even with the predator stalking the city, the pace slackens in the middle section.

Still, all that can be fixed. Lincoln wishes he had someone to high-five or bump chests with. He briefly considers calling Amy at home but decides no, it's better to approach her in the clarifying light of day. So he sits down at his computer and types out some suggestions. By eleven that night, he has written a dense, five-page memo. He prints it out and reads it over with yet more vodka. With the late hour and his alcohol-fueled energy, he drifts for a moment into an odd misperception: he imagines that *he* has written the novel and some brilliant editor has grasped his vision perfectly, exactly understanding his meaning and purposes and making brilliant strategic suggestions to realize the novel's greatness. No, Lincoln scolds himself. Mustn't get proprietary, that's the worst thing an editor can do. It's Amy's book. And so he goes to bed and lies awake for most of the rest of the night, reworking her sentences in his head.

On Sunday morning, he calls her at home. "It works," he says when she picks up. On the other end, he hears what sounds like someone being gagged or strangled. "Amy?" he asks, alarmed.

Heavy breathing, then, in a voice Lincoln hardly recognizes: "It's me, celebrating. I've got the world's worst cold."

"It sounds like it."

"But you liked the book?"

"Yes. Quite a nice job." Here, Lincoln dials back, going into his practiced editor mode. Much work remains to be done, and it's important that the author not come to believe the original draft is an untouchable masterpiece. "Good characters. Strong story. Really quite enjoyable."

"Ooooohhhhh!"

"Naturally," Lincoln says coolly, "I have some suggestions."

"What are they?"

"I've got a memo. I'll e-mail it."

"Fantastic!"

"Drink lots of tea," Lincoln tells her, quoting the only medical advice his soon-to-be ex-wife ever gave him.

Lincoln sends the memo. Two hours later, Amy calls. Curiously, her voice sounds almost normal now, as if reading the memo has had the cleansing effect of powerful menthol. "There's a lot of stuff here," she says gloomily.

"Well, of course. Because the book is so good, it sparked a lot of ideas." You've got to be a salesman with this sort of thing.

"I'm not sure I agree with all of them."

"You don't have to. They're just suggestions."

"Like adding more sex."

"Now, that's important."

"I don't want to write a sex book."

"It won't be a sex book. It's a book about people. But you've got to get them out of the lab, so to speak. Anyway, in this day and age, lots of literary books have candid sex. Think of *Vox*. Or *Middlesex*."

"Haven't read them."

"Or Updike or Roth. The sex isn't gratuitous, it's part of the context."

"I can't do porn."

"It won't be porn. It will be discreet and naturalistic."

"And you want to cut some of my favorite scenes."

"This is a work in progress. Nothing in my memo is carved in stone."

Lincoln waits while Amy goes through a sneezing jag on the other end of the phone. She continues, "I mean, that scene where Professor Hazeltine comes in and orders everybody in the office to drop what they're doing and join him in a tai chi session on the lawn—that really happened. How can you say it's like a cartoon?"

Lincoln knows he has to take control of the situation. "Look, consider the memo, sleep on it, then do what you can. Those are only suggestions. But I guarantee that if you don't take at least some of them into account, the book isn't publishable."

Amy says nothing. In the silence, Lincoln worries that he's been too harsh. Fiction is all so subjective. Who's to say he's right about anything he proposed? He adds, "God is in the rewrite."

"All right," she says at last. "I'll see what I can do." The deathbed voice has returned.

Amy doesn't come to work for several days, and when she finally appears, she looks pale and frazzled, and her nose still bears traces of the raw, red battle scars inflicted in her fight with the cold. She volunteers no bulletins, that day or over the course of the next few weeks, though several times when she and Lincoln pass in the office, she makes a face, scrunching her nose, as if she's caught a whiff of something unpleasant. The one time they find themselves alone together in the elevator, he asks her how it's going. She rolls her eyes. "I'm trying."

"I'm available to help," Lincoln reminds her.

"It's just hard to change when you've got things in your mind one way. I can hardly sleep for thinking about it." Before Lincoln can respond, the doors open on the twelfth floor to Duddleston and a cadre of his lawyers about to head off to a meeting somewhere.

But in his gradually improving state of mind, Lincoln really does believe that Amy can do it. He's made some calculations, and if they can get the manuscript in shape by the first of the year, he'll propose crashing it for the spring list so they'll be able to publish just in time for the start of beach-reading season. In his head, Lincoln has already started to compose the press release. ("Pistakee Press, Chicago's premier book publisher, is proud to introduce *The Ultimate Position*, Amy O'Malley's stunning first novel of young women coming to grips with the wide-open sexuality of today's college generation.") He assumes that the book's backstory—a pretty young U of C grad drawing on her experience with a sex survey—will grab the attention of the talk shows and newspapers. And in a particularly incautious moment, he imagines Jeff Kessler of Malcolm House opening his *New York*

Times to the Arts section, scanning the story about the surprise, sexy best seller from the small Midwestern publisher, and stopping at the name of the clever editor who spotted and marshaled the book. With a new maturity nurtured in pain, Lincoln quickly stifles the fantasy.

Lincoln doesn't mention the book to anyone, and he regrets having discussed it months ago with Flam—on something like this, operating beneath the radar is so much easier. Of course, with his nose for angst, Flam hasn't forgotten. One night, while he and Lincoln are having hamburgers at John Barleycorn, Flam asks out of the blue how the book is coming. "Still being written," Lincoln dodges.

"Wasn't that going to be your ticket out of here?" Flam presses.

"That was a long time ago."

"Just last summer."

"I meant metaphorically."

Flam takes a bite of hamburger and considers. Barleycorn is quiet on this chilly December night, and the strings of Christmas lights and holiday ribbons look as if they've been hanging for decades. "I sort of liked that project," Flam says finally. "I thought it was one of your better ideas."

The semicompliment emboldens Lincoln. "What do you think of the title *The Ultimate Position*?" he asks.

Flam abruptly halts a bundle of fries on its way to his mouth. "You're going to call the book *The Ultimate Position*?"

"Maybe," says Lincoln, retreating. "One of the characters claims to be searching for it."

"The ultimate position for sex."

"Yes."

"Perfect."

"You like?"

"It's perfect!"

Lincoln feels an easing in his upper back, between his shoulders. A steel rod that had somehow been implanted there for the last six months flexes, bends.

Flam continues eagerly: "That's it, that's modern man—you know, his senseless, hopeless quest: sweating and wrestling and testing out all these uncomfortable arrangements, trying to figure out how to maneuver things just right. The Ultimate Position."

Something occurs to Lincoln: Is Flam talking about me?

The next morning, Amy sends the rewrite. "I'm finished," her note says simply. Attached are all fourteen chapters.

Lincoln immediately prints the manuscript. At 213 pages, it has a pleasant heft. He makes himself a cup of coffee, then sits down to read. Within the first few pages, he feels his excitement draining. His stomach turns raw, and he abandons the coffee half-finished. He skims some pages, reads, then skims some more. Amy has hardly changed a thing. She's rewritten an occasional sentence, added a brief scene here or there, overexplained a few elements that were elusive in the original. If anything, the book has deteriorated.

Her efforts to inject real sex into the pages have an awkward, even prophylactic quality. "He placed her naked across the large, firm pillow, laying her on her back, as if carefully draping an expensive fur coat. Then he dropped to his knees in front, entering only the first two inches of her vagina, so he could directly massage her G spot with his erect penis." The book's sluggish midsection has practically stalled with the addition of background information on Mary's annoying boyfriend. By evening, Lincoln can't push himself to finish and instead goes out alone to a movie.

He reads to the end Sunday morning, after he's been through the *Times* and the *Tribune*. He's sitting in the nubby chair, Amy's manuscript plopped atop a scattering of newspaper sections, when his cell phone rings.

"Well?" asks Amy.

"How do you know I've finished it?"

"I know you, John."

He wonders at the implications of the remark, then decides to ignore it. "Well, I think the book's still got a lot of promise," he says.

"I don't like the sound of that."

"To be candid, there's more to be done."

"Like what?"

"Like…most of the things we talked about before."

"I can't. I'm exhausted." Click. She's gone.

Lincoln sits. His arm aches, and now his eyes hurt. Maybe he needs to see an optometrist, get a prescription for glasses. In five minutes, Amy calls back. "I'm going to quit my job," she says.

"Why, for God's sake?"

"I hate publishing."

Lincoln senses that the best way to calm this tantrum is to play it out. "So what are you going to do instead?"

"Maybe teach English."

"But you'll be dealing with books, and I thought you hated publishing."

"A waitress. I used to do that, and now I'm old enough to serve liquor."

"Would you really be happy spending your life as a waitress?"

Click.

Lincoln continues to sit, and Amy doesn't call back. His disappointment has seeped into his muscles and his bones—it's not just his aching arm and tired eyes, his entire body feels weighted and dull. Like Amy's manuscript. Did it actually once hold promise, or was the whole thing just an inflated dream, the absurd escape fantasy of a man imprisoned?

Lincoln's chin falls to his chest, directing his gaze to the front of the *Tribune*'s Sunday travel section, discarded on the floor. The top half of the page is taken up by a photograph of a lonely hut in the middle of a frozen lake, a square blot of human scale in a vast frigid landscape. The story is about ice fishing in northern Wisconsin. Why? Who in his right mind? And, yet, the image of cold, stark isolation suggests a purity of purpose that draws Lincoln. Life in the Midwest, reduced to its quintessence. He picks up the paper and reads. The article is full of the usual travel-writing inanities, all celebration, no skepticism, with a half dozen ice-fishing enthusiasts (all enormously fat, judging by the inside pictures) trilling on about the glories of their sport. Still, that bleak photograph calls to Lincoln. He will take his gift week of vacation and check into a motel in northern Wisconsin, away from all distractions, all temptations, and he will dedicate every waking moment to rewriting Amy's book.

It will be his walkabout, his forty days in the desert, his punishment and his salvation. He will be following the great literary tradition. Like Thoreau at Walden Pond, he will go to the wilderness and return with…well, something that will propel him the fuck out of this place.

WINTER:

Lunker Sex

19

Three days before Christmas, Lincoln rents a car and drives eight hours north to Lac du Flambeau, Wisconsin. A few miles out of town, he stops at the Lunker Motel, which looked clean and relatively comfortable ("Good heat in winter!") on its simple website. From the sound of the name, Lincoln assumed that the motel was owned by a good Wisconsin German family, but the lady at the reception desk quickly sets him straight. "It means a big fish," she says, amused at his ignorance. She points outside, and indeed, the motel sign along the quiet road features a huge, curling fish in neon. "You know, like a *lunker* walleye!"

"Ah." Lincoln smiles. A new word. The trip is off to a promising start.

"I guess you aren't a fisherman," she says as Lincoln fills out a guest card. She's a hefty woman, middle aged and ruddy faced, with incongruously yellow-blond hair, and she's wearing a brown crew-neck sweater over a plaid flannel shirt. She ought to be named Lunker, Lincoln thinks.

"No, not a fisherman," he confirms. He hands her the guest card, which she studies carefully.

"Chicago," she pronounces. "Passing through on business?"

"You might say." Only Amy knows his true purpose. He didn't even tell Flam he was going away.

"A salesman?" the curious woman presses. "It's pretty quiet up here this time of year."

"No. Well, in a way, yes," Lincoln fumbles. Lying makes him feel like a criminal on the lam, hiding out in a cheap motel. He flashes her a broad smile that manages to quell the interrogation.

The motel is one long strip of rooms divided in half by the reception area (and, Lincoln eventually discovers, the owners' apartment in back). Because business slows around Christmas, the heat has been shut down in the west wing. Lincoln gets room 14 at the far end on the other side. A couple of pickup trucks and a van are parked along the walkway, but several empty units separate him from his closest neighbor. Excellent.

Except for its cable-fed TV, room 14 offers few amenities—thin wood paneling, flimsy dresser, small desk, undulating king-size bed. The dark brown carpeting has an unfortunate texture that feels damp to Lincoln, and the radiator fills the room with such intense, dry heat that he constantly has to turn it down, then push it back up again when the Wisconsin cold seeps in. The place also lacks Wi-Fi, so Lincoln is limited to e-mail on his cell phone. Overall, though, the Lunker is all he had hoped.

He arrived in midafternoon, and right away, he sets up his operation. He puts his laptop on the desk and attaches a small printer, which he places on the floor. He hides the paper copy of the manuscript in the top drawer of the dresser, then on his computer he copies all fourteen chapters of the book separately, labeling them as he goes "Amy/edit/1," "Amy/edit/2," and so on, creating a version of her work that he can chew up, discard, and rearrange as he likes.

Finally, he opens up "Amy/edit/1" and contemplates the first sentence. "Mary Reilly considered the slender, attractive young woman…" Lincoln sits on the rickety desk chair, his fingers poised on the keyboard. Nothing. He scrolls down the text, substituting a word here or there, nibbling at an occasional sentence. After an hour of fitfully backing up and going forward, he comes to the end of the chapter. He's hardly changed a thing.

In a misguided effort to find his muse, he cracks open the fifth of vodka he's brought along. Still nothing after several glasses. In the crack in the window curtain, he can see snow falling through a shaft of light on the walkway. Glancing up once, he thinks he sees a blurred figure quickly pull away. Mrs. Lunker (as he's taken to calling her in his head)? Is she spying? His trips up and back to regulate the radiator become a measure of his lack of inspiration: The room's climate moves from desert heat to tundra cold and back again, with hardly a word altered. Someone with the flu moves in next door and rattles the paneling with thundering coughs. Lincoln realizes he's getting drunk. Buford said happy people were more creative, and now Lincoln feels so glum he could hardly write his name.

At last, he shuts his computer down. He tells himself that after a long drive, what he needs is dinner and a good night's sleep. When he checked in, Mrs. Lunker offered a pair of dining options—a supper club a few miles away or a bar with a microwave just down the road. He's in no condition to drive, so Lincoln bundles up and walks along the slushy shoulder until he comes to Iggy's Ice House, a wood-shingled structure plopped in the middle of a desolate parking lot.

Iggy's is empty except for one customer and a jowly bartender. Lincoln sits at the bar four stools down from the other customer and orders a glass of red wine. The bartender, a model of bored efficiency, offers up the dining options—a bratwurst or a hamburger, each heated in a clear plastic bag in the microwave. Lincoln asks for one of each. The sandwiches have a damp, spongy texture and taste faintly of oatmeal, but Lincoln needs the fuel and orders a second round. As he eats, the other patron, an elderly man, glances over occasionally, flashing a wrinkled smile. He waits politely for Lincoln to finish his second bratwurst before leaning over to ask, “You staying down at the Lunker?”

“Yes,” says Lincoln.

The old guy nods happily at the news. He has a neat, grandfatherly style, with a head of carefully combed white hair and a brown sweater-vest pulled over a red-checked shirt.

“From Minneapolis?”

“Chicago.”

Now Gramps throws his head back with a wide smile. These rural Midwesterners are so easy to please, thinks Lincoln.

“You a writer?”

What the fuck? “What makes you think that?” asks Lincoln.

The man’s blue-gray eyes sparkle. “You aren’t an ice-fisherman. Nobody’s making sales calls this close to Christmas. We get writers. They hope the solitude will give them inspiration.”

Lincoln thinks: so even my last desperate gestures are nothing but cliché. “How often?”

“Ohhhh.” The man drags out the moment. It’s hard to figure his age. He could be in his eighties, maybe older. He has the air of someone who takes care of himself. “Not so many in the end. But we had a fellow here last year around this time. He was working on a book about his dead brother.”

“Really?” Lincoln signals for his check. Time to escape. “A biography?”

“No,” says the old man. “His brother’s ghost. How it comes back to visit.”

Lincoln throws some bills on the bar.

The man continues, “He ended up killing hisself. When the thaw came in the spring, he walked out to the edge of the open water and threw hisself in.”

“Who?” asks Lincoln. “The writer or the brother?”

“Why, the writer.”

So the path taken by Thoreau has been trampled by wackos and suicides. “I’m actually editing someone else’s book,” Lincoln explains, as if to forestall an intervention by the old man and the good people of Lac du Flambeau. "I'm just an editor."

"Ah! That's good." The old man smiles. "Giving it your own stamp."

"Right." Lincoln waves good night, and the moment he steps outside, the slap of frigid air on his face loosens an idea: his own stamp. Of course. He'll convert Amy's novel to first person. Why didn't he think of it before? There's energy that way and drive. First novels are almost always first person; the voice is more natural, more intimate. "I" as a verb—someone, somewhere has said that, and it's true, you build action just following the narrator's psychic evolution. I, I, I, I. That's it!

As he hurries back to the motel and flops straight into bed, Lincoln is aware, vaguely, that this inspiriting idea has washed up from his alcohol-sopped imagination and may not survive the harsh morning light. Nonetheless, he sleeps better than he has in weeks.

20

LINCOLN RISES EARLY THE NEXT MORNING. IN THE CHILL, gray North Woods dawn, after gobbling aspirin and grabbing coffee and doughnuts from the spread laid out in the Lunker's reception room, he comes to grips with his idea from the night before. Using first person means Lincoln has to channel Mary Reilly, Amy's protagonist. As he sits at the little desk in room 14 and starts to work, Lincoln finds it surprisingly easy to drop into the head of a twenty-one-year-old woman, smart and opinionated, emerging from a sheltered life and eager for experience.

He works straight through to noon, almost finishing the first chapter, when there's a knock on his door. "Mr. Lincoln?" calls out Mrs. Lunker. "Do you want me to clean your room?"

Fresh sheets, new towels. "Sure," Lincoln answers. He'll take a break for that.

The proprietress enters pushing a cart. "I usually have an Indian girl do the cleaning, but I let her off this time of year since things are slow," the woman explains. Talking to Lincoln, she glances past him and around the room, looking for evidence of his mysterious activities. Her nervous manner suggests that she knows he's a writer and that she hasn't forgotten last year's suicide. "Were you able to get your work done this morning?" she asks.

Lincoln realizes he had better clear out while she is there. "Yes, thanks. Now, I think I'll run and get a bite to eat," and he's out the door before she can continue her cross-examination.

The room sparkles when he returns, and he works feverishly through the afternoon. He struggles occasionally to express Mary Reilly's thoughts, particularly when the subjects turn physical and intimate. But Amy has provided some of that material in the original, and Lincoln can simply jigger the language to bring it around to first person. Besides, having to speak through the voice of a young woman teases out Lincoln's imagination. He finds he can make observations about colors, appearances, moods with a fluency he hardly expected. Editing a book last year on the costume collection at the History Museum has given him the vocabulary to talk about clothes. And, he reminds himself, he grew up listening to a mother and a sister. After a while, he gets cocky. As a modern man, he holds that the sexes aren't really that different, but he starts to believe that for purposes of fiction, the differences favor a woman's voice. Women are more confessional, more honest about themselves. They're willing to appear vulnerable. Men are guarded, stiff. So much to hide. If Mary Reilly were a man, the book would be a fraction as long, a CliffsNotes version of the story. Every now and then, Lincoln worries about how Amy will react to his changes, but he tells himself he hasn't really altered the substance of her book, just redirected it slightly. And she can always rewrite his rewrite, if it comes to that.

Lincoln works late into the evening, and he pounds away virtually nonstop the next day, Christmas Eve, even waving away Mrs. Lunker when she comes to clean. On Christmas morning, coffee and pastries are laid out as always in the reception room, but the kind woman is concerned about Lincoln's dinner. The few restaurants in Lac du Flambeau are closed, and even Iggy's

Ice House shuts down for the day. "Everyone spends Christmas with family," Mrs. Lunker warns.

Lincoln worries that she's about to invite him to dine with her and her husband, a brooding, silent man who rarely looks up from the newspaper classifieds. "Oh, I'll find something," he assures her.

Later, when she comes to clean, she gives him a sheaf of printouts, with maps to three restaurants that are open. She's been searching the Internet. "I've eaten at the Fireplace Inn," she says of one of the three. "A little expensive, but very nice."

"Thank you, thank you," Lincoln tells her. "Merry Christmas!"

"Merry Christmas!"

In fact, Lincoln is on such a roll that the McDonald's in neighboring Minocqua will do him just fine. By the afternoon, he's already up to Amy/edit/5. He's been virtually alone now for three days with Mary Reilly, and her voice and sensibility have taken over part of his brain. He tells himself it's as if she's whispering in his ear. He looks up from his keyboard and knows how she'd respond to the mauve curtains covering the window ("Don't make me look at them!"), to the Brueghel print of a village scene in winter hanging above the bed ("Are all the Lunker rooms so classically decorated, or did we get lucky?"). She speaks to him through long-ago remarks—things said by his sister, his mother, his ex-girlfriends, his soon-to-be ex-wife, and Amy herself. Lincoln jots them into a notebook he's keeping and then tunes them and sprinkles them through the text. On his brief forays out of the motel room, he regards the icy, piney landscape through Mary Reilly's eyes (she sees it as harsh, repressed, male) and turns his car radio to a classical music station out of respect for her aesthetic interests.

Even writing about sex from her point of view starts to come easily. Again, Amy has provided the basics, but Lincoln surprises himself at his gush of articulation as he imagines sensuality from the other side. The descriptions emerge (to his ear) as candid without being clinical—far less self-conscious than they would be if he were speaking through the voice of a man. He even lets Mary Reilly spout on at one point about vaginal contractions when she has her first big orgasm. Is Lincoln out of his mind? Perhaps, he admits to himself. But rereading the scene he's just written provides an affirmation of sorts: he gets a hard-on.

On the day after Christmas, Lincoln's cell phone rings. "How's it coming?" Amy asks without a greeting.

"OK." He's startled and slightly annoyed to be pulled out of his Mary Reilly trance. "I'm moving right along."

"I want to come up there."

"Here?"

"Yes."

"But…I'm not done yet. I need a couple more days, then I'll bring it down."

"I can't stand it. I feel like part of me is being raped and ravaged up there, and I'm stuck here. I'm coming up."

"What about work?"

"I'll call in sick."

"But I need solitude. It's going to be a great book, but I'm at it sixteen or eighteen hours a day. If we start going over the manuscript now, the whole edit will screech to a halt."

"I can be reading the beginning while you're finishing the end."

"But…"

"John, this is *my* book, *my* life."

Amy won't relent. In the end, Lincoln can only manage to put her off for a few days. She'll borrow a friend's car and drive up New Year's Eve, a Thursday. They have to be back in the office on January 4, a Monday. Lincoln will try to finish most of the rewrite before she gets there.

The mere thought of her arrival slows him. Mary Reilly checks out of the motel (in a pique of jealousy?), and Lincoln has trouble hearing her voice. What's more, his feverish confidence begins to cool. He rereads the first chapter and finds he's no longer so certain about the tone he's imposed on the manuscript. He edits some of Mary's more intimate thoughts and descriptions, tempers her flights of intellect (she's still an undergraduate, after all). Moving forward, he bogs down trying to inject some realistic drama into the section where Mary starts to suspect that her new friend is somehow linked to the sexual predator. What does Lincoln know about crime? Looking for inspiration, he wastes part of an afternoon skimming novels by John Grisham and James Patterson that he buys at a Minocqua bookstore.

At one point, Lincoln writes in Mary Reilly's voice:

I considered the emptied coffee cup Jennifer had left behind, searching for evidence in my own ineffectual way, studying the delicate red half-moon of lipstick stain as if it were a fingerprint.

Looking the sentence over, he realizes he's borrowed the lunar lipstick image from an Anthony Buford poem, "Dirty Dishes." Lincoln deletes the line, wondering how that could happen.

Still, he labors over his computer and slowly, slowly, the pages fall away.

On Thursday morning Amy calls to say she's on her way. The day is cold but clear. She should get in around four. That afternoon, Lincoln prints out copies of the twelve chapters that he's finished, and then he fitfully keeps working. When Amy hasn't arrived by six, he calls her cell. She picks up after three rings. "Where are you?" he asks.

"Where the fuck is Lac du Flambeau?"

"You're lost?"

"Even MapQuest doesn't know where to find it."

Lincoln gets out his road map and patiently talks her through the route. Finally, at seven, the phone in his motel room rings for the first time since he arrived. "I'm in eleven," Amy tells him.

"Welcome to the Lunker," Lincoln says. "It's too late to work today—let's go to dinner."

"I really sort of want to see what you've done to my book."

"It's New Year's Eve," Lincoln presses. "I've got a reservation."

Reluctantly, Amy accedes.

Lincoln spends five minutes warming up his car before he sees Amy emerge from room 11. She's bundled in a sky-blue ski jacket, with a blue wool cap pulled down on her head. For a moment Lincoln is taken aback. This isn't Mary Reilly. Days ago, Lincoln had embarked on the rewrite by associating Amy with her protagonist, but in his edit, he's elaborated on Amy's terse physical descriptions, and he's turned Mary into a fragile, spiky creature—a physical manifestation of her delicate, questing sensibility. In contrast, the woman walking toward him looks robust and athletic, the picture of healthy determination. She could be about to slip over the edge of a mountain slope and ski down a double black diamond.

"I don't think I've ever been in your car before," she says brightly when she slides into the front passenger seat.

"This is a rental," he tells her.

"You rented a car to come up here?" She looks surprised.

"Why not?"

"What about your own car?"

"My wife—my ex-wife—needs it for work."

"She got the car?" Amy marvels.

In his head, Lincoln completes her thought: his wife gets to cuckold him, then clean him out—what kind of a wuss is he? "I think you'll like the restaurant," he says as they pull out onto the road.

Lincoln has made reservations at Mrs. Lunker's recommended Fireplace Inn, a cavernous supper club a few miles away. The restaurant has set out a lavish New Year's Eve buffet, tables lined up along one wall and crowned with a feast: huge platters of herring and other pickled fish, trays of deviled eggs, five kinds of salads, a spread of cheeses, three selections of potatoes, rice, sliced meats, breads, salmon, turkey, some sort of teriyaki-inflected chicken, and—the climax of the affair—a roast pig. Amy is impressed. "How much did this cost?" she asks as they make their first pass through the buffet, standing in a long line of large, cheerful people dressed, despite the season, as if they are about to play a round of golf. Lincoln shakes his head as if it's nothing, and in fact, it was cheap by Chicago standards—thirty dollars a person, tip included. "It's Wisconsin," he says.

Amy restrains herself through dinner. She passes on gossip from the office, talks about Christmas with her family, avoids references to Lincoln's personal life. It's only after they have made their third excursion to the long buffet (this time venturing to the lethally caloric dessert region) and are finishing their second bottle of wine that she brings up her book. "I think it works," Lincoln tells her. "By now I'm so close to it that I don't quite trust myself, but it seems to me that you've got a voice and a story that are really quite special."

"You think?" A pink flush roars upstream from Amy's neck through her cheeks to her forehead.

"Quite special," he repeats conclusively. "I'm going to recommend it to Byron for publication."

"Publication." She turns over the word slowly. "How much editing did you have to do?" she asks after a few seconds.

"Not really so much." Lincoln is forking apart a pastry thing shaped like a swan and filled with sweet, heavy whipped cream.

"Did you cut a lot?"

"I did some trimming, but I bet you'll hardly notice."

"Rewriting?"

"I tried to fill out a few scenes—you know, enrich the descriptions—but nothing that gets in the way of your story."

Amy takes another sip of wine. "John, you've been up here for a week. What have you been doing?"

Might as well unload it, thinks Lincoln, finishing off the swan. So he launches his carefully rehearsed speech about the advantages of the first-person narrative—the energy it provides, the chance to explore character, to play with American vernacular. The great tradition it follows.

Amy turns pale. "You've changed my book to first person?" she gasps.

"It's not that big a thing."

"Not that big a thing!" she cries. "It's the whole thing!"

Around them, several tables of large Wisconsin families look over to see what the commotion is about.

"Just read it with an open mind," Lincoln tells her. "If you don't like it, you can change it back."

Amy leans forward and clutches at the table. "I can't believe you eviscerated my novel without even asking me."

"I didn't…"

"What am I? Just some researcher?" she interrupts. "Some notetaker for the great artist?" Her face has immediately gone red again, and her eyes are firing BBs at him.

"Give it a chance…"

"I want to read it right now! Tonight."

"It's New Year's Eve. You've already drunk a bottle of wine."

"Tonight!"

Lincoln settles the bill and follows Amy out of the restaurant. She rides in silence back to the motel, her arms folded across her chest, ignoring Lincoln's efforts to soothe her. At the Lunker, several pickup trucks are clustered around room 8, where there seems to be a small party going on. Amy waits outside Lincoln's room while he retrieves the twelve chapters that he's finished. "I really think you should get some sleep and start reading in the morning," he advises as he hands her the manuscript.

In the harsh light of the motel walkway, Amy glances at the top sheet. "You've changed everything!" she cries.

"It's all negotiable."

"*Everything!*" Amy's fury suddenly dissolves into despair. Tears spray from her eyes. Lincoln watches as the outpouring floods her cheeks and spreads huge dark patches over her ski jacket. She wheels and runs to her room.

He follows, but she's inside behind a door slammed shut before he can catch her. He's standing alone, considering whether to knock, when Mrs. Lunker wanders out of room 8, a plastic cup in her hand. "I hope we're not making too much noise for you," she says.

Lincoln shakes his head.

"Just a few old friends from town." She lifts her cup. "Would you like to join us?"

"No, no thanks," says Lincoln backing away. "I think I'll just turn in." Quickly, he heads toward his room.

She calls to his back, "Happy New Year!"

The cold yellow light of the walkway, the soggy whelps of delight coming from room 8, Amy's heartbreaking expression of betrayal—the scene has opened a crushing epiphany: Lincoln is a delusional fool. Of course Amy will hate what he's done. It's her book, and he's treated her thoughtful words as if they were just a starting point for his brilliance. What was he thinking? He knows how writers feel about their work. How could he be so clumsy, so selfish, trampling on a good-hearted innocent? He imagines Amy sitting at the desk in room 11, her tears splashing on the pages.

Lincoln gets in bed with Grisham. Before, Lincoln had disdained the simple prose as obvious; now, it seems smart, dramatic, economical. At midnight, Mr. and Mrs. Lunker and their townie fraternity pour into the parking lot and whoop up the New Year. Lincoln waits for them to quiet before turning off the light, but it takes him another hour to drop off, and even then he sleeps fitfully.

A rap on his door awakens him. It's still dark outside. The garish red numbers on the digital clock by the bed say 6:02. Lincoln turns on the light and mopes his way to the door. He opens it just a crack, and Amy pushes past with the manuscript in her arms and drops onto the desk chair. She balances the book in her lap and buries her hands in the pockets of her ski jacket, staring blankly toward the ugly mauve curtains. She's still wearing the print skirt and tan sweater she wore to dinner last night.

"Well?" Lincoln asks. He feels exposed, standing in the chill room in his underwear.

"I can't say it's terrible, and in fact it's probably better, but it's not me."

Her tone is depressive yet resigned, better than Lincoln could possibly have hoped for. "Were you up all night reading it?" he asks, pulling on a pair of jeans.

"Yes."

"You didn't sleep at all?"

"I didn't move from the desk."

"Jeez, you must be exhausted." Lincoln sits on the bed across from her.

For the first time since she entered the room, she looks at him. "It isn't me, John. It's you. Or some awful hybrid of the two of us. I don't talk like that. I don't *think* like that."

"But it *is* you," Lincoln pleads. "It's all you. I just tried to fill out some of the spaces and follow your blueprint."

"I don't *sound* like this." She fumbles with the manuscript, and Lincoln notices that she's folded down corners, marking things she wants to recall. From a few feet a way, it looks as if half the pages have a dog-ear. "Listen." She reads: "'He put his hand over mine, but I insisted that I had to go. I knew I was starting to sound like a nag, and I knew Stephen had a way of doing that, drawing out my shrill, anxious side, a manner of behaving that would only come from a woman. It was a tendency that I hated and that Stephen seemed to enjoy nursing in me.' " Amy stares at Lincoln. "*I* would never write something like that."

Secretly, Lincoln is relieved. He'd been afraid she would enter into evidence a passage so outrageous that the verdict would be inevitable. The one she chose actually sounds reasonable to him.

"But you can change it," he tells her. "Rewrite it. Get comfortable with it. I just wanted to give the book an injection of energy."

"Or what about this?" In her rush, as she flips through the pages, the manuscript spills from her lap and scatters at her feet. She continues rummaging and finds more offense. "The silvery moonlight on the lake—the way it pulsed with the slight movement of the surface—made me think of sex." She tosses the page at Lincoln and it drifts down atop the chaos on the floor. "I'd never say anything like that."

"But it's not you, it's Mary Reilly," Lincoln points out.

"Or the sex stuff." Amy has moved through her depression and is getting angry. "This, this..." She drops from the chair to her knees and shuffles through the pages, then reads mockingly: "I stood beside the bed and let him undress me, kissing me between my breasts, on my belly button. I wanted to apologize for not losing those four pounds gained over the winter, but I was too turned on to talk."

She throws this page at Lincoln, too. " 'Apologize for not losing four pounds'? No woman would write that."

"Well, you can change it," says Lincoln weakly.

"The whole book's like that now," says Amy. "I can't rewrite everything you rewrote." She gets to her feet and walks across the carpet of pages to the other side of the bed, where she lies down on her back. "It's hopeless," she tells the ceiling. "I'm not made for this. I actually finished reading half an hour ago and I've just been thinking. I have to go somewhere else with my life, do something else."

Lincoln considers her lying there, wan, motionless, stretched out like a body laid out for a funeral. "Like what?" he prods gently.

"Social work. I like helping people, so maybe I should go back and get a degree in social work. Or maybe something else. I don't know." She trails off in weariness. "I just know that I'm not a writer."

Something in her tone of voice lingers in the dry air of the motel room, an uncertainty, the hint of a question. She repeats, "I'm not a writer," and Lincoln realizes: this is going to work. Amy is going to go for it.

21

Amy needs reassurance. Sleep would help, and a shower. But she mainly needs Lincoln to tell her repeatedly and from various angles over the next two hours that she indeed has the talent and sensibility to be a writer. He talks of her gift for storytelling, her skill at sketching character. He reads aloud sections of her book that he particularly likes (her words, not his, of course). He reminds her that some of the greatest writers relied on the strong hand of an editor—think of Maxwell Perkins carving the narrative out of Thomas Wolfe's verbosity. And Lincoln promises that he can make it happen—he can convince Duddleston that Pistakee should publish this terrific first novel.

Still stretched out on the bed, Amy alternates between basking in Lincoln's praise and worrying that she's a fraud. "How can I defend it, how can I even talk about it, if whole chunks come from you?" she asks. "I feel like a plagiarist."

"So make it yours," he tells her. "Take it from here."

"Maybe I'll just fuck it up again."

Lincoln sits beside her on the bed and takes her two hands in his. He feels for a moment as if he's stepped into a scene from a Victorian novel, the dashing soldier called home from the front to bid farewell to his dying lover. "You can do it," he promises. "Put yourself in front of your computer and type."

They find a Walgreens, miraculously open on New Year's Day, and buy a flash drive, on which Lincoln copies the first twelve rewritten chapters. Amy retreats with it to her room. Around noon, she appears at his door with her computer. By now she's showered and changed, but she still hasn't slept. "I can't work alone," she tells him. "I get too discouraged." So she sets herself up on the bed while Lincoln writes at the desk. After an hour or so, he goes out for sandwiches. They eat on the bed, wrappings and bags of chips and cans of pop spread out picnic-style. Then they work through the afternoon.

She's accepted the first-person voice, and she warily accedes to most of his changes and additions, usually with small fixes of her own. The interior monologues bother her, even those that Lincoln has lifted almost verbatim from her third-person description. "It loses all its subtlety when Mary says it directly," Amy argues. "People don't talk to themselves like that. Third person gives you some distance to round out the observations."

"It's the directness that speaks to the reader," Lincoln tells her. "That's part of the hook."

"It seems…loud."

"You've got to believe in your words. Let yourself go."

Amy's as eager about the book as I am, Lincoln tells himself, and it occurs to him—he's surprised that he's never realized this before—that he finds ambition in women sexy. He watches her working, sitting cross-legged on the bed (how does her back hold up?), staring fiercely into the computer screen, her eyes bright and intense despite a night without sleep. Does he look that alive when he edits?

Their biggest problem comes with the sex. Their sensibilities are simply different. To his ear, her descriptions sound like romance material, all swoons and euphemisms. She thinks he's channeling porn. They compromise their way through the first sex scene, when Mary Reilly plays out a fantasy in her mind and touches herself in her bed one night. But later they hang up over Mary's first intimate encounter with Stephen, her boyfriend.

"This is awful!" Amy screams. She reads aloud: " 'He nuzzled me in the neck, burrowing under my hair, and I felt myself getting damp.' Ugh!"

"What's so awful?" Lincoln asks.

" 'Damp'? That's a terrible word. Completely unsexy."

"Wet? Moist? Change it," Lincoln says.

"I'd never say that. I'd never *think* that."

"It's Mary thinking it, not you."

"No woman would think that to herself. That's a man's fantasy. You're turning my book into an article for *Maxim* magazine."

"I thought woman were more candid about sex, the physiology of it."

"But they don't go through a mental checklist of their bodily reactions."

"It wouldn't be strange for a man to notice he had an erection."

"But he wouldn't announce it to himself: 'Hey, waddyaknow! I'm erect!' "

It's late in the afternoon by now, dark outside. Lincoln has heard vehicles pulling up, people talking on the motel's walkway. Mrs. Lunker warned him that with the weekend, rooms would be filling with ice fishermen.

"Maybe we should call it a day," Lincoln suggests. "We've made a lot of progress. Let's go have dinner."

"No, I want to get this right," Amy insists. "If we can't get the sex right, nothing is going to work."

So Lincoln sits next to Amy, and together—building the scene word by word—they describe how Mary Reilly goes from necking with Stephen on the sofa in her apartment to rolling around half-undressed on the soft carpet to having hurried and clumsy sex on her bed. Though Mary Reilly encourages the encounter, the sex for her is unsatisfying. For Lincoln, looking at the computer screen over Amy's shoulder, catching whiffs of a fresh, flowery fragrance coming off her hair, tossing back and forth descriptions of states of arousal, brushing hands as he types in a few words himself, creating at last several airy paragraphs they can agree on—it all amounts to one of the most erotic experiences he has ever had. Amy apparently has the same reaction.

Just moments after Stephen has prematurely climaxed, and Mary, on her back beneath him, is left with nothing but the chapter-ending discovery that cobwebs have gathered in a ceiling corner of her bedroom, Lincoln and Amy fall into a frantic embrace. As they rush to rapturous, thrilling, and emotionally cleansing sex, he has only enough presence of mind to take the most essential precaution: he hits SAVE on Amy's computer.

Afterward, lying together in the motel bed, Amy says, "I suppose that was a mistake."

"I suppose so," Lincoln agrees. "But it couldn't be helped."

"I'm not going to apologize."

"Who would you apologize to?" Lincoln asks.

"Good point." Amy considers for a few seconds. "You're not married anymore."

"Well, almost."

"I suppose I could apologize to Duddleston. He'd be furious."

"He must never know."

Amy kisses Lincoln on the shoulder. "I'm not going to feel guilty, and neither should you." She rests her head on his chest.

They lie that way for several minutes. From her slow breathing, Lincoln thinks she has fallen asleep. But suddenly she says, "John?"

"Hmm?"

"Why are you rubbing your arm?"

Lincoln stops. He didn't realize he was doing it. "Just a habit," he says.

Amy sits up on one elbow and looks hard into Lincoln's face. "John, you must tell me how you broke your arm. Now."

Lincoln wants to resist. The incident brings up memories and emotions that he's purposely closed off. He never talks about it. But he can see that Amy's electric, been-up-for-thirty-six-hours intensity won't be denied. So as they lie in bed, Amy nestled against him, Lincoln tells her his somewhat less reflective, considerably abbreviated, but nonetheless largely reliable version of the following true story:

How John Lincoln Broke His Arm

The summer before his senior year of high school, John Lincoln spent almost every evening with his best friend, Will Dewey. The Deweys lived near the Lincolns in the comfortable Washington suburb of Bethesda, and both families owned second homes in rural West Virginia, where the moms and kids moved every June when school let out. That summer of 1993 was the last that John and Will spent in the country. Afterward there would be trips to Europe and internships in far-flung cities—the sorts of experiences that would lead the boys permanently out of the nest and pull them apart from each other. But that summer they still lived at home, working for county road crews, earning just above the minimum wage.

Will and John had been friends forever, so inseparable that their classmates ran their names together as if the boys existed only in combination; Will and Johnny became Ouija, as in the mysterious board game. And in fact, the boys felt joined—privileged members of a kind of suburban aristocracy. Their families were prosperous, but more than that, the boys sensed that their parents were special—more sophisticated and creative, more alive. At parties—and their families were always throwing parties when the boys were young—their fathers reigned as the smartest, wittiest men in the room. At school, compared to the moms of the other kids, the mothers of Will and John seemed younger, prettier, more stylish. While the boys' classmates trudged home in the afternoons to watch TV or maybe take a tennis or ballet lesson, Ouija's mothers whisked their children off to cultural experiences—a visit to the Corcoran Gallery, a tour of Ford's Theater. Dinner-table conversations at both houses featured firsthand anecdotes about some of the most important people in the country. It helped that the boys themselves were bright and athletic, but through their friendship, they nurtured in each other the idea that they stood out—together they were a well-defended team against self-doubt.

Their summers encouraged the notion since in West Virginia their families were more privileged in almost every way than the local people. Will and John got to know some of the children from the nearby towns, mostly through sports, and the two Bethesda boys had occasional playdates with one or another West Virginia child. The boys had been well trained to be thoughtful and generous to others and to hide any sense of superiority. But they couldn't help seeing how different their lives were.

That feeling of shared status peaked that last summer, and in some ways it no doubt echoed an attitude enjoyed by seventeen-year-old boys everywhere. The combination of near independence, physical prowess, and intense sexual desire creates a lush environment for breeding arrogance. Looking back years later, John Lincoln even came to think that he reached his peak on a particular August Friday night when, once again, he and Will set off together on an adventure. A few weeks before, Will's father, a doctor with a flamboyant streak, had bought himself a red Porsche convertible, and for the first time, he let Will take it out for the evening. Of course, as on every other evening in the country when the boys borrowed a more modest family car, there was really no place to go. Sometimes they would find a basketball game, sometimes they would drive to the movie theater several towns over. But mostly they just cruised the country roads, scooping the loop, as they put it, going from one small town to another in a kind of circle, ceaselessly looking for excitement.

That night, with Will driving the open car, they embarked on the usual round. After checking out the A&W drive-in in Concord—nothing but a handful of families with small children sitting at picnic tables on the concrete patio—the boys headed for the hamburger stand in Granite City. Soon the Porsche's speedometer was hitting seventy-five on a straight stretch of road.

"One of the guys in my crew wrecked a mower this morning," Will said, shouting, his words swept away by the wind roaring over the convertible. "Drove it right over a big rock. Snapped the blade."

"What happened?"

"We all stood around and looked at it."

"The crew chief didn't get pissed?"

"The chief was out, so an old guy was in charge, and he always expects everything to go wrong. He used to be a miner. He's from Hungary, and he hardly speaks English. 'Sumbubbabitch.' "

"What?" John could barely hear.

"That's all he ever says: 'SUMBUBBABITCH!' "

John laughed. The leathery new-car smell of the Porsche's interior made him feel giddy.

Bill's Burgers in Granite City was squeezed between an abandoned tire store and a Shell station that had closed for the night. A single pickup sat in the mocking brightness of the parking lot. The boys bought their hamburgers at the stand's small, screened window, then used the Porsche's hood as a table to avoid the risk of sullying the sparkling new interior. After a while, the short-order cook, a young man wrapped in a dirtied white apron, stepped outside to smoke a cigarette. He recognized the boys and walked over.

"Hey, nice wheels, Ouija," he said. His name was Theron, and he knew Will and John from basketball games. Once they'd brought along a friend from Bethesda who'd used their joint nickname, and Theron had been alert enough to pick it up, wielding it afterward with a slight edge of mockery.

"My old man's," said Will.

"That's some old man," Theron reflected.

"The only one I got."

Theron inspected the car, and Will did an adequate job of parrying questions, though Theron clearly knew far more about the workings of an automobile than either Will or John did.

"You boys just cruising?" Theron asked.

"Looking for action," John said.

Theron grinned. He was a few years older than the boys, and smoking had already started to stain his teeth. "I heard there's a hot stripper at a carnival at Gunther," he said.

"No shit." John worked to contain his excitement.

"You ought to check her out."

"Maybe we will."

Theron dropped his cigarette on the pavement and crushed it with his sneaker. "Well," he said, sighing, "I better get back behind the grill. I hope you enjoyed the hamburgers."

"Needs more pickle," Will called after him.

Gunther lay thirty miles or so deeper into the Blue Ridge, well beyond the boys' normal loop. But the prospect of seeing a stripper was too good to pass up. The road climbed in curves up the side of a gentle mountain, then cut through a pass and wound down a wooded valley. The sky overhead was a bedsheet of stars. John slouched in the bucket seat, sliding closer to his friend so they could talk without fighting the wind. The trip took nearly an hour, and their conversation covered girls, sex, college prospects, *Basic Instinct*, politics, sports, Nirvana, the LA riots, and much, much more. Reflecting on it years later, John sometimes wondered—where did all the opinions, the ideas, the *vitality* come from?

In Gunther, they parked diagonally in front of the bank and walked to the edge of town. The carnival had colonized a rubbly vacant lot. Strings of colored lights enclosed a dusty encampment of booths, tents, and rides. The boys bought Cokes and wandered the grounds. Crowds filled the paths, and speakers on lampposts layered the place with blasts of tinny rock music. Will and John passed up countless games of skill—a noisy rifle range where cork bullets bounced off flat, metal ducks; a pitching contest that invited contestants to throw baseballs covered in black tape at stacks of bottles; a small basketball court. "Gyps," Will said knowingly. "Rigged to make you lose." In the lot's far corner, the boys came upon a tent with a sign out front announcing Boris The Wrestling Bear and promising twenty-five dollars to anyone who could pin the creature within five minutes. But there was no sign of a stripper.

The boys sidled up to the man running the Tilt-a-Whirl. "Say," John said politely, "we heard there was a strip show here."

The man yanked a long lever on his machine and waited for the Tilt-a-Whirl platform to start its rotation. "You're looking for a strip show," he repeated finally. He studied the boys from under the brim of an Atlanta Braves cap.

"Yeah." John tried to sound cool about it.

"This here's the Holmes Carnival," the man said, "and Ted Holmes, he don't believe in that sort of entertainment. It's a family carnival."

"There's no stripper?" Will couldn't hide his disappointment.

"Nope." The man gave the lever another yank, raising the speed of the machine. The riders screamed from their spinning seats.

Will and John skulked away. "Fuck," muttered Will.

"Theron must have been fucking with us, that prick," John said.

"That fuckhead."

They walked a bit farther, and John said, "Sumbubbabitch." The boys laughed.

They needed to head home before Will's dad started worrying about the car, but as they circled toward the exit, they passed a small crowd gathered in front of the tent with the wrestling bear. A barker wearing a cowboy hat was standing on a wood platform in front, bantering through a microphone, trying to lure someone to take on the animal. "Come on, I thought West Virginia was full of brave mountain men," the barker taunted. "No one wants to make twenty-five dollars?" He held the microphone close to his mouth, so every breath and smack of his lips echoed unpleasantly out of the amplifier.

Someone down front in the crowd yelled for him to bring out the bear so they could get a look at it. The barker tossed a few more insults at the crowd, but eventually he turned and yelled something into the tent. After a few seconds, a black snout nuzzled aside a flap, and a black bear ambled onto the platform, followed by its handler, a stocky man wearing red trunks and tights. The handler held a chain that linked to a muzzle on the bear's head. When they got to the barker, the handler yanked the chain, and the creature stood on its hind legs. The crowd whooped.

A man yelled, "That bear's skinnier than my wife!"

"But can you pin your wife?" the barker snapped.

More laughs and hoots.

The boys edged forward to get a better look. Upright, the bear looked precarious, and it actually appeared to be smaller than the handler, though its real size was hard to gauge since its curved upper spine and bent knees gave it a stooped and almost arthritic posture. John studied the low, square hips, the rounded shoulders, the forelegs held awkwardly at the sides. He had an overwhelming sense of recognition, and he whispered to Will, "That's no bear. That's a man in a costume."

"How can you tell?"

"Look at the way it moves. Look at the body. That's an actor."

Will stared and nodded. "You may be right."

The barker still couldn't lure any takers, and he tested various pitches. He said Boris came from the forests of deepest Siberia. "This is your chance to fight the Russians." He raised the prize money to thirty dollars. He started singling out onlookers, teasing them, challenging their virility. Still no takers. Scanning the crowd, the barker spotted Will and John. "Lookee there, two college boys," he cried. "You fellows got brawn *and* brains," the barker taunted. "You ought to be able to outthink a bear."

The crowd gawked and laughed. John shook his head self-consciously. A squat old man in overalls piped up, "They don't want to mess up their haircuts." More laughter.

The barker sensed an opportunity. "Tell you what," he said, marching to the front of the platform so he loomed over the two of them. "Here's the deal. I'll let you two wrestle him together. Two against one."

Will and John looked at each other.

"How about it?" the barker asked the crowd. "Isn't that a deal? Two college boys against a bear!"

People screamed, urging the boys to go for it. Anonymous hands slapped their backs. Will said to John, "What the hell, it's a man in a costume."

John wished he could consider it for a few seconds, maybe talk it over. But the noise and the attention demanded a quick response. Besides, it was almost impossible not to slide along on the excitement and momentum. He looked up at the barker. "Yeah, sure," John said softly.

"We've got a match!" the man cried as the crowd of West Virginians cheered. The barker leaned over to help hoist the boys onto the platform, and after thrusting the microphone in their faces to ask a few perfunctory questions, he announced, "Get your tickets now!" Then he led the boys through the flap into the tent.

The wrestling ring was a canvas square about twenty feet on a side contained by a fence of wire mesh about six feet high.

Plain wood bleachers rose around the sides. The bear was already squatting in one corner of the ring next to the dour handler, who was sitting on a three-legged stool. The barker, all business now, handed the boys bulky overalls. "Put these on over your clothes," he ordered.

The overalls smelled stale and felt heavy.

"Now these." The barker gave each of them an old, worn football helmet. John got the Packers, Will the Redskins.

"I feel like I'm in a space suit," John said when they were fully outfitted.

The barker thrust a clipboard dangling a pen into Will's hands. "Sign that, both of you," he ordered.

"What is it?" Will asked.

"Waiver of liability. Just sign it."

Frowning, Will studied the document for a few seconds, then handed the clipboard to John. "Your dad's the lawyer," Will said.

John glanced over the legal mumbo-jumbo. In the dim light, the small type was hard to read. "What the fuck," he said and signed his name on a line at the bottom. Will signed right below him.

The barker wanted to make one thing clear: "Listen. It's thirty dollars total, not thirty dollars each. You pin him, you split the money. Clear?"

The boys nodded.

"And no funny business," he added. "No punching or kicking. Keep your fingers away from his mouth and eyes. If either of you gets out of the ring for any reason, the match is over. If you want to quit, just yell. One round, five minutes. Understand?" From under his cowboy hat, the barker scanned the tent. The bleachers had mostly filled up. "Now, let's go." He opened a gate in the wire mesh and led the boys inside.

John and Will moved to their corner of the ring. Surrounded by the wire fence, John felt as if he were in a cage. His heart drummed against his chest. This had happened so quickly. It comforted him that Will was beside him, but John was only there because of Will, who had inherited a touch of his father's flamboyance.

"How you feeling?" Will asked just then.

"Good."

"Here's the thing. We can take this guy. High-low. You hit him high, I'll hit him low."

"OK."

The barker stood in the center of the room and bellowed an introduction for the team called the College Boys. The crowd responded with a mixture of whoops and boos. Will hammed it up, clasping his hands over his head, turning slowly, nodding and grinning. John gave a clenched-fist salute and let it go at that.

"And in this corner," the barker continued, "we have the champion—trained in the forests of Siberia, undefeated in his last twenty-two matches, a star of stage and television—he's tough, he's smart, give a hand, folks, to Boris the Wrestling Bear!"

A honking chorus of cheers filled the tent. The bear just sat, its head lolling slightly back forth. The handler unhooked the chain from the muzzle and gave the creature a soft slap on the back of the head. The bear lumbered on all fours into the center of the ring. The handler said something in a guttural language, and the animal rose on its hind legs. The handler assumed a boxing stance, and for a minute or so, they danced around each other. Every few steps, the handler slapped the animal sharply on the snout, setting off an angry shake of the furry head. But the bear stayed upright and moved with a light step, lifting and placing its feet carefully, as if crossing a stream on rocks.

John was less certain now that he was watching a man, but he couldn't fit what he was seeing—the lean, square torso, the agility upright, the nimble forelegs—into his idea of a bear.

After circling the canvas with the boxing exhibition, the animal and its handler retreated to their corner, and the barker returned to the center of the ring. "One round, five minutes, thirty dollars if the College Boys can pin him. Are we ready?"

The crowd hollered its answer.

"Let's have a clean fight! Here we go!"

Someone sounded a gong, and the match was on.

The boys moved warily into the ring. The bear sat on its haunches in the corner until the handler barked something and the animal roused itself and plodded on four legs toward the center. As the boys closed in, the bear planted itself in a defensive posture. Will slipped around behind. John dropped into a wrestling crouch, knees bent, hands in front, and dodged around, feinting, as if looking for an opening. In fact, he was frozen—he couldn't for the life of him imagine attacking this muzzled creature, whatever it was. He wondered if he could eat up five minutes just pretending to prepare to make a move. But the crowd quickly grew restless for action. After several men stood and shouted insults, Will suddenly launched himself at the bear's hindquarters, knocking the beast on its side. "Go!" he cried to John. As the bear flailed to right itself, something in John—some hunting instinct, some passion for his friend, for his species—pushed him to throw himself at the animal's chest. He landed with a thud, bouncing on the surprisingly springy torso, scrambling to wrap his arms around a thick furry shoulder.

The bear rolled quickly on its back, kicking aside Will, then swung its hips behind John, who clung to a foreleg. The dense coat of fur had a greasy quality, and the animal, now righted, easily slipped out of John's grasp and loped to the side. The boys climbed to their feet while jeers and cheers echoed around the tent.

The two of them glanced at each other but didn't say anything. John could see from his friend's face that this first encounter had hardened Will's determination. Again they circled their adversary, Will edging to the bear's back. Touching the beast had eased John's wariness, and as he moved in, he stared hard into the creature's black, unblinking eyes. He'd grown up with dogs, and he'd played the stare game with them countless times, and always the animals grew bored and turned away. But the bear didn't waver, and John thought he saw a glint, a depth behind the glassy blackness. A man, John told himself.

The handler called out something, and the bear rose on its hind legs. Lurching toward John, the animal caught him by surprise and planted its forelegs heavily on John's shoulders. John tried to pull away, lost his balance, and wrapped his arms around the animal's neck. The two staggered, head against helmet, like clumsy dancers in an intimate embrace. John's chin pressed against the animal's shoulder just below its ear. The fur gave off a musty, dead odor that caught in John's throat. With the snout just inches from his own ear, John could hear deep, heaving grunts. Where was Will? This was the setup for the high-low move. The grunts got louder and mingled with screams from the crowd, the commotion muffled by the painfully tight football helmet. At last, Will saw his chance and rolled into the back of the bear's hind legs. John and the animal tumbled together violently onto the mat, bouncing, heaving. In the frenzied crash, the grunts in John's ear clarified for an instant: "Big shot," the creature growled—or seemed to. "Big shot."

The force of the impact loosened John's grip, and again the animal twisted free and scrambled off to the corner beside its handler. Will and John pulled themselves up off the canvas. The crowd thrilled at their humiliation, screaming and stomping on the wood planks of the bleachers, inflating the tent with scorn at the cocky upstarts. Back in their corner, Will put his mouth close to John's ear. "That thing smells like shit," he said. He'd lost his steely face. "That's a real fucking bear."

"It's not," John shouted back over the noise.

"How do you know?"

"It was talking to me."

Will's eyes got big. "Are you sure?"

"Positive."

Of course, John wasn't. But he thought he'd heard those words, and something familiar in the body he'd been hugging had bolstered his suspicion that human flesh and bones were hiding beneath the fur.

In the other corner, the handler talked to the bear and stroked its head. John formulated a plan. Years ago, on a children's TV show, he'd seen a man climb into a gorilla suit that had a single zippered seam running around the waist. If John could get his hand on the seam of the bear suit or, better yet, unzip it, he could expose this act for what it was.

"I'm gonna go for the zipper," he told Will.

"What?"

"Zipper," John shouted, as the bear came toward them, its head back and its snout pointing to John like a gun. "Now!" John cried, and the boys pounced, Will going for the hips, John tackling the shoulder. They knocked the creature off its feet and fell on top, but the bear quickly rolled onto its side, it's legs splayed defensively against the canvas. Will embraced a thigh and John clung to the animal's back, his face buried in the stinking fur at the nape of the animal's neck. Looked at close, John saw that the hair of the coat wasn't just black, but an explosion of shades of black and dark brown.

For several seconds, the grapplers held their places, the bear solidly anchored, the boys awkwardly hanging on. Time was running out. As the crowd screamed, John reached with his right arm around the bear's side and slowly walked his fingers through the tough hide, feeling for a zipper. Nothing. The bear lay still, as if taking measure of John's move. The grunts stopped. John pressed, his arm extended and exposed. If only he could get to the zipper. Suddenly, the creature bucked. John bounced back and a furry right foreleg came down with a vicious karate chop on John's probing forearm. He screamed. The bear shook free and scudded away. John lay on his back, hugging his arm to his stomach. The pain came in waves. He couldn't stand to look down, so he stared straight up into the bright lamp attached to the top of the tent. Will's face appeared above him. "You OK?" Will asked.

John forced himself to look. His right forearm had a bulge about four inches below the elbow and then made a slight dogleg to the left. "I think it's broken," he said.

The crowd had fallen silent. "Hang in there," Will told him.

The barker appeared above John, the thin face in a scowl under the cowboy hat. "I told you no funny business," he snarled. He knelt and pulled away John's good arm. For a few seconds, he studied the situation, then carefully placed the good arm back. He stood and walked away without saying anything.

With Will looking anxiously down at him, John tried to say, "Sumbubbabitch," but for some reason he couldn't form the word. So he closed his eyes. He lost track of time and may have fainted. After a while, he saw a bright-red throbbing light broken by spidery veins on the inside of his eyelids. Will lifted John's head and took off his helmet. When John opened his eyes, the throbbing red light covered one side of the tent wall. "Easy now," Will said, putting his arms under John's shoulders, lifting him.

Two cops stood behind Will. "We'll get you to the hospital, son," one of them assured. The barker's cruel face peeked over the cop's shoulder.

Still clutching his arm to his stomach, John walked in a cluster of helpmates down an aisle and then outside. The air felt frigid. John realized he was washed in sweat. The cluster swept him to a police car, its red light spinning. The cops helped him into the backseat and closed the door. A silent crowd stood around. As the police car pulled out, John saw Will's anxious face fall away from the window, and John had a panicky need to have his friend beside him. He wanted to scream out, to stop the car, but he was beyond that now. The car eased forward. The flashing red light streaked across a gaudy landscape of game booths, food stands, and clumps of gawking West Virginians, and John knew he was entering a place he had only heard about, but now he could never leave. He hugged his throbbing arm.

It's late by the time Lincoln finishes the story. Amy's head lies heavily on his chest, and he absently combs her soft hair with his fingers. He feels relieved—emptied, but unburdened.

"Did that really happen?" Amy asks without looking up. Lincoln can hear the toll of the all-nighter in her voice.

"More or less."

"What kind of an answer is that?"

"Yes."

"Did you ever find out if the bear was real?"

"My father tried to check. They insisted it was a real bear."

In the unit next door, an ice fisherman is watching *American Idol* with the volume too high. Amy falls quiet. Lincoln thinks that perhaps she has dropped asleep at last. But suddenly she lifts her head and scolds, "That didn't ruin your childhood, John."

No, it didn't. But when he thinks back before the bear, he remembers—he *thinks* he remembers—how he used to operate with a kind of natural grace. Patterns unfolded, doors swung open. His path was clear—or, more to the point, he didn't have to think about the path. It was just there, beckoning. Afterward, he faced uncertainty, missed chances, bad luck, and bad decisions. For all his talent and privileges, he was somehow unprepared for a world where you had to make hard choices, dig deep down to find what was really moving you. The bear introduced him to that. It was as if the creature were telling him that he didn't really know, didn't really get it. Sumbubbabitch.

No, Lincoln thinks, the wrestling match didn't ruin his childhood. But it ended it.

22

FOR THE NEXT TWO DAYS, LINCOLN AND AMY WORK FURIously on the book, punctuating their efforts with interludes in bed. She spends the days and nights in room 14, only returning to 11 to shower and change. The collaborative editing goes remarkably smoothly. Once, defending a scene he'd added, Lincoln says the action will make the book more commercial, more likely to "grab readers," and over time "grabby" becomes code to express the sensibility he's trying to impose. Even Amy uses the word without rancor. At the same time, Amy robustly defends the literary merit of some of the material that Lincoln has deleted—language and ideas that she insists would make the book appealing to "thinking readers," as she puts it. They end up retrieving sentences, paragraphs, even several sections from the computer file containing her original manuscript. Jokingly, they talk about joining the yin and the yang, the "thinky" and the "grabby." Secretly Lincoln suspects there's actually something to the notion.

As for the real-life sex, they assure each other that this is just a passing occasion—curious circumstances have brought them together, and there's nothing beyond the diversion and pleasure. Lunker sex, they call it, honoring the location, and they acknowledge that it must end when they leave for Chicago. There's not even much discussion of the matter, the dictates—jobs, ages, outlooks—are so obvious. One afternoon, as they lie in bed in a becalmed after-moment, Amy admits that she feels too young to link up with a divorced man trailing an ex-wife. Stung by her candor, Lincoln reminds himself of Amy's naïveté, the slightly annoying sense he's had from the start that she's an intern at life. With equal candor, he tells her that what he needs now, after the disastrous end to his marriage, is a mature woman, someone who's been through several serious relationships and knows herself and her emotions. The strong bond Amy and Lincoln have built in two days of intense editing helps them accept each other's confessions with grace.

In keeping with their continuing policy of discretion, they try to hide their relationship from the curious proprietor of the motel, though inevitably, the maneuver fails. "I ran into Mrs. Lunker outside, and I had to tell her that I was your girlfriend," Amy admits on Saturday morning.

"Why'd you do that?" Branding the relationship makes Lincoln feel uneasy, as if unnamed it could disappear into the past.

"What else could I say? My bed has been untouched for three days. She asked where I've been sleeping, and I didn't want her to think I was a slut."

"Hmmm." Why didn't Amy think to muss the sheets? Why didn't he think to suggest it? After a moment Lincoln says, "You know, that's not really her name."

"You call her that."

"Not to her face. I just named her that because of the motel. I think her real name is Geiselbrecht, or something."

Amy considers for a moment. "No wonder she gave me a funny look," she says.

By Saturday night, they have completed all but the last three chapters, which Amy will finish in Chicago. That night, their last in Wisconsin, they go out for a celebratory dinner at the Fireside Inn. Lincoln is feeling buoyant about the book, and he plans to thank Amy over dinner for her hard work and her forbearance of his occasional insensitivity. But they've barely finished ordering two steaks, and the hovering waitress has just disappeared, when Amy beats him to it. "No matter what happens to the book, John, you've been incredibly helpful," she says. "I can't tell you how much I appreciate all you've done." She locks her eyes on his and keeps her voice soft and low.

Her sincerity unsettles Lincoln: in his mind, his motives have been selfish, even crass. "Well, let's see if Duddleston goes for it," Lincoln responds. "That will be the test of my help."

Though the Fireside Inn has put away the teeming buffet, the restaurant again bustles with diners, many tables filled with what Lincoln assumes are three or even four generations of a family. Over one bottle of wine, then another, he and Amy natter on about the book, the office, the U of C, Amy's family. By dessert, Lincoln even allows himself to reflect a bit on what went wrong in his marriage. ("It was as if we were still dating, without the newness or anticipation.") Sitting at their two-person table in a corner of the busy restaurant, Lincoln feels cushioned by the hordes of hefty, cordial Wisconsinites, by the huge steaks and mounds of mashed potatoes, the overheated air, the low, ambient murmur of conversation. By the vision of Amy's soft breasts behind her tan sweater. Afterward, they return to the motel and enjoy one last night in bed together. Early that morning, Amy whispers to him, "I'm glad we don't call it Geiselbrecht sex."

They drive back to the city separately. In the office on Monday morning, Lincoln finds that work has piled up. Professor Morgenthau's manuscript has returned from the copy editor, whose corrections must now be checked. Meantime, Gregor's idea for a cover design needs rethinking (why use a photo of a modern battleship on a book on a about the management theories of the Founding Fathers?). Lincoln has missed the deadline for writing jacket flap copy for *Walking Tours of the Windy City*, and Pistakee's distributor has left a message: he desperately needs advice for his sales reps on how to pitch bookstores on Antonio Buford's collection of poetry.

Lincoln hunkers down, and by midafternoon he's polished off the flap copy ("To appreciate the greatness of a glorious city, you need to walk its streets with a master of its history, its people, and its hidden treasures. No one knows Chicago like the University of Chicago's Norman Fleace…"); he's mothballed Gregor's battleship; and he's lobbied the baffled distributor on behalf of Buford's poetry ("Think of it as the newest literary extension of rap…"). Lincoln is working his way through *Revolutionizing Business* when Duddleston walks in.

As the boss sits gingerly and asks about Lincoln's vacation, a yellow alert goes off in Lincoln's head: Duddleston is being tentative—that usually means trouble. After a minute or so, speaking in the deliberate, rehearsed tone that confirms the danger, he gets to the point: "Over the holiday, I took some time going over the numbers. And we had an OK year. Up a little from last year, actually—not much, but up."

"That's good, given the climate," says Lincoln. Duddleston has always closely guarded Pistakee's financials, speaking of them only in generalities.

"Good, yes." The owner pauses. "But not a growth pattern that's healthy. Recession or no, that's not a trajectory that takes us where we want to go. If we were a publicly traded company, I wouldn't buy our stock."

"I see."

"Pistakee is seven years old, and we continue to tread water."

Lincoln nods gravely. Where is this going?

"I know publishing is a tough business—I knew that coming in. And the economy hasn't helped lately. But, frankly, I expected more."

"As you should." Lincoln nods, his anxiety rising. Is this the end of Pistakee? What happens to me?

"So I spent an afternoon with Jerome Geelhood, the consultant. You remember him?"

"Of course." How could Lincoln forget? Jerome Geelhood turned twenty-five years of failure in assorted publishing ventures into a business that offered hackneyed and obvious advice for high fees.

"And after a lot of thought and running the numbers various ways, we came to the conclusion that Pistakee needs to grow its list. We need more volume—in print and in digital, when it comes to that."

"Grow?" repeats Lincoln witlessly, whipsawed by the change of direction. He was already formulating questions about severance pay and temporary health insurance.

"We currently publish twenty books a year," Duddleston explains. "We need to ramp up to thirty. That will help get the attention of the distributor and the bookstores, and it will speed the building of our backlist. And as you know, the more books you publish, the greater the odds that one will break through and turn into a hit."

"Right," says Lincoln.

Duddleston leans forward and puts his hands on his knees. "The difficult thing," he says, looking grim, "is that for this to work, we can't add head count. We're going to have to handle the additional books with our current staff. That means the editors—you, Hazel, and Warren—are going to have to take on a bigger load."

"I see." Though hugely relieved that he still has a job, Lincoln works his face into a frown.

"And as the executive editor, obviously, the biggest burden will fall on you."

"Right." Lincoln strokes his chin; meanwhile, his mind races: an opening for *The Ultimate Position*! After a moment he says carefully, "You know, just off the top of my head, one thing we might consider is buying a few more polished manuscripts from real writers. Not that, say, Professor Fleace and Professor Morgenthau can't write, but their books need more massaging to get them up to publishing speed. That's what eats up the editors' time. We might look for books that are close to being ready to go."

Duddleston sits back, pleased that his key employee is on board. "Good idea. Excellent. I'm sure those books are out there. Let's talk about it at the next editorial meeting."

"Will do," Lincoln promises.

The two smile and nod at each other, and the moment lingers a bit too long. For all his fluctuating anxiety about staying in his boss's good graces, Lincoln has slowly come to understand that Duddleston—self-conscious about his lack of publishing credentials—is reciprocally wary of his executive editor. Finally, Duddleston says, "I realize you already carry a big load, Abe, and now I'm adding to it. So here's what I propose. I've asked Matt to draw up a profit-sharing plan for you. I'm not offering it to either of the other editors, so please consider it confidential. But if we can bump up that margin by a few points by the end of the year, there'll be a bonus in it for you."

"That's very generous."

"It's only fair. Matt will talk to you about the terms when we get them worked out." The owner rises. "And welcome back. I think it's going to be a great year."

"I agree," Lincoln tells his boss heartily.

Alone again in his office, Lincoln wrestles with the urge to call Amy with the good news: her book is now a prime candidate for the new, expanded Pistakee list. But he restrains himself—Mrs. Macintosh's radar ears sit just a few feet from Amy. Lincoln returns to checking the copy edits in the manuscript of Morgenthau on management, though he violates one of the Founding Fathers' principal tenets, according to the professor ("Focus on *one* thing at a time. There was no multitasking at the Constitutional Convention!") by staring at the pages while mentally buffing arguments on behalf of publishing *The Ultimate Position.*

Over the next week, he and Amy exchange the final chapters by e-mail (carefully using their personal Gmail accounts). Lincoln finds that collaboration is harder over a distance; cyberspace can't match the immediate give-and-take of working side by side (and finishing off a polished chapter with a stirring orgasm). Apart, they drift into their separate regions of the cosmology, Amy drawn to the thinky-yin, Lincoln determinedly grabby-yang. In particular, Amy prefers her dreamy, gossamer ending: Mary Reilly concludes that her mysterious friend, Jennifer, has fantasized her sexual adventures, leading Mary to spin off into an unsatisfying Fitzgeraldian riff about wonder and imagination being the underpinnings of a rich life. Lincoln wants certainty: Jennifer is a wacko (albeit an alluring one), and the cops catch the sexual predator (who's completely unconnected to either woman). The collaborators compromise by mixing both versions, a solution that Lincoln finds somewhat clunky, but he reasons: what the hell, if a reader gets that far, we're at least offering more, not less.

The choreography of the book's presentation has to be precise. Lincoln has decided he will leapfrog the editorial committee on Thursday and take the manuscript directly to Duddleston. From a personnel perspective, the move makes arguable sense: since the author is a Pistakee employee, the internal dynamics of the committee could be awkward. But Lincoln has a stealthier motive: he suspects that the owner/editor-in-chief will be flattered by the mano a mano approach, the suggestion that only Duddleston, that sage U of C English major, has the discernment to recognize the literary quality of this unusual (for Pistakee) book.

But making the pitch in Duddleston's office with Amy sitting outside could be awkward in itself, so Lincoln waits until Friday afternoon, when Amy goes off to do photo research for an oxymoronic book Hazel has brought in on Chicago fashion. Duddleston prefers to read on paper, so Lincoln prints out a copy of the novel—232 pages double spaced—and at three, he puts the manuscript under his arm, marches through the hallways, nods to Mrs. Macintosh (who may have been napping on this quiet afternoon—her chin pops off her chest when Lincoln walks by), and presents himself in the boss's doorway. "Got a second?" Lincoln asks.

Duddleston looks up from studying an ominous spreadsheet that's almost as wide as his desk. "Sure."

"I think I have a spot of good news," Lincoln teases.

Duddleston looks bewildered. He's not used to such upbeat introductions.

"We have someone with extraordinary talent right here at Pistakee," Lincoln continues. "Your assistant, Amy, has written what I think is a remarkable book. Smart, sexy, literary. It's a great read, and Pistakee has the inside track to publish it."

"Amy? No kidding!" Duddleston's tense face relaxes into a wide smile. "What's it about?"

"Well, it's a novel." The owner's face tightens again, and Lincoln hurries on. "It's about a young woman's awakening, coming to understand herself and her sexuality. It's set in a university town, and there's some criminal intrigue. Amy has done a marvelous job straddling the literary and the commercial." Lincoln tries to sound casual, yet impressed, hoping his confidential tone will plant the suggestion: Pistakee better publish the book or Amy will take it to a big New York house and make a fortune.

"A novel? Did you know she was working on it?"

"No," Lincoln lies. "Not until she brought it to me."

Duddleston squirms. "I mean, that's great—great for Amy, but I don't think the book's for us. Remember, we decided to stick to nonfiction. It says so right in our mission statement."

Two years ago, as the crazed search for mission/vision statements was finally winding down in the rest of corporate America,

Pistakee's top staff wasted two days with a relentlessly cheery facilitator in a chill meeting room at an overpriced resort near Galena coming up with seventy-nine typed words on a sheet of paper that promptly disappeared somewhere, utterly forgotten. Except, apparently, by Duddleston.

"Yes," Lincoln responds thoughtfully, "but I think the mission statement also talks about publishing books that speak to Midwestern readers about their times and their culture, and that's exactly what Amy's book does, albeit using fiction as the vehicle. So in that sense, this exactly meets the intent of the mission statement."

"Hmmm." Duddleston resists. He warily eyes the manuscript in Lincoln's hands, as if worried that the executive editor will force it upon him, breaching some line of propriety. "I don't really have confidence in our ability to evaluate fiction. None of the novels we published before really went anywhere. I mean, what's good? What will sell?"

"But it's all storytelling, just in alternate modes." Lincoln hesitates, then shifts into what he hopes will be the closer. "You said yourself the other day that Pistakee has to expand its list, and this is exactly the sort of book that we can acquire cheaply and produce efficiently. Very cleanly written. Needs almost no editing. Just take a look. It's good!"

Duddleston chews the inside of his lower lip and stares balefully at the manuscript. For a moment Lincoln even feels bad for his boss. Just a few months ago, Lincoln pressed a book of poetry on him, and Duddleston went along (not even bringing up the noxious mission statement), mostly to appease his most accomplished and hard-working employee. Now, Lincoln is back with a novel. But Lincoln's fleeting sympathy doesn't prevent him from holding out the wad of pages, virtually forcing Duddleston to take the manuscript or risk appearing stubbornly indifferent to the work of his own assistant. The boss places it on the south end of his big desk atop a pile of papers that appear to have been there, undisturbed, for months. "I'll give it a look," he says.

Lincoln smiles benevolently on the prickly Mrs. Macintosh as he makes his escape.

23

THE AGONIZED WAITING. AFTER SEVERAL DAYS OF SILENCE from Duddleston, Lincoln starts to feel like someone sitting in limbo until the results come back on a scary medical test. Does his career, his happiness, really pivot on the whim of an obsessive-compulsive literary hobbyist? Lincoln tries to reason himself back from his anxiety, but Amy doesn't help matters. As a week ticks down with no news, she calls Lincoln at home one night. "It's bad," she says. "He won't even look me in the eye. You know how they say that a jury has brought in a guilty verdict if they come back from deliberations and don't look at the defendant? I'm the defendant."

"Maybe he hasn't read it yet," Lincoln offers feebly.

"I just don't want him to say it's terrible. He can turn it down, fine. But I don't want him to say it's terrible and ruin my confidence."

"Don't be ridiculous. You and I know ten times as much, a hundred times as much about literature as Duddleston does. And we think the book's good."

"But he's the owner. What we think doesn't count."

Lincoln can't really argue with that.

To make things worse, the weather turns, and suddenly a quiet, ineffectual January fills out its true Chicago bones. In the space of a few days, a moderate snowstorm, five or six inches, precedes a temperature drop to the single digits, followed by a brief, slush-producing spike, then sleet, another deep freeze, more snow, wind. Each panel of the *Tribune*'s little seven-day weather cartoon features nothing but cruel, gray clouds spouting precipitation like the quills on a porcupine. Getting anywhere is a chore. Lincoln takes to wearing his heavy, black Timberland Classic boots all day every day, the little toe on his left foot developing a painful corn from rubbing against the stiff leather. Since the owners don't live in any of the three-flats on Lincoln's block, no one takes responsibility for shoveling the snow out front. The manic pattern of freeze/melt/freeze produces a long stretch of treacherous, iced sidewalk that even Lincoln's fierce boots won't grip. After seeing two people go down ahead of him one morning, Lincoln bails out and starts dodging cars in the snow-narrowed street. That evening on his way to the L station, his head buried in his shoulders against the barbed wind whipping down wide LaSalle Street, passing similar headless, bundled, human forms, mummies fighting for life, Lincoln wonders: Why the fuck did the Indians settle here in the first place? Why stop in Chicago? Why not keep going, down to Arizona, Florida, Costa Rica, someplace where Mother Nature offers at least modest hospitality?

That night, a basement door in his building blows open and a pipe freezes, forcing the management company to shut off all water. Lincoln gets up in the morning and can't make coffee, can't shower, and has to get by with a single flush. He ends up cabbing it to Flam's apartment to borrow the facilities. The old friends haven't seen much of each other in the last few months, and Lincoln suspects that Flam misses those weeks they shared as roommates after Lincoln's marriage fell apart and before he got his own place. Flam is eager to recount his latest romantic interest, and while Lincoln dries off from his shower and shaves, Flam hovers outside the bathroom and talks through the thin door. His new love, by his description, is a busty and brilliant young college dropout who works in the men's department at Macy's.

"Had a date yet?" Lincoln calls through the door.

"Working up to it," says Flam, without irony. "So far, I've bought three ties and a Calvin Klein dress shirt."

When the conversation turns to news of the *Tribune*, Flam reveals that starting in the spring the vastly reduced weekly book section plans to devote a page a month to online and digital publishing. "Oh, Christ," Lincoln groans.

"It's all going electronic eventually, anyway," Flam presses. "Already there are plenty of these online packagers who can help you get your book published on whatever platform you want."

"Without editing," Lincoln says, talking to his reflection in the mirror as he shaves. "The stuff they publish is junk, worse than a vanity press."

"Some of the books have become hits," Flam points out. "They find their audience. The Internet is direct, writer to reader. No intermediation. Why should smug assholes like you and me decide what the world wants to read?"

It's still early in the morning, and Lincoln is out of training for Flam's provocative arrogance. He says nothing.

"These days, everybody is a writer," Flam pronounces to the door. "It's easy."

When Lincoln finally emerges from the bathroom, Flam asks, "By the way, how's the sex novel coming?"

"Still coming," Lincoln dodges as he throws on his clothes and hurries to get away.

Duddleston often takes manuscripts home to read over the weekend, but after a second Monday passes without word from the boss, Lincoln begins to despair. Late that afternoon, Tony Buford calls. "I'm on the lineup for the poetry slam at the Funk Hole in Wicker Park tonight," he says. "I can bring one guest who gets a free pitcher of beer. Want to come?"

"Are they still holding those things?" Lincoln asks.

The question annoys Buford. "The famous one is every Sunday night at the Green Mill. This slam isn't at that level, but it's a good program. How about it?"

"Ahh." Lincoln attended a few poetry slams in college, when the events were relatively fresh on the scene. By some accounts, the slam is one of Chicago's worthier recent inventions: Poets declaim their work in a bar, and the audience shouts its assessment. "I think of slam poems as, say, angrier than yours," Lincoln says, reasonably.

"They invited me," Buford snaps.

Lincoln needs a diversion. Why not? "OK, I'll meet you there."

The Funk Hole is a dim, almost windowless bar that decades ago served as the ersatz living room for punch-press operators, steelworkers, truck drivers, and the like back when Chicago was a manufacturing town and this neighborhood was a working-class enclave. Since the artists, the kids, and then the money started moving into Wicker Park, the crowd in the bar has changed, though the proprietors wisely retained the authentic grunge, and even Lincoln shudders to imagine what a harsh, bright light would reveal.

Standing inside the doorway, peering through the gloom, Lincoln sees scattered tables that, surprisingly, are mostly filled. A line of customers stands at the bar. After a moment, Buford spots him and beckons from deep in the room. "Already ordered your pitcher," the poet says, when Lincoln joins him at a small table up front. "Old Style. Sorry. That's the deal."

"No problem," Lincoln tells him, pouring himself a glass of the watery brew.

Buford looks impossibly scrubbed and tended for the venue—hair trimmed close to the scalp, shirt collared and starched. He's eschewed a tie, but he's wearing what's probably the only tweed jacket in the place, perhaps the only tweed jacket in all of Wicker

Park. Talk about undaunted courage. "Have you been to a slam before?" asks Lincoln, who himself has dressed down in old jeans and a plaid flannel L.L.Bean shirt.

Buford puts on a peeved frown. "Of course. Performed a few times, too." Softening, he says, "Never here, though."

"I haven't been to one in years," Lincoln admits. "I guess I thought they had fallen out of fashion."

"I know, I know. Harold Bloom said slams would be the end of art." Buford shakes his head. "More death cries from the *ancien régime*." Quickly, he brightens. "Hey, brought a fan club," he says, and he gestures toward several tables of bright faces situated toward the back. A handful of the kids see him and wave. "Some of my students—the ones old enough to drink. I'll introduce you later."

The program starts twenty minutes late. A skinny young man wearing a wool knit cap and with his sleeves rolled up to expose the tattoos on his forearms welcomes the audience from a microphone just a few feet from Lincoln's chair. The host explains the Funk Hole protocol: Eight poets get three minutes each in each round. Over three rounds, judges randomly selected from the audience will whittle down the contenders to reach a winner. "Everybody get it?" he asks.

A chorus of affirmation.

"Before we get started," the man under the wool cap continues, "I'd like to acknowledge a special guest with us here tonight, someone who works tirelessly to keep Chicago's literary lights burning."

Dear God, thinks Lincoln, his heart leaping. Did Buford tell them I was coming?

"Marissa Morgan!" cries the host, and he points to a table on the side, where Lincoln can see the blogger's huge, purple-rimmed glasses and overeager smile. "I'm sure everyone in this room reads her blog, *Big Shoulders Books*. Keep up the good work, Marissa." Wool Cap leads the audience in rousing applause.

Lincoln's shame—entirely private—at his momentary hubris immediately gives way to a more practical emotion: terror that Marissa Morgan may actually write about this event. Will Lincoln's poet come under public scrutiny? Worse, will Buford's connection to Pistakee (and Lincoln!) be exposed? And all this time Lincoln had been hoping that *Still Life* would pass silently to remainder bins.

The opening poet in the first round turns out to be a youngish woman in a wheelchair who swerves her vehicle around the tables on the way to the front. Wool Cap lowers the mic, and she recites a poem that describes in piercing detail the car crash that left her paralyzed from the waist down. Lincoln finds the poem quite powerful, though he doesn't see anything very poetic about it—he can imagine the passage as several well-crafted paragraphs in a personal essay. The audience applauds politely.

The action gets rolling with the next contestant, a wiry guy with a ratty gray ponytail who looks as if he could be left over from the Funk Hole's past existence. Shouting and punching the air, he declaims a poem about the night his army unit ravaged an Iraqi village, and he and another soldier unloaded their weapons on a crude, mud-brick house that they suspected of harboring insurgents. The audience whoops and hollers along with him—whoops even at the end, as the poet describes a lone, human cry emerging from the mayhem.

The vet gives way to a potbellied ex-con drug-dealer who poetically rails about the brutal injustices served by the cops who raided his apartment. He yields to a lumpy woman promoting the liberation of children ("Run, boys and girls! Run down that hall! Shout, boys and girls! Shout through the walls!"). The audience is fevered and noisy, and the pitchers of beer are flowing.

Between poets, Buford confides, "I have a bit of an advantage here because my poems are so short. I can probably recite five in three minutes, if there aren't too many interruptions."

He's seventh in the first round. When Wool Cap finally calls his name, Buford gives Lincoln a sporty nod and hops up to the mic. One of the kids in back shouts out, "Go for it!" and an anticipatory silence falls over the revved-up audience. Buford starts with "The Remote," his poem about the channel changer. He recites with the professorial manner Lincoln has come to know well—open, searching, somewhat cerebral. At first, the crowd seems befuddled. It remains deadly silent, save for the end of the poem, when a lone shout of "Yeah!" comes from the vicinity of Buford's students.

The poet then moves to "North Wells Between Grand and Illinois," and the heckling starts. First there's an outbreak of hissing, then a cry of "Get it going!" answered from the other side of the room by "Get the hook!" Hooting laughter competes with Buford's words ("The tile shop flaunts its shiny square baubles/all corners and edges, a Tuscan intrusion…"). Gripping the mic like a rock singer, Buford forges on, reciting from memory. When "Throw Rug" opens to outright booing, Buford's students rally to his defense. "Let him speak!" "Shuddup!" Soon, the scene erupts into an aural melee—stomping, whistling, cries and shouts, and laughter fill the decrepit room. A man a few feet behind Lincoln uses his hand and mouth like a trumpet, blowing farting noises in the direction of Buford. Even the two bartenders, an almost matching set of young women dressed in black, stop pouring drinks to enjoy the scene. Still, Buford soldiers on, looking out on the sea of chaos with no visible hint of recognition.

When his three minutes expire, everyone in the room stands and cheers, the tables of DePaul students waving and screaming, trying to drown out the derision. Lincoln glances across the room and sees that Marissa Morgan is on her feet, too, applauding and laughing. A skirmish breaks out in back near the students, and the sound of bottles breaking and chairs scraping the floor interrupts the commotion, but the violence is quickly tamped down, and Wool Cap retakes the mic and settles the crowd.

"Whew!" whispers Buford as he sits again beside Lincoln and the noise dies.

"Way to hang in there," Lincoln says.

"What a show!" the poet exclaims, his face lit and vibrant.

Lincoln thinks: No wonder he's undaunted. The poor sap is clueless.

Of course, Buford doesn't survive the first round. When Wool Cap reads out the four poets who will advance, Buford utters a soft, "Aww."

"Well, you gave it a good shot," Lincoln says.

Buford rallies immediately. "This was great! Very exciting! A good omen!"

"You think?" Lincoln can't hide his skepticism.

"History is full of artists whose works are shouted down," Buford points out, as if it were Lincoln himself who was clueless. "The audience rioted at the first performance of *The Rite of Spring*."

"Yes," says Lincoln cautiously. "Of course, that was the avant-garde. The author was way ahead—"

"It's all art," Buford says, intercepting the potential insult. "Who's to say what's avant-garde and what's retrograde? Everything moves in big circles, anyway. Besides, what's important here is the attention. This could be great for sales. You might want to increase the print run."

"Ahh."

There's a break before the start of the second round. When Buford says he wants to go thank his loyal students, Lincoln uses the occasion to take his leave. "You don't want to see how it ends?" asks Buford. "My money's on the ex-con."

"You can let me know."

Buford grabs Lincoln's hand. "Thanks for coming," he says. "It really meant a lot for me to have my editor here."

Lincoln tells him he wouldn't have missed it for the world.

The next day at work, Lincoln checks in periodically at BigShouldersBooks.com to make sure Marissa Morgan hasn't immortalized the fiasco. Nothing for most of the day. Then, late in the afternoon, she drops in a long, varied post—news of a bookstore closing, author readings, a brief Q&A with a woman from Naperville who's publishing a vegetarian cookbook. Scanning the text, Lincoln's eyes catch on the last item:

Action at the Funk Hole

> Poetry slams are supposed to be energized affairs, but the Funk Hole's event Monday night took it to an extreme as the crowd reacted so violently to a DePaul professor's poetry that a fistfight broke out between supporters and detractors. The short, quiet, rather domestic poems by psychology professor Antonio Buford stirred a disdain among some listeners rarely witnessed before by this observer, though a vocal group of DePaul students heartily supported their professor. Afterward, Professor Buford seemed unfazed by the reaction. He described his poetry as "Emily Dickinsonish," and he said Pistakee Press is bringing out an edition of his work later this spring. "My editor is John Lincoln, the best literary editor in Chicago," the professor told me. "He gets it." No one was hurt in the altercation. Iraqi War vet Edward X. DeLeo was eventually declared the slam's winner.

Lincoln stares numbly at his computer screen. The report will live in perpetuity in cyberspace, he and Buford locked forever in a literary embrace. What if Jeff Kessler at Malcolm House decides to check up on Lincoln with a quick Google search? What if Duddleston sees the item? After years of nurture and careful investment, his beloved publishing house has been made a laughingstock.

Lincoln's depression eases slightly after he spends half an hour testing various phrases on Google and finds that only the most targeted search ("John Lincoln + Antonio Buford") lifts the item onto the first page of results. Is he safe hiding in Google's algorithm?

On Thursday morning at ten, the editorial committee gathers in the conference room for its weekly meeting. Duddleston is late arriving. Lincoln sits beside Warren Sternberg and across the table from Hazel Lanier, who has brought a manila folder thick with proposals about children's books. Just as Duddleston enters carrying Amy's manuscript under one arm, Hazel looks brightly at Lincoln and says, "I read about your poet in Marissa Morgan's blog!"

"Uhhhh." Lincoln can't speak.

The boss glares at his employees as if he's caught them in flagrante. "Can I see you alone for a moment," he says to Lincoln.

Duddleston leads Lincoln down to Lincoln's office and shuts the door behind them. The boss doesn't bother to sit, so the two of them stand uncomfortably in the small space. A whorl of wrinkles between Duddleston's eyes makes Lincoln think of a tornado. "Have you spoken to your writer Antonio Buford lately?" the boss demands.

"Ah, yes." (So it's happened: Lincoln's world has come to an end.)

"He keeps calling Matt Breeson, telling him we should increase the print run of his book. He's being a real pest." Duddleston doesn't try to suppress his disdain. He learned long ago in the screaming chaos of the trading floor never to pick over decisions already made, contracts already bought or sold. They've settled on printing one thousand books. End of discussion.

"I told him it wouldn't happen." So this isn't about the blog?

"He thinks you're distracted by your divorce—you're too distraught to focus on the problem. I hope we haven't made a mistake getting involved with this guy." The thought fuels the tornado, which grows and spawns several others that rage across the plains of the boss's forehead.

"It'll be all right," Lincoln assures with no good reason.

"I hope so. Now, as for this." Duddleston places Amy's manuscript on the corner of Lincoln's desk, then strokes it as if it were a small dog. "I read Amy's book," he says.

"Oh?" Stay calm.

"It's very sexual, isn't it?"

"Well, not unduly so, I think. It touches our cultural moment, the sexualization of quotidian life. And, of course, there's the coming-of-age phenomenon. Done literarily…" In his anxiety, Lincoln babbles.

"Oh, it's very well written," the boss interrupts. "I was impressed. A bit shocked, I must admit. Our innocent little Amy." He can't suppress a boyish grin. Duddleston married relatively late, in his early forties, and his two kids, a boy and a girl, are just entering adolescence. Lincoln wonders if the good Presbyterian walked chastely through his own young manhood or if he's simply forgotten.

"Good writers have rich imaginations," Lincoln suggests.

Duddleston puckers his lips, forming a thought. "I just don't know how to judge it. I mean, if I were in a bookstore, would I pick this up?" He pretends to consider, sniffing the air. "No."

"But do you ever read fiction?"

"You're right. Not often, not often."

"See, I think this can be a good test for us. I've got some ideas how we can promote it. We can use it to really pump up our skills in social media."

Duddleston nods coolly, and Lincoln quickly tacks sideways. "We can publish incredibly cheaply," he points out.

"I suppose it would be good for staff morale," Duddleston muses. "Publishing a book by one of our own."

"Exactly! Who knows what sort of talent you'll stir up." Lincoln gets a disheartening vision of Matt Breeson marching in with a three-hundred-page police procedural or Hazel Lanier with a picture book of children and kittens.

Fortunately, Duddleston is already on to another issue. "What do you suppose we should pay Amy?"

"Well, she doesn't have an agent." It occurs to Lincoln that he has a serious conflict of interest here, since he's hardly in a position to defend Amy's financial stake. But never mind. She'll be happy enough just to see the book in print. "We can give her a small advance—maybe a thousand dollars—and a standard contract, then if the book's a success, she'll get her payoff with the royalties."

Duddleston offers a genuine smile. "Well, what the hell, let's do it," he says. "But it's only a test. We're not back in the fiction business yet."

"Right." Lincoln wants to let out a whoop. Instead, he follows Duddleston's lead and places his hand on the manuscript. Nice puppy.

On their way back to the editorial meeting, Duddleston says, "Let me tell Amy, if you don't mind. I want to see the look on her face."

For Lincoln, the two-hour meeting passes in moments. When he returns to his office, he's still too wound up to sit down. He wanders to his porthole window and glances down at the alley below. With its grim layer of gray and flattened snow, its sombrous pyre of black bags of garbage, frozen now in the cold, the view provides a useful antidote to Lincoln's joy. This is only a tiny first step, he reminds himself. A whole Everest of obstacles stretches between here and the success of which he's dreamed. Still, still...you've got to start somewhere.

Of course, he's too careful to seek out Amy. But at around three that afternoon, he's at his desk when she walks by outside his door. She pauses and looks up and down the hall. Certain she is alone, she turns to him, sticks out her tongue, and shakes her head and body violently, her tongue flapping wildly around her lips, her arms flying in all directions. She maintains the bedlam performance for maybe five seconds before stopping abruptly, straightening her skirt, and walking on like a proper young woman.

24

THERE IS SO MUCH TO DO. THE TIMELINE FOR *THE Ultimate Position* has to be telescoped to meet Lincoln's plan to publish the book for summer. He sends the manuscript out for copyediting to the elderly woman, a *Tribune* vet, who handles Pistakee's manuscripts, and he orders Gregor to design a cover. ("Maybe something that brings together the sex and the mystery," Lincoln suggests, and the designer produces a picture of a pair of shapely legs in glittery stilettos marred by drops of blood. Lincoln sends it back.) He scribbles some promotional copy for a last-second addition to the Pistakee catalog, and he prepares a press release to go out with advance copies. The distributor has to be coaxed to crash yet another Pistakee book (with the Cubs' season ending ignominiously, *Wrigley Field: A People's History* died on third). All this—on top of all the chores for Lincoln's other books. He's working weekends again and staying late at the office, but he appreciates being busy. Locking up one night, the last person to leave the twelfth floor, Lincoln realizes he's hardly thought about Mary for days, and he hasn't even been bothered by the soul-crushingly gray February weather.

That night, while Lincoln is eating half a roast chicken from Dominick's and watching yet more snow decorate the maple branch outside his living-room window, Amy calls. "Are you at home?" she asks in a tight voice.

"Yes."

"I'm coming over."

"What—"

The phone clicks off before he can get the question out.

Ten minutes later, she rings the front-door bell. Lincoln buzzes her in and listens as her anxious steps pound the wood stairway up to his floor. He opens the door, and she brushes past and drops onto the sofa, shedding snow as she goes. She doesn't bother taking off her mittens or cap or even unzipping her ski jacket. "My parents hate the book," she says, burying her hands between her thighs and rocking up and back. "They hate it, hate it, hate it."

"Whoa." Lincoln sits across from her in the nubby chair. "Slow down. What did they say?"

"They hate it. I told you."

Lincoln recognizes this outburst as an indictment of him. He wants to tell her: Who cares what your parents think? Worry about the *New York Times Book Review.* Instead, he says, "Try to be more specific. What exactly didn't they like?"

Amy takes a deep breath. She's wearing a funny little pill-box ski cap that looks incongruously jaunty given her distress. "Mostly the sex," she says in a slightly calmer voice.

"There's less sex in your book than in half the novels published these days," Lincoln reminds her without too much exaggeration. "The copy editor is at least seventy-five, and she's entirely unfazed."

"My mom read all the sex scenes as if they were autobiographical," Amy says glumly.

"Well, there you go. What did your father say?"

Amy smiles sheepishly. “He didn’t actually read it. He said he couldn’t bear to.”

“So what’s the big deal?” Lincoln throws up his arms. “Your parents are reacting exactly like parents. They can’t stand that you’re grown up enough to know about sex.” (Lincoln thinks: of course, if the parents lived in Manhattan, the kid could write a memoir about seducing an entire barnyard and as long there was a guaranteed first printing of fifteen thousand, Mom and Dad would be thrilled.)

“I know,” Amy says. “But I’ve always been a good girl, a perfect girl—I’m not used to disappointing them.”

“Well, blame me,” Lincoln offers. “Tell them I made you add the sex.”

She smiles sheepishly again. “I did, sort of. My mother suspected it. In fact, she thought you wrote most of the sex stuff.”

“What did you tell her?”

“I said it was more of a collaboration.”

“So?”

“She said that made it like teenage sex—we both get to fool around, but I’m the one who gets stuck with the baby.”

Lincoln makes a mental note not to tangle with Mrs. O’Malley. “It’ll be fine,” he promises. He brews up a pot of cinnamon-apple-spice tea to soothe Amy’s nerves. By the time he walks her out into the cold to catch a cab, she’s excited again about the book, and Lincoln is feeling particularly buoyant—after all, the reaction of her parents has affirmed one of his stereotypes about the provincial attitudes of the Midwest. He’s got a feel for the marketplace, he tells himself. A good sign for the book.

Two weeks later, walking down the narrow interior stairway of his building on his way to work, Lincoln meets the old woman who lives on the first floor. She’s just returning from walking her Chihuahua. “Sun today!” she crows with remarkable vigor while the annoying dog sniffs at Lincoln’s pant leg. “Maybe we’ve put the worst of winter behind us!”

"Let's hope!" Lincoln rejoins, taking care not to trip over the dog or its leash.

When he opens the front door, the blue sky and mild air hit him with such a rush of liberation that he actually considers playing hooky from his job for the first time in his life. The trouble is, he can't think of anything to do—at least nothing outdoors that would let him bask in this premature breath of spring. Besides, he's got things he's looking forward to at work. Gregor has promised to bring in another idea for the cover of *The Ultimate Position*, and Lincoln has vowed to read the book one more time in galley pages. So instead of taking off on a frolic and detour, he luxuriates in the weather on the walk to the L station, where a nearly empty train is just pulling in and Lincoln gets a seat. His luck holds when he arrives at the office and Mrs. Macintosh calls to tell him that Duddleston wants to see him in the conference room right away. Good thing I came to work, after all, Lincoln tells himself.

The conference room's narrow, windowless space gets stifling in summer and even in winter carries the musty odor of stale air and old cups of coffee. Aside from editorial meetings, the staff uses the room mostly to go over projects—picture books, for example—that need to be spread out on the long wood table. The moment he opens the door, Lincoln sees that this meeting is something different. Duddleston is seated on one side of the table, between a man Lincoln knows only as a Duddleston lawyer and a woman, Jane Something-or-other, who's the office manager for a small investment firm in which Duddleston holds an interest and who handles HR issues for Pistakee. Naively, Lincoln thinks: the company is finally adopting the new health-care plan, and they need to bring Pistakee's executive editor into the loop.

"Please sit down," says Duddleston, pointing to a chair on the opposite side of the conference table. His voice is chill and flat.

Lincoln sits, and he stares across the table at three unsmiling faces. Behind them on the whiteboard, someone—probably

Hazel, who teaches a class here in writing children's books—has scrawled and underlined "Connecting to the fantasy reality."

"You know Jane Hemer," Duddleston says, nodding toward the woman, "and this is Martin Canon; he's a lawyer."

Lincoln nods and reaches over to shake the man's hand, but the lawyer makes no effort to meet him halfway. It's only then, with his arm stretching awkwardly while the lawyer sits like a marble statue, that Lincoln realizes: me.

The lawyer speaks in a low, emotionless voice, using words that have clearly been scripted: "On good evidence, we have reason to believe that you have had sexual relations with a lower-level employee at Pistakee Press. Is this true?"

With his heart pumping blood at a furious pace, Lincoln's mind spins. He thinks first: Shouldn't they read me a Miranda warning? Don't I get a lawyer? Then he wonders if he can call his father. No, Lincoln's on his own. How did they find out? Can he bluff? He frantically tries to play out in his head the chess game of lies and obfuscations that would follow from a denial. How far could he take it? Or could he just deny and refuse to say more—be like one of those fundamentalists who reject evolution against all evidence? But the precise, inelegant language of the accusation ("sexual relations") brings Lincoln back to memories of the humiliating falsehoods practiced by Bill Clinton under duress.

"Well, what do you say? Is it true?" demands Duddleston after Lincoln has sat mute for almost half a minute.

Lincoln has been a cad and a cheat; his moral compass is skewed by ambition, and he holds an arrogant disregard for great masses of perfectly decent, well-meaning people. He will fib to get his way and dodge the truth to avoid confrontations. As much as anyone, he practices the blinding self-justification that seems to have become a defining element in the character of Americans born after World War II. But pressed to the core, when it comes to taking responsibility for an action that involves himself and others in a crucial way, Lincoln will not lie. "Yes," he says.

Duddleston shakes his head in disgust. Jane Hemer, who seems to draw an intense pleasure from this fast-moving drama, emits a small, vaguely sexual sigh. Canon, the lawyer, stays on mark. "You have broken a fundamental rule of this company," he says, "and your employment is immediately terminated." He turns over a sheet of paper that is sitting in front of him and pushes it across the table. "This letter waives any future right of recourse against Pistakee and promises that you will never disclose anything material about the company or say anything in any way disparaging about it or its principals. If you sign the waiver, Pistakee will give you six weeks severance and agree to make neutral acknowledgements of your employment here. We will tell people you resigned." He waits while Lincoln stares blankly at the sheet, its lines of type blurred to his eyes. The lawyer continues: "Otherwise, you will get nothing. You're out, and you're fired."

Lincoln hesitates, then lifts a corner of the document and fingers its thick, rich texture, built to last. He's far too stunned to think, to reason. Instinct alone remains. "No," he says, flicking the sheet back across the table. He signed a waiver before he wrestled the bear. One is enough for a lifetime.

The lawyer lets slip a hint of emotion, a slight, almost immeasurable elevation of the eyebrows. Surprise? Admiration? It passes in an instant. The eyebrows slam down like a steel gate. "You will be escorted to your office and allowed to take your personal belongings only," he says. "You will not take anything that belongs to the company. You have ten minutes."

As if answering a bell, the three people on the other side of the table stand in unison. Jane Hemer hands Lincoln a packet of material about health care and his 401(k). Duddleston opens the conference room door, and the three antagonists watch Lincoln rise unsteadily and step out of the room. In the hall, the paunchy building guard waits, holding several empty boxes. He nods in the direction of Lincoln's office and follows while Lincoln scuffles in a fog through the corridors. His legs are rubbery. He feels as if his clothes are propping him up. He and the guard pass no one, see no one. Lincoln wonders: Is everyone hiding? Do they all know? When he enters his office, he pauses briefly in the middle of the room, trying to get his bearings. This place where he's spent so many hours reading, editing, daydreaming, where he's breathed the air and left untold traces of his DNA—already it seems changed. He thought it was his, but it belongs to the countless ghosts of people who occupied this building before and the countless who will follow.

Lincoln senses the guard at his back. The man used to tease Lincoln, telling him he worked too hard since he was always the last to leave Pistakee's offices at night. Now, Lincoln can feel the man's stony efficiency. Walking around the desk, Lincoln opens several drawers and stares at the files. He considers the clutter of books and manuscripts on his desk. Then he gestures for a box from the guard, and he carefully packs the family pictures sitting atop his bookshelf, including the shot of Mary and him in Tuscany. Why hadn't he put that photo away earlier?

"Let's go," he says.

"That's it?" the guard asks. "You don't want any of them books?" He points to the volumes lining the shelves.

"Let's go," Lincoln repeats, leading the way out of his office.

Kim is off today and a temp, another young woman, watches from the reception desk as Lincoln and the guard wait for the elevator. They ride down in silence. Out on the street, the guard shows a surprising burst of energy, pushing past Lincoln to hail a cab that happens to be passing. Lincoln puts his box of photographs in the backseat, then slides in beside it. The guard pulls a twenty-dollar bill out of his pocket and hands it to Lincoln. "Mr. Duddleston gave me this for your cab ride home," the guard says. "I think he thought you'd have more stuff."

Later, Lincoln wishes he'd refused the money. But his mind is stuck in slow motion, and by the time he thinks of handing the bill back, the guard has disappeared into the building.

What do you do at ten in the morning on the first mild, sunny day in weeks, when everyone else in Chicago is at work and you have just been fired? For an hour or so, Lincoln lies on the sofa in his apartment, holding his right arm. He's not exactly thinking, although his mind is bombarded by thoughts. It's as if his head has tuned to an awkward wavelength that, amid static, pulls in fragments of sentences, glancing ideas, memory pictures from throughout his life: Missing a free throw at the end of the Chevy Chase game. "A brilliant editor." His mom asking, Why don't you go to work for the *Washington Post*? as if it were that easy. George C. Scott as Patton talking about the monumental triviality of the latest infraction for which he is being punished (why does Lincoln love that old movie? Nixon loved it, for fuck's sake). "That sounds like a small book," his father had said. The ultimate position. Duddleston's cold, gray eyes this morning, as dead as pasteboard. "Connecting to the fantasy reality."

Finally, Lincoln gets up. He changes into his jogging gear and goes for a long run north along the lake, dodging patches of ice and puddles, exhausting himself. Returning, he walks the last two blocks to recover his breath and finds Amy standing in a splash of sunlight, leaning against the railing on the steps to his building. "I thought you might be jogging," she says.

Lincoln is soaked in sweat. "What are you doing here?" he asks.

"I came to see how you were doing."

"I don't know," he admits. But then the endorphins from his run kick in, and he regains a touch of bravado. "Oh, I'll be all right. I'm just pissed."

Amy ratchets her face into a twisted frown. "Duddleston is a fool. We've always known it, and this just proves it."

In fact, Lincoln doesn't quite agree. Duddleston's standards, on everything from business to hanky-panky, have been open and consistent from the start. That's not the manner of a fool. "I'm mostly pissed at myself," Lincoln says. "I feel as if I made some basic mistakes early on and they've been compounded over the years. This is just the logical culmination. Bad luck, dumb choices, take them step-by-step, and they lead exactly to this point. In Chicago."

"That's stupid, John," Amy says with real anger in her voice.

For a moment, Lincoln considers arguing with her. Isn't he at least entitled to cultivate bitter self-pity at a time like this? But the February breeze is starting to chill his damp body, and after all, Amy cared enough to come up here to check on him. "Do you want to come in?" he asks. "I can make you a cup of tea."

Amy hesitates, then shrugs. "Sure."

She follows him up the flight of stairs, Lincoln leaving little drops of sweat on the wood steps. In the apartment, he directs her to the living room sofa and heads to the kitchen to put on water. "Cinnamon apple spice?" he calls out.

"OK."

The run has cleared his head somewhat, but he senses a huge, smothering depression hovering just beyond the edges of his consciousness. Worse, somehow, than the cloud that descended after Mary asked for the divorce. Everyone fails at romance. This was his career. "Does all of Pistakee know?" he asks. Keep talking. Use Amy as a diversion.

"Duddleston sent out an e-mail," she answers from the living room. "It just said you've left the company. No explanation. They were already putting your files in boxes when I left."

Lincoln takes down the teapot and drops in two little pillows of tea. He rewashes two cups, scrubbing to erase the coffee stains on the inside. That's odd, he thinks—back when he had a job he wouldn't have taken the time for the extra cleaning. "Where did you tell them you were going just now?" he calls out over the running water. "It won't do your career there any good if Duddleston thinks you're up here giving me solace."

"I didn't tell them anything," Amy says from the living room. "I didn't have to because I quit."

Lincoln shuts off the faucet and goes to the living room. "You're shitting me," he says.

Amy has shed her jacket and kicked off her shoes, and she's sitting in a corner of the sofa, her legs pulled up beneath her. "What else could I do?" she says calmly. "It was as much my fault as yours."

"Yeah, but you still had a job."

"I couldn't stay under those circumstances." Her chin thrusts out; her eyes spark. Lincoln has come to recognize that look of defiance. "Sexual harassment?" she says. "What kind of an opportunistic cynic do you think I am?"

He sinks into the nubby chair. "Not at all..." he starts, then falters. What exactly did he expect? That she'd know that life constantly serves up injustices to others, but that it rarely avails anything to sacrifice yourself, at least beyond a few expressions of pity, perhaps a message of condolence? In other words, that she'd react as he likely would in her place? "What did Duddleston say when you quit?"

"He said I was making a mistake. That it wasn't my responsibility, which of course is bullshit."

"And your book?"

"Canceled. Which is stupid, too. As if the fact that we fucked has anything to do with the merits of the book."

"Yeah," Lincoln says, echoing her disgust, though in fact it had occurred to him that the fucking—or, more accurately, the anticipation of it—had been the antecedent of some of their best writing/editing sessions.

"I think the water is boiling," Amy tells him.

When he returns with the tea, Amy explains how they were found out: Matt Breeson, that tedious suburban pop who likes trying to outsmart a good mystery, happened to notice that both Lincoln and Amy had submitted credit-card statements that contained simultaneous charges from the Lunker Motel in Lac du Flambeau, Wisconsin. Neither employee had claimed reimbursement for the expense, but the match was there to see, listed on the bills, along with a handful of expenses (highlighted by yellow Magic Marker, as per company policy) that indeed belonged to Pistakee. Was this disaster foreseeable? Lincoln's MasterCard bill had been three pages long, with scores of charges (he was still adjusting economically to the separation from Mary). Amy had never before put in for expenses, but in an emergency a few months ago, she'd used her Visa card to buy ink for the printer in Duddleston's office. Neither Lincoln nor Amy had given a thought to the risk before turning in the documents. When Breeson saw the contemporaneous charges, he called Mrs. Lunker, who was happy to acknowledge the attractive young couple who had spent every night in Lincoln's room.

"How does Matt get off pawing through our credit card bills?" Amy asks indignantly. "There's a privacy issue there."

"We were idiots," Lincoln tells her, and Amy can't really argue with that.

As they talk and finish the tea, the midday sun fills the living room with a dense, sweet light. Lincoln's perspiration has dried, and even though he knows he probably smells bad, he has that salty, baked feeling—satisfying in a languid way—you get after swimming in the ocean and drying yourself in the warm sea air. Amy's blue jeans show off the taut curve of her hip, and several layers of T-shirts emphasize her breasts. Her short, brown hair is slightly tussled, and her low-maintenance makeup regimen has left her face fresh and vibrant. Lincoln realizes that the events of the morning have flummoxed his perceptions, but he thinks she's never looked more alluring.

"What are you going to do now?" he asks.

"Who knows?" Amy says. "Duddleston said I could keep the advance, so I've got a little cushion. I can always be a waitress for a while. I suppose I'll go back to school eventually."

"In English?"

She frowns. "I'm sort of down on books right now."

"Maybe you should send your manuscript to an agent," Lincoln suggests halfheartedly.

"No," she declares simply. "This is enough."

Lincoln rises and moves toward the sofa. Some impulse, exposed by trauma, pushes him to her. "Do you realize what we have been through together over the last six months?" he asks.

Amy stiffens and puts her feet on the floor. "Don't sit down," she tells him.

"Why?"

"Just don't, John. I know where it's heading." She hops up from the sofa and grabs her coat from the closet.

"But what difference does it make now?" he pleads, aware of how pathetic he sounds.

Amy talks while she slips into her coat. "Look, John, this has been an incredible experience. But one thing that is abundantly clear is that we are terrible for each other. The combination brings trouble. Bad chemistry, or something. I can see that clear as day, even if you can't."

"Ahh." Lincoln is wholly unprepared to argue on behalf of their romance, and anyway, how much rejection can one man take in a day, a *half* day?

Amy pauses to smooth her hair in the reflection of a framed photograph of the Chicago skyline at night, a wall hanging that came with the apartment. Then she hurries to the door. She glances back at Lincoln, standing listlessly in the middle of the room. "Stop rubbing your arm!" she orders. He obeys. And then she is gone.

25

TELLING HIS PARENTS IS THE WORST. AFTER TWO HERMETIC days and nearly sleepless nights, Lincoln slugs back a shot of vodka and calls home. By then, the weather has returned to the winter norm, and as he waits on the phone for someone to pick up, Lincoln stares out his living room window at a world with the color and hospitality of concrete. His father's first reaction, after a long, heartbreaking silence, is to ask if Lincoln wants to sue. For a moment, Lincoln is cheered—his father believes in his essential innocence! But as they talk, Lincoln realizes that no, that's not it—in his father's eyes, Lincoln has finally sunk to the bottom. Now he's just another blundering client who needs to be rescued from his own stupidity.

Beyond that, his father's clipped advice turns practical: hurry up and get another job, anything, anywhere, so you can close this embarrassing gap in your résumé and avoid questions by future employers.

His mother wants to know about the young woman who was Lincoln's partner in this disaster. Was it a serious relationship? So soon after his break-up? (Lincoln sees past the questions: Before, his mother only worried about his career. Now, with the divorce and this colossal misjudgment, she has to worry about his personal life. Where did she fail?) Her ultimate advice is practical, too: squelch the romantic activities until you get the rest of your life in order.

Afterward, Lincoln sits in near catatonia in the nubby chair. He's thirty-three years old, fifteen years out of the house, and still ravaged by the unspoken disappointment in the voices of his parents. Shouldn't he have anticipated this years ago? Couldn't he have arranged some kind of psychological inoculation?

Two days later, Mary calls. She's heard. (How? From her parents, via his. Tracing back the game of telephone makes Lincoln feel even more desperate—like a hospital patient, someone who's lost control of his life.) "What'll you do now?" she asks.

"Find something else. I've got to have a job."

"But what? What's your strategy, your plan?"

"My strategy?"

"You should use this as an opportunity, Linc—take the time to assess your career, evaluate your strengths and your weaknesses. Turn this to your advantage."

Lincoln knows she means well, but he feels so beaten down he can't fight petulance. "You're going to fit right in at business school," he says sullenly. "You're already talking like a careerist."

"Don't be like that. You've got to fight this."

"Right."

"Look." Mary's tone is clipped, impatient. She asks nothing about the details of his offense, doesn't seem to care whether he was carrying on an affair while they were still together. "Why don't you move to New York? That's where you've always wanted to be. You hate Chicago. Why not just pick up and go? What better time?"

So it's not enough to divorce him; she wants him to leave town, too. "Maybe I will," Lincoln tells her. But how? With no place to live, no job, thousands of journalists and editors out looking for work, and now, a badly stained résumé. Plus, no money, at least, until they sell the apartment—and given the economy, that's not going to happen soon. Mary still lives there in exchange for paying the hefty mortgage, and recently she warned him that sales are dead in the immediate neighborhood. Even Lincoln's divorce lawyer has advised him to stick around until all the papers are signed. "So what are *your* plans?" he asks Mary, dodging.

"You know, the same," she says elusively. "Business has been slow." She pauses. "I'm taking an interesting macroeconomics course in the general studies program at the U of C."

Lincoln meant what are her plans with that dickhead Jerry Cirone, but never mind. While he wants to know, sort of, he doesn't want to learn that they are planning marriage or swanning off on an exotic trip or still fucking. He and Mary talk listlessly for a few more minutes before she signs off with an admonition: "Don't slide into depression, Linc."

The petulance, at least, rouses him out of his lethargy. He spends hours a day on the Internet, first fruitlessly checking the job sites and then wandering aimlessly, following links, pursuing odd facts, Googling everyone he's ever known. Lincoln decides that depression isn't really a problem when you've got the Internet as a constant distraction. The greater risk is that you'd just sit there, occupied but accomplishing nothing, oblivious to the demands of life until you waste away. Lincoln imagines the Comcast man coming to reclaim equipment after the bill goes unpaid for several months and finding Lincoln at his computer, a desiccated skeleton in a decaying bathrobe, one rigid claw of a hand still resting on the touchpad.

Sometimes, toward the end of the day, Lincoln returns to the constantly updated media job sites and after again seeing nothing suitable, he casually explores sites featuring other categories of work—the law, for instance. Maybe he should go to law school after all. It's probably not too late. But then Lincoln thinks of the law students he knew at the U of C—pasty drones forever testing each other in tedious arguments. Where's the pleasure of creation in that? (Besides, he's Googled his old pal Will Dewey, now a litigation partner at Mannheim, Rogers & Baer in Washington, and the smug, ageless face that pops up on the firm's website makes Lincoln shiver.) Or maybe he should make a complete right turn and go into health care. Administrators, nurses, even medical PR positions—despite the recession, openings are all over the job sites. But who's he kidding? He hates hospitals.

After several fruitless days, Lincoln decides to test the water and applies for a research position with a small financial empire based in the northwest suburb of Arlington Heights. The company responds with some interest, and in a phone conversation with the recruiter, Lincoln makes plans to go for an interview. He asks if the headquarters is near the train station.

"What?" croaks the recruiter, a man whose voice until that moment had been soothing and pliant.

"No problem, I can rent a car," says Lincoln, clumsily trying to recover.

"You don't own a car?"

Lincoln slides around the issue and finishes the conversation, but an hour later he calls back to cancel, saving himself what would certainly be a wasted trip. He thinks: In Manhattan, not owning a car is a sign of practical intelligence, not to mention evidence of your concern for the environment; here, they treat you like a homeless person.

Lincoln seriously considers teaching—maybe he can turn his knowledge of books into a gig. One afternoon, he e-mails a résumé to a private school in Indiana that's looking for an English teacher. But Dean Thornburgh at Foster Prep responds almost immediately with a note, thanking Lincoln for his interest, while explaining that the school insists on at least three years of teaching experience.

Sitting at his computer on this early evening, the rest of Chicago returning in darkness from a day at the office, Lincoln realizes that he's relieved at the dean's message. The harsh alchemy of his trauma combined with the deluge of Internet trivia has brought forth an insight, a small clarity that's bracing to his fragile confidence: being an editor is the perfect job for him. Coaxing, nitpicking, spotting holes, cutting excess, sharpening logic, recognizing talent, turning cynicism into something productive, acting like a know-it-all. Editing is what he was born to do.

And then he gets a lead. Flam puts him in touch with the young proprietors of a Chicago-based Internet outfit that publishes mysteries and thrillers through its website, iAgatha.com. Flam says their operation is coming along well enough that they are looking to add an experienced editorial hand.

Lincoln calls, and the webbies arrange to meet him at a Starbucks in Wicker Park, near the team's office. Beforehand, Lincoln visits iAgatha.com and studies the "About Us" section. In photos, the three proprietors, two men and a woman, each ham it up PI style in fedoras and trench coats, and the woman has clamped a curving, Sherlock Holmes pipe in her jaw. At 11:00 a.m., though, no one in the Starbucks near the L station on Damen is wearing a fedora. The place is filled with scruffy young people, pierced and tattooed, sporting hair that looks as if it's been electrified, all eagerly occupied with things to do or discuss. A month ago, Lincoln wouldn't have thought twice about mixing with this crowd. Now he feels acutely his difference in appearance, attitude, employment. He takes his coffee to a corner table and wonders what turns these people took that he missed, how he failed to see the signs. After a few minutes, he's approached by a slender young fellow whose straw-colored hair looks natural enough, but it's completely flattened on one side, as if he's just climbed out of bed. "John Lincoln?" he asks tentatively.

"Yes."

"I thought so!" the young man exclaims triumphantly, and Lincoln winces at the confirmation that he's the squarest-looking person in the place. "I'm Jimmy. Come over and let me introduce you." He leads Lincoln across the room to a table occupied by Sammy, a stout young woman with a streak of pink flowing through her dark hair, and Wade, another slim young man with colorful tattoos wrapping around each arm. "Sammy for Samantha," the woman explains.

Lincoln shakes hands around. "Sorry about the mess," Jimmy says. "We're just having breakfast." Plates of muffins, sweet rolls, and other Starbucks treats cover the small table.

Jimmy seems to be the leader of the group, and he provides a bit of background: they are three recent college grads (surprise—all from Loyola!) who came together in school around a shared love of detective stories and police procedurals. "We're all from cop families," Sammy interjects. In time, all three tried to write in the genre without having any luck selling their manuscripts to publishers. So they created iAgatha.com to bypass the official publishing world—exactly the sort of model, Lincoln thinks, that Flam says is taking over.

For a hosting and administrative fee, the site allows authors to upload their manuscripts and then sell them as PDFs or print-on-demand books, with iAgatha taking a cut. Jimmy explains that they'll have the technology in place for e-book versions in a few months. Early on, the iAgatha crew had a stroke of marketing genius by making all first chapters available free—readers found the site and returned to browse. "We're big on Facebook," Jimmy crows. "Last month we sold five hundred and eleven books."

"Is that enough revenue to sustain you?" Lincoln asks.

"Here's the thing," Jimmy confides. "We're selling a lot of ads. We get traffic from all over the world—people don't come just to read the books, but to talk on our message boards about mystery stories and anything that has to do with crime and cops. That's a very specific audience that some advertisers want to reach. They started coming to us—publishers, book dealers, stores that sell cop paraphernalia."

"Gun stores?" Lincoln asks.

"We're all for gun control," Jimmy explains, "but they have a First Amendment right to advertise; you understand that, don't you?"

"Of course," says Lincoln.

"Now we've added a couple of blogs that are drawing even more traffic. One in particular, by Draco DiVergilio, do you know him?"

"No."

"He's from Chicago, a big mystery writer, sells a lot of books through regular publishers. That's not his real name, by the way. But he blogs for us twice a week, all about the mystery genre."

"He's very opinionated," Sammy offers. "Likes to put things down."

"People love to argue with him," says Jimmy. "So our traffic is really spiking."

Lincoln sips his coffee. He's barely ten years older than these kids, but he feels a gaping cultural divide. They seem pleased by their success, but not entirely surprised. The Dot-Com Bust and now the Great Recession are just blips of history to them, not judgments on greed and mass hysteria. Was this Bill Gates at the dawn of Microsoft? Steve Jobs in his garage building his first computer? "How exactly could you use someone like me?" Lincoln asks.

"Mr. Flam told us you are a brilliant editor," Jimmy says. "The best book editor in Chicago."

"Well, I don't know about that." Lincoln blushes under the compliment.

Jimmy is all earnestness. "See, we're thinking about adding an editorial services function to our business. Most of the people who write for us are amateurs. A lot of them don't want any editing—they think their books are perfect. That's fine. But some writers want advice, feedback. Sammy and Wade and I, we're not really qualified to do that. But we thought that if we offered up a real editor, some people would pay for the service. We'd divide the fee—say, twenty-five percent for us and the rest for you."

"How much would you charge?" Lincoln asks.

"We weren't quite sure, but we thought maybe charge by the size of the manuscript. A penny for every two words. What do you think?"

Lincoln taps his dormant math skills to do some quick calculations on a Starbucks napkin. At that price, a lean, fifty-thousand-word manuscript would bring in $250. But it could take him hours just to give the thing a good read. Double the time to come up with an analysis, make margin notes, prepare a memo, and later look over the author's rewrite, and you're probably talking at best twenty dollars an hour after iAgatha takes its cut. At Pistakee, Lincoln was making more than that and getting benefits, too. He's not in a position to haggle, but he recalls the toll it took on his psyche to deal with the Bill Lemkes, the Professor Fleaces—and they, at least, had nominal claims to writing skills. Who knows what kind of sentences he'd get from that bookkeeper for the car-parts store in Moline who thinks he's the next Mickey Spillane?

When Lincoln looks up from the napkin, iAgatha's three proprietors are staring at him with eager, open, absorbent faces, as if he were a Zen master come to deliver Wisdom. "I think you had better make it a penny for every word," Lincoln suggests.

"Cool!" says Wade, the first time he's opened his mouth.

And so Lincoln has a new job, barely two weeks after losing the old one.

The iAgatha gang works out of a one-room office in the Flatiron Arts Building, a wedge-shaped structure at the intersection of North, Damen, and Milwaukee, the bull's-eye at the center of the arty Wicker Park/Bucktown area. The three principals sit in front of computers at gray, industrial desks scattered around the room. The walls feature three large whiteboards covered with techno-jabberings and lists of names that mean nothing to Lincoln. Two small windows on the east side look down on the busy intersection and across Milwaukee Avenue to Café Absinthe, a veteran restaurant. The bathroom is down the hall.

Jimmy arranges the import of another gray, industrial desk for Lincoln and sets him up with a spare computer, a nifty Mac Pro. "You know, you don't have to work here," Jimmy points out. "You can work out of your home."

"I may," Lincoln tells him. "But let me just get a feel for things."

The founders of iAgatha have divided up the work according to skill sets. Wade handles the technology issues. Sammy deals with the writing clients and the blogs. Jimmy sells the ads and does the bookkeeping. On Lincoln's first day, he and Jimmy puzzle out the wording and design of the announcement that iAgatha now offers editorial services ("Need an experienced editor? We can help!"). With the news and terms posted on the site, they turn to adding Lincoln to the "About Us" section (he chooses not to pose for his photograph in the fedora, which is hanging on an old-fashioned hat rack in a corner of the room). By the time they get back to the home page, iAgatha's offer of editorial help has its first client, Vijay Sharma, of Jaipur, India.

"What time is it in India right now?" Lincoln wonders aloud.

"We get people at all hours, from everywhere," Jimmy says matter-of-factly.

Lincoln downloads Vijay's manuscript, prints it out, and spends the rest of the day reading. The story is set in the waning days of the Raj. An Indian private eye, also named Vijay, gets summoned to the home of a wealthy Indian couple whose handsome teenage boy has been suspiciously disappearing at night. Can Vijay find out what he's up to? Before the detective has a chance to get to work, the boy turns up dead, apparently the accidental victim of a bizarre sexual ritual. Of course, after pages and pages of sleuthing, Vijay fingers the culprit—an aristocratic British lieutenant, whom he ultimately clubs to death with a cricket bat in an act of self-defense after an epic battle at the local officers club.

That night, Lincoln stays up late on the Internet, refreshing his history of the British Raj, catching up on the Indian caste system, tracking details of the country's geography and climate. By the time he sends off his three-thousand-word diagnostic memo the next day, he's already spent almost twenty hours on the book, and three new manuscripts are awaiting his services, one from Prague and two from California.

He gets right to work on the Prague story (Cold War; Czech policeman who'd been a student during the Prague Spring; KGB bad guys) and anxiously watches for the response from Vijay Sharma. In his memo, Lincoln tried hard to restrain his darker impulses and to stay positive, encouraging. But given his experience at Pistakee, he can't help wondering if he lacks the touch for gentle criticism—he worries that turned loose on a manuscript, he's like a feral creature that instinctively gnaws flesh. The resolution comes a few hours later. Vijay is thrilled. He's ecstatic. He's reread Lincoln's memo three times, and he's astonished at the perception, the attention to detail, the wisdom of the suggestions. "Mr. Lincoln," he writes, "you have truly entered my vision and realized exactly what I want to do with this book. Your empathy is miraculous." Wade confirms that the message was sent at 3:00 a.m. Jaipur time, which turns out to be a rather normal period of the day for Lincoln's clients to e-mail their responses. Indeed, in the coming weeks Lincoln sometimes wonders whether he's providing editing services to aspiring writers or an intense form of sympathetic companionship to very lonely people.

No matter; they all seem terrifically happy with his efforts, endlessly grateful for his attention. Even the one person whose manuscript is such incomprehensible gibberish that Lincoln suggests putting the book aside ("Let it percolate in a drawer for a few years; many writers do that with early efforts") and to whom Lincoln offers to refund the down payment, won't take the money back—he so appreciates Lincoln's straightforward honesty.

Meantime, Lincoln gets far more efficient. He learns to speed-read manuscripts, focusing on plot points and dramatic scenes. He discovers that he has five or so boilerplate pieces of advice that he can adjust to meet the specifics of almost any story. And he forces himself to suppress his contempt for the endlessly incoherent sentences, the leapfrog logic, the tired ideas, the delusional hopes of the people paying for his help. “Everybody is a writer,” he recites to himself, his new mantra, a quote from Flam.

Though he usually works at home, he believes in the sustaining value of discipline, so he’s careful to keep up the morning routine left over from the days when he went into an office: rise early; read the newspaper over breakfast; shower; dress (always casual, of course). For the sake of variety, he’ll occasionally stop by the iAgatha office after lunch to check in and print out manuscripts; sometimes he’ll stay to work at his gray desk for a few hours. The proprietors are friendly but busy. There’s little water-cooler-type talk, at least when Lincoln is around, and in fact, he rarely hears Wade say anything but the occasional “Cool.” Several times when Lincoln arrives he finds a note on his desk: “Antonio Buford called. Wants you to call him.” But Lincoln ignores the messages. At least that is behind him.

At John Barleycorn a few weeks into the new job, Flam asks for details. “They’re nice kids,” Lincoln responds. “Very low-key. Very dedicated. And they’ve built an enterprising little company.” He pauses for a bite of hamburger. “Of course, the stuff I work on is dreck.”

“How do you stand it?” Flam asks.

“In some ways, it’s easier to be gentle with the rank amateurs,” Lincoln says with a shrug. “They know not what they do. And the business is going great. I’m backed up with work, and the kicker is, the books I work on sell much better.”

“Readers recognize good editing after all.”

"No. I think the difference is that I write the sales blurbs for the books I edit, and my blurbs are better than anyone else's. It's all about promotion."

Flam smiles. He's let his hair grow since Lincoln has seen him last, and blond locks now curl behind his ears and fall unpleasantly over his shirt collar in back. Lincoln wonders if his friend has given up in some way or whether he's just trying out a new, more visually eccentric persona. "Maybe if you stick around, you can get some equity," Flam suggests. "They go public, and who knows? Internet stocks are making a comeback."

Lincoln has considered and rejected the idea. "I can't wait that long," he says. "I'm hanging in until I get a grubstake together, and then it's off to New York, with a job or without. Mary's right—I've been complaining long enough. Time to close out Chicago."

Flam lets out a snort. "I've heard that before."

"I mean it," Lincoln snaps, but he knows the skepticism is deserved—he's been griping about Chicago and talking about leaving virtually since he arrived, half his lifetime ago. What does that say about his initiative, his drive?

Still, he continues to work hard. There is always work. If he feels a slight emptiness now in the rituals of his occupation, a tamping of his angry desire to make a mark, he at least knows the psychic value of staying busy. Put him at a desk in front of a manuscript, and he is a dray horse, head down, muscles straining, moving forward. On the best days, he tries to think of the latest iAgatha manuscript as his private Lewis and Clark Expedition. Maybe, he tells himself without irony, this counts as being engaged.

SPRING:

The Land of Lincoln

26

LEAVING THE IAGATHA OFFICE ONE AFTERNOON, LINCOLN turns north on Damen Avenue, and the sweep of his eyes catches a well-dressed black man, a relatively rare sight in this gentrified neighborhood of hip entrepreneurism. Lincoln takes several steps before he realizes that he's just seen Antonio Buford.

"Hey!" cries the poet.

Lincoln wheels, and Buford hustles up, but instead of the placid features, the impeccable manners, the poet's face is knotted like a fist and he waves a finger under Lincoln's nose. "You owe me a book," he blurts.

"What are you talking about?" Lincoln asks. He's never seen Buford so riled.

"Pistakee canceled my contract."

"Jeez, I'm sorry," Lincoln tells him. "They fired me, and they must be eliminating all my independent decisions."

"You can't do that—take a writer right up to the line and then drop him on his head."

"I'm out of it now."

"That bookkeeper, that guy Breeson," Buford sputters. "I asked him how many white writers they canceled, and he didn't have the nerve to tell me."

"I know of at least one."

Buford wants heat, reaction. Lincoln's detachment triggers another outburst. "I'll sue," Buford fumes, wagging his finger again.

From behind Lincoln, a large, red-faced and jowly cop suddenly appears. "Is this man bothering you?" the cop asks Lincoln from the side of his mouth.

Buford scowls and immediately steps back.

Lincoln says, "No, officer, we were just having a little argument about business."

The cop stares down Buford. "Well, keep it civil. We don't like scenes on the street around here."

"Yes, officer," says Lincoln.

"Yes, sir," Buford mumbles.

The cop backs off, then turns and walks north on Damen. Lincoln watches Buford watch the officer go. Poor bastard, thinks Lincoln. No wonder he ignores race in his poems; if he thought about it, he'd be angry all the time.

"Listen," Lincoln says, "there's a Starbucks down the street. Let me buy you a cup of coffee."

Buford hugs himself in the cold. "Well, tea," he says.

The Starbucks teems, as usual, but Lincoln and Buford find a small, empty table in a corner. "I'm sorry I yelled at you," Buford says when they've settled in. "I just needed to vent. I'm mad and frustrated."

"And your poetry-yoga sessions don't soothe the pain?" Lincoln teases.

"That's just twice a week, and..." Buford registers Lincoln's sly smile and stops himself. "You prick," the poet says, but he laughs. "At least I don't have to contend with getting fired for sleeping with the help."

"Who told you?"

Buford dunks his tea bag. "The literary community in Chicago is pretty small."

"Marissa Morgan's blog again?" Lincoln hasn't bothered to read it lately.

"She didn't write it, but she told me."

"It was a mistake," Lincoln admits. "On the other hand, it probably couldn't have been helped."

"Then it doesn't really count as a mistake," consoles the happiness professor. He sips his tea. His earlier burst of temper seems to have passed gently. "At least you've found a landing spot," Buford offers. "I didn't realize you knew the detective genre."

"I don't, but I'm learning." In fact, in trying to sharpen his skills, Lincoln has spent time sampling the canon—Chandler, Hammett, Cain. He found them stylish, smart, and very American, but tired of them quickly—the withheld information, the manipulated intrigue. "I don't think I have the gene for enjoying that kind of fiction," Lincoln confesses. "When it comes to literature, I'm Calvinist—I want a novel to teach me something, about life, about the world."

"What about pleasure?" Buford asks. "What about reading purely for entertainment?"

"Like thrillers? I get impatient. Too much coincidence. Too many people doing stupid things."

"Dickens uses coincidence," Buford points out. "And Shakespeare understood how people's emotions let stupidity rule. Think of Claudius—poisoning his brother, then marrying his wife. Now, that was a stupid man."

"But Dickens, Shakespeare—they didn't wrap the whole story around those things," says Lincoln. "Life is more complex than that."

Buford shows off a teasing smile. "I think you're giving life too much credit, old buddy."

Lincoln sits back in the flimsy Starbucks chair. Old buddy. That's the second time Lincoln has heard Buford use that fusty locution. Remove the menace, and the well-spoken poet sipping the cup of Tazo Earl Grey on the other side of the little table becomes an almost Edwardian figure. It couldn't have been easy growing up that way, South Side or anywhere. Maybe that's why he's so eager to get published, Lincoln thinks—to wave a success under the noses of the bullies and skeptics, the cops. We're all just kids looking for chances to show off.

After a pause, Buford says, "You know, I don't want you to publish *Still Life* on your website." When Lincoln frowns but says nothing, the poet continues, "I want a hardcover. That's what I've got my heart set on."

Buford lets this pronouncement settle. After a moment, he leans forward in alarm. "You OK?" he asks, reaching for Lincoln's arm.

"Just a little gas." Lincoln pats his stomach. But in fact, Buford's remark has loosed an idea that's struck Lincoln to stupefaction—a thought so obvious that it confirms the role in life of both coincidence (to be working at an online publisher at this moment) and stupidity (for not thinking of it before). Of course. Publish Amy's novel on iAgatha.com. Lincoln must have been so shell-shocked that he didn't think of it before. The book's not really in iAgatha's genre, but so what? It's the Internet—anything goes. For an instant, Lincoln lets his imagination romp: Published by iAgatha, Amy's book becomes a social media sensation, virally spread around the world. Online sales boom. The big New York publishers get wind of the phenomenon and vie to bring out a print edition. Lincoln, the impresario of this coup, can write his own ticket. Redemption.

He pulls himself back to Starbucks. "Listen," he tells Buford, "If I were you, I wouldn't give up on Pistakee. Those folks are very risk averse. Maybe you should have your brother the lawyer make a call."

Buford nods. "I've considered that."

"Just one phone call." Lincoln stands. "And now I've got to run."

Buford still looks mildly alarmed. "You sure you're OK?" he asks.

"I'm fine. I'm glad you looked me up."

Buford stands and reaches in his pocket. For the third time in their brief relationship, he hands Lincoln a business card. "I really think your spirit could use some soothing," Buford says. "Here. This really works. Trust me." Decorated with a sketch of a tiny bouquet, the card reads in part:

POETRY & YOGA
The mind-body solution
for taming stress
Prof. Antonio Buford

"Why don't you give me a try?" Buford says.

"I may," Lincoln promises, stuffing the card in his pocket and hurrying out to set his redemption in motion.

But first he's got to find Amy. An e-mail bounces back. Her old cell phone is disconnected. A visit to her building reveals she's already moved out. Lincoln searches the Internet listings for O'Malleys in the south suburbs, hoping to locate her parents, but several dozen households show up with that name. Eventually, he bolsters himself and calls Kim at the switchboard at Pistakee. She sounds surprised but mildly pleased to hear from him. Between putting him on hold to take other calls, she shoots her questions about what he's been up to. Finally he blurts his query—does she know where to reach Amy?

"Wow, you're not dating anymore?" Kim gasps.

"No." (Unspoken: we never were, you moron.) "That's not really the way it was. I was just sort of her…mentor."

"I heard she was working in a restaurant, but I don't know where," Kim confides.

Lincoln can't believe he's stumped in an age when everything from your credit card to your DNA is out there for the taking. He's about to start calling down the list of south suburban O'Malleys when he hits on a long shot. He calls the English

Department at the U of C and explains to a friendly secretary that he's an alum and a book editor and he's very eager to locate a certain recent graduate whose work he admires. "Do you happen to know Amy O'Malley?" he asks.

"Amy!" the woman cries. "One of our favorites. She was in just last week."

"Oh, good," Lincoln says in a paternal voice, trying not to sound like a sex maniac or a serial killer, since the secretary is probably not allowed to give out personal information.

"She was asking for a recommendation. She's applying to graduate school."

"Marvelous. In English, I assume."

"No," the secretary says, "I'm afraid we've lost her. Social work. She wants to get a masters in social work."

So it happened, Lincoln thinks. I drove her out of the writing business. "Did she by chance leave an e-mail address or a telephone number?" he asks innocently (but really, how often does a sex maniac target English majors?).

"I don't have anything. Maybe Professor Weinberg knows, but he's out this week."

"Darn," says Lincoln.

"She said she has her days free because she's working nights at a restaurant."

"Did she happen to say where?"

"Ohhhh." The poor woman really wants to help. "She said it was a sushi place on the North Side. Oh, I'll never remember the name. Something Japanese. She said she was the only Caucasian waitress there. Let's see...I think she said it was on George Street."

"Thank you," says Lincoln. "Thank you."

"I hope you find her. Do you want to publish her?"

"We'll see, perhaps. We'll see."

With a little Internet scouting, Lincoln narrows the likely spot to Mika Sushi at George near Seminary, a restaurant he's never patronized. That night, a Thursday, he takes a cab there. The restaurant is bright and modest, one large room with unadorned white walls and a sushi bar on one side. It's doing a good business this evening. Lincoln gets a small table in front. Moments later, Amy emerges from the kitchen carrying two platters of sushi, her face gripped in fierce concentration as she maneuvers her load through the swinging doors. Lincoln is jolted by a shot of nostalgia—or *some* resounding emotion. He remembers that intense look from the Lunker Motel when they were locked together on the rewrite, and he feels an overwhelming impulse to run up and throw his arms around her. In fact, the urge hits him so powerfully that he's afraid if he actually did it he'd squeeze hard enough to crack one of her ribs. What's that about? When Amy spots him, he beckons her with a nod and a smile, but she throws him a look of exasperation and hurries to a table in the back. Feeling slightly embarrassed, Lincoln orders a beer from his waitress and pretends to study the menu. A few minutes later, he senses Amy standing beside him.

"I can't talk to you, John," she says. "We're busy tonight."

"No problem. Just checking in." He smiles again but can't penetrate her hostility.

"You're never that innocent," she tells him.

"Hey, I just wanted to catch up. We've been through a lot together."

"And I've worked hard to put it all behind me."

Lincoln's waitress comes up. She's a stunning young Japanese woman dressed, like Amy, in Mika's uniform of a white blouse and black skirt. She seems to think that Amy wants to steal a customer because she positions herself between Amy and Lincoln and pulls out her notepad. "You order," she says to Lincoln in accented English. Amy wheels and disappears into the kitchen.

Lincoln eats his sushi dinner while reading an old paperback of William Kennedy's *Ironweed*. ("Riding up the winding road of Saint Agnes Cemetery in the back of the rattling old truck, Francis Phelan became aware that the dead, even more than the living, settled down in neighborhoods." Now, there's a classy opening, Lincoln thinks.) At one point, Amy approaches his table. "This is stupid," she says.

"Why?"

"You're going to get me fired again."

"You quit, remember?"

She retreats once more to the kitchen.

Lincoln can't parse her anger, but he knows Amy well enough, has felt the heat of her ambition at close enough hand, to be fairly confident that he'll win her over eventually—if not tonight, then another night or another. As he's paying his bill, she comes by yet again. "I get off in an hour," she tells him tartly. "Meet me at the Golden Nugget on Clark." She walks away before he can respond.

At the Golden Nugget, an overbright and characterless twenty-four-hour diner, Lincoln nurses a coffee and his Kennedy at a booth near a window. Despite the iciness from Amy, he worries that when he sees her, he'll get hit by another nostalgic thunderbolt, or whatever it was, so he keeps an eye on the street to prep himself for her arrival. Assortments of noisy young people wander in and out, refugees of the bars in the neighborhood. Amy shows up just after an hour. She hangs her coat on a hook and slides into the booth opposite Lincoln. Again, something inside explodes, and he worries that she can hear his heart drumming against his chest. He'd forgotten—or, at least, shelved in his memory—Amy's physical allure. The trim blouse and skirt of the waitress uniform emphasize her gentle curves, and she's cut her hair and combed it behind her ears in a sleek style that seems very Japanese to Lincoln. This is *business*, he reminds himself. Stay on message.

"I know why you're here," she says, sounding world-weary.

"You do?"

"You want to publish my book on your stupid website."

This sets Lincoln back momentarily. "How did you know where I was working?"

"Word gets around. Nothing escapes Google."

"Well..." he starts.

She interrupts. "Can I get something here?"

Lincoln calls over the waitress, and Amy orders tea. Waiting for it to arrive, she delivers her speech. "I've spent a lot of time thinking about my career, my plans, what I want to do. And I've decided I want to help people. I've got this sympathy that I want to exercise. That's what makes me happy. That's my calling. This whole writing thing—it was a fantasy that was never really me. I mean, everyone writes short stories in college, and the smart ones move on to the real world. All I needed was a little taste of the publishing business to come to my senses. God, John—the egos, the selfishness, the *failure* rate. Who needs it?"

"You have talent," Lincoln urges.

"I was clueless when I met you. So naïve. I've grown up."

"That was six months ago."

"Disappointing my parents, the whole disaster at Pistakee—you can learn an incredible amount from trauma."

Lincoln reads this as a swipe at their age differences. He's the old washout, thwarted in his hopes, cuckolded in his personal life. Covered with calluses that block out insight, lock in ignorance. Her insult pains, but he braces and pulls out his own speech. "You *are* talented. That's not idle flattery. How many other people at twenty-two years old have written an entire novel? That took talent *and* discipline. You deserve to get your book out there. Other people should see it. Let it compete in the marketplace. I think it's good, but if it isn't, then you'll know. You can move on without any regrets or second thoughts. But you should at least try—try once. And the thing is, this is so simple and painless. We'll post it. And maybe no one will even notice. Chances are, no one will notice. Your parents will probably never even know. Unless it's a hit, of course, and then they'll be proud. But don't quit now. Don't turn into a loser before your time."

As Amy sits there, a slight, impulsive smile flutters around the edges of her mouth. Lincoln assumes his flattering argument has won her over. "You are relentless, John," she responds after a slight pause. "You tire me out just to listen to you. You never let go. You're going to be eighty years old, living in some miserable, smelly one-room apartment, and you'll still be maneuvering to get your big literary break. You're perfect for Chicago. You always talk about New York, but you belong right here."

"Now you're trying to hurt me," Lincoln says, not kidding.

"Haven't you read history? The people who built this town were all just like you—Easterners, driven by ambition, mostly to impress the folks they'd left back home. They built the place out of a swamp, and when it burned down, they built it back up again. They were literally mad with ambition. But you know what? We only hear about the ones who made it big. Think of the hundreds of thousands of guys like you who wore themselves down to the bone promoting their great plans and never got anywhere." She pauses after this outburst, then adds, "That's the real Chicago. And we never hear about them."

In the neon brightness of the diner, Lincoln thinks he sees little tracer bullets of light firing on him from Amy's soft brown eyes. He's too wounded to say anything, but he feels his face sagging, his whole covering of flesh slipping from his skeleton, puddling at the bones of his feet.

Amy says, "Oh, go ahead, publish the fucking book. I can't stand to see you this way."

"Really?" Lincoln is slow to rebound.

"Just don't use my name." She glances around the room, as if looking for something. "Use Alice. I always liked that name. Say the book is by Alice Somebody-or-other."

"Ahhh." The idea trampolines around Lincoln's mind. Why *not* use a pseudonym? Many have done it before. Who cares? "OK!"

"But keep me out of it," she orders.

"I promise."

She meets his look of flushed excitement with a frown registering somewhere between disgust and resignation. "Then it's all yours," Amy tells him.

27

LINCOLN WORRIES, SLIGHTLY, ABOUT IMPOSING *THE ULTIMATE Position* on his new employers—the book doesn't exactly fall within the mystery/thriller range, after all—but the iAgatha gang is happy to post it, and they offer to dispense with the upfront fees because the author is Lincoln's friend. Even before the book goes up, Sammy reads the manuscript and pronounces it outstanding. "I really think this is the best thing we've published, literarily," she says. "It's so well-written, and so *sexy*. I'd like to meet the author."

Her name is Alice Upshaw, and she's not so much Lincoln's friend as a casual acquaintance, a friend of a friend who came to Lincoln because he's in publishing. She's young-ish (Lincoln isn't sure of her exact age), single (he, too, is impressed at her remarkable sexual fluency), and shy almost to the point of being a recluse. "I promised to do everything in my power to protect her privacy," Lincoln tells his colleagues. The author blurb he writes says simply, "Alice Upshaw lives in Chicago. This is her first novel."

Lincoln offers to pay for a designer to create an attractive cover, and Sammy gives the job to a Wicker Park friend. Inspired by the title, the artist comes back with a lovely line drawing of a bell curve that morphs into the shapely silhouette of a woman.

The Ultimate Position gets posted in late March. On the day it goes up, Lincoln stays away from the office—he's made such a point of playing the calm, elder statesman of the publishing business that he can't stand to have his colleagues witness his anxiety. Alone in his apartment, he gets no work done, returning again and again to the iAgatha website to check on sales (the first copy gets bought within an hour!), then taking long, diversionary walks on the slushy streets of the North Side, forcibly removing himself from access to his computer. When Lincoln returns to his apartment at about seven that evening, *The Ultimate Position* has sold a total of three copies.

Over the following days, sales poke along at a slightly elevated iAgatha rate—seven by the end of the first week—but lag most of the outright entertainments that Lincoln has edited, despite enthusiastic promotions on Facebook and Twitter. He tries rewriting the marketing blurb, virtually eliminating any mention of Jennifer's pursuit of pleasure in favor of hyping the mystery of the sexual predator. Sales drop to two the next week, and one purchaser posts a comment: "This book belongs on an English department curriculum. I quit college to get away from crap like this. Take it off the site!"

"I suppose I should accept that as a compliment," Amy tells Lincoln when she calls two days later. "I've been looking around iAgatha, and I'm not sure that's the sort of company I like to keep."

"That's not you at the party," Lincoln reminds her. "That's Alice Upshaw."

"I feel protective of the poor girl."

"Did you just see the comment?" Lincoln asks. "Most authors check sales every day, if not every hour."

"I wasn't kidding when I told you I was moving on. I never told my parents the book was being published, my friends, anyone. Remember, you promised to keep it a secret."

"No one will ever know."

"No one will ever read it," says Amy with a genuine laugh.

"The book could still get hot," Lincoln points out, somewhat defensively. But the books that become iAgatha successes inevitably catch fire immediately, following an alchemic law that none of the principals can explain. *Warranty for Torture*, for example, a plotless hodgepodge about an ex-con who inflicts revenge on the savage prison guards who tyrannized him, sold almost a hundred copies the first day on its way to more than two thousand, an iAgatha record that continues to climb. Jimmy, Wade, Sammy, and even Lincoln have pored over the elements of the book's success—the writing, the title, the blurb, the author's bio (he's a middle-aged criminal lawyer from Cleveland whose expertise on the grotesque infliction of pain remains unexplained)—without finding any wisdom. Gorier iAgatha offerings have languished.

Lincoln's bruised defiance prompts Amy to console him. "I feel bad for you, John. You put so much work into this and had such high hopes. I hope you don't get too discouraged. You'll still find your hit; I know you will."

"Thanks," he tells her. "I'm doing fine." In fact, he may not be doing *fine*, but he's doing *OK*, a close distinction that Lincoln has pointed out to himself over the last few days. The paltry response to *The Ultimate Position* hasn't devastated him. He's disappointed, but less so than he once would have imagined. Losing your wife to another man, getting bushwhacked in your job—setbacks like those don't just temper your moods, Lincoln realizes, they crowd the space you have to dream, to fantasize, to seek pleasure. Too many memories, regrets, fragments of conversation, thoughts left unsaid. It's a wonder anyone gets anything done. At least he's doing *OK*. "It's sweet of you to think of me," he tells Amy.

"Good-bye, John," she says in a way that sounds final.

And then *The Ultimate Position* stages a rally. Sammy happens to talk up the book to Draco DiVergilio, iAgatha's annoyingly overbearing blogger. He likes it and devotes a posting to it, calling the novel "a mind tease with more terror and sex than ever shows up in any *Friday the 13*th movie." Draco concludes: "*The Ultimate Position* provides a lesson to all you wannabe thriller writers serving up buckets of blood and heaps of body parts: just as the brain is the greatest aphrodisiac, so is it the best source of thrills."

Draco's comments give *The Ultimate Position* a nice boost—34 copies the first day, 112 within a week. A handful of readers complain in comments that the book is too highbrow to count as a real thriller, but the majority of people who weigh in on iAgatha.com seem to like it, and several salute the psychological depth of the characters. One person, commenting under the handle hotpants911, makes the point, "Alice Upshaw shows that sex can be as mysterious and scary as murder!"

Out of curiosity, Lincoln searches out the bona fides of Draco DiVergilio, that condescending asshole and discerning critic. A little work on the Internet yields the secret that he is really Edmund Hermanson, U of C '82, BA English. God bless the old alma mater, Lincoln thinks.

Around that time, Lincoln visits the iAgatha offices, and Jimmy pulls him aside. "I was getting ready to pay Alice Upshaw her first royalties, and I saw that all the contact information is for you," he tells Lincoln quietly. "What gives?"

Lincoln has planned for this contingency. As far as he knows, aside from Amy and him, the only people who saw the manuscript of *The Ultimate Position* were Duddleston, Gregor, the elderly copy editor, and Amy's mother. Mrs. O'Malley would never out her daughter as author. Gregor, the original cover designer, never reads a manuscript; he just works from what the editor tells him. The copy editor has subsequently moved to Arizona. And Duddleston? Even if, through a huge coincidence, he were to come upon the published book, Mr. Personal Discretion would never volunteer the secret—at least not without checking with Amy.

"Alice wanted it all to go through me," Lincoln explains to Jimmy. "I told you, she's neurotically private, and she didn't want to risk any detection."

"But the checks?"

"You can send them to me, and I will pass them on. I'll get a receipt from her to prove that I made the payment."

Jimmy cocks his head and carefully considers Lincoln. Over the course of working at iAgatha, Lincoln has come to realize that for all his mussed hair and youthful enthusiasm, Jimmy is quite shrewd and protective of the tiny publishing empire he has helped build. Plus, he's the son of a cop.

Lincoln adds, "There's not that much money at stake, anyway. If there's any kind of a problem, I'll make good on it."

"Whatever," says Jimmy, and he walks away.

Half an hour later, as Lincoln is leaving, Jimmy follows him into the hall, where they are alone. "So," he says, suppressing a smirk, "are *you* Alice Upshaw? Did you write that book?"

"God, no," says Lincoln, who has prepared for this question, too. "It's all Alice. Well, I gave her editing advice, but it's her book. Do you think I could write from a woman's point of view like that?"

"I suppose not," says Jimmy, amused by the situation. "But you know, there are some pretty weird people in Wicker Park."

"Not me," says Lincoln, adding after a silly laugh, "at least, not in *that* way. I'm just honoring the promise I gave Alice."

"Your secret is safe with me," Jimmy assures.

Lincoln considers alerting Amy to the uptick in her book's fortunes but chooses against it. She'd sounded so settled, so confident in her decision to move on in her life that he's wary of intruding. He feels a bit like an unwanted suitor. Besides, he suspects she's logged in to see what's going on, and she hasn't called to talk about it. He mails her a check for royalties with the simple note attached, "Buy yourself a bottle of good Scotch!"

He's been reluctant to press the book on Flam, but Flam asks about it several times, so—with Draco's nod bolstering Lincoln's confidence—he finally prints out a copy and sends it over to his friend at the *Tribune*. Then he hears nothing for a week. Finally, Flam calls: he's been too busy with book review work to read it, but he's about to go on a cruise up the Nile and he'll pack the manuscript.

"A cruise?" Lincoln asks, startled.

"Yes. A deal came up, and I've always been interested in Egyptology."

"You're going by yourself?"

"Why not?" Flam asks defensively. "I don't need a companion to certify my pleasure." Then he pauses and lets his guard down. "Besides, a cruise may not be a bad place to stir some romance—you know, meet a mature single woman traveling with her mother."

"Maybe in a nineteenth-century novel."

"You're too callow," Flam says. "You miss the transcendent verities."

"Send me a postcard," Lincoln tells his friend.

Ten days later, a postcard arrives. On one side is a photograph from 1887 showing two men—they must be English—in khaki traveling suits and pith helmets standing in front of the Great Sphinx at Giza. The men are tall, slender, slightly stooped—in shape and aspect, both are dead ringers for Flam himself. The note on the other side is brief: "Trip a delight. Ship infested with eligible spinster daughters, many trailing fat dowries. You may never see me again. Enjoying *The Ultimate Position*. Strong start. Eager to get to the sex parts. F."

By then, it's early May. With Draco's help, the book has sold 325 copies, but sales have tailed off. It's been more than a week since anyone has posted a comment. Lincoln understands the dynamic: *The Ultimate Position* has enjoyed a modest, brief run, and now the world has moved on. When he thinks back on the expectations he once built around the book, he feels slightly chagrined, as if at the end of a play he had stood to applaud noisily, urging the actors to repeat their bows, while the rest of the audience only tapped their palms together politely and shot him sullen stares from their seats, already worrying about getting their cars out of the garage, racing home to tuck in the kids, having a drink before bed. Still, he senses that he's learned something, even if he can't put it into words. In a small way, Lincoln's ordeal has eased. His arm doesn't ache as often.

28

LINCOLN TURNS THIRTY-FOUR ON A SATURDAY BY HIMSELF. His sister sends a card. His parents call. (His father, not unkindly: "By thirty-four, the die is pretty well cast. If you're going to change direction, it had better be soon.") Nothing from Mary. That morning, as usual, he tunes in WBEZ, the local NPR station, while he does the dishes and gets dressed. In the shower, he goes over his plans for the day—he'll do a few hours of work on an iAgatha manuscript from a lady in Lodi, California, and then take a bike ride up along the lake, past Evanston and on through the bejeweled towns of the North Shore. No real destination, just good exercise.

When Lincoln steps out of the shower, someone he knows is talking in the living room. Startled and anxious, Lincoln wraps himself in a towel and hurries out to see who's there. It's Tony Buford, being interviewed on BEZ. Apparently, Pistakee has published Buford's book of poems after all—Duddleston must have decided that publication was easier and cheaper than dealing with a lawsuit. Now the book is doing well by poetry's standards—Buford mentions casually that Pistakee already has gone back for a second printing.

How could Lincoln have been so wrong? He'd been embarrassed by the book and dreaded publishing it. Contemplating his monumental misjudgments, Lincoln stands dripping on the hardwood floor and grips the back of the sofa to steady himself.

The unctuous young woman conducting the interview fawns over the poet, lavishing compliments and pressing for the personal details that nursed his genius. "I've always been drawn to the masters of the everyday realm," Buford explains. "That goes back to some of the early Japanese practitioners of the haiku, who found solace in the quotidian life beneath the capricious hands of fate. And then all the way up through the plain-speakers of modern times, Robert Frost, Gwendolyn Brooks, Billy Collins."

The BEZ interviewer says breathlessly, "One of the fascinating things about this collection, if you don't mind my saying so, is that here you are, an African-American man from the South Side, this repository of black life and culture, and, really, there's very little that relates specifically to the African-American experience in any of your poems. Would you care to comment on that?"

"See," says Buford, "with the leaps in education, in mobility, and of course, with the advent of the Internet providing the democratization of information, we as a country are moving beyond simple classifications. Our common experience today is without hyphens, just American."

When the young woman asks Buford to read from *Still Life*, Lincoln discovers that Buford has amped up his presentation since the disastrous poetry slam. Now the poet declaims with the exaggerated excitement and wonder of a kindergarten teacher trying to interest a squirming class. After a minute or so, Lincoln turns off the radio in the middle of a poem about radishes. With Buford's voice still looping inside his skull, Lincoln hurries to dress and get onto his bike. He spends the whole day pedaling along the lakeshore, doing all he can to wear himself down to an exhausted nub.

That evening Lincoln stretches out on his sofa to soothe his aching muscles. Sipping vodka, he drifts through the day's *Tribune*. Several years ago, the paper moved the truncated books section to Saturday, and Lincoln sees that there's a page devoted to online publishing, just as Flam mentioned a few months ago. Glancing over the columns, Lincoln stops short and takes a slug of vodka. The *Tribune* has reviewed *The Ultimate Position*.

He recognizes the byline: Alden Fieldstone, an English professor at Beloit College.

The professor begins by worrying that online and digital publishing is too easy—too many careless books are being produced. "A good case in point is *The Ultimate Position*, a bildungsroman cum thriller cum sociological treatise cum sex manual written by a Chicagoan, Alice Upshaw." Fieldstone proceeds to obliterate the book, calling it "banal" and "tedious," crammed with "internal monologues that sound like Samantha from *Sex and the City* babbling to herself on the way home, alone, in a taxi after she's drunk too much and failed to pick up a man." Fieldstone concludes:

Ms. Upshaw has glommed together the beginnings of some fresh ideas about women's sexual exploration in the postfeminist era; she shows flashes of inventive language. None of her budding talent mattered, however. I suspect that it was too simple to publish the manuscript without a serious editor adding the slow layering of thought provided by the old-style book business. On my optimistic days, I hope that the new world of publishing will come to appreciate the value of strong editing. But for now, I fear we will be saddled with more techno-facilitated books like *The Ultimate Position*, which in its carelessness proves to be badly misnamed—*The Awkward Position* would be more like it.

Lincoln looks up. He has trouble focusing his eyes, and he hears a low buzzing in his ears. He feels as if he's been pummeled, although there's no overt pain.

He lies that way for more than an hour, getting up only once, to replenish his glass of vodka. His cell phone rings at about ten.

"Have you read it?" Amy asks.

"An hour ago."

"Just *an hour ago*?"

"It's been a long day. I was out."

"Well, what do you think?"

Lincoln knows he has to play this carefully. He can't read her voice—is she devastated? Furious? He says weakly, "Actually, there are a couple of phrases we could cull from here for an ad: 'fresh ideas about women's sexual exploration;' 'inventive language.' "

"John, that's one of the worst reviews I've ever seen," Amy cries, but she's laughing.

"Yeah, you're right, it is pretty bad."

"Thank god my name isn't on it." Another laugh.

"Yeah, you lucked out."

"And the *Tribune* doesn't usually run critical reviews."

"No, not very often."

"Aren't you friends with the editor of the book review? Isn't he your best friend?"

Lincoln lets go of a deep breath. He knows how easy it would be for suspicions to start swirling in Amy's mind, conspiracy theories. "It doesn't work like that," he explains. "The editor can assign the book, but he's pretty much got to take what comes in. Flam can't just impose his opinions." He pauses. "Besides, he's been away for a couple of weeks."

Yes, Flam has been away, but in bits of Professor Fieldstone's observations, Lincoln detects echoes of his friend. Is Flam trying to tell him something?

"Well, I'm really glad I made you keep my name off the book," Amy repeats. "Poor Alice Upshaw! If she were around, she'd be humiliated."

"The pathetic irony," Lincoln continues, "is that the book got *huge* editorial help—at least as much as I ever gave a book in print. Probably more."

"That's not ironic," Amy corrects him before hanging up. "That's just fucked."

Lincoln, too, is glad that his name isn't on *The Ultimate Position*, but he worries that his colleagues at iAgatha may see the review and wonder about the quality of editorial advice he is being paid to hand out. No problem. The iAgatha principals don't read newspapers, and the books they publish are so obscure that no one has bothered to set up a Google alert on the titles. The review passes unnoticed, with no impact on sales. So much for the adage that any kind of publicity is good publicity. Like almost everything else in Lincoln's life, *The Ultimate Position* has turned out to be a sparrow fart.

The mystery of the one seeming exception gets solved a few days later. Lincoln is visiting the iAgatha office when Sammy yells over to him, "Hey, that guy who kept calling you here is in the news."

She's staring at her computer screen. Lincoln looks over her shoulder. She's opened an item on the Huffington Post Chicago site. Beneath the headline "A Picture Is Worth a Thousand Books," a photograph shows Michelle Obama's mother, Marian Robinson, sitting stiffly in a tall wing chair in a slightly formal interior setting, perhaps the White House. Clearly visible on her lap is a copy of *Still Life* by Antonio Buford. Thanks to Gregor's serendipitous cover design, the title pops visually. The HuffPo account reveals that the book had languished until someone happened to send a copy to Mrs. Robinson. By chance, an AP photographer snapped her reading it, and sales took off. The White House wouldn't comment on the book's success, but Buford told the reporter, "I have heard through friends that Michelle's mother reads from it to Malia and Sasha every night."

Lincoln lets out a low, soft whistle.

"You know him, right?" Sammy says.

"Yes," says Lincoln carefully. "Yes, I know him."

"Maybe we can get him to write a mystery for us," Sammy enthuses. "Wouldn't it be fantastic if he could get the president to endorse one of our books?"

Lincoln thinks: I'm surrounded by children.

Partly to avoid being pressed to recruit Tony Buford, Lincoln stops dropping by the iAgatha office—it's more efficient to work at home, in any case. Needy writers (the supply is endless) continue to populate his iAgatha inbox with their artless manuscripts. Several clients are already back with their second book, and Vijay Sharma, Jaipur's answer to James Patterson, has warned that his eponymous private eye is about to launch his third assault on the corrupt Raj. Lincoln has developed the ritual—no matter the quality of the finished manuscript—of sending the books he edits off into the world with a simultaneous note of encouragement to the author: "Something you can really be proud of!" "1,000% improved!" "A pleasure to see the novel take shape!" He thinks of these remarks as the verbal equivalents of smiley faces, but he's astonished how often the authors respond with earnest gratitude.

And the work pours in. Some days Lincoln only leaves the apartment to jog or ride his bike. Occasionally, he joins Flam for dinner at Barleycorn. (The Fieldstone review remains unremarked between them. Flam is perhaps regretful, and Lincoln prefers to leave open the suggestion that he never saw it, the *Tribune* being such an insignificant player in the world of letters.) More often, though, Lincoln eats alone at home and then turns to another hour or so of editing after dinner. His clients need him.

On one such night, he finishes up an edit memo for a public defender in Florida (premise: the DA prosecuting the murder actually committed it) and then opens the iAgatha home page to see what else has come in. On a whim, he clicks on *The Ultimate Position* for the first time in several weeks to see what's happened to sales. They've skyrocketed! More than one thousand in the last week alone. Lincoln scrolls down through the comments to try to find some explanation and sees a reference to a website, JennifersUltimatePosition.com. Right away, Lincoln senses trouble. He types the address into the computer and up pops a crude site with a constantly evolving cartoon of a busty naked woman assuming a variety of sexual poses—presumably as a prelude to testing their relative advantages. The title "Jennifer's Ultimate Position" scrawls across the top of the page, and on close inspection, Lincoln sees that each letter is formed by tiny naked women poised for sex.

The site explains itself in big type right at the top: "For millennia, men and women have sought the secret holy grail of ecstasy, the perfect sexual position for maximizing pleasure for both partners. Most of us have searched quietly over the years in private, but recently a beautiful and forthright fictional character, Jennifer Blythe, in a visionary new novel, *The Ultimate Position*, brought the pursuit of the Ultimate Position into the open. With Jennifer's inspiration, we can share our insights. This site is dedicated to questers."

Scores, probably hundreds, of people have weighed in with their nominations, many of them described in intricate physiological detail and most accompanied by photographs or crude line drawings. Many postings have attracted long commentary tails. A link on the side goes directly back to the iAgatha site and the sales page for *The Ultimate Position*.

Lincoln searches for indications of the site's proprietors. No names, no hints. Then he lingers briefly over the submitted illustrations (does the erect male penis really bend in that direction?), before sending off an e-mail to Jimmy: Why didn't anyone alert me?

Jimmy texts back quickly but elusively through his new iPhone: "We actually just recently noticed it ourselves!!!"

Lincoln texts to Jimmy: "Isn't somebody monitoring sales?"

Now, Jimmy is slower to respond, though Lincoln knows the iPhone is welded to Jimmy's hand. After about twenty minutes (time to allow a consultation with the other principals?): "Sales are going great, and we were afraid you would want us to take the book down."

Lincoln: "Why would you think that?"

Jimmy: "Because that site is pretty nasty, and we were afraid Alice Upshaw would be mad."

Lincoln lets the correspondence drop. Yes, Alice would be mad. Furious, in fact. But what's Lincoln to do? If he insists that iAgatha stop selling the book, he'll probably raise more questions with Jimmy and the others about this mysterious author.

Lincoln returns to JennifersUltimatePosition.com. Some of the illustrations are rankly pornographic, but most of the really raunchy stuff comes in the comment tail, as men (obviously) weigh in on the merits of the nominations. The remarks, defiled by typos and misspellings, provide a raw profile of the male psyche. For example, there's the substantial niche who seem to assume that women derive pleasure from being doused on the face with ejaculate. Doggie style, if not outright anal, is widely popular, and an unpleasant faction favors S&M (apparently, a Wi-Fi connection has reached Hell, and now the Marquis de Sade can post through eternity). Lincoln browses for several minutes looking for a posting that's clearly from a woman. No luck—if women are visiting, they aren't leaving DNA. Lincoln is far from a prude—he's visited plenty of porn sites—but this site is supposed to be devoted to equality of ecstasy. He clicks off when he starts to feel really cruddy about the passions lurking in his gender.

Still, half an hour later, when Jimmy texts, "How about it? Can we keep on selling the book?" Lincoln responds, "Yeah." What good would halting sales do now? The damage is done—pages live forever on the Web. He'll ration out royalties to Amy so the spike in sales won't be apparent, and maybe she'll never know. With luck, the whole faddish commotion will fade in a few weeks.

It doesn't. Sales don't increase, but they stay steady at the elevated pace. Questers for the Ultimate Position apparently keep buying. It pains Lincoln to see the work that he and Amy labored over so earnestly—in which they invested their literary sensibilities—turned into a manifesto for sexually adventurous frat boys. He checks in every day, perhaps the first editor in the history of publishing to hope to see a decline in the fortunes of one of his books.

One afternoon, he comes in from a jog along the lakefront and plops into the chair in front of his computer. He has a message in his e-mail inbox from Cheryl Romano, the enterprising young arts columnist for *The Reader*, an alternative Chicago weekly. "Dear Mr. Lincoln," she writes. "As you certainly have noticed, the novel *The Ultimate Position* has become a minor hit and inspired a pornographic website, JennifersUltimatePosition. I'd like to find out how the writer, Alice Upshaw, feels about it. Your colleague, Jimmy Englehardt, said you know Ms. Upshaw. Could you put me in touch?"

Lincoln ignores the request. Cheryl Romano probably pursues a dozen stories a week. If he stays low, maybe she'll move on to something else. But the next afternoon, she returns to his inbox. "Dear Mr. Lincoln, You no doubt saw my e-mail from yesterday and disregarded it. So I will come right to the point: Are you Alice Upshaw?"

This is not a crisis—not yet. Lincoln spends an hour or so crafting a brief reply. "No, Cheryl, I am not Alice Upshaw. Some authors simply prefer to stay out of the public eye, to let their work speak for itself. Frankly, I think we should respect that attitude—as unfashionable as it is these days—particularly in instances, such as the present, when anonymous opportunists have crudely hijacked the material. *The Ultimate Position* should be allowed to manage on its own."

Two sentences of fact, two of mild opinion. No lies. His father the lawyer would admire the skill. Lincoln clicks the SEND button, and within seconds Cheryl Romano responds: "Oh, come on, get off it."

Now, Lincoln is worried. Someone (Jimmy?) has obviously planted the suggestion that Lincoln is Alice. What if Cheryl Romano, despite his denial, writes an item that points the finger at him? Local bloggers will get on the case no doubt—there's never enough to write about in Chicago. He sees himself led down a pathway of more evasions and half-truths until he's finally strangled by his own obfuscations.

Lincoln calls Jimmy, who denies, somewhat unconvincingly, that he's Cheryl Romano's source. Jimmy promises that if she calls, he will join in assuring that Lincoln is not Alice. "And tell Sammy and Wade, too!" Lincoln orders.

"Will do!"

Then Lincoln sends another e-mail to Cheryl Romano. He warns that she would be making a colossal blunder by identifying him as Alice. He types, "Alice is a talented artist of some fragility and needs and deserves her privacy." On reflection, he thinks, no, that will just encourage the frenzy, and he deletes the sentence. Instead, he types, "A mistake of that sort will attach to you and drag down your career, if not end it."

Harsh, but possibly effective, since she is just starting out. Lincoln pushes SEND.

Then nothing. He waits with some anxiety until Wednesday evening, when the latest edition of *The Reader* gets posted on the Web. After Lincoln visits the site on and off for several hours, the issue finally appears, and he clicks through to Cheryl Romano's column. An item about an upcoming show at the Museum of Contemporary Art and another short piece on a new jazz program on the Loyola University radio station. Nothing about *The Ultimate Position.*

Lincoln clicks off feeling slightly amused. Chicago. The reporters here are sheep.

29

A WEEK LATER, A THURSDAY, A FEROCIOUS POUNDING WAKENS Lincoln early. At first he thinks he's dreaming, then he imagines a neighbor has started a construction project. There's a pause in the commotion, and Lincoln glances at the clock: 6:22. Then the hammering erupts again. His door.

Lincoln rolls stiffly out of bed and lurches to the living room in his underwear. More pounding. He opens the door a crack. Amy stands on the landing, her face scarlet, her right arm cocked to pound some more. She waves a newspaper at Lincoln. "Have you seen this?" she demands.

"What?"

"*The Reader*. They've outed me." She slaps the paper against his chest. "They've turned me into a porn star!"

Lincoln opens the door wide. He's aware that he's naked except for his boxers, that his eyes are pasted with sleep and his breath is sulfurous.

Amy stomps into the apartment. "Listen," she orders and starts reading aloud. "No one ever accused the University of Chicago of being a hotbed of sexual adventure, but it turns out a young female English major has written a book that's turning on male fantasies around the globe..."

"Wait!" says Lincoln holding up his hand. "Wait. Let me read it."

Amy slams the newspaper into his palm. "I've lost my job. My family thinks I'm a slut. The *Tribune* trashed my book. And now I'm a secret pornographer, and everybody knows it!"

"Just hold on," pleads Lincoln.

"You've ruined my life," she cries. "Is this what you wanted?" Her face is so red and pulsating that Lincoln can't be sure whether her head is going to explode or just start gushing blood. "Are you happy now?"

The question echoes for Lincoln, hooking something, a memory.

When he remains blankly silent, she repeats, turning up the volume, "Are you happy now?"

She stands with her knees slightly bent, one leg in front of the other, her arms tensed at her sides. Amy never played sports seriously, but she's assumed a classic athletic posture, poised for either offense or defense. Lincoln recalls the tautness of her body, the grace with which she romped across her bed that first night together. Afterward, she'd asked…the echo. We live in circles. "Sit down, take your coat off," he tells her.

"I don't want to take my coat off, and I can't sit. I'm too upset."

"Suit yourself," he says soothingly. "But give me a minute to get dressed, and then I'll read it."

Lincoln goes to his bedroom and pulls on a pair of jeans and a T-shirt. In the bathroom, he takes a pee, splashes water on his face, and brushes his teeth. When he returns to the living room, Amy is standing beside the door, as if she's about to leave. Her hands are in her coat pockets. Her hair is uncombed, and of course she's not wearing makeup. He looks to see if she's been crying, but her eyes are clear and angrily focused on him.

"All right, let's take a look," he says in the tone of an examining physician. He picks up the copy of *The Reader*, this week's edition, and sits in the easy chair. Cheryl Romano's latest column carries the headline "Mystery Solved."

No one ever accused the University of Chicago of being a hotbed of sexual adventure, but it turns out a young female English major has written a book that's turning on male fantasies around the globe. At least the evidence points to that young literary grad, who has managed to keep her identity secret until now.

The mystery first unfolded two months ago when iAgatha.com, a local online publisher, released *The Ultimate Position*, a book in which two college girls "explore the outer edges of sexual pleasure," as the promotional blurb put it. The purported author was named Alice Upshaw. No one seemed to pay much attention except some weirdo webbie types (as yet unknown), who built a porn site, JennifersUltimatePosition.com, based on the sexual journey of one of the book's characters. The site allows viewers to upload their wildest fantasies. Why am I not surprised that all those viewers turn out to be men? Anyway, sales of *The Ultimate Position* suddenly rocketed, which raised the question, Who is this siren of sexual extremes, this pornographer's muse, this mysterious "Alice Upshaw"? For weeks, Chicago's literary community has been asking that question.

Now a source tells *The Reader* that a sexy novel titled *The Ultimate Position* was scheduled to be published by the Chicago house Pistakee Press this spring. It was written by an associate editor at Pistakee, Amy O'Malley. The book was suddenly withdrawn when the author abruptly left the company. The reasons are not known, but she left on the same day as a Pistakee editor, John Lincoln, who soon turned up as a writing coach at iAgatha.com. Hmmmm. The source said, "It's the same book, word for word." Lincoln was elusive with me in several e-mails, but my source said, "He was, like, Amy's mentor."

And who is Amy O'Malley? She graduated cum laude last year. A classmate recalls, "She was really obsessed by literature, but I don't remember her being into sex at all. This is really weird." O'Malley is apparently lying low—she could not be reached.

But, hey, Amy, don't be shy. Porn is the money engine of the Web, and now you're a star! All the guys want to get a good look at the temptress who's stoked their fantasies. Come out and take a bow!

Lincoln is finished reading, but he doesn't look up. The paper has found a photo of Amy, probably something from an old U of C yearbook. The picture is not much bigger than a postage stamp, but there she is—the mussy, layered hair, the unpainted face, the overserious frown of childish concentration. Lincoln can't take his eyes away. The Ruffed Grouse.

"Well?" Amy demands. "Well?"

"You could look at it this way," Lincoln offers weakly. "*The Reader* still has a decent circulation. You'll sell a lot more copies of the book, make more money."

Wrong argument.

"My mother saw it!" Amy shrieks. "Her friend called to warn her! They've both looked at that awful website! I feel...I feel...violated!"

Lincoln scrambles for something to cool her fever. "Look," he says firmly. "The whole thing is nonsense. In the first place, this article is stupid—calling you a porn muse. You're a writer. And you wrote a good book that's not pornographic, it's literary. In the second place, well, none of us can control our reputations anymore. Anything we do—it's just out there, for anyone to make of it what they will. Through Google, on Facebook. You can't control it. You'd go nuts trying to."

Amy starts to protest, but Lincoln holds up his hand. "And the third thing is," he hurries on, "nobody cares! A hundred years ago, *ten* years ago, the world would have been horrified. But now everything's fodder, everything about everybody. We all have our turns at being demeaned. You've heard of Andy Warhol's fifteen minutes of fame? Now, everybody gets fifteen minutes of infamy, and afterward no one gives a shit or even remembers."

Lincoln's logic seems to calm the scene. Amy purses her lips, thinking. The scarlet on her face eases toward pink. She drops onto the sofa. Lincoln is secretly congratulating himself when she says mournfully, "But you promised you'd keep me out of it."

"I tried," he offers helplessly.

"You were always the miserable one," Amy says vacantly, addressing him but talking to herself, as if he is such a failure as a human being that his presence doesn't even register; he's a dust mite, a flyspeck. "You were the one who hated everything, who was too good for everything. Not me. I was fine. Whatever happened, it was an adventure." She shakes her head slowly. "I don't want to be like you."

Lincoln has never seen her this way—hollow, lifeless. "Amy?" he says, worried.

She stands. "I've got to go."

"You don't want any tea or breakfast? I could cook eggs."

She hurries to the door.

"Amy, are you all right?" Lincoln asks.

She steps outside quickly, as if she's suddenly realized that Lincoln and his apartment are scenes of contagion that she must flee. She turns to him and says flatly, "Missionary position."

"What?"

"I wanted to tell you after I saw that awful website. The girl my freshman year who searched for the Ultimate Position? In the end she decided it was the missionary position. I didn't tell you before because I thought you'd be disappointed."

"Jesus," gasps Lincoln.

"Now you know." Amy starts down the steps but stops and looks back. "Please leave me alone," she says, then hurtles off, clasping the banister so she won't fall. Her footsteps, pounding on the wood stairway, rain down on Lincoln's head like blows until she is out of the building.

30

LINCOLN HIDES OUT IN HIS APARTMENT. THROUGHOUT THE days following Amy's visit and well into the anguished, aspirin-glutted nights, he sits at his desk, trying to cocoon himself with work. He often feels chilled, for no good reason other than his frozen spirit, and since he can't wrap himself in electronic manuscripts, he drapes a scratchy L.L.Bean blanket over his shoulders, looking like FDR in Warm Springs, waiting for death.

Marissa Morgan and other Chicago bloggers follow up on *The Reader's* report, and even the *Tribune's* culture blog runs an item. Most accounts summon a gassy tone of moral outrage aimed at Lincoln—the "mentor," the presumed impresario of the deception—chiding him for his lack of honesty, for supposedly trying to put one over on the world. Somehow, without Lincoln's realizing it, utter transparency has become the obligatory ethical standard for all behavior that reaches the public, and violators face censure and shame across cyberspace, the digital equivalent of pillories and stocks. Marissa Morgan sniffs that Lincoln, "one of Chicago's most experienced book editors," has broken the "publisher's pledge of intimacy" with readers by lying about the name of the real author. An overheated blogger on a politically lefty site sees the evil profit motive behind the whole plot and likens Lincoln to the "fat Wall Street leeches who nearly brought down the economy"—as if selling a book by Alice Upshaw instead of Amy O'Malley was the equivalent of peddling worthless financial instruments that no one understood. The *Tribune*'s post pursues the cranky theme introduced by Professor Fieldstone and wonders if the Internet's "democratization of writing means that book publishing will become as tainted with fakes and fraud as voting in Chicago."

Lincoln tries different tacks with the writers, speaking frankly to some, on background to others, refusing to comment to still others. No matter. Nothing draws eyeballs like outrage, and Lincoln represents a plump and easy target. Soon he comes to feel a bonding with James Frey. Several times Lincoln visits the Oprah website to study photos of the author's woeful face as he undergoes the necessary public debasement at the hands of the talk-show star.

But it's not simply the bad publicity that torments Lincoln—he realizes now that he can handle the dents in his reputation, that there was actually truth in the little speech he gave Amy about everyone being demeaned and nobody caring. Rather, what pains Lincoln is that he's dragged Amy down with him, pulled her into his pathetic game. Blindly pursuing his ambition, he's corrupted an innocent. He can't stop thinking about her helpless exasperation, the cry of a child: "But you promised…!" Lincoln feels as if the last threads of his honor, his *virtue*, are tearing away.

This, too, shall pass, Lincoln's father had assured. No, Lincoln thinks. The Chinese may be entering their century, but they got that aphorism wrong. "This" remains and just keeps getting worse.

Tony Buford calls the day Marissa Morgan weighs in. Lincoln hasn't heard from him in weeks and had come to assume that the poet's bonhomie was an act that lasted only as long as Lincoln could be useful. But Buford starts right in with support. "Silliness," he announces without identifying himself.

"Uhhh." Lincoln recognizes the voice, but he's sunk to crippling, perhaps terminal, befuddlement.

"It's all silliness," Buford repeats. "I sent Marissa a note saying as much. What's your crime? Pseudonyms have a great tradition in literature—Mark Twain, Lewis Carroll, George Eliot. Hell, even Stephen King sometimes writes under Richard Bachman. The opportunism is astonishing."

"Opportunism?"

"Beat up on the little guy. The Marissa Morgans of the world would never think of going after Stephen King."

"I think the Internet has changed the culture," Lincoln suggests, rallying slightly from his stupor.

"Exactly. The feeding frenzy has become the norm, the ritual. Devour, lest ye be devoured. I keep thinking of Shirley Jackson's 'The Lottery.' " Buford pauses. "You surviving?" he asks.

"Sort of."

"That's not good enough. You've got to stay positive."

"Right."

"Take this moment as a learning opportunity, a chance to train yourself to keep focused. Think of it like going to the gym for a good workout."

The exhortations echo others Lincoln has heard—from Mary, from his father—and they only raise the tempo of his constantly pounding headache. To deflect Buford, Lincoln congratulates him on the success of his book.

"I couldn't have done it without you," the poet responds.

"Looks like you got some help from Marian Robinson, too."

Buford snorts a quick laugh. "I see the public stoning hasn't cured you of your cynicism," he says. "Well, if you must know, Mrs. Robinson is an acquaintance of my mother's. Whether that made a difference—who knows the way publicity works? But it all started with you. And I reminded Marissa of that. The point that everyone misses is that you're a great editor."

"Or was."

"Don't go there!" Buford admonishes. "Stay positive!"

Lincoln says he'll try.

Flam worries enough about his friend that he comes one night bearing two steaks and a bottle of 1999 Chateauneuf du Pape. "The whole thing is ridiculous," Flam says as they eat at the little round wood table in Lincoln's kitchen. "That *Tribune* blog—it was stupid on about six levels. Talk about making up news."

Lincoln shrugs. Pep talks can't reach him these days.

Flam has formulated his own media analysis to explain the suddenly toxic situation. "Sex," he says. "You add sex to the equation, and the bloggers go nuts—they can spin it any way they want."

"Sex," mumbles Lincoln.

"And another thing," Flam continues. "I find it interesting that the opprobrium has fallen entirely on you. I mean, where's the author in all this? It's as if the template for this offense carries the underlying presumption—like in sexual harassment cases—that the older male seduced the naïve girl into the vile deception."

Lincoln sips from the good wine. Oddly, he's been drinking less lately—some nights, his mind is racing so hard he just forgets to pour a drink. He tells Flam, "Maybe they can't find her. *I* could hardly find her. She's hard to get hold of."

Flam chews a piece of steak thoughtfully. "Maybe she's talked to them for background, and the price of her cooperation is that they keep her out of it," he suggests.

"I don't think she'd do that," Lincoln says after a moment. "She'd tell them how it was. She's loyal, even though she doesn't need to be."

"You really like this girl, don't you?"

"I feel I let her down."

Later, they sit in the living room. They've finished the wine and moved to the bottle of vodka Lincoln keeps in the freezer. The alcohol has loosened Lincoln, and they reminisce about their days together at the *Tribune*, their nights on the town before Lincoln met Mary, their rivalries, arguments, the pleasure they've shared in belittling the city that became their home. It occurs to Lincoln that, though they still qualify as young, they are like a couple of old men on a park bench, recalling friends and adventures long departed.

Lincoln declares finally, "Flam, I'm getting out of here. I know I've said it before, but now it's for real." There's no joy in the announcement, which Lincoln has been planning all evening. Just resignation. He's leaving in defeat. "The iAgatha folks are giving me a bonus because *The Ultimate Position* sold so well. As soon as the money comes through, I'm going to New York. Just going. No prospects, no plan. I may have to camp out in Central Park. But I'm going. My Chicago days are over."

How many times has Flam sat across from Lincoln—in a bar, at Barleycorn, at some other cheap and dim restaurant where they've eaten badly and drunk too much—and heard the same thing? This time, Flam says, "I know."

31

THREE DAYS LATER, A MONDAY, LINCOLN IS AT HIS COMPUter when his cell phone rings at around eleven in the morning.

"John?"

"Yes."

"This is Jeff Kessler from Malcolm House. You're a hard guy to contact."

Lincoln throws off the L.L.Bean blanket. "Yes, well, I've changed jobs," he blurts.

"I know. That's in part why I wanted to talk. But we didn't have your phone number or a private e-mail address. Finally, my assistant called the book editor at the *Tribune*, and fortunately, he had it."

"Flam?"

"Yes, I think that's it. Strange fellow, isn't he?"

"Sort of an acquired taste."

"Yes, well, here's the thing. We're looking to hire an editor, and with your background in online publishing, I thought it made sense for us to talk."

"Of course." (Talk? Lincoln thinks: I'll scream, beg, pray, filibuster.)

"Do you suppose, in the next week or so, you could fly in for a visit? We'll pay for the ticket, and I'd like you to meet some of the other editors in the office."

"Of course."

"Let's make ourselves clear: This is just talk so far, but I assume you wouldn't object to relocating? You'd be willing to move to New York?"

Glory Hallelujah!

That Friday, dressed in his lone gray suit and a blue tie he fished from the far reaches of his closet, Lincoln takes an early flight from O'Hare to LaGuardia. It's an in-and-out trip—leaving just enough time for a round of interviews before Malcolm House, with typical New York efficiency, has booked him on a five-o'clock return flight. Lincoln's luck holds from the start: the whole of the country east of the Mississippi is basking in a glorious, cloudless high. (He thinks: the heavens have opened for me at last.)

He was tempted to alert his parents—they certainly deserved a spot of promising news—and he wished he had a discreet way to let Mary know, just to prove he wasn't completely stalled. But he decided not to get ahead of himself, reasoning that a show of optimism could amplify eventual disappointment. So (save for an evasive conversation with Flam, who naturally was curious about the call from Malcolm House) Lincoln has savored his glad tidings alone. On the taxi ride in from LaGuardia, Lincoln worries that his excitement will be too obvious, that he'll expose himself for the outsider he's become. But by the time he's crossing the sinuous Triborough Bridge, with all of Manhattan laid out alongside, a cruise ship ready for boarding, Lincoln accepts his simmering stress. The quickened heartbeat, the surging adrenaline, the elevated metabolism—they soothe, and he wonders if in fact they represent his natural state, given that he's a New Yorker at heart. When he steps out of the cab in front of the Malcolm House building, a glassy fifties box on East Forty-Ninth Street, he almost collides with a stunning brunette motoring along the sidewalk in a pair of towering stilettos. “Excuse me!” she snips, glaring. Lincoln can only smile.

In the lobby, Lincoln registers with security and takes the elevator to the twenty-ninth floor. The reception area has been redesigned since Lincoln’s intern days, but the huge blowups of classic Malcolm House book covers and the enormous signage behind the receptionist’s desk signal that this is an enterprise with permanence, with reach. At just after eleven, he is ushered down several meandering corridors and into Jeff Kessler’s large office. None of the cushiony, clubby trappings here—just glass and laminate and sharp angles. Everything gives off a polished shine, as if all fingerprints, indeed, any trace of human physicality, have been scrubbed away that very morning. (Lincoln remembers the eraser bits that drifted through his Pistakee office like sand dunes, somehow always missed by the night cleaning crew).

The publisher is a tall, slender man, still only in his midforties, with an olive complexion and shiny black hair and a breezily elegant manner. (Lincoln recalls that Kessler could enthuse equally about opera and the Knicks). He’s dressed this day in a slim navy suit and red tie. Lincoln takes a seat in a sleek chair—stainless steel tubing interwoven with a kind of rubbery string. For a few comfortable minutes, they catch up and chat about acquaintances from Lincoln’s days as a Malcolm House intern, and then Kessler gets down to it.

“When I heard you’d gone to an online operation, I thought you might be interested in an opportunity here,” the publisher says.

“How did you know I’d moved?” Lincoln asks.

Kessler flatters with a sly smile. “I keep an eye out on promising up-and-comers.”

Lincoln blushes. Imagine—those agonizing hours with Professor Fleace, et al., and Jeff Kessler was watching out, like a guardian angel.

"What sort of talent did you find out there—out there in the Land of Lincoln?" the publisher asks.

"At iAgatha, not much," Lincoln says carefully. "I'm afraid it was mostly amateurs. I did work on one book that I thought was quite good, though. And it ended up selling pretty well."

"Was that the one about the sex positions?"

This is getting intimate. Kessler knows Lincoln's CV line by line. "Well, yes," says Lincoln. "Though the book was quite a bit more than that."

"Brilliant marketing," Kessler says. "The website, changing the author's name. Brilliant."

"I, ahh…actually, the website just popped up. I can't claim it was my idea."

"I didn't read the book myself," Kessler continues, ignoring Lincoln's disclaimer, "but one of our editors here did. Peter Falcone. I want you to meet him later. He dug it."

"Great."

"And how is your former publishing house—Pulaski, is it?—holding up in the downturn?" Kessler asks.

Lincoln blathers on for a minute or so about niche publishing and backlists built on timeless reference books.

"I saw from the Internet that you even made a hit out of a collection of poems," the publisher says.

My God, thinks Lincoln, the world has turned upside down. "A small hit," he says sheepishly. "By poetry standards."

Kessler shakes his head and laughs. "Another marketing coup—getting Michelle's mother to show off the book."

Lincoln decides to shut up and go for the ride.

"So what caused you to leave your old job?"

Of course, Lincoln has anticipated this question and carefully considered his response. Lying, even hedging, won't do. Candor is the only way. So he carefully explains that after he'd separated from his wife, he and the author of *The Ultimate Position*, a company employee, developed a brief, intimate relationship while he was editing the manuscript. She was not a direct report, and afterward, she acknowledged her complicity, resigned in solidarity, they remain platonic friends, etc.

Kessler listens closely, leaning back in his chair, holding the palms of his hands together as if praying, a wan smile playing on his lips.

"The Midwest," he says conclusively when Lincoln is finished.

"Exactly," says Lincoln, hugely relieved.

They chat for a few more minutes about books, agents, writing programs, even the Bulls vs. the Knicks, and Lincoln senses he's holding up well in the game of volleying insights and observations, his skill level elevated by the Olympic virtuosity of his partner. Finally, when Lincoln pronounces *The Devil in the White City* "a newspaper clip job—but a masterful clip job" and wonders aloud "what other potential best-sellers are buried out there in the archives," Kessler smiles upon him benevolently.

The publisher stands. "Let me introduce you to a few of my colleagues," he says. "And I will be in touch. I'd like to make a decision soon."

Kessler has arranged a talking tour. He deposits Lincoln with Rhoda Zimmerman, a grand dame of quality fiction who lectures for several minutes on the gender crimes of Lincoln's (former) homeboy Bellow. She then directs Lincoln to Elizabeth Warner, the young refugee from *Time* whose hiring dismayed him last fall. She is polite but harried, and she rushes through a perfunctory conversation before walking Lincoln down the hall to the office of Peter Falcone.

Lincoln has been hearing about Falcone for several years—blog posts, *PW* references, even the occasional items on *Gawker*, usually references to book parties that spilled into downtown clubs and collected a seasoning of movie stars and rockers. Oddly, Falcone is a visual echo of Kessler, with a narrow face, dark complexion (permanent tan or Mediterranean pigmentation?), flowing black hair combed behind his ears, and a navy suit and lavender tie. He's about Lincoln's age, maybe a couple of years older, and he sits behind a glass-topped desk clear of everything but a laptop and a phone—there's not even a cup for pencils, scissors, or other implements of a vanishing age.

"Hey!" Falcone says in greeting when Lincoln appears. "Malcolm House intern made good!" He stands to shake hands. Firm grip, strong baritone, angled, almost conspiratorial smile. Lincoln can see why the blogs love this guy.

They trade bona fides (Falcone easily bests Lincoln with a Brown economics degree, a dalliance at Goldman Sachs, an introduction to publishing through the agent side at ICM, and then a quick rise at Malcolm House). They seem to hit it off, and at exactly twelve thirty Falcone pronounces, "Let's have lunch!" (In Chicago, Lincoln reflects, everyone wants to eat at noon, before his appetite ever has a chance to sharpen.)

Falcone leads Lincoln to a small, modern Italian spot on Second Avenue, already noisy though it's only half filled. The curvy young hostess knows Falcone and seats them at a table near the front window. Their curvy young waitress (Flam would love this place, Lincoln thinks) drops off a menu for Lincoln. She already knows what Falcone will order (salmon spinach salad and a bottle of San Pellegrino). Lincoln follows suit with his host.

"Tell me about Amy O'Malley," Falcone says abruptly once they've settled in.

"Jeff said you read her book," Lincoln responds, slightly disconcerted.

"Yeah, I did." End of statement. No compliment. No assessment.

"She's bright," Lincoln proffers. "Lively style. Young, but promising."

"What's she look like?"

Lincoln pauses. What's this about? "She's attractive," he says, nodding, then quickly adds, "And she managed to survive the

University of Chicago's English department without disappearing into all that poststructuralism and genderizing crap."

"Did you fuck her?"

Lincoln is speechless. He slurps his water, buying time. Finally, he says, "We had a brief fling." (A *fling*? How sappy! How Midwestern!)

Apparently reassured, Falcone proffers, "It wasn't a bad book. Had some energy, some life. Did you have to do a lot of work on it?"

"Well, yes, there was a lot of line editing, even some rewriting. But she was there every step of the way."

"You do a lot of that heavy line editing?"

"Most of my manuscripts take a lot of work."

Falcone emits a snort. "I hardly bother anymore. Acquisitions are what count. Who can you sign up?" He leans across the small table. "As for line editing, I'll let you in on a secret. Readers don't notice."

"I know things are changing," Lincoln says.

Falcone sits back. "Don't get me wrong. I love books. I love authors, too—at least some of them. But the publishing business has to face facts. The game's new. Now, it's all names and marketing."

The rest of the lunch goes well. Lincoln and Falcone chatter through dessert and several rounds of espresso, talking about books, writers, sports, wives, marriages. (Falcone, too, has come through a divorce and for financial reasons has retreated to a studio sublet on the Upper West Side.) They don't finish until after three o'clock, and Lincoln has to rush to catch a cab to the airport. In front of the restaurant, Falcone shakes Lincoln's hand. "You're not what I expected," he says. "I'll put in a good word."

A little over an hour later, Lincoln is in line at his gate at LaGuardia when his cell phone rings. It's Jeff Kessler. "Good. Got you before you got away," he says.

"Just waiting to board."

"Listen. You made a strong impression here. I'm not going to beat around the bush. We'd like to offer you the job."

Lincoln can only burble, "Wow." The line at the gate starts forward.

Kessler runs through a few rudiments, including salary, which generously eclipses what Lincoln is currently making, though his instant calculations suggest he'll be exiled out of Manhattan or closeted in a studio sublet, like Falcone. "Well, what do you think?" Kessler asks.

"Ahhh." Lincoln is so awash with surprise and joy that he can't even blurt out a simple "yes." He's broken the tape at the end of his grueling marathon, and he's too exhausted to think. And just then a gate announcement blasts through the intercom, and Lincoln can't find the pocket where he stashed his boarding pass.

Kessler rescues. "I understand. It's a big move. You should think about it. Just let me know on Monday."

"I'm so flattered. Thank you."

"Have a good flight back," Kessler says.

As soon as the plane lifts off, Lincoln realizes how tense he's been. He feels limp and drained, almost as if he's recovering from a fever. He sits back and closes his eyes. A phrase from an Anthony Buford poem, "Falling Asleep," floats into his head: "Nature's gift of oblivion." He got that right, thinks Lincoln, just as he drifts off. He awakens as they are crossing Lake Michigan. His first thought is that he's blown it. He should have said yes to the job immediately. Now Kessler will doubt his enthusiasm. But maybe not, maybe Lincoln lucked out. Maybe a touch of hesitation shows worldliness, sophistication. His father, the fierce negotiator, always said never jump at the first offer. Maybe on Monday Kessler will even dangle a slightly higher salary, allowing Lincoln to upgrade from a studio to a small one-bedroom.

From Lincoln's window seat, the spires of Chicago come into view. The plane takes a northern route, swooping past the city before circling and pointing toward O'Hare. The angled sun casts a sepia light on the cityscape. Lincoln looks down. Chicago's cluster of big buildings looks so...contained, so *knowable* from three thousand feet. For all the third-biggest-American-city hoopla, the famous downtown stands like an outpost, a small redoubt on the vast, flat surface. Lincoln has a sudden flash of the pride those early Chicagoans must have felt in setting their flag here, in this swampy, windswept, unwelcoming prairie. The thought leads him back to his conversation with Kessler, then his lunch with Falcone. Something nags.

Did he fuck Amy? No! Well, yes, but he would never put it that way, never treat it as if it were the natural, transactional outcome of his work. He feels sullied now for having responded to the question at all. If Amy knew...Lincoln vows to himself that he will never, ever, get drawn again into an exchange like that. Half an hour later, coming home in a taxi, stalled in traffic, Lincoln wonders if it's that misstep with Falcone that has slightly deflated his joy at being offered the job.

When he gets to his apartment, Lincoln doesn't have the energy to go out for dinner, so he toasts himself with a large vodka on ice and calls out for a pizza. Checking the iAgatha website, he finds that three new manuscripts have come in for him, including Vijay Sharma's latest. "I have been writing feverishly and can't wait for you to work your magic," says Vijay in a note sent at 2:00 a.m. Jaipur time.

In bed that night, Lincoln churns dreams until about five in the morning, when he awakens with one of those sleep-induced moments of utter clarity: he will go to New York—that is of course what he wants, but he will take Amy with him.

32

AMY HAS MOVED TO PILSEN, A SLIGHTLY SKETCHY, LARGELY Mexican neighborhood south of the Loop that's enjoyed an influx of offbeat galleries and promising restaurants. Her plain, rectangular three-flat—subdivided into at least six apartments—sits in the middle of an unshaded block of similar buildings that crowd the sidewalk and provide a feeling of density missing from much of the North Side.

A taxi drops off Lincoln at nine thirty in the morning. The block is quiet. As he stands on the sidewalk, an older, overweight Hispanic woman carrying a cloth bag walks by, considering him warily. Lincoln smiles. He waits for the woman to reach the corner, then marches directly to the entrance of Amy's building. The intercom shows Hispanic names in every apartment but one, 2B: A. O'Malley. Lincoln rings the buzzer. He can hear it sounding distantly, deep within the structure. No answer. He waits, then thumbs the buzzer again. Thirty seconds pass, a minute. Suddenly, a scratchy bleat of static erupts from the inept intercom.

"Amy, it's John," says Lincoln into the speaker, enunciating clearly.

"Kxxxkkkxxx."

"What? I can't hear."

"Kxxxkkkxxx."

"Let me in! We have to talk."

"Kxxxkkkxxx." By now, with his excellent language skills, Lincoln has translated the static: "Go away!"

"Please!" he begs.

But the intercom is silent, offering not even the closure of a click.

Lincoln could stand at the building entrance and try to slip in when someone leaves, but then he'd be left pounding on Amy's apartment door. Or he could wait for her to come out and accost her on the street. He decides to reappraise over coffee at a diner a few blocks away on Halsted, but as he heads in that direction, he thinks of the alley. (Ah, those Chicago alleys.) He walks down the potholed and littered passageway and comes to the back of the three-flat. Looking up through the rusty filigree of a fire escape, he can see what must be a window to Amy's apartment. If he could get up to that window—if Amy could see him, she'd read his sincerity. He'd get his chance to plead his case.

The first-floor windows are boarded up, no doubt to prevent burglaries, so there's nothing but a blank wall of siding for the bottom fifteen or so feet. But a concrete ledge juts out about ten feet up, presumably marking the support between floors. If he could get to the ledge, he could use his athleticism to hoist himself and grab a bottom rung of the fire escape. He'd be like a monkey hanging there, but his devotion would be on full display.

The alley is lined with the city's black garbage containers, hard plastic boxes about four feet high with two large wheels on one side of the bottom. Lincoln rolls one over just beneath Amy's window. He steps back and vaults onto the top, balancing on his knees. So far, so good. Bracing himself against the wall, he carefully stands. Because of the wheels on the bottom, the container lacks stability, but Lincoln keeps his legs apart and stays on the balls of his feet. Then he reaches up with his left hand to grip the concrete ledge. He's just poised to make his move to the fire escape when the hard plastic top of the container collapses like a trapdoor, dropping Lincoln into a loose pile of garbage and toppling the fragile contraption. He lets out a shout as he falls and lands on his back, fortunately cushioned by the garbage that is spilling into the alley. (So many banana peels—or are those plantains?)

Before he can scramble to his feet, a man leans out of a building across the alley and yells something in Spanish. Then another head appears in another window. More Spanish screams.

Above him, Amy opens her window and looks down on the pitiful scene. She yells something in Spanish to the heads across the street. Lincoln catches the word *amigo*. Then she tells him sourly, "Clean up that crap and then come around to the front. I'll let you in."

Several more heads appear in windows across the street. It's as if they have skybox seating to observe his little fiasco of a show. All watch silently as Lincoln pushes the garbage—dark, smelly, semiliquid, much of it pouring out of paper grocery bags—back into the container. His pants are wet in patches and his hands are foul, but he carefully picks up the last stray pieces before waving cheerfully to his unsmiling audience and walking around front again. Amy buzzes him in and greets him at her door on the second floor. She's wrapped in a white robe, and it looks as if she's hastily run a comb through her hair. "You smell like shit," she tells him. "Go wash up."

The apartment is a railroad flat, one long hall with rooms off the sides. Amy directs him to a tiny bathroom, spotlessly clean but crammed with jars of makeup, tubes of shampoo, and assorted cosmetics. Lincoln goes to work with a ball of scented soap and finishes by squirting some perfume onto the dark stain in the back of his pants. He emerges smelling like a nineteenth-century fop.

"In here," Amy calls out from a room down the hall. Lincoln follows her voice and finds her sitting on a worn, blue sofa, her legs crossed and her arms folded across her chest. Standing a few feet away, also wearing a bathrobe and with his arms folded, is Tony Buford.

"What?" gasps Lincoln. The facts of the situation are too terrible for his mind to grasp at once—he has to absorb their implications slowly, let the awfulness seep in. Amy and Buford are seminaked together early in the morning. They were unconnected, in separate compartments of Lincoln's life, but they were his friends. Doesn't this count as a hideous betrayal? How long have they been carrying on together behind his back? Is he always, in all ways, a cuckold?

Amy doesn't offer any solace. "Well, what is it you wanted?" she demands.

"I…ah…" Lincoln stares at Buford, who appears to be as peeved as Amy.

"You've interrupted my yoga lesson," Amy says impatiently.

Lincoln looks from her to Buford. For the first time, he notices two mats open on the floor. "Yoga?" he says. "I thought…"

Amy rolls her eyes. "Jesus Christ," she grouses.

"I'm a professional!" Buford exclaims, furious. "An academic and a yoga teacher. You never took me seriously."

Trying to compose himself, Lincoln notices the man's pencil-thin bare legs, the way his maroon U of C bathrobe can almost wrap two times around his slight torso. "We got off on the wrong foot," Lincoln says.

Amy doesn't want to see this confrontation escalate. "Maybe we should cancel the lesson for today," she tells Buford.

He starts rolling up his mat. "I practically handed you success," he mutters at Lincoln, "and you were too pigheaded to recognize it."

Amy motions Lincoln not to respond. Buford tucks his mat under his arm and marches down the hall to another room. When he's gone, Lincoln tells Amy, "I didn't realize."

"I found his card in your apartment—in the bowl by the door where you drop your keys," she explains. "He's an excellent yoga teacher, and he's giving me a break on the price because I'm your friend. Do you know how expensive a private yoga lesson is otherwise?"

"What about the poetry part?"

"I told him we could skip that."

"I hope I haven't spoiled it for you."

"He'll recover." Amy softens. "He really does like you. And he thinks you're a brilliant editor."

Buford emerges a few seconds later, dressed now in a polo shirt and blue jeans and carrying his mat and a small athletic bag. "For a guy as smart as you are, you can really be a jerk," he tells Lincoln.

"Right," says Lincoln.

"Your problem is you think too much. You're doing all this thinking, and you don't see what's right in front of you."

"I'm sorry," Amy tells Buford. "I'll come to your class Monday."

Buford sighs and disappears down the hall. Amy and Lincoln hear the door close behind him.

With her yoga lesson canceled, Amy gets back to business. "Well, what was it you wanted?" she asks coolly.

Lincoln looks around. Amy has enlivened the room with several hanging pictures and a bookcase of her bottle collection, but the narrow space only admits light from that one window in back. The mood is funereal. "Can I sit?" he asks. He's feeling shaky, both from the weight of his cause and the blundering way it's played out so far. He gestures to a wood chair, where there'd be no risk of transmitting the stain on his pants.

Amy nods grudgingly.

Lincoln sits, takes a deep breath. First he says, "I've been offered a job in New York, with Malcolm House."

Amy perks up. "Really? Congratulations. That's nice. That's what you've always wanted."

"Yes, right. Well, here's the thing." As he prepares to deliver his plea, Lincoln balks. Amy looks so cool, determined, unyielding. Get on with it, he urges himself. "I know this is sort of out of the blue," he bumbles, "but I really only realized myself this morning." He stares at her, then blurts, "I was hoping you would come with me."

Amy sits sharply back, looking stunned and pained, as if she'd been hit by a telephone book. "Why?" she demands.

Lincoln has coached himself to avoid the L word—too abrupt, too weighted. Words are too easy. "Because we should have this adventure together." He takes another deep breath. "I know you think we're a bad mix, but that's not true. We're a great team." (Did he really say that?) "I mean, I've never felt smarter, never felt more alive than when we were working on your book. I never felt more *engaged*." (Stop him! He's out of control!) Lincoln blinks, resets himself. "Buford's right—I do think too much. And at the time, I didn't realize what was happening, because I was so addled with ambition. But it wasn't the book, it was *you*."

Amy rocks on the sofa, her gaze goes blank.

"Come with me," Lincoln urges. "You deserve New York, too."

"Sumbubbabitch," Amy mumbles.

Lincoln sits back. "What did you say?"

"Sumbubbabitch."

"I gave you that."

"So?" Amy glares at him. "It fits. Why can't I use it? If anyone has a copyright, it's the old man on the work crew."

Lincoln thinks: What else from my blather has stayed with her? You toss these things out and think they drop into a black hole, but then something catches. "No problem," he says. "I was just..." He stops himself.

"Anyway, I like that word," Amy says gently. "It fits."

In the slight mellowing of her tone, Lincoln catches a hint that her intransigence may be weakening. Five years of failed marriage has taught him that this is his tiny window. He gets up from the chair and sits beside her on the sofa. He puts his arm around her shoulders and rubs his forehead against the mussed hair on the side of her head. "I've missed you," he whispers.

"You don't know," she says quietly.

"Yes, I do," he insists. "I want to be with you."

"You don't know," Amy repeats. "I'm pregnant."

"Pregnant?"

"You know—with child."

Lincoln stares, dumbfounded. "Me?"

"Of course you, you idiot. You're the only man I've slept with in the last year."

This is coming too quickly. Lincoln's faculties are overloaded. "But how? You said you were on the pill."

"It turns out the pill is not infallible. Well, maybe I missed a few days back when I was in a tizzy to finish the book. My gynecologist warned me, but who ever thinks of it?"

His mind galloping, Lincoln nonetheless manages to do the crude math. Around five months. "You don't look pregnant," he says, as if that were determinative.

"Not when I'm bundled up."

Lincoln melts into the sofa. "Holy shit." The words come out in feeble puffs. Pregnant. Lincoln remembers the efforts he and Mary went through when they were trying to start a family—counting days, checking temperatures, visiting doctors. Nothing worked. Now, this. Just at the moment of his triumphant departure. Is Chicago like quicksand? The harder you struggle to get away, the more it sucks you in?

Amy says, "I wasn't going to tell you." She stares at him, alarmed, then reaches over and touches Lincoln's left arm. "Oh, I should never have told you, John. You should see your face."

Her touch anchors him. "But why? Why not tell me?"

"Because." She carefully pulls her hand away. "This was my mistake, not yours. I let it happen. And this isn't 1955, when people who didn't plan to be together, who weren't *meant* to be together, ended up getting married. I can do this. It will work out."

Is it really that simple? Lincoln feels as if he's floating away. He's adrift in a vast and bottomless sea.

"Besides," Amy continues, "you want to go to New York, you *are* going to New York. I need to be here, in Chicago, where my family can help. There are lots of single mothers in graduate school."

The turn to the practical gives Lincoln something to cling to. "Have you told your parents?" he asks. He knows Amy well enough to know abortion was never an option.

"Of course. I'm not doing this alone."

"I'll help in any way…" He lets the comment dangle when he realizes how hapless he must sound.

Amy comforts. "Everything's fine. Really. I love my obstetrician. She says the baby and I are going great." With an effort, a hint of the life she's carrying, Amy pushes herself up and stands beside the sofa. "And, now, you really must leave. My mother's coming, and we're going shopping for baby clothes." She lifts her arms, palms up, in happy wonder. "There's so much preparation! Today we're hunting clothes, tomorrow a crib. There's a sale at Land of Nod."

Also with an effort, Lincoln heaves himself up out of the soft cushions. Light-headed, his legs rubbery, he shuffles behind Amy to the door. He has so many questions, so much to digest, to work through. But he knows he must flee—he desperately needs the bracing slap of the cold spring wind to get his mind back in focus.

Amy is not quite finished with him, however. "I don't want you to think I've done this casually, John," she tells him. "I've thought about it a lot, talked about it a lot—with my parents, my doctor, even a family friend who's a lawyer. Everyone but the priest." She laughs. "It's better this way."

Lincoln offers a dazed nod.

"Don't worry," Amy continues. "I won't hide you. When the baby wants to know who her daddy is, I'll tell her—tell her *nice* things. Maybe she'll even want to come to visit some day. But you've got no obligations."

Even in his muddled state, Lincoln realizes he has gleaned a spot of information. "Her?" he asks.

"The baby's a girl," Amy says, and her face blossoms into a huge smile.

When Lincoln remains speechless, Amy goes on, "That's one reason why I was so upset about getting outed about the book. I don't want my daughter to be wandering around the Web one day and reading about her mother being a pornographer."

Lincoln thinks he's solved another mystery. "So you steered Marissa Morgan and the other bloggers to me?"

"Of course not," Amy scolds. "I'd never do that. Marissa found me, but I wouldn't talk to her. It was Kim, the Pistakee receptionist. She kept nagging me while I was still there, so I finally let her read the manuscript. She loved it, and she always wanted to talk to me about it. She had a friend from Iowa in the production department at *The Reader*. And Kim's the only one clueless enough to talk to a reporter."

"Kim," Lincoln repeats. Of course.

"But five minutes after I left your apartment, I was thinking about the baby," Amy continues. "I didn't even know why I came over."

Drawing from a last, buried repository of bravado, Lincoln says, "Maybe you came over because you wanted to see your baby's father."

Amy's smile disappears and she opens the door, ushering him out. "I like you, John," she says, "but I don't want to spend my life with you." Just before she closes the door firmly behind him, she adds, "Have fun in New York."

33

LINCOLN LEAVES AMY'S BUILDING AND TURNS RIGHT, HEADING east. He has a dim understanding that if he turned left in his condition, he'd probably just keep walking, one foot ahead of the other, over and over, across the despoiled prairie until he tumbled off the bank into the Mississippi itself. Pointed east, though, after a few blocks he comes across Halsted, a familiar artery, and he takes a Number Eight bus home.

Back in his apartment, Lincoln occupies himself by inventorying what he'll be taking to New York, making a list on a yellow legal pad. There may be enough that he needs to hire a moving company—Malcolm House will pay. Books, stereo, clothes. A few pieces of furniture—maybe he can even reclaim some items from his old apartment. Mary owes him that much. But soon he wearies of the exercise. It can't distract him from rerunning his conversation with Amy, and it doesn't allay his sense of loss. Finally, searching for a way to ease his restlessness, he takes a look at Vijay Sharma's latest offering (might as well do the guy a favor, since he launched Lincoln's online career), and reading the absurd but heroic adventures of the Indian private eye, Lincoln finds a way to make the hours pass.

In midafternoon Flam calls. He wants to know how the trip to New York went.

"Well, they offered me the job," Lincoln reveals.

"No shit. That was quick. I'm impressed."

"Thanks."

"You must be feeling pretty good."

On the prompting, Lincoln does a quick check of his systems. No, he's not feeling all that good. "You bet!" he dissembles.

"How about celebrating over dinner tonight? The champagne's on me."

Lincoln has no plans, but he's not in the mood for an evening with Flam, and he lacks the energy to exult over the move to New York when he can't extinguish this outburst of melancholy. He begs off dinner and asks for a rain check.

After he hangs up, Lincoln suddenly wonders what Amy is doing tonight. Having dinner with her parents? Going out with friends? Another image slices into Lincoln's thoughts: Amy rubbing noses with a fat-cheeked baby, both of them laughing, the baby waving its arms, the two of them, in that moment, utterly complete in their love.

New York! Lincoln tells himself. New York, New York, New York—his incantation to get out of this emotional warp and back into his own reality. And it works, for a time. He wants to attach himself to a great publishing house, edit profound writers, maybe even write a book or two himself. Bask in the pride of his parents. Wave those credentials in front of his rivals. Be somebody.

Returning to Vijay Sharma's manuscript, Lincoln thinks of Peter Falcone. Hah! What would he think of this epic pile of subcontinental swill? Falcone would never even look at it. He'd be wining and dining agents and famous authors. And that is now Lincoln's destiny. No more Vijay Sharmas! But late that night, after a delivered dinner of spicy Kung Pao chicken washed down by too much vodka, when Lincoln finally comes to the end of Sharma's book and the eponymous hero rescues the kidnapped young woman from the cult of religious zealots by hiding in the coffin in which the terrorists were planning to bury the poor girl alive for daring to seek a liberal education, Lincoln erupts in sobs. The melodrama! The glory! Teardrops splatter Lincoln's shirt as the lionhearted private eye machetes his way through swarming fanatics and carries the beautiful, terrified victim to freedom. Lincoln puts his head on his desk and lets the waterworks flow.

When he gets up the next morning, Lincoln goes through his usual Sunday routine: scrambled eggs, English muffin, a pot of coffee, the *Tribune*, the *Times*. While glancing over the *Times* business section, he suddenly thinks: baby cribs. Amy is going to get one today. Haven't there been stories recently about dangerous cribs—the slats are too far apart or the adjustable rail accidentally drops? After a few minutes on the Internet, he finds that, yes, some older cribs have been blamed for deaths, and even some newer models have been recalled. Does Amy know? He returns to the paper, but over the next half hour, the concern itches until it suddenly erupts in a full-blown panic: he's got to warn her. He tries to call, but she doesn't pick up. He sends an e-mail, listing the varieties of cribs that have caused trouble. But what if she doesn't check her e-mail before her shopping excursion? In his agitated state, Lincoln has little trouble convincing himself that there is only one thing to do: he has to find her and tell her.

He showers and dresses quickly, then hurries outside to catch a cab. The driver, a dark-complected man of some Eastern nationality, soon picks up on Lincoln's anxiety—the lugubrious sighs when they don't crash a yellow light, the groans when a lumbering truck pulls in front. "You in a hurry?" the driver asks.

"Yes, I'm afraid so," says Lincoln.

"What can be the hurry on Sunday morning?"

"It's a personal thing."

"Sunday morning is the only time Americans slow down. The rest of the time, always in a rush. In my country, every day is like Sunday morning."

"Where's your country?"

"India."

"India," Lincoln murmurs. The word jars loose an absurd question: "Do you know of a writer named Vijay Sharma?"

"What does he write?"

"Books. Thrillers."

"No." The driver shakes his head. "I mostly read newspapers."

That ends the conversation until they reach Amy's block. As Lincoln is paying, the driver says, "Vijay Sharma. I'll remember that name and look him up."

"You won't regret it," Lincoln says, and he realizes that his mind and his mouth are on two different tracks. He really has to get his bearings. He stands on the sidewalk for a moment. A spot of sunlight flowing down the east-west street warms his face, calming him. Then he walks to the entrance and makes his second siege of Amy's building. But this time he sits on the buzzer for more than a minute with no response. Too late—she's already left.

Now what to do? Lincoln walks back to the curb, fumbling with his BlackBerry. She mentioned Land of Nod, but where the hell is that in Chicago? While he waits for Google to come up on his phone, a taxi starts backing toward him from down the street. The cabbie who dropped him off has waited. "Still in a hurry?" he asks in his lilting English.

Lincoln hops in the back and finds Land of Nod on his BlackBerry—900 West North.

The driver knows the place. "Ah, no wonder you're in a hurry," he says, laughing. "A baby!"

The trip takes only fifteen minutes on the Sunday morning streets. "Congratulations," says the driver when he drops Lincoln off in front of the store. It's a tawny, one-story warehouse of a building in the shopping maze that's sprouted around North and Clybourn. Lincoln pushes through the doors, and a sparkling new world opens up to him, all pastels on white with accents of stained wood. The atmosphere of cheer even survives the relentless track lighting. The space is divided into alcoves, cubbies, and three-sided rooms, and Lincoln wanders among the furniture and other baby paraphernalia. From a distance, he spots a middle-aged woman reading the tag on a white-slatted crib. She's small and slight, with short auburn hair and a splash of freckles. Very well kept-up and youthful and wearing a light, beige spring coat. Amy's mother?

Bracing himself, Lincoln approaches and inquires gently, "Mrs. O'Malley?"

She turns to him pleasantly. "Yes?"

"I'm John Lincoln…Amy's friend."

Her soft features harden, and Lincoln feels her probing gaze—examining, poking, covering all six feet two of him, up and down several times. He thinks of a Louisville horseman evaluating a prospective stallion. (Well, in this case it's really too late for that.)

"The editor," she says finally, a trace of Ireland in her voice. "This is a surprise." Smiling tentatively, she offers a delicate hand, and Lincoln gives it a firm but careful shake. "Is Amy expecting you?" she asks.

"Not really."

"Well, let's find her," Mrs. O'Malley says, with the air of efficient authority that has steered a classroom for two decades. She leads Lincoln through the slalom of beds and cribs until they come upon Amy, standing, with her hands on her hips in front of a bunk bed done up with a celestial theme. She's staring in exasperation at Lincoln.

"I came to warn you about the crib," he explains.

Amy winces. "What are you talking about?" But as if his response, whatever it is, will be nonsense, she doesn't stop for an answer and says to her mother, "Why don't you give us a minute."

Amy used to grumble that her mother hovered, but here Mrs. O'Malley shows admirable discretion. "Nice to meet you, Mr. Lincoln," she says, amusing herself by drawing out the formal address for the father of her grandchild.

"Me, too," he says.

She ignores his non sequitur and leaves quietly for another area of the store.

When she's out of hearing, Amy says angrily, "John, why are you here?"

"I came to warn you about the crib," he repeats and sputters on for a minute about some of the alarming facts he gleaned.

When at last he runs out of horror stories, Amy says quietly, "Don't you think I know all that? Don't you think I've spent hours reading up about cribs—and about baby furniture and baby clothes and baby food and *everything there is to know about babies*!"

"Yes," he says weakly.

Amy drops heavily onto the bottom tier of the celestial bunk bed. "John, why are you doing this to me?" she asks pleadingly.

The question—direct, pained, bristling with blame, yet somehow acknowledging the helplessness they both suffer when fate and character intertwine—hits Lincoln like a hard wind. He plops down beside her. As she stares blankly across the narrow room, where a framed poster announces, GO ASK YOUR MOTHER—BY ORDER OF THE MANAGEMENT, Lincoln absently starts combing her hair with his fingers. The velvety softness, the heat of her mysteriously changed body, the polar swings of emotion he's undergone in the last few days—he feels light-headed, his eyes loose in their sockets, his spine soft. Is this the start of a swoon? He fights his way back to lucidity, and it's as if he's breaking the surface of a lake, bursting into the fierce light of the sun. "I want to be with you," he insists, and Lincoln knows from the unanticipated urgency in his voice that he means not just the pregnancy, but beyond—the disrupted nights, the afternoons at the playground, the messy dinners, the pleasures, the woes, life before the three of them, in all its unarrangeable sprawl.

Amy says softly, "You don't, John. That's sweet of you, but you really don't."

"But I *do*," Lincoln sputters like a desperate child. "I really do." For all his frantic plotting, he senses that everything that came before has led to this accidental moment—as if nature has finally intervened and is giving him one last chance. "I do!" he cries again.

Amy laughs at his artlessness and places her hand on his cheek. He covers her small hand with his. "Listen," he says, recovering enough to lay the groundwork to make his case. "Let's have dinner tonight. We'll talk."

"I can't, John," Amy tells him gently. "I'm working."

"Fuck that. Call in sick. We've got to talk." Lincoln presses her hand against his cheek. He's not going to let her go until she agrees.

She pats her stomach with her free hand. "I can't drink," she points out.

"So what? I won't either."

Amy studies him intensely. Lincoln can't imagine what his face is telling her, but he keeps pressing her hand. He'll never outlive the pain if she removes her hand now.

"But what about New York?" she asks finally. "I won't leave Chicago."

"Fuck New York."

Amy pulls away. "I can't believe you said that."

Lincoln can't either. But he said it, and now the words and the logic pour out, as if the flood tide had been building for two days. "I mean, I love New York, but ever since they offered me the job, I've been thinking—is that really what I want to do? It's as if I got visited by the Ghost of Christmas Future. A lot of boring lunches with agents, all that maneuvering to get ahead of rivals. Pretending I'm a big deal just because of my job. I'll probably just go home and drink, turn into an alcoholic. Talk about growing old alone in a smelly apartment! I need to be editing manuscripts, trying to improve things. That's what I'm good at." He reaches for her hand again. "I could go, I *would* do it—if it weren't for you, but I'm embedded in Chicago now. I'm a part of it, and it's a part of me. You're here."

"You're like Gatsby," Amy teases. "You lived too long with a single dream."

For the second time in less than twenty-four hours, Lincoln gushes tears, using Amy's hand to mop his sloppy face while she laughs at his childish display. She pulls his head close with her free hand and whispers, "I didn't really mean what I said yesterday—that I didn't want to spend my life with you. I'm just confused. It's all happened so fast. I don't know what I think."

Lincoln's body goes soft. Every muscle, every cell, has been tensed. "We'll talk," he says. "And talk and talk and talk."

Amy takes a deep breath and pulls her hand away. "But now you have to go. My mom's waiting."

"Do you want me to help?"

"God, no."

"But we're having dinner tonight," Lincoln reminds. "You promised."

"I'll call you later." Amy stands. "Go wash your face," she instructs, motioning toward the restroom. "New parents won't want to see you cry."

In the restroom, Lincoln douses himself with cold water. What has happened? He has leaped from taking Amy with him to New York on a romantic lark to settling with her and their child in Chicago. And he did it without even thinking. It just… came to him. He's found someone he loves. They are having a baby. Doesn't that trump everything else?

When he emerges from the bathroom, Amy is still standing beside the bunk bed, looking slightly puzzled. "Let me shop with you," Lincoln asks again. "I should be there."

Amy shakes her head. "No, no, no, this is better." Then she collapses onto the bunk. "Oh, John, I'm so confused. I convinced myself of one thing, and now I don't know. How will we live? Maybe you *should* go to New York."

This is a test. Lincoln knows he's being tested. By Amy? Her subconscious? The world? He places his hands on either side of her head. He lifts her face, nuzzles her nose with his, kisses her lightly on the lips. "We can do this," he says. "We'll do it *together.*"

Amy hesitates, smiles. She takes Lincoln's right hand between her palms. "You aren't rubbing your arm," she points out.

"See!"

She laughs and leads him by the hand to the store's entrance, then stands on tiptoe to kiss him. "I'll call you after," she says.

Lincoln backs out, and through the glass door, Amy blows him another kiss.

A few hours later, Lincoln goes for a bike ride. After the shocks of the last few days, he needs his rock to settle himself. He keeps thinking of that moment years ago, lying on the filthy canvas in West Virginia, at the end of his encounter with the bear. He had an overwhelming sense that his course had veered suddenly, taken an unexpected new direction, and that, if you viewed his life from afar, as a line, it would forever angle in a small way, like the forearm he was clutching close to his chest. Now he has that sense again. He doesn't know where the direction leads—there is much to be discussed, much to be arranged, but that is Lincoln's métier. He can pull this off.

The day offers the first real sweetness of summer. Blue sky, soft air, the sort of weather that lets Chicagoans imagine that the dismal winter, the endless cold and gray, the delayed pleasure—it all pays off in the end (a deal that seems worth it until November). Lincoln pedals over to the lake, then north along the bike path. He passes his rock, circles, and comes back to perch. Already, several families are picnicking behind him, their grills firing, their kids of assorted heights and widths kicking soccer balls. The lake is quiet, and though Lincoln knows the water is bitterly cold, the smooth expanse of sun-blessed turquoise looks inviting enough to swim in, or maybe drink. Lincoln stares east, as always. A squad of gulls swoops over the water in indecipherable but precise flight patterns, then settles on the surface just a few feet away. Beyond, he sees an early-season sailboat, a brilliant white triangle, catching a wind from somewhere, dipping over the horizon. Who would have thought—the curve of the earth, evident even here, in this low-slung, landlocked enclave. Chicago. There's so much he has to learn.

Lincoln wonders where he should take Amy for dinner tonight. Someplace special. Gibsons, that's it. Gibsons, the city's favorite steak joint. Amy loves red meat, and now she's eating for two. Gibsons is always festive, always memorable—visiting ballplayers drawing crowds in the bar, waiters hauling around great trays of beef. Amy will like that. He sees her smiling. He imagines pulling her under his arm and kissing her just on the top of her forehead, where the tiny, unruly hairs always escape her control. But Gibsons is a busy place. He'd better call for a reservation. He pulls out his cell phone.

Behind him, a child squeals in pursuit of a ball. And Lincoln thinks: yes. Yes, I am happy now.

ACKNOWLEDGEMENTS

I owe many thanks to many people. Lucy Childs Baker and Frances Jalet-Miller offered outstanding advice and remained warmly loyal. Ed Park provided an acute and friendly editorial eye. Richard Cahan, Shane Tritsch, and James Ylisela Jr. helped nail down Chicago facts and history (any lingering mistakes are entirely my own). Billy Clyde Puckett, the protagonist in Dan Jenkins's wonderful 1972 football novel, *Semi-Tough*, refers constantly to the "dog-ass Jets." That tic inspired my protagonist to speak of the Chicago Cubs with similar regular disparagement. Above all, I owe a measureless debt of gratitude to my wife, Gioia Diliberto, who has been making me happy now for thirty-two years.

ABOUT THE AUTHOR

Photo by Katrina Wittkamp

Richard Babcock is the former editor of *Chicago Magazine* and *New York Magazine* where he spent more than three decades as both an editor and contributing writer. Raised in Woodstock, Illinois, Babcock graduated from Dartmouth College in 1969 and from the University of Michigan Law School in 1974. Beyond editorial duties in magazines, Babcock has spent many years working as a founder of *The National Law Journal*, a weekly newspaper for attorneys. Today, Babcock lives with his wife Gioia Diliberto, an acclaimed biographer and novelist, in Chicago. Babcock stays close to his roots in journalism as a teacher of narrative journalism at Illinois's Medill Northwestern University and Knox College. His other great endeavor is a life-long attachment to the Chicago Cubs, a team he warmly credits for schooling him in the "nuances of failure and loss." *Are You Happy Now?* is Babcock's third novel; his first, *Martha Calhoun*, published in 1988; and his second, *Bow's Boy*, published in 2002.

Made in the USA
Charleston, SC
23 December 2012